REDEMPTION

Other titles by S. Usher Evans

THE RAZIA SERIES
Double Life
Alliances
Conviction
Fusion

Empath

THE MADION WAR TRILOGY
The Island
The Chasm
The Union

THE LEXIE CARRIGAN CHRONICLES
Spells and Sorcery
Magic and Mayhem
Dawn and Devilry
Illusion and Indemnity

REDEMPTION

DEMON SPRING TRILOGY
Book Three

S. USHER EVANS

Sun's Golden Ray
Publishing
Pensacola, FL

DEMON SPRING TRILOGY

Resurgence
Revival
Redemption

DEMON FALL TRILOGY

Reawakening
Resurrection
Reclamation

Demon Art by Ashley Gonzales, Zeefa Studio
Line Editing by Danielle Fine, By Definition Editing

Sun's Golden Ray Publishing
Pensacola, FL
www.sgr-pub.com

For ordering information, please visit
www.sgr-pub.com/orders

DEDICATION

To Charlotte
From your Nitney

CONTENTS

DEMONOLOGY

The following is a brief introduction to the five kinds of demons found in the human world. The International Coalition for Demon Management (ICDM) is charged with protecting humans from unwanted demonic transformation, but we can't do it alone.

Learn the signs of demonic coercion and don't become a victim.

ATHTAR

First Seen: 1500 BC, Syria
Magical Element: Void
Original Sin: Pride
Original Demon: Bael

The oldest and rarest demons, Athtars live in the Underworld and appear during Demon Spring. They have the ability to manipulate time and space. If you encounter an athtar demon, seek shelter as quickly as possible, and alert your local US Division office.

ELOKO

First Seen: 400 AD, Democratic Republic of the Congo
Magical Element: Earth
Original Sin: Envy
Original Demon: Biloko

Eloko demons use the sound of a bell to hypnotize their victims into a false sense of security. If you think an eloko is trying to coerce you, stomp your feet or clap your hands to disrupt the magic, then run away.

KAPPA

First Seen: 600 BC, Japan
Magical Element: Water
Original Sin: Greed
Original Demon: Mizuchi

Kappas mostly live near water, and will create an illusion of a house or structure. When the victim enters the illusion, it will break and the human will be drawn underwater, given the option to transform or drown. When near bodies of water, familiarize yourself with existing structures, and watch for others coming in and out.

LILIN

First Seen: 200 AD, Germany
Magical Element: Air
Original Sin: Lust
Original Demon: Freyja

Lilins use a mixture of pheromones and glamour (illusion) to lure humans into sexual intercourse, then transformation. If you think a lilin is trying to coerce you, pinch yourself or think of something unsettling, then run away.

NOX

First Seen: 1400 AD, Mexico
Magical Element: Fire
Original Sin: Anger
Original Demon: Mot and Xo

Nox demons use the human's innate fear of demons to construct terrifying nightmares, and the human agrees to transform to cease them. To combat a nox demon, take a deep breath and remind yourself it's only a vision.

PROTECT YOURSELF

If you encounter any demon or supposed demon, contact your local US Division of the International Coalition for Demon Management right away to report the incident.

UNITED STATES DIVISION
INTERNATIONAL COALITION
FOR DEMON MANAGEMENT
#demonspring

CHAPTER ONE

In all her years on this planet, Cam Macarro had never thought she'd find herself speeding down Interstate 10 in the wilds of Texas with a sleeping demon in the passenger seat.

Then again, there were a lot of things Cam was having trouble believing lately.

For starters, her best friend and partner Jack Grenard had been taken by the King of the Underworld, Bael. Jack had been on the run with Anya, who also happened to be Bael's estranged lover. Cam had finally caught up with them in the parking lot of a hotel in New Orleans when Bael arrived, ready to reclaim his woman. But Anya surprised all of them by declaring she was finished with Bael.

Unsurprisingly, Bael wasn't one to take no for an answer. And before Cam knew what was happening, he and Jack were gone.

And Anya and Cam were now on a mission to get him back.

Supposedly, anyway. Anya had been vehemently opposed to Cam's involvement in the rescue mission, claiming Cam wouldn't last a minute in the Underworld. But Anya had also been passed out since they'd high-tailed it out of New Orleans, so Cam was pretty sure she'd be needed.

"Slow down," came the quiet voice of the demon. "You'll get pulled over."

"Nah," Cam said, leaning back in her seat. "There aren't any cops along this stretch."

"So you say."

"So I know. I've driven this route a few times," Cam said. She cracked her shoulders, brushing away the exhaustion. "So this schism. How sure are you it exists? I thought Bael was the only one who could bridge the worlds? How come the noxes have one?"

"I've heard Xo created it when she gave birth to her son," Anya replied. "That, at least, is plausible, as we didn't hear of it until after the little bastard was born. She's an original demon, and their son was never a human."

Cam shook her head. "Then how come nobody knows about it? Wouldn't all the demons be clamoring to come through it all the time?"

"It's a nox secret, and they'd like to keep it that way," Anya said. "Bael may not even know it's still there. He likes to believe he's the only one with the power to open a portal."

"Because he could control who went through it, right?" Cam

said. "Yeah, I got the measure of him. But you're sure it exists? Like…really sure?"

"I've never seen it, but I trust my source. What I don't trust is whether the noxes will let me through the door."

"Why?"

"They don't like me."

"Does anybody?" Cam said, a little louder than she'd intended. The demon sighed, falling back into her own thoughts. Cam snuck another glance between watching the road—there was a definite sadness there.

"I really hoped he would let me go," Anya said after a moment.

"What?"

"Bael. I wanted him to let me go."

Cam snorted. "Hoped or fooled yourself into believing it?"

That sparked the first bit of fire she'd seen from her passenger. "Excuse me?"

"I mean, you've been running from the guy since the 1880s. You wouldn't have been doing that if you thought you could just walk away from him."

"It's complicated."

"I mean, it's really not."

Anya curled back into herself. "I don't wish to discuss it further."

"Yeah, that might've worked with Jack, but that shit doesn't fly in this car," Cam said. "After all, it's your fault Jack was taken."

"I know." She laughed, but there was no humor in it. "Trust me, I know."

"So..." Cam squeezed the wheel. "What happened between you two?"

"That's our business."

"Did I or did I not just say that shit doesn't fly in this car?" Cam took a swig of cold coffee. "Besides, when Jack gets back, he'll tell me anyway, so you might as well just deal with it and spill everything. Starting with why the hell he followed you in the first place."

"You'll have to ask him that," she said. "But the long and short of it is: I thought I was cursed to repent for all the people I'd killed over the past few thousand years. Jack thought he could help me. But there was no curse." She loosened a breath. "I think he always knew that. Just wanted to help me see it."

Cam's anger dampened at the softness in Anya's voice. Perhaps the demon wasn't as unfeeling as Cam had originally thought. "That's Jack. Loyal as hell." She shifted in her seat. "You never answered my question about what happened between you two."

She inhaled and lifted her shoulder in a half-shrug. "Perhaps I just don't have an answer for you. Everything changed last night. I found out the curse wasn't real. Jack..."

"Jack what?"

She blew air out between her lips. "If the curse wasn't real, then that meant I felt everything. Every ounce of guilt I carried with me for every person I'd killed. The way I felt about Bael."

She sighed and her face softened. "And that also meant that what I felt for Jack wasn't…wasn't because of some curse either."

Cam leaned into the steering wheel. "So you do love him, then? For real?"

"I don't know if I'd call it love," she murmured. "But I had begun to care about him. Otherwise, Bael wouldn't have done what he did." She shivered. "Jack's a good man. He doesn't deserve this. Even if I didn't feel something for him, I'd still want to get him back home."

Cam squinted at the road, trying to figure out if that was an acceptable answer. "Did you fuck?"

"I know you did."

Cam nearly slammed on the brakes. "*What?*"

"Jack told me," Anya replied. "Said it was a mistake. Do you feel the same way?"

"Of course I do," Cam said, her heart thumping in her chest. "What I want to know is why *you* know. My sister didn't even know, and they were married for three years. Did you do something to him?"

"No. I don't know why he told me."

"Liar."

Cam waited for another back and forth, but Anya retreated into her thoughts.

"Look, that shit was private," Cam said after a long pause. "I don't like that he just shared it with you."

"There was a mutual trading of secrets," she said, staring out the window.

"And that makes it all right?"

"It was Jack's to share, so I suppose it does." She pinched the bridge of her nose. "Can we put a pause on this conversation? I have a splitting headache."

"Yeah, and I have a pain in my ass," Cam said. "I don't want to be here any more than you do. But if we're going to work together, no more secrets, okay?"

"We aren't working together," Anya said, sounding tired of the conversation. "You can't go into the Underworld. You're human. Even if they didn't sense you immediately, which they would, you wouldn't survive the back and forth of demonic energy."

"Jack survived."

"I already told you he only survived because he was under Bael's protection. The demons around him kept their miasma reined in. When I go to the Underworld, they're going to be doing their best to stop me from getting to Jack. It's not a place for a human."

"I have the talismans," Cam said, flashing her wrist where five coins hung from a leather rope.

"They didn't do much against the belus," Anya replied. "Look, you can go as far as Mexico City, but once I enter the Underworld, I have to go alone."

"And how do you expect to even walk? You've been sleeping the whole damned time we've been in the car," Cam said.

"This is temporary. I just overdid it a few times with Jack."

"I'll say."

"I meant with our escapes," Anya said with a glare that Cam felt more than saw. "I probably shouldn't have been using my magic at all, and we had to disappear a few times. I haven't had a chance to recover fully…if I ever can."

"But going back to the Underworld should make you stronger, then, right?"

"One would hope."

Cam didn't like the sound of that, but decided to let it go as they passed a sign for the US-Mexico border. "I don't have a passport, so how the hell are we going to do this?"

"Just keep driving. I'll get us through the border."

"I thought your magic was too weak to use?"

"I can get us fifty feet."

The queue of cars was coming up fast.

"Anya…"

"Keep driving."

Cam heard a sharp intake of breath beside her, and the world outside the car decelerated. The engine's low roar deepened, sending sound vibrations into Cam's chest. The wind moaned against the windshield, and the cars around them slowed to a crawl, even as Cam's speedometer read eighty-five.

Then, the world flew toward them, cars and busses and trucks on the highway zooming in their direction. Cam squeezed her eyes shut, bracing for impact, but it never came. The low hum of the engine sped back up to normal, the wind no longer moaned, and Cam cautiously opened an eye—just in time to swerve out of the way of a car in the slow lane.

"*Shit!*" Cam said, nearly flying off the road as she overcompensated. But she steadied the car then pressed a hand to her still-thumping heart. "That was..." She glanced at the slumped-over figure in the corner. "Anya?"

"M'fine," slurred the demon.

"Are you?"

Light snoring was the only response.

CHAPTER TWO

Jack knew Sara was dead.

Three years ago, he'd arrived home after a long day at work to her bloodied corpse on the floor. The image had been burned into his memory—a constant reminder of his failures as a man, husband, and Division agent. He could still feel her cold body limp in his arms, sticky red blood covering his clothes as he cradled her. He would never forget the weight of her coffin as he and her cousins carried her to the gravesite, or the sound of her casket lowering into the ground.

Yet, Sara stood before him, as real and alive as he was.

Her black, curly hair spilled over her shoulder in a low ponytail. Her brown skin was freckled as if she'd just spent the day in the sun. The smile on her lips was hesitant, like she wasn't sure what to expect.

"Aren't you excited to see me?" Sara asked.

Jack fought the urge to drink her in like a man in the desert. This was Bael's twisted joke. His torture wasn't gong to be physical, it seemed.

"Jackie, what's wrong?" she said, her voice both soothing and devastating.

"This is sick," he croaked. "You aren't real."

She put the food down on the table and crossed the room. Jack backed away as if she were venomous, but he smacked into the wall.

She slid her fingertips across his face—so familiar, so wrong, and forced him to look at her. "I'm as real as you are."

Jack listened for the sound of bells and waited for the smell of flowers but found neither. But he knew, he *knew* this wasn't real. He repeated that mantra in his mind as he stared into the beautiful brown eyes of his dead wife. If, even for a moment, he thought otherwise, he'd be lost.

"If you won't kiss me," she said, with the audacity to look hurt, "will you at least eat? I've made your favorite dinner."

Jack shook his head. He couldn't put anything in his mouth, not when his stomach was threatening to revolt.

"Then why don't we talk?" she said, sitting down on the other chair. "Come, I want to hear your voice. I've missed you."

"You're dead."

"I'm not dead," she said with a shake of her head. "Bael has brought me back to you. He's God-touched, so he can do that. I'm your gift."

For a brief, beautiful moment, Jack allowed himself to

believe that could be possible. But a strong voice in his mind that sounded a lot like Cam blew a raspberry at that idea. Bael was no God, and as much as Jack wished it were true, the Belu Athtar could not bring people back from the dead.

"Bullshit," Jack said. "You're a demon. Lilin glamour is what this is. And it's fucking disgusting."

"Jackie," she said, taking his face in her hands. "Please listen to me. It's really me, I promise."

"It's not," Jack said, a treacherous tear falling down his cheek. "I know it's not you. You're dead."

"I've come back to you."

She pressed her lips to his and he thought he might die. Everything about her was the same, down to the way she tasted. It was so hard to resist, but he did, pushing her away.

"Jack," she whispered, backing up. "What is it? Why won't you kiss me back?"

He clenched his jaw, not trusting his words.

"Is it her?"

Her. Anya. Just thinking of her awoke a storm of guilt. The last thing he remembered before blacking out was Anya telling Bael she no longer wanted to be with him. She and Jack had begun something new the night before, something neither thought was even possible. But he couldn't think about her right now, not when he was struggling against this image of Sara. Not when he still had no idea what she was to him, or what he was to her.

"Do you love her?" Sara asked, cupping Jack's cheek. Her

brown eyes had filled with tears. "Jack, didn't you promise to love me forever?"

"This isn't real," he whispered, closing his eyes.

"You slept with her, didn't you?" Sara said, sliding up under his arm. It was so familiar, and it tore his heart even farther apart. "I don't know what's worse. You slept with another woman, or that she was *demon*." She took Jack's face and forced him to look at her. "Jack, didn't you even care about what happened to me?"

"This isn't real," he spat out, instead of the thousands of words he'd had built up in his head. This had been what he'd wanted for years, to have one final conversation with Sara. But *this wasn't her*. This was Bael.

"You'd rather believe I'm not real because you're in love with your demon woman?" A tear fell down her cheek. "That's it, isn't it?"

"I don't believe you're real because I put your casket in the ground."

"I told you, the Belu Athtar can bring people back from the dead. He found me in the afterlife. He asked me to come back to you. He was worried you'd strayed from your marriage vows." Sara stared at the table. "Did you enjoy sleeping with her? Did she feel like I did?"

Jack inhaled. Maybe if he answered, she'd be satisfied and leave him alone. "She didn't feel like you. Like Sara."

"Was it better?"

He grimaced. "It was different."

She lifted her gaze to his, everything about her so painfully real. "Do you love her? Did you forget about me?"

"I never forgot about you—Sara. And I didn't get a chance to be in love with Anya."

"Anya…" Sara dropped her gaze again. "Her name is Anat. And she killed thousands of humans, Jack. Humans like me. How could you fall in love with something like that? How could you give up everything you stood for? Your grandfather stood for? I bet he's ashamed of you." She snorted. "I know I am."

He couldn't find his tongue.

"I wish Bael had never brought me back to see what you've become. The Jack I married would never have done any of this." She rose from the table. "Enjoy your dinner."

The door shut behind her and Jack released a loud sigh of relief. With Sara out of the room, his mind was calmer, although it still shook with the aftereffects of the onslaught. Whatever kind of magic Bael was using was potent—it wasn't just lilin glamour. Maybe he'd added in some nox miasma too, for she was ripping his worst fears from the back recesses of his mind.

He rested his head in his hands and let himself feel everything. Then, when the demon returned, Jack would be better prepared to handle the magic and words thrown in his direction.

Or, as prepared as he'd ever be facing the ghost of his wife.

CHAPTER THREE

"I'm not carrying your Colibrí-sized ass into the hotel," Cam said. "So you'd better wake up and walk yourself in."

Cam had been driving for hours, but exhaustion had finally caught up with her, so she'd pulled over at a motel for the night.

Anya cracked open an eye. With a sharp intake of breath, she pushed herself out of the car and held herself against the door for a moment before taking a first step. Her knees buckled, but Cam was quicker, hoisting her up.

"Just what I wanted going into the Underworld. A demon who can't even stand up."

"This isn't my ideal situation either," Anya replied quietly. "Also, you aren't going."

"Might have to," Cam said, adjusting her against her side. "Since it's clear you're weaker than you thought. You said moving fifty feet wouldn't be a big deal."

"I didn't think it would be." She chewed her lip with a furrowed brow. "Maybe I am a lot worse off."

"Well," Cam grunted, "hopefully we'll get you nice and healthy before you face Bael. Or maybe it won't matter, because he'll smile at you, and you'll fall back in love with him then we'll all just be fucked."

If Anya had a response, she didn't share it.

"And I suppose I'm paying for this, too," Cam said.

"I have money," Anya murmured. "Black bag in the trunk of the car."

Cam left the demon the side of the car and went around to the back. She cracked open the trunk, revealing two identical duffle bags. In the first, she found a stash of weapons, and in the second the second, several wads of cash.

"Ever heard of a bank?" Cam said, counting out a few hundred.

"Banks are too risky with Bael chasing me," Anya said, rubbing the sleep form her eyes. "We had to be extra careful with where we left a paper trail. Anyway, that's Jack's money. He did that gig."

"Vigilante work," Cam said. "Is this the one with the Academy kids?"

Anya narrowed her eyes. "How did you know about that?"

"Apparently, Jack told Myra to tell me he was still alive," Cam replied with a smirk. "It was good timing too, because I was about to consider him a lost cause." Cam's smirk faded. It was the night some athtar had slaughtered thirty people in a fast food joint. The same night Jack had broken into his own house and left a note apologizing for stealing all Cam's research material. One little sign that kept Cam's trust in her partner alive. "You didn't kill those people, right?"

"What?"

"In that restaurant near Charleston," Cam said. "That wasn't you, right? And Wani? And—"

"I haven't killed a human in over a hundred and thirty years," she said, placing her hand on her chest. "Wani... Well, it wasn't by my sword, but I take responsibility all the same. If we hadn't gone to see him, Bael wouldn't have had reason to kill him." She paused, then added quietly, "I suppose you could blame the humans' deaths on me as well."

"How's that?"

"Jack thinks Bael was trying to send me a message," Anya said. "That I had no allies. He was trying to turn the humans against me. The demons, of course, believed there to be a bounty on my head."

"All so you'd crawl back to Bael," Cam said with a shake of her head. "I can't imagine living with someone so fucked up."

"He wasn't bad all the time," Anya said. "There were centuries when he never—"

"Yeah, I'm gonna stop you right there," Cam said. "You hear that? That little wistful sound in your voice? The one that's about to tell me that your abusive ex isn't all bad, that he doesn't hit you *every* day? That's why I'm going with you to the Underworld. Don't trust that you won't fall victim to all the bullshit you did before."

"I'm going to get Jack home," Anya said, sounding a little hurt. "I wouldn't abandon him."

"You *just* said—"

"I know what I said," she snapped. "I also know that if I wanted to abandon Jack, I wouldn't be here, listening to you insult and belittle me. I'd be taking my fifteen thousand dollars and disappearing."

"And that's all well and good, but I remember what happened in Atlanta," Cam said. "How he told you he forgave you and wanted you to come back home. You fucking *melted*."

"I didn't melt," Anya said. "And things are different now."

"Are they? I still hear you making excuses for him."

Anya inhaled and exhaled, as if she were steeling herself against whatever she wanted to really say. "You have my word that I'll bring Jack home. However the rest of it occurs is not your concern."

"So you're saying you're going to go back with Bael, then?" Cam asked, gripping the steering wheel in anger. "You're going to bring Jack home, then spend the rest of your life getting the shit kicked out of you."

"The only way I can keep Jack safe is by making Bael happy. Otherwise—"

"Wow," Cam said, folding her arms across her chest. "You know you could, of course, kill the mother fucker and we could solve this *whole* problem."

"You'd like that, wouldn't you?" Anya said, folding her arms across her chest.

"Yeah, I kind of would, considering he's holding my *entire family hostage* basically. And he keeps kidnapping my best friend. But hey, forgive me for thinking an athtar could think of anyone but herself."

Anya was silent for a moment. "I am thinking of Jack. Do you really think someone as weak as I am could stand a chance against Bael? The only way I can secure his safety is to keep Bael satisfied until Jack dies a happy old man."

"Then what?"

"Then…I don't know."

"Sounds like you need a better plan," Cam said. "C'mon, let's get inside before you pass out."

After checking in, they settled in a pair of queen beds in a room that smelled faintly of smoke. Cam stared at the ceiling, her mind and body still rolling at eighty miles an hour down the interstate. So much had happened that day that she'd forgotten half of what she'd been worried about.

Not even two months ago, she'd been settling Jack in Atlanta, working on schmoozing her way toward a mid-level director position for the US Division of the International Coalition for Demon Management. Then they'd stumbled across La Colibrí and things had just gone to shit. He'd run off in search of her, and Cam had stumbled upon a mystery of her own. The five iron talismans that hung around her wrist had been a gift from her grandmother. Cam had been told they were an old wives' tale. But she'd always suspected they could be more useful than helping her combat demonic miasma, so she'd started along a path to introduce them to ICDM headquarters.

Only, it turned out they *could* be weaponized, and the aforementioned King of the Demons had put a gag order on her family for the past umpteen generations to keep it hidden. A gag order he'd been kind enough to remind Cam of when he came to retrieve his girlfriend the day before.

Cam could picture his face as clearly as the ceiling above her. The disarming smile, the way he'd so casually threatened to slaughter her entire family if she continued to talk about the talismans. And he would make good on that promise. After all, he'd slaughtered an entire contingent of Division security guards in one second.

How the *hell* were they supposed to defeat that?

Emotions bubbled up inside her, and it took all her strength to keep tears at bay. She'd been crying entirely too much lately. Perhaps she just needed to get laid or something.

Instead, she grabbed her phone and left the room, seeking a quiet place to stare at the moon and figure some things out. Per Anya's request, her phone had been off since they'd decided on this ill-advised mission. Anya had even suggested (rather forcefully) that Cam toss the device entirely. But nobody was following them anymore. Bael had closed the schism. The athtars were back in the Underworld. And the Division was probably glad to be rid of both her and Jack.

Once the phone booted up, it began pinging with the hundred or so emails Cam had missed. It was an odd feeling to no longer care what Deputy Director Kim thought, not to worry about whether Director Navarro was going to let her continue on in Atlanta. Those worries and thoughts had since evaporated in the face of much bigger problems.

She unlocked the phone and dialed a number, closing her eyes.

"Hola?"

Her heart constricted in her chest. "Hi, Mama."

"Cam? Cam! Oh my God, where are you? What's going on?" Her mother spoke in rapid-fire Spanish, a testament to the chaos Cam had left behind. How Jack could've survived this as long as he did was beyond her.

"I'm fine," Cam said. *For now.* "Listen, Bael…took Jack. To the Underworld."

Her mother was silent. "And the demon woman?"

"She's…well, she and I are gonna get him back."

Cam braced herself for another onslaught, but there was only a quiet sigh. "The hole in Atlanta is closed."

"Yeah, well," Cam glanced around. "Apparently, that's not the only one. La Colibrí says she knows a way in."

"Are you sure you can trust her?"

Cam had asked herself the same thing a thousand times. "I don't have any other option."

Elena made a tutting sound. "Baby, I think… Maybe, it's time for you to let him go."

Tears rushed to Cam's eyes, and she struggled to keep them out of her voice. "Mama, you know I can't do that."

"Sara would understand."

"But that's just it," Cam said, wiping the wetness from her eyes. "It's not just about Sara. It's about every human who's ever been hurt by a demon. We're all..." She licked her lips, wondering how far she should veer into the truth.

Instead, her mother surprised her. "...So María told you, hm?"

"You know?" Cam said, sitting up straighter. "About the talismans?"

"Of course I know. Where do you think you get it from?" Elena said with a sad chuckle. "Believe it or not, your mother used to be a pretty fierce Division agent in her own right. I felt, as I'm sure you do, that it was wrong to keep these from humanity, no matter the cost."

Cam stuttered for a moment. "What changed?"

"I had a baby girl named Camilla," Elena said. "The moment you came into my life, I understood what María was saying about sacrifice. The greater good. Bael has killed in our family before and I couldn't risk him going after my children."

"But what about Sara?" Cam said, standing. "Mom, she could have been saved if we knew about the talismans—"

"And how many more would've died?" Elena said. "Bael is a powerful demon, my love. How many lives have we saved by toeing his line?"

"Yeah, well, that's part of why I'm headed down there," Cam said. "I want to get Jack, but man... I also want La Colibrí to slice his motherfucking head off."

Elena, by now used to Cam's tongue, simply sighed. "Do you think she's able to do that? She's been his lover for millennia."

"Yeah, and apparently, he's been beating the shit out of her," Cam said, sitting down. "You shoulda heard him yesterday. Talking about how much he loves her. I would've believed him, except for how damned terrified she is of him. And she told him to let her go."

"So he took Jack instead?"

"Yeah," Cam said. "It's so sick. He treats her like garbage, but even now, she won't even agree to kill him when we get down there. I'm afraid he'll bat his eyes at her and she'll puddle at his feet."

"Mm," Elena said, thoughtfully. "Perhaps not."

"You aren't here, Mama."

"The heart is a forgiving place, my love. But in this case, her actions speak louder. She's clearly going with you to the Underworld."

"But what if she goes back with Bael?"

"If she were going to do that, she would have already," Elena said. "She wouldn't have run with Jack all over the world in search of a resolution to her curse. She wouldn't have told Bael she was leaving him. Bael wouldn't have taken Jack unless he thought he was a threat. It sounds to me as if she's a woman working to break free of a bad situation, but needs some help getting there."

Cam slumped against the wall. "I wish that we'd never met

her. I don't want to be in the middle of this."

"But you are, my love. And maybe that's exactly where you're supposed to be. If anyone can make Anat realize what needs to be done, it's you."

"Well, I do have very little patience right now," Cam said with a laugh. "She owes me a lot after what she and Jack put me through. Least she could do is behead her ex."

Elena laughed, and it raised Cam's morose spirits. "Good to know you've still got your priorities straight. I'm so very proud of the woman you've become."

This was starting to feel like a goodbye call, so Cam swallowed her tears and steeled herself. "We're headed to Mexico City. Do you think…?"

"I'll put in a call to your grandmother. I'm sure she could put you up for a night. She may even have a few extra talismans lying around you could use."

Anya's warning rang in Cam's ear. "I'm not sure it'll be helpful where I'm going, but a good meal would be a nice send-off."

"Call me the moment you get back," Elena said, her voice filling with emotion. "Cam… I love you so very much."

Cam closed her eyes, letting one tear drop down her face. "I love you too, Mama. Tell Dad I said…"

"He's better off not knowing until you return," Elena said with a watery laugh. "But I'll give him an extra hug for you tonight."

"Thank you." Cam wiped the tears from her face. "Gotta

run. Love you."

"Be careful."

⊱❦⊰

"Where the hell did you go?" Anya said, sitting up when Cam walked into the room.

"Relax. I just made a phone call," Cam said, waving her phone.

Anya stiffened and flew out of bed wearing nothing but a long, white t-shirt. With frenzied speed, she yanked her pants on while snapping up the few things scattered around the room. "Are you *insane?*"

"Calm down," Cam said, holding up her hands. "It was just to my mother—"

"And Bael—"

"Is in the Underworld, remember?" Cam said, inching further into the room. "And he's waiting for you to come down there."

Anya dropped her toiletry bag and sank down on the bed. "Sorry. Habit."

"Hell of a habit," Cam said, sitting on the other bed. "You okay?"

"Yeah, just… bad dreams I guess." The demon stood and undid her pants, letting them fall gracelessly to the floor and leaving her dressed in the white shirt that hung to her mid-thigh. "I'm sorry, really."

"Hey, shit happens." She curled her legs beneath her. "He's really far in your head, isn't he?"

Anya leaned against the headboard. "It's not just him." Then she half-smiled at Cam's quirked brow. "Okay, it's mostly him. I've been on the run for so long, I don't know what it's like to be the one doing the chasing."

"It's a lot harder to chase than to be chased," Cam said. "Trust me, it was no picnic trying to figure out where you two would be going next. Thank God you guys stayed put in New Orleans long enough for someone to recognize you."

Anya snorted. "I told Jack it was stupid to not be more careful. But he wanted to call Bael's bluff. I guess he was right all along. Bael knew where I was. He'd always known where I was. Even before I met you and Jack, he knew I was alive."

"And you didn't…know that?" Cam said, sitting up. "The demon-maker connection is pretty well documented."

"Athtars are different," Anya snapped, pointedly staring at Cam.

"Are they, though? Or is that another lie Bael told to keep you all under his thumb?"

Anya didn't answer right away. "Not everything out of his mouth is a lie, you know."

"I kind of think it is," Cam said. "There's a rule that my grandmother taught me when I was young. When you get the measure of someone, expect them to act that way forever. You'll never be disappointed."

"What if they improve?" Anya asked.

"Then you'll be pleasantly surprised," Cam said. "But that rarely happens, you know. Bael is a liar. He's a manipulator.

He's going to do everything in his power to maintain control for as long as possible. So no, I wouldn't put it past him to keep pertinent information away from you."

Anya didn't respond, just glared at the ground as if unable to come up with a better response.

"Wanna talk about it?" Cam asked. "I'm not sleepy anymore anyway."

"No, I don't," she snapped. Then, after a brief pause, "We need to rest. If you need a nightcap, there should be a bottle in my weapons bag."

Cam sat up, a bit confused by the sudden change of character. "Thanks."

"I may be well enough to drive some tomorrow. But I'd prefer to save my energy."

"Get me some coffee, and I'll be right as rain," Cam said, but still crawled out of bed to hunt down the bottle. At the very least, it would help quiet her racing thoughts. Cam carefully sifted through the various swords and knives in Anya's weapons bag. Something white caught her attention, and she pulled out a man's shirt, identical to the one Anya wore to bed. On it, she caught a whiff of Jack's usual scent—a mixture of his shower gel and musk. She also found the mostly empty bottle of whiskey, from which she took a long sip. It burned, but the fuzzy feeling almost immediately took effect.

The demon woman's breathing had slowed as Cam crawled back into bed with the bottle in her hand. Again, Cam noticed the white shirt—Jack's shirt. This demon was sleeping in Jack's shirt.

Perhaps there was something to what her mother had said after all.

CHAPTER FOUR

Cam rustled, then settled to sleep, but Anya couldn't doze off. The dream she'd been having left her wide awake. She'd been reliving the last death she'd caused—Ekur. The sight of him falling backward. The smell of his blood. The knowledge that *she'd* done it of her own free will.

"You did what you had to. If you didn't kill him, he would have killed you."

Jack's voice floated through her memory. She curled up tighter against the pillow, inhaling the faint smell of the man who'd comforted her that night. When she'd become so dependent on him, she had no idea. But there she was, missing him with an ache that wouldn't relent. Smelling his t-shirt like a woebegone teenager.

In the short time they'd been together, he'd become the only stable thing in a world that was constantly shifting. There were no pretenses behind his smile, no ulterior motive. He'd come because he wanted to help her, then stayed because he wanted her.

Something she was still having a hard time believing.

But now he was gone, and she was lost again. Unlike before, when she'd had the threat of the curse to keep her tethered to an identity, now she had nothing. She lacked the courage to even accept why she was on this journey in the first place. The truth lurked behind the intent of their travels, watching her with blood red eyes and sharp teeth promising pain. Pain if she completed the task, and more if she didn't.

She'd *known* falling for someone else was a bad idea. Bael had shown his jealous nature with Ayumi, the servant girl who Anya had befriended once. Now, with Jack? She could only imagine the torture he was going through. She prayed Bael would save his worst punishments for her. But that had never been the case, no matter how much she begged for it.

And yet, even as she feared and hated Bael, some part of her accepted the situation—even justified it. After all, Bael had rescued her from a mortal life filled with pain. And she'd repaid him through betrayal.

The day Anya had met Bael had been a day like any other in the hot, humid village near the Mediterranean Sea. Anya had been around thirteen—old enough to have started her monthly bleeding, which was the cause of everything.

Her father was a gambler, a drunk, and owed money to

nearly every man in the village. Anya had no idea why her father had chosen the particular man she was to wed, but she did know he was probably three times her age, and had grandchildren. Perhaps it was simply the timing. The day he'd discovered her bloody linens was when he'd announced her impending nuptials.

Protesting had been a futile effort; there was nothing she could do. She was expected to lie on her back and do whatever her new husband said, regardless of how she felt about it. But she spoke her mind anyway, awaking his wrath. But as her father raised his voice in argument, spittle flying from his grotesque mouth and his hands bruising her delicate skin, the world began to shake.

Her father fell to his knees and she bolted from the house. Ignoring the shrieking of the people around her, she ran as fast and as hard as she could. Why, she still had no idea. Perhaps it was just delaying the inevitable. Perhaps she was hoping the shaking would demolish the village and everyone in it. Or maybe she thought it was the end of the world, and she wanted to see her sanctuary one last time.

Huffing and puffing, she crested the hill and stood atop it as the world slowly stopped trembling. The crystal waters were rougher than usual, shaken by what Anya now knew was an earthquake, but still breathtaking. She'd been coming to the idyllic blue water since she could toddle. It was the one place she could go to escape her miserable life—one place unsullied by her father and the miseries of the village.

The sound of gravel crunching beneath feet roused her and

fear sent daggers into her heart. Would it be her father, finally come to take her? Or her betrothed?

The man who stood before her was neither. His skin was golden brown, like hers. His hair was long and thick, hanging to his elbows. But what struck her most was the bewildered look. As if he'd just stepped into a world he didn't recognize.

He spoke to her in a strange tongue. She backed up a few steps, too afraid to turn and run. She'd known nothing but cruel men, and there was nothing to make her suspect this man would be any different.

She steeled herself, crawling back into the space in her mind that held the sea and serenity as the man approached closer. He placed two soft hands against her cheeks and wiped away her tears. Her eyes fluttered open to look into his. There was kindness there—something she had only seen from her mother, who'd died when she was young.

The man spoke again, and although she didn't understand him, when he offered his hand to take her away, she readily accepted.

They didn't return to the village; rather, he brought her into a world of vibrant colors and beautiful mountains that stretched for miles and miles. Her champion continued to speak in the language she didn't understand, but it didn't matter. He'd saved her, and she would do whatever he said without question. And when he kissed her the first time, her young heart soared.

Along with that kiss had come new feelings—that invasion of demonic energy that had scared her at first. But she'd trusted

Bael, her savior, that he wouldn't hurt her, and she'd allowed the kernel of magic to take root. She had known, somehow without being told, that becoming a demon was the only way to escape her father and the life that she'd led in that village.

"Do you accept this gift?"

"Yes," she had replied.

Glorious pleasure pulsed through her. It was the first time she'd ever felt so alive, so perfect. The man's words began to make sense in her addled brain, promising riches and beauty if she'd just submit to him, if she would stay with him and be his Lady. And she, a mere peasant girl, readily accepted.

She had awoken a woman, but had still very much been a girl. Bael took great pleasure in doting on her, washing her hair and making her simple dresses. It was just the two of them in Ath-kur then, no servants, no other belus. And for Anya, it was heaven.

Then, one day, Bael asked if she wanted to return to her village.

"No," she'd said definitively. "I don't ever want to see that place again."

"But my lady," he cooed, taking her into his arms. "You are strong now. Wouldn't you want to see all those who hurt you destroyed?"

Did she? She still had nightmares about her father's beatings, and still worried he might show up and ruin their paradise.

"You could kill him," Bael whispered, as seductive as ever. "Him and everyone else. Show them the true power of an athtar.

You are the most incredible, the most powerful creature. They will tremble at your feet." He held her face in his hands. "I want them to fear you as much as I love you."

And though she didn't want to at first, she'd returned with Bael and slaughtered every single person in the village, just to hear Bael sing her praises.

It had been a long three thousand years since then. At times, Anya felt every year, and others, she remained that scared teenager who yearned for Bael to rescue her once more. No matter how many centuries passed, she still saw that long-haired, disheveled man who'd cupped her cheeks and carried her away to a fantasy world like a knight in shining armor.

Would she ever be able to separate the two? Could she slay the monster while she still longed for the man?

That was the question she kept asking herself as she silently cried herself to sleep.

CHAPTER FIVE

The whiskey had done the trick, because the next thing Cam knew, it was nine in the morning, and Anya was shaking her awake.

"Brought you this," she said, placing a large cup on the beside table.

"Thanks," Cam said, rubbing her face. "Didn't mean to sleep in."

"It's been a long few days," she said, sitting down on the bed. "How long until we reach Mexico City?"

"From here? Maybe another five hours," Cam said, stretching her tight shoulders. "We can crash with my grandmother. She's about an hour outside the city."

Anya furrowed her brow. "Is that advisable?"

"She's not like my Great Aunt María, if that's what you're worried about," Cam replied. "Polar opposite, in fact."

"I meant, are you willing to..." Anya's shoulders sagged. "Never mind. I suppose no one would be looking for us."

"Because we're not on the run."

"Because we're not on the run," she repeated with a shake of her head.

"But I appreciate you looking out for my grandmother," Cam said, before taking a long sip of coffee. It tasted like an old tire, but it would get her up and out the door. "Maybe you aren't as bad as I thought."

"Don't let our conversation last night fool you," Anya said, although there was very little heat in it. "I'm still the Lady of Destruction."

"Who brought her friend a cup of coffee?"

"Who brought her *driver* a cup of coffee."

"Sure," Cam said, with an exaggerated wink. "Now I see why Jack stayed."

Anya's eyes grew wide for a moment, then she walked out of the hotel room.

Several hours later, they reached the outer limits of Mexico City, and the roads began to look a little more familiar. The García clan had been in Mexico City for hundreds (perhaps thousands) of years, but the current familial home was in the mountains, surrounded by lush green forest. It was easy to miss the turn onto the small road that cut through the greenery, and Cam nearly did as she veered around a corner.

The car whined and complained the whole way up, but the

drive was worth it. Aptly named Hacienda los Xoxoctic, or Green House in a blend of Spanish and Nahuatl words, the pink clay home towered out of the mountainside, with a large overhang held up by concrete columns, tile steps, and a front garden filled with green bushes and multi-colored flowers.

"I don't know which house is more impressive, yours or Jack's." Anya muttered from the passenger side.

"Mine, obviously," Cam said with a smirk. "This one predates Jack's by a good hundred years."

Anya nodded to the house. "That must be your grandmother."

Juana stood in the doorway, a wide grin on her old, wrinkled face. She, like the rest of the García clan, was short and stocky, and gray hair spilled in glorious curls down her back.

"Camilla, my love!" she exclaimed the thickly-accented Spanish favored by those from Mexico City. "Do you know it's been exactly twenty months since I've last seen you?"

Cam got out of the car, the smile on her face matching the one in her heart. "Been a little busy. I'm sorry."

"Your family is always more important than that Division you work for. Remember that," she said, holding out her arms for a hug.

Cam embraced her, breathing in the scent of childhood and summer, and probably something delicious for dinner. She hadn't realized how much she'd needed such an embrace. But coming to la hacienda always dissolved the adult part of Cam to reveal the gangly teenager she always felt like inside.

"You, demon." Juana said to Anya. "Go in the backdoor."

Anya shot the woman a glare, but hoisted all their bags and marched toward the back.

"There now. We have some privacy," Juana said with a smile.

"Anya isn't going to be a problem," Cam said. "She's on our side."

"Mm-hm," Juana said with a snort, then her face lightened. "Come, let's get you settled. I know you've had a long drive."

Cactuses lined the stone entrance into a surprisingly modern home filled with local art and concrete floors. Long, vine-covered outdoor walkways separated each of the different rooms housed in their own buildings.

Cam stood in the center of the buildings and drank in the view. The house overlooked green, nobbly mountains that rose into the blue sky. Other houses dotted the countryside, but here, Cam could've been the only person in the universe. It was a nice reprieve from the weeks and months of stress.

"Did you bring your suit?" Juana asked. "The pool needs some attention."

"No, we're just here for a night," Cam replied.

"Then off to the Underworld?"

She pursed her lips. "Mama needs to learn to keep her mouth shut."

"You above all people should know, Camilla, that mamas know everything," Juana said with a slight spank to Cam's behind. "And don't be disrespectful to your mother."

"It's not that," Cam said, Bael's warning creeping into her

mind. "I don't want anything to happen to her. I'm dealing with some scary stuff here."

"Bael isn't so scary," Juana said with a look only an old, wise grandmother could pull off. "He's an insecure little boy who needs others to make him feel good about himself."

Cam gaped.

"I've been speaking ill of the king since I was a little girl," Juana said simply. "I do not fear him, and thus he has no power over me."

"But he can stop time—"

"And I have a talisman that can kill him," she said with a quirked brow. She nodded to the door, where two arrows were crossed over the entrance. "Those have all five symbols inscribed on them. No demon can walk through my front door."

"That's why you wanted Anya to go in the backdoor?"

"That, and I think she's scum," Juana said with a chuckle.

"I can sleep in the car, if it's inconvenient for me to be here," Anya said, placing the bags down. She wore an impassive look, but Cam could tell she'd been a bit hurt.

"My grandmother is a bit ornery," Cam explained in English.

That earned a thumb to her side. "I'm fluent in seven languages, granddaughter," Juana replied in the same.

"Since when?" Cam asked.

"Since always." The old woman cackled. "I just let you and your sister think otherwise so you'd tell more secrets."

Cam's mouth hung as she thought of the conversations she

had with Sara in the house. Many of them revolved around the various boys they were flirting (then sleeping) with, as well as the proper way to sneak in and out of the bedroom window.

Juana whistled to herself as she bustled off to the gourmet kitchen. "I've got a pot of Pozole de Frijol on the stove, when you ladies are hungry."

"Well, I can see where you get it from," Anya observed.

"Get what?"

"Everything."

Despite the frosty greeting, Juana had welcomed Anya to her dining room table and fed the both of them a hearty meal of bean soup. Afterward, Juana kicked them both out of the kitchen promising a spanking if they lifted a finger to help with the dishes.

Anya retreated to her room, muttering something about a shower, but Cam ventured out onto the porch. The pool was lit with an eerie blue glow, mirroring the large full moon in the sky. Cam removed her socks and shoes, rolled up her pants, then dipped her feet in the cool water. For the first time in years, everything was quiet—in her mind and in her world—for one beautiful moment.

"Your grandmother is an interesting individual."

Anya appeared beside her, wearing a fresh set of pants and shirt, her long, black hair dripping from a shower.

"Between my family and Jack's, neither of us has ever been wanting for love," Cam said. "Or a ration of shit."

Anya looked up to the sky. "I've contacted my friend. She'll meet with us tomorrow night."

"Is she going to get us in to see the noxes?" Cam asked.

The demon sat down next to her. "One can only hope. Otherwise, I'll have to find a few noxes and threaten them within an inch of their life."

"We could skip the meeting and do that anyway," Cam said.

"You forget I'm operating at a sliver of my strength," Anya said. "I don't wish to walk into the Noxlands with even less power. They would sniff me out and slaughter me before I could mount a defense. It's better to try diplomacy, if we can."

"Diplomacy, who needs it?" Juana had joined them out on the patio.

"We do," Cam said with a small laugh. "I'm not interested in taking on the noxes either."

"The noxes aren't so bad."

"You also said that about Bael," Cam reminded her.

Juana smiled, the wrinkles of her face growing deeper and giving her the look of a cheshire cat. "They say the first demons were humans expelled from this earth for original sins. Pride, envy, greed, anger, lust. God chose the worst offenders, so as to save the rest of humanity from those sins."

"Do you believe that?" Cam asked.

She shrugged. "I believe evil still lives in men's hearts, and not all demons are full of their supposed sin. You, my dear, do not strike me as a prideful woman."

Anya half-smiled. "I used to be."

"Yes, but then you did something else. Choices, my dears, are what makes a life." She nodded toward Cam. "You and Jackson could've held illustrious careers in the highest ranks of ICDM. Instead, you both decided to help people. Jackson chose to help this demon woman at the expense of his career and, I'm sure, your sanity."

"You're not saying Bael can change, are you?" Cam asked dubiously.

Juana smiled. "Bael would first have to recognize there was a problem, wouldn't he? I don't think him capable of such self-reflection."

Anya snorted. "You're right about that."

"But the noxes. Oh, they are fascinating creatures. I can't speak for the demons who killed our Sara, for they don't live under the thumb of Lotan in the Underworld." Juana's eyes narrowed with unspent anger, then softened again. "But while those who've lived amongst us are still frightful, they're not wholly evil beings."

Cam shook her head. "That's not what—"

"My sister María tends to believe whatever truth will keep the humans from asking too many questions," Juana said with a chuckle. "It makes her job harder when they press back, you know."

"Yeah, I know."

"My grandmother told me stories of the noxes," Juana said, sitting back in her chair. "They emerged, a man and a woman from the mountains. They wore robes like gods, and carried no weapons. From the story *I* was told, they came in peace. They met with the Aztec emperor and offered immortal life to any human who wished to join them in the Underworld. Many went willingly to become stronger to protect their families."

Cam looked at Anya. "Is this true?"

"We didn't interact much with noxes," she said, gaze focused on the pool.

"Ah, yes, but I assure you, Bael knew what Lords Mot and Xo were doing. It was by his hand that the Spaniards left Cuba for Tenochtitlan. More than a few elokos and kappas were with them on that journey," Juana said with a growl. "And the rest, as they say, is history."

Cam stared at the water, surprised that she could still be surprised. "But if Bael was responsible for that, then why did he let someone bring the talismans along?"

"Our ancestor," Juana said with a nod. "Bael has very little patience for the details of the wars he wages. He also shares nothing with those who carry out the details. So much can happen under his nose." Juana looked at Anya and winked. "As I'm sure you know, Lady Anat."

Cam leaned back onto her palms, letting her feet swirl in the water. "So this bullshit has been going on for centuries. Humans have been proxy fighting these demonic wars for Bael."

"Oh, don't blame Bael entirely, my love. Humans have been doing a good job of fighting their own wars, too." Juana chuckled.

"So why did the noxes kill Sara if they're supposedly so

peaceful?"

"For the same reason Nunzia was killed. Vicente has become too complacent in his lordship, far away from the nox den in Mexico City. He'd become more allied with Bael than his own prince. And Bael lets them do what they please."

"And that's why I have to go to the Underworld. This shit has to end," Cam said.

Anya made a noise and pursed her lips. "Cam, you can't go with me."

Juana just laughed. "You should know by now, demon, that telling my granddaughter not to do anything is the best way to ensure she'll do it."

Cam just grinned.

CHAPTER SIX

Jack had no idea what time of day it was, or how long he'd been stuck in Ath-kur. But he'd eaten four meals, which was his gauge for the passage of time. Other than the first, terrifying meal delivered by Sara, his attendants had been a kappa and eloko, both looking more human than demonic. It had given him time to recover and reflect on this brand of torture, and how best to fight it. After all, it was only a matter of time before she came back. Bael wouldn't let him get too comfortable.

With nothing to do but think, Jack had plenty of time to wonder about Bael's end game. Was he simply biding his time until he grew bored of toying with Jack? Would he let Jack die in this place—either from old age or a broken heart? Or was he waiting for Anya, perhaps to prove to her once and for all that Bael was the only man she should be with?

Jack had his doubts that Anya would come. She was skittish

on a good day, and had spent most of their time together belittling him and keeping him at arm's length. Bael had given her a get-out-of-jail free card. She could very well disappear into the ether and live unhappily until the lack of athtar magic killed her.

Or she could put her freedom and life at risk to rescue him.

The door opened, revealing the demon-dressed-as-Sara, wearing a white lace nightgown and carrying a plate of food with a bottle of wine perched on the edge.

"Hi, Jackie."

"'Lo," he grunted, walking himself through the steps he'd prepared in the interim. He let himself be surprised by her appearance, to be happy to see her walking and talking. Then he reminded himself forcefully that she was *not* real. He kept Bael's face in the forefront of his mind, which made him both angry and maintained a grip on reality.

"I thought we might try again," she said, putting the tray on the table. "Bael was kind enough to send along a bottle of wine. He so wants us to make amends with each other."

"I'm sure he does," Jack said.

"Have a glass with me?"

Jack peeled himself off the bed, sensing things might go better if he played along. He had set very small goals for himself —first and foremost, preventing more psychological torture. Once he'd figured the game, he could play it, and then, eventually, escape.

Sara smiled as she poured him a glass of wine and placed his plate in front of him then gave herself a glass. "This is nice."

"Mm." Jack took a bite, hoping to avoid making conversation with her as long as possible by keeping his mouth full.

"I'm glad you're eating," she said, swirling the wine in her glass.

Jack swallowed. "It's rich food. I should be let out of this room for some exercise."

When she leaned back to laugh, he caught a glimpse of her cleavage, and he could practically predict what she'd say next. "We don't have to leave to exercise."

"Not sure I'm ready for that," he muttered, diverting his gaze to the pork loin on his plate.

"Oh right, I forgot. You've moved on to another woman." She took a sip. "She isn't good enough for you. Not after the way she treated you."

"What do you know about that?" Jack asked.

"She asked you to give up everything just to keep her happy."

"That's…not what happened at all," Jack said. "I chose to go with her. She needed my help."

"And yet…" Sara gestured around the room. "She's not here. She left you here, Jack. So why are you holding onto her so tightly when I'm right here?"

He had no answer that he was comfortable voicing. It was getting harder to remember this Sara wasn't real, especially as she slid her hand across his.

"It wouldn't be cheating if you're sleeping with your actual wife, you know."

"It's not about cheating," Jack said, before stopping himself. This argument was a logical fallacy, as his wife was dead. This was Bael. But he couldn't help himself. "Besides that, the vow was: 'til death. And you died. So there you go."

Her eye widened, then filled with tears. "Jack, how could you say something so horrible to me? I came back to life for you. And you…you act like you never loved me."

"I loved my wife," Jack said forcefully.

"Past tense." She looked at the ground. "So it's true. You've really moved on."

"What do you want me to say?" Jack said. "I *died* that night. I've been walking around like a dead man for three years until something finally got me out of bed. And you want me to feel guilty for that? You want me to…"

"I don't want you to feel guilty, Jack. I want us to get back to where we used to be. I want us to be a family." She squeezed his hand. "We were going to start one, remember? I just want to pick up where we left off. Forget about whatever else happened while I was away."

"While you were *dead*," he said through gritted teeth. It was getting harder to resist and remember the truth.

"I'm back. I'm here. I want you. Please, stop fighting me."

Jack stood up abruptly, knocking over the table with a clatter. The sound broke whatever spell she'd had over him, leaving only his panting and her quiet whimpers. She'd fallen to the ground, the red wine staining her white chemise like blood.

It was too much to look at, so he turned away from her.

"The least you could do is apologize," she whispered, gathering the fallen food and putting it back on the plate. "You've changed, Jack. You never used to get angry with me."

Her voice, so quiet, so perfect, tore him up inside. He closed his eyes, reminding himself this wasn't real—she wasn't real. She was dead. This conversation, the one that he'd had in his mind a thousand times since her death, wasn't real.

Soft hands slid across his hips to rest against his chest and she pressed herself against his back as she held him.

"I want you back, Jack."

And he let her hold him, telling himself that it was playing her game and praying it wasn't because his defenses were slipping.

CHAPTER SEVEN

After spending the morning and early afternoon resting and eating more food than Cam had eaten in months, she and Anya set off downtown to meet with Anya's friend. Before they left, Juana gave Cam a handful of nox talismans to take with her.

"Just in case," Juana said.

"It won't be necessary," Anya replied, looking over her shoulder. "Cam can't go with us."

"So you say, demon. So you say."

It took Cam an hour to drive into the city, and another half-hour to find the neighborhood where they were meeting Anya's friend. It was in a demonic part of town, strangely empty for the early evening. There was a faint magic in the air, the kind that lifted the hair on Cam's neck. She toyed with the talismans in her pocket. They didn't seem to help the nervous feeling in her stomach, so she strapped on her macuahuitl—the club-like weapon designed by her ancestor with sharp teeth that sprang out at the click of a button. And for extra confidence she took Jack's knives and rested them in her lap.

They were all that was left of her partner after Bael had taken him. She was looking forward to giving them back soon.

"So tell me about this 'friend' of yours," Cam said, to distract herself. "Who is she? Is she a nox? How come she's your friend if they all hate you so much?"

"She has…special privileges. She's a very old nox who was extremely close to the belus."

"How old?"

"2500 years, perhaps."

Cam furrowed her brow. "How's that possible? The noxes weren't seen in the human realm until the sixteenth century."

"Bael brought a group of humans to Mot and Xo as a peace offering once," Anya said. "She was in that group. Xo was especially fond of her."

"And she calls you a friend after you killed her maker? She must be one forgiving person."

"She's useful," Anya murmured, looking at the knives in Cam's hand. "Gave those to Jack."

Cam examined the knives more closely than before. The leather handles were different from the black kevlar on all modern Division weapons, and the blades were a bright silver versus a dull metal and balanced evenly. Cam wasn't a weapons expert by any means, but she recognized good craftsmanship when she found it.

"Why? His knives were fine."

"He'd been struggling in fights," Anya said quietly. "I thought he was carrying too much emotional attachment to his knives, so I brought him to her. She quickly diagnosed the problem, gave him new weapons, and he was on his way."

"Yeah, he was pretty shaky," Cam replied. "But it was because he was out of practice."

She shook her head. "As long as he carried the guilt of his wife's death, he wouldn't be able to use his old knives. Too many bad memories."

Cam opened and closed her mouth. When Jack had arrived in Atlanta, Cam had been more focused on getting back to normal. On having her partner back so she could continue her career climb. And she'd *yelled* at him for being so indecisive and off balance. Anya, on the other hand, had seen past the struggle for what it really was.

Some best friend Cam was.

"It's time," Anya said.

She and Cam earned some looks for their weapons from the few passersby on the street. Cam wasn't sure if they were demons or just humans who wanted to tempt fate in this demonic neighborhood. Either way, the onlookers gave Cam and Anya a wide berth.

"Down here," Anya said, leading her through an alley. The hair on Cam's neck rose slightly as the nox magic became more potent. A growl emitted from one of the dark doorways, and Cam pulled the knives from her holster, readying them.

Anya held her hand up. "Easy, Cam. She's a friend."

"Friend?" came the snappy reply. "That's not what you said a few weeks ago."

The nox prowled in darkness more like a cat than hellbeast, but her claws were definitely out—toward Anya.

"You knew it was a lie or you wouldn't have come when I emailed you," Anya said.

"And what is this? Two appearances this decade?" the woman purred with a deadly smile. "Color me surprised."

"I need your help, Oce," Anya replied evenly. "Please."

The anger melted off the nox's face. "Well, since you're asking so nicely…" Her yellowish gaze turned to Cam, then lit up like a kid on Christmas. "And what happened to your other human?"

"That's what I need your help for. Bael… Bael took Jack to the Underworld."

Oce chuckled. "And why, pray tell, did he do such a thing?"

Anya clenched her jaw then thought better of it and lifted her chin higher. "Because I asked him to let me go."

The demon's eyes grew to the size of saucers, and she lost her air of playful mystery in favor of gaping disbelief. "This is welcome news indeed. Shocking, but welcome."

"It wasn't so much a tell-off as a tearful goodbye," Cam replied with a snort.

"Believe me, human, I've been waiting for such for centuries," Oce replied with that same air of incredulousness. "I'm very proud of you, Lady."

"Yeah, well, look at the good it did me," Anya said with a scowl. "He took Jack, and now I have to return to the Underworld anyway. Exactly as he wanted me to. I fail to see how any of this is positive."

"We're wasting time," Cam said, stepping forward. "Look, do you have a way into the Underworld or not? Our gate in Atlanta sealed up, and we need alternate means."

Oce's gaze slid back to Cam, and she quirked a smile. "And who might you be, who speaks so boldly in front of the Lady of Destruction?"

"This is Jack's partner," Anya said. "The one with the demon talismans."

Oce's eyes lit up and she clapped her hands. "Oh, I've heard much about you! And your talismans…"

"Yeah, well…" Cam looked at her feet. Bael's threat against her family was still very clearly at the forefront of her mind. "There's not much to tell about them."

"Bael has forbidden talk of it among the humans," Anya replied with a wave of her hands. "For obvious reasons."

"Because they could actually fight back?" Oce said with a shake of her head. "I hope you know, human, that once Anya beheads Bael, you and I will have a very long chat about your talismans."

Anya sucked in a breath but didn't argue with Oce. "First, we need to get to Ath-kur. Do you think you can help us?"

Oce pursed her lips in thought. "You know they don't like you in La Madriguera."

"She said she'd grovel to get us past," Cam said.

"Groveling may not even cut it," Oce replied. "Our lady killed the belu noxes. There are some in our family who will never forgive her for it." She tilted her head. "But there are others who might be persuaded, if your purpose for using our portal meets our needs."

Cam glanced between them. "Meaning?"

"Meaning I have to swear I'll kill Bael," Anya said in a whisper. "Oce, that's too much to ask."

Oce shrugged. "I'm merely offering advice to help you in your journey. If you opt not to take it, that's your decision."

"Hell, *I'll* swear to kill Bael," Cam said, glancing between the two of them. "We just need to get inside."

"For the last time, Cam, you *aren't* going," Anya replied with a shake of her head. "You'll draw more attention to me than I need."

"I don't give a shit about what you need," Cam barked. "My partner is being tortured."

"I told you I'd get him back," Anya replied.

"You also said Bael wasn't all that bad."

"I care about Jack," she snapped.

"Really?" Oce said. "You…actually care about this human? And you're admitting it?"

Anya's cheeks had grown pink, and she carefully considered her words. "He's a good man."

That must've been some secret code, because Oce's face blossomed into a smile once more. "I'll take you to La

Madriguera and do my best to vouch for you."

"Thank you." Anya turned to Cam. "Return to the car."

"Like hell I will," Cam said, placing a firm hand on Jack's knives. "I'm going with you."

"Can you help with this?" Anya said to Oce. "Tell her La Madriguera is no place for a human."

"I believe the miasma will do what it does," Oce said with a small shrug. "Eventually, she will succumb and turn back. But we must go now."

"Fine," Anya said with a hefty eye roll. "Let's just get going."

"Succumb, my ass." Cam glowered at the two demons' retreating backs, but followed them down the maze of alleys and narrow streets. Now, the magic was potent, so Cam stuffed her hand inside her pocket, grasping the five extra nox talismans. It took the edge off, but she had a feeling they would be no match for the power she was about to encounter.

Even with the protection, bad thoughts and memories stirred in her subconscious, eliciting a fluttering of anxiety in her chest. She inhaled and exhaled. She was descended from demon hunters who'd been tangling with noxes for centuries. Fighting them was in her blood. Normally, this little pep talk worked. Now, with all she knew about the talismans and her family, the strong voice had a note of doubt.

If Anya noticed Cam's nerves, she made no mention of it, and for that, Cam was grateful.

They turned a corner, and Cam was hit with a wave of nox magic, pouring out of a large open door flanked by two statues of fully-transformed noxes with sharp teeth and fur. They were so lifelike that Cam expected them to move.

"These come from the noxlands?" Anya asked, looking a little green herself.

Oce nodded. "Carved by our best artisans. It's an effective deterrent to humans and demons alike."

"Why?" Cam said with a small shiver. "Because they're scary?"

"Because they're imbued with the same magic I am," Oce said with a smile. "Everything in the noxlands is."

Cam wasn't looking forward to experiencing the noxlands for herself, if two stone statues could make her feel this shitty. But she wasn't going to share that sentiment with Anya. "Let's go."

Oce shrugged, patting the two statues on the head as if they were beloved pets. Past the entrance, Cam was enveloped in darkness, the light from the outside world fading with every downward step. She stretched her fingers and skimmed the cool wall to keep her balance. The last thing she wanted was to trip over her feet and faceplant in front of the noxes. Just the thought awoke a storm of fear—

"Knock it off," Cam muttered to herself.

"You all right?" Anya asked.

"Fine."

Anya closed her hand over Cam's shoulder and squeezed. "Jack would understand if you turned around."

"I'm *fine*," Cam said, trying to shake her hand to no avail.

"Worry about your own shit."

"I am," Anya said. "You're my shit right now."

Oce stopped abruptly, and Cam would've knocked her over, if not for Anya's grip. The nox turned and flashed a smile in the darkness. "Stay here. I'll announce your presence."

"No need," came a voice from inside. "We can taste their stench in the air."

Light flashed at the bottom of the stairs, and fear climbed Cam's spine. Oce released a sigh of frustration and continued the descent into the room below, Anya and Cam right behind her. The antechamber arched high into the air, a cavernous space that resembled something out of a horror movie. Cam wasn't sure if they were underground, but she was definitely claustrophobic. Only the pressure of Anya's hand kept her from spiraling out of control.

That was, until she saw the gigantic hellbeast sitting on the other end of the room.

Cam had never seen a fully transformed nox. She'd read about them at the Academy. She'd studied photos and paintings. But they didn't do the Clydesdale-sized creature justice. His fangs, not unlike the stone statues above, were a brilliant white, dripping with drool, and probably a foot long. His paws, resembling those of a wolf, bore nails that could probably slice Cam in half without trying. She wasn't sure why the beasts needed magic to make humans fear them if they looked like this.

"Lord Cerberus," Oce said, stepping forward with a sweeping bow. "It is an honor to be in your presence once again."

The yellow eyes narrowed, and Cam got the distinct impression he didn't consider it an honor to see them at all.

"Lord Cerberus—" Anya began, but was drowned out by a loud chorus of human cries and dog barking.

Cam finally tore her eyes away from the monster at the front of the room. There were *more* hellbeasts filling the dark space. Some of them were human, others were half-human, half-beast. Yet others resembled their lord with large claws and teeth. They were outnumbered. If this started going south, would they get out of there alive?

"It would be better if you didn't address him, Lady," Oce said with a gentle look over her shoulder.

"Fine," Anya muttered.

"Lord," Oce smiled easily, "I apologize for the intrusion."

"As well you should," said the beast, his gaping mouth taking on almost a human appearance as it moved. "We have tolerated your friendship with the athtar, but this is too far."

Oce quirked a brow. "My friendship with the athtar was blessed by the nox prince himself, Lord. He remains our leader, not you." A low growl was his response, and Oce chuckled, placing a dainty hand on her hip. "You don't wish for me to embarrass you in front of our nox family again, do you? Let me speak, and we'll avoid it."

Cam would've liked to see the diminutive nox take on such a fierce hellbeast. What kind of monster would *she* turn into?

The nox lord gnashed his teeth together. "Speak."

"The athtar wishes to use our gate into the Noxlands," Oce started, holding up her hands to silence the growing outrage. "She has decided to switch sides. She will return to Ath-kur to kill the so-called King of the Underworld."

The room went silent.

"I understand you may think she's lying or that this is lunacy, but..." Oce glanced over her shoulder at Anya, who wore a face of stone. "I believe this is our chance to rid ourselves of that athtar despot for good."

"And how do we know we can trust her?" Cerberus began. "Bael has closed his schism to the Underworld. She could be on her way to reconcile with her lover."

"If I was going to reconcile, I wouldn't have waited until the door was closed," Anya drawled, earning a chorus of growls from the room.

"Trickery!"

"Kill her where she stands!"

"Noxes," Oce said, her small voice echoing in the space and silencing the rest of them. "I understand this is a lot to ask. But I believe her to be speaking the truth." She straightened and lifted her chin at Cerberus. "So what say you, Lord Cerberus? Will you grant them access to your gateway?"

The monster cracked a smile. "Not in this lifetime."

More growling, barking, and roaring from the peanut gallery as the noxes celebrated their lord's decision. Anya placed her hands on her swords at her back, her eyes flaring with anger, but Oce held up one hand. "Please, lady. Allow me to resolve this."

"I'm only asking permission to be *diplomatic*," Anya said, loud enough for Cerberus to hear. "Otherwise, I'll find the gateway and kill everything in my path as I go through it."

The noxes at the edges of the room moved closer, and Cam's heart slammed against her chest. "Anya, probably not the smartest idea to antagonize them."

"I don't give two shits what's smart," Anya growled, releasing her swords from their sheaths. "These assholes think they can keep something from me?"

"Ladies, gentlemen. Calm yourselves."

It was as if a blanket of calm fell over the room, and the growling and barking ceased. Only Anya was still ready for the fight, her swords perched in her hands. The man who'd spoken looked fully human, and, Cam thought, fully handsome as well. Black ringlets set off dark brown skin and a bright white smile that seemed wolfish and sexy at the same time. The man breezed through the room, placing a calming hand on those who were still upset about the intrusion. He stood next to Cerberus, dwarfed by the monster's size, and yet, it was clear this was someone used to commanding respect.

"And you are?" Anya drawled.

"He is an underworlder," came the snarl from Cerberus. "And we're so anxiously waiting for the nox prince to call you home, sir."

"Please, Lord Cerberus, we are family. Levi is appropriate." He bowed to Anya. "I am the nox prince's close personal confidante, and liaison to the human realm."

Cerberus growled, one of his teeth spanning the length of the man's forearm as he patted the monster on the side of the muzzle. "Stay out of this," he snapped to the man.

"I'm not trying to overstep, my lord," Levi said with a tut. "But I believe we have a unique opportunity here. It's not often we'll have the Lady of Destruction in our debt. We should extract a favor for allowing her entry."

Anya finally put away her swords. "Fine. What do you want?"

"Apologize for the death of our belus."

The swords came back out instantly. "*Fuck off*," she growled as Oce placed a restraining hand on her arm. "Anything else, but not that. Never that."

"Levi, it's clear there's bad blood on both sides," Oce said with a glare. "I'm sure you can understand that such an apology would be difficult to obtain."

Levi shrugged. "Then I guess you aren't that interested in getting down to the Underworld. Perhaps you can wait until your lover creates another schism in four years."

"For shit's sake, apologize," Cam said to Anya.

Oce glanced over her shoulder and smiled. "You can still speak with all this miasma? You're a lot stronger than most humans."

"Don't get me wrong, I'm fucking scared as hell," Cam said, unsure it was wise to announce such a thing when every eye on the room was on her. "But this is important. Whatever they did to you can't be worth all this!"

Anya's gaze slid to her, and Cam was surprised to read sadness in it. "Mot and Xo killed my daughter. Their deaths were warranted."

Cam's mouth fell open, and Levi made a disgusted sound. "That's a lie," he spat. "The belus were peaceful and grateful to keep away from the cosmic shitshow that went on in Mount Zephon."

"Oh, really?" Anya said. "Then who did it? Who took my daughter from me before her fifth birthday?"

"Let's see," he said, tapping his hand against his cheek. "Who amongst the demons has a track record for killing thousands, including babes and toddling children? Who amongst the demons is legendary for his obsession with his own power?"

A muscle twitched in Anya's cheek, but her eyes narrowed. "Bael is many things, but he would never hurt his own child." She leveled her sword at the man. "This conversation is over. If the price to get past you is to apologize for the death of Asherah, then it is too high. I'll make my own way."

"The price is for you to realize you erred," Levi said with an easy shrug. "But if your pride is too great, then here is where your journey ends."

"W-wait a minute!" Cam said, her voice echoing. "Are you telling me your ego is worth more than Jack's life?"

Anya flinched for a moment, then shook her head. "Even if I got on my knees and apologized to the belu's son himself, they would never let us pass."

"But you won't even try it, so I guess we'll never find out," Cam said with a glare.

"You don't understand," Anya said quietly, glancing at the beasts around them. "My daughter was a *child*. The noxes killed her in cold blood. I can't ever forgive something like that. You can't ask me to."

"What if it wasn't the noxes? What if Bael did it?" Cam said.

"He did," Levi said.

"Bael would never," Anya said, almost too quickly. "He mourned for his daughter as much as I did. He would never hurt someone he loved."

And with that, she turned and marched out of the room.

CHAPTER EIGHT

"So that's it?" Cam said, as soon as they hit the top step and the sticky summer air of the human world hit her face. "You're giving up just like that?"

"I'm only giving up asking," Anya said with a look at Oce. In a blur of motion, Anya's sword was drawn and at the nox's throat. "Where is the entrance?"

"Put down your sword, lady," Oce said with pursed lips.

"Not until you tell me where the gate is," Anya said. "I don't care what I have to do, but I'm going in."

"I understand," she said, gently pushing the blade away from her neck. "The gate lies beyond Cerberus below."

"Like…on the other side of that giant monster?" Cam said, cocking her head. No wonder the magic had been so thick in there.

Oce nodded. "Cerberus is not as old as I, but he's not one to be trifled with. Belu Xo gave him the sacred honor of defending the schism with his life."

"Well, if he's not going to move his fat ass then I guess he's going to lose his head, isn't he?" Anya said. "I'm not apologizing."

"Then perhaps we can barter for something else."

Levi was back, leaning against the entrance of the nox den with that same casual smile. As he walked by Cam, she got a whiff of his expensive cologne, and an up-close look at the way his body moved under his shirt. If she hadn't been on a mission to get her partner back, she might've become tongue-tied.

"I don't need your help," Anya said with a glare.

"I'm well aware," Levi said with a laugh. "I'm surprised you even came to us in the first place. It seems so unlike the lady I've heard about."

"I thought it prudent," Anya said. "But if you aren't going to work with me, I'm going to have to do things the hard way."

"Fair enough," he said. "But I'd prefer it Lord Cerberus kept his head. So I'm willing to barter something else to expedite your journey." His brown eyes swept to Cam and his smile widened. "I want your human to hand over the object she was using to resist our considerable magic down there."

Cam swallowed, gathering the charms in her hand. "You want my talismans?"

"Just the nox one," he said. "And I'll make sure it returns to you once I've finished with it."

"What do you want with it?" Anya asked.

"I simply want to understand what it is, and to share the design with my kin around the world," he said.

"Yeah, like that's going to happen," Cam said, putting her hands on her hips.

"But I thought you wanted to save your Jack?" Levi asked. "You asked Anat to forgive the noxes for the death of her child—which, for the record, wasn't our fault. Why is this any different?"

"Because maybe Anat isn't the only one who's got some grievances against you assholes," Cam said. The more she thought about it, the angrier she became, which was an effective deterrent to the nox magic. "One of your 'brethren' killed my sister. So if you think I'm going to give you *any* advantage over us—"

"I assure you, noxes do not kill humans," Levi said with a shake of his head.

At that, Cam had to laugh. "Are you kidding me? The D.C. lord all but admitted to it!"

"Then why wasn't he dealt with by your authorities? Don't you have a council for that sort of thing?"

"Go look at our arrest numbers and tell me how much power they have," Cam snarled. "Have you been living under a rock for the past few hundred years?"

"Technically, as I've been in the Underworld." But the demon actually looked troubled by this news.

"This is ridiculous. I don't have time for this," Anya said. "I have to get to the schism—"

"*We* have to get to the schism," Cam said.

Anya pinched the bridge of her nose. "Oce, can I count on you to manage this human until I am gone?"

"Oh, no," Oce said, holding her hands up. "This is your battle to fight, my love. And far be it from me to stop this human from doing *anything*."

"Damned straight," Cam said with an affirming glare. "I'm going with you, and that's final. And don't even *think* about using your athtar magic to disappear, because I know you don't have a lot of it." Anya turned to Cam with wide-eyed horror and dread slipped down Cam's chest. "I mean…"

"Oh, it's no secret that the Lady of Destruction is a mere shadow of her former self," Levi said. "Hence why I'm offering to help. After all, it wouldn't do for her to expend all her energy just to get inside, right?"

"Cam, we're going," Anya said, taking her by the arm. "This place reeks of dog."

"Hey, let go," Cam said, pushing off her hand as they rounded the corner. "Why are we leaving?"

"Because I don't want Oce or that smug little prick in my way," Anya said, her gaze focused on some unseen point. "They'll probably be expecting me to come down there, swords blazing."

"…I mean that's what you're going to do, right?" Cam asked.

"Not against twenty noxes high on Underworld magic and a

monster as old as Cerberus," Anya said heavily.

They reached the car, but neither of them got inside. "So what's your plan, then?"

"You and your plans," Anya said, running her finger along the top of the car.

"That's code for you don't have one, right?"

Anya opened the door and sat down, looking almost defeated. "Not one that doesn't involve a reckless and probably unsuccessful full-frontal assault on La Madriguera." She slammed her hand against the dash. "Goddamn it."

"So...that's why you hate the noxes? They killed your daughter?"

Anya nodded. "And asking me to apologize—"

"Is bullcrap, yeah, I know," Cam said. She sat down, but didn't turn on the car. They were seemingly out of options. Anya needed more power to get past Cerberus, but she couldn't get more until they were in the Underworld. It was the worst Catch-22…

Cam straightened, an uncomfortable solution popping into her mind. It would actually solve a number of problems, but it would be about as reckless as Anya running down to the nox den and trying to kill Cerberus.

"Turn me," she whispered.

"I'm sorry?" Anya replied, blinking a few times.

"Turn me into an athtar," Cam said, louder. Stupid, stupid idea. But it also made a stupid amount of sense. "You need power. Spawning increases a demon's magical strength by twenty percent."

"It's not always that much."

"But it's more than you have. And if I'm there pumping demonic miasma into you, you'll grow even stronger, right?"

"In theory," Anya said, shaking her head violently. "But you're just talking crazy. You have no idea what you're saying."

"I know exactly what I'm saying," Cam said, turning in her seat. The idea was starting to sound less stupid and more like a silver bullet. "If you turn me, I can go with you."

"Exactly why I *don't* want to turn you," Anya replied. "There's a good chance I won't make it out of there alive—"

"So take me with you and double your chances," Cam said. "I'm a damned field agent. I won tons of awards at the Academy for combat—"

"Jack would never forgive me if I let something happen to you."

Cam was taken aback for a moment. "Really?"

"Of course," Anya said. "He talked about you a lot. I'm going to bring him back, then you two can...well, get back to the business of being inseparable again. But if I let you go, and Bael or someone else..."

"Look, I appreciate you looking out for me," Cam began. "And for what it's worth, I really appreciate that you helped Jack battle his inner demons with Sara. I guess I can see why he might've become attached to you. And I guess I can forgive you for keeping him from me for so long."

"I hear a 'but' coming..."

"*But* you've got one thing wrong. You aren't *letting* me do shit. He's *my* friend, and more importantly, if I don't do something to stop Bael, he's going to continue threatening my family and all of humanity. So, as far as I'm concerned, if something happens to me, you're absolved of any guilt there. And Jack would see it the same way."

"Turning you into a demon isn't something to be taken lightly," Anya said. "It's irreversible."

"Unless you die, or you kill Bael," Cam said. "Or I die. In any case—"

"In any case, you should leave this up to me."

"This isn't your decision. It's mine," Cam said, a little softer. "And I'm telling you to do it. Turn me into a demon. It's a win-win for all of us."

Anya stared out the front of the car, indecision written all over her face. She didn't speak for a long time, but finally licked her lips slowly. "When we find Jack, you *have* to tell him this was your idea."

"I will," Cam replied with a half-smile. "He wouldn't believe it otherwise."

"And when we find him," she continued slowly, "you will get him to safety."

"Of course—"

"I mean," she interrupted softly, "if it comes down to it, you will leave me behind and get him back home."

Cam swallowed. "What does that mean?"

"It means I'm fully expecting Bael to kill me," she replied

dully. "There's no going back to him now, not after I've left him twice. I had hoped to bargain with him—I would give him my life if he would spare Jack's. But if you're going—"

"So you're not even going to try to fight him? Not fight for Jack?"

She didn't say anything for a few moments, staring at the empty streets with an unreadable expression. "I have loved Bael for three thousand years. He gave me...He gave me *everything*. As much as he's done to me, I can't erase what he's done for me, either. Fighting him? Raising my sword against him?" She shook her head. "If it comes down to it, if it means Jack would be safe, I would. But my heart is praying that won't come to pass. I'm praying that Bael will take my life as payment instead. Just in case... I have to know you'll get him home."

Cam wished she had something to say that could change Anya's mind, to make her believe she was worth fighting for. But that was a journey the demon would have to take on her own. And just as her mother had said, Cam would need to be there to guide her.

"I promise I'll get him to safety," she said, after a moment.

"Thank you," Anya said, her shoulders sagging in relief. "Thank you."

Cam nudged her with a half-smile. "So how does this work, exactly?"

"I'm not completely sure," Anya replied. "I've never done this before. I mean, other than getting transformed myself."

"Oh." Cam reached for her phone. "Think we can Google

instructions?"

"I mean, I know the mechanics," Anya said with a chuckle. "I watched Bael transform more than a few athtars in my time. But he never let any of us transform others. He wanted to be the only source."

"Of course he did," Cam said with an eye roll.

"What I mean is becoming an athtar isn't as comfortable as, say, turning into a lilin. They can mask the effects of demonic transformation in the fog of pheromones. For athtars, you have to want the transformation more than your body wants to reject it." She swallowed and thought for a moment. "You will feel like something is invading your body, something you know will control you. Will change you. But think about why you've agreed to this process in the first place." She chuckled. "For most athtars, Bael tells them to think about the power they will obtain. For you—"

"Saving Jack," Cam said with a swallow. "Will it hurt?"

Anya shook her head. "No, the opposite. Once you accept the magic, it'll feel like…complete bliss. It's submission. All your worries, your fears, all the uncertainty, you'll hand off to me. The demon inside you will make you think that I'll take care of everything for you."

Cam furrowed her brow. "Will you?"

Anya snorted. "That voice is a liar. I'll do my best to make sure you don't die. But I would've done that anyway."

Cam was still glad to hear her say it. But it did beg a question. "What did you think about?"

"Freedom," Anya replied sadly.

Ironic. "I'm ready. Let's do this."

Anya placed her hands on Cam's cheeks, pressing her thumbs against her cheekbones. The demon's eyes glowed black, and the world slowed down. Cam's own heartbeat grew louder. Was this the right thing to do? Was this a line she should cross?

But the lines were gone. If Cam wanted them back, if she wanted to end Bael's stranglehold on the world, if she wanted Jack home and happy and healthy, she had to do this. Even if it meant she was doomed to an eternity of being a demon. She'd gladly pay the price for her best friend and family.

"Open your mouth."

Every instinct told Cam to keep her lips clenched shut, but she dropped her jaw almost mechanically. Anya's cool breath filled the inside of her mouth as her lips grazed Cam's. Something magical tickled the back of Cam's throat, and she fought the urge to cough.

"Accept it. Think of Jack."

No. This ill-advised idiocy would be done in honor of Sara. To make sure some other sister never lost her best friend because the humans were too afraid of Bael. She kept the sight of Sara's casket in the church in the forefront of her mind as the magic moved down into her stomach.

Tingling broke out from her gut, spreading through her body with agonizing slowness. It was like the world's best and worst orgasm, filling her with slow, aching need.

"Do you accept this gift?" came the voice of the only person who mattered anymore.

"Yes," Cam whispered.

The tingling exploded into waves of pleasure that rippled across her body. Cam fell backward against the carseat, hearing herself cry out. There was no other sensation, nothing could compete with the incredible feeling undulating across every inch of her.

Except pain, excruciating pain, coming from her wrist. With hooded eyes and heavy limbs, Cam unhooked the latch and let the bracelet fall away. The pain immediately subsided, and the pleasure took over. Her body twitched and trembled as the magic filled her from head to toe.

Slowly, the feeling ebbed away, leaving Cam with a buzzing in her ears and the feeling that she could fly to the mountains. Her lungs filled with air as she flexed her fingers, slowly reacquainting herself with her body.

"How do you feel?" Anya's low voice asked.

"Like I need a cigarette," she said, suddenly very tired. "I don't know if I could survive a lilin transformation."

She raised her head toward Anya and blinked a few times. Anya looked...well, healthy for lack of a better word. Her skin had darkened to a golden brown, and her hair was perfectly coiled in black ringlets, instead of the frizzy mess she kept pulled back. Her lips were flushed pink, and even her eyelashes seemed darker and thicker.

"You okay?" Cam asked with a yawn.

"Yeah," Anya said, looking at Cam. "You?"

"Perfectly..." She released a loud yawn. "Peachy... We gonna go fight the noxes now?"

Whatever the answer to that question was, Cam didn't know, because sleep overtook her.

CHAPTER NINE

Screw a cigarette, Anya needed a fifth of whiskey after that.

When the energy came to her, it was like an afternoon shot of caffeine. Or waking up from a century-long nap. The world had grown duller in her lethargy, but now, everything was bright and vibrant. Her heart pulsed strongly in her chest, and she was so awake, she might not need sleep for another month.

Her new athtar, on the other hand, was passed out in the backseat of the car, snoring quietly and twitching every so often. It was odd for the shoe to be on the other foot—Anya wide awake, the human asleep.

Except she wasn't human anymore. She was Anya's.

It was a very particular feeling to have made a demon. Prior to the transformation, Anya had been tolerating the human's presence out of respect for Jack. But now, there was an affection there, almost motherly in nature. It was that care that had made

Anya pull Cam from the car and put her in the backseat where she could spread out and sleep it off.

She considered going back to Juana's house, but that might invite more questions. Anya was already on fragile ground where the older woman was concerned; bringing back her granddaughter-turned-demon would be disastrous. So they remained in the dark alleyway as the night stars twinkled above them, and Anya considered this new reality as a demon with a… well, *spawn.*

Anya had always hated that term. It made her think of an insect or a filthy creature from a swamp. To hear other demons throw it around so casually just proved how little they thought of themselves.

And yet, spawn seemed apt. Especially as Anya now had a very clear connection to Cam. The demon-maker connection.

It was the oddest part of this new situation. If she concentrated, Anya could even hear her slow, steady pulse as she slept. Was this the feeling of a master to neophyte demon? Was this why Bael doted on and loved his new athtars so much? Would this feeling remain strong, or would it lessen over time?

Most importantly, did Bael maintain this connection with her?

That Anya had lived thousands of years as an athtar and didn't know the answer was unnerving. The extent of her knowledge seemed to be only as much as Bael cared to share. In hindsight, that seemed rather foolish.

Instead of pressing him for more information, she'd trusted

him implicitly. She'd accepted that he had her best interests at heart, and that every word of love and adoration that came from his lips was the truth.

For the first few decades, Anya and Bael were very happy together. The other belus visited their world from time to time, more to listen to Anya speak of life in her village. They told her of their origins, how they'd once been humans banished to this world for their sins.

She'd grown close to Mizuchi, the kappa, and Freyja, the lilin. Mizuchi was a quiet man who showed her how to catch fish in the streams that ran through Ath-kur, and how best to serve them for her king. Freyja taught her the best ways to serve Bael in the bedroom, introducing Anya to the many ways people loved each other. Anya understood that Freyja had been intimate with Bael before her arrival, but she wasn't a woman to be loved by one person.

Bael seemed content to let Anya serve him. That was, until one day, he announced he would like to return to the human realm once more.

"Are we not a little lonely here, my darling?" Bael asked, running his hands down her bare shoulders. "Would you not like some servants to bring you water and feed you?"

Anya had been happy doting on Bael, finding the work fulfilling. She'd seen some of the rich men in her village with servants and slaves, and had always thought she might end up as one. But she pushed aside her discomfort. How could she say no to Bael?

So Bael had used his great power to create a schism, and they'd walked into the human world hand-in-hand. The land was much different than her village—cold and barren. The trees were scraggly and empty, the fields dry and crumbling, the sky gray and unwelcoming.

"Come, my darling," Bael said, gathering her in his arms. "Let's meet the locals."

Bael swept into the village with a smile on his face. At first, he was treated with scorn, fear, disdain. But he found a young boy and turned him, the same way he'd turned Anya. Almost immediately, the rapid-fire words of the villagers began to make sense, as all the knowledge the boy held flooded into Anya's mind.

Bael seemed to have known this would happen, because he turned to the small crowd that had gathered to witness the boy becoming a demon.

"I want to offer you a deal," he said. "Everlasting life, power beyond your wildest dreams. The glory of living in the Underworld—"

"Lies!" shouted an old woman from the back of the crowd. Anya could remember every detail about her face, down to the mole on her left cheek. She was hunched with a fur slung over her shoulders. Her wiry gray hair hung in her face, but her old eyes were alight with fury. "Evil has arrived in the village. All who go with this man will be doomed!"

"Anat," Bael said, not losing his smirk. "Will you please take care of this woman for me?"

Anya froze. "T-take care?"

"She is bothering us. Show these humans what happens when you cross the King of the Underworld."

He'd begun using that name in confidence, mostly in their intimate moments. Anya had called him so, just to keep him happy. But now she wondered if he'd had grander plans than hearing it shouted in the throes of pleasure.

"Bael…" Anya said, looking at the woman. "She's causing us no harm with her words."

Bael sighed, and fear shot down Anya's back. Was he going to be cross with her? She'd tried so hard not to displease him, but this seemed too much for even her to do.

"Why are you trembling, my love?" Bael spoke in their usual language, so the villagers wouldn't understand. He gently took her by the shoulders. "Does my command terrify you?"

"I don't want to make you angry," she confessed, "but this woman, has she done anything wrong? Enough to deserve—"

He slid his hands down her shoulders, resting intimately on her hips. "She has embarrassed me. It is enough."

Anya swallowed, her face growing pale. "But—"

"If you love me," he said, taking her face in his hands, "you will show this village what it means to disobey me."

She heard a double meaning in his words, and her heart skipped a beat. But she still couldn't bring herself to take the sword. "M-my lord—"

"Do you not remember how *good* it felt to take revenge on

your village?" Bael asked. "Remember how powerful you felt striking down those who'd hurt you? Aren't you grateful to me for granting you that power?"

"Yes." Anya thought about the village often, but kept her regrets to herself. She'd returned four years after Bael had taken her, and she'd slaughtered all those who'd stood by while her father beat her. But even now, she still remembered their faces—had counted every life she'd taken. She didn't want to add to it.

"Then show me," he said, placing his sword firmly in her hands. "Show me your love by accomplishing this task. Show me how *grateful* you are that I saved you from that village. Show me I wasn't wrong to choose you."

A sliver of fear coursed through her, and she raised the sword. "You were not wrong, my lord. I shall do as you ask."

"Good girl."

Anya wiped away a tear, glad for Cam's snores. The old woman's face had haunted her dreams for months, the sound of her death echoing through the years that had passed since. It was the beginning of Anya's body count—one she'd kept up for the next few millennia.

Bael had brought a hundred humans back that first trip, gathering the belus around a table and offering them their pick of the flock—as long as they swore fealty to him. It had been his first step toward becoming the true King of the Underworld. The noxes and elokos had walked away, opting to keep their sovereignty. Mizuchi was grateful for the influx of intellect and stories of the human realm, and Freyja was happy to have new blood to sleep with.

The only athtar Bael took from that expedition was the young boy who would grow into Bael's second general, Bojan. He was a faithful servant of Bael's until he wasn't. Then Anya had the odious task of taking him down.

Another face that would remain etched in her mind forever.

CHAPTER TEN

Cam jerked awake, something poking into her back. She'd been having the best dream ever, although the particulars escaped her. The sky above was pink—was it dawn or dusk?

"Morning."

"A-Anya?" Cam croaked, sitting up. "Did I…fall asleep?"

"You did," she said with an uncharacteristically warm smile. "How do you feel?"

"Like I just had the best sex of my life." The words flew out of her mouth before she remembered why.

Anya just snorted. "Now you see why you have such a hard time keeping the humans away from demonic transformation."

"So does this mean you should buy me breakfast?" Cam asked.

Anya handed her a pastry. "It's a bit stale. Thought you'd be up already."

"My hero," Cam said, stuffing the pastry into her mouth. "Feel like storming the castle now?"

Anya smirked. "I don't feel that much better. Not enough to take on Cerberus by myself. But perhaps now I have enough magic to get us to the schism. We may have to attempt it in a few jumps—and sneak down there first."

"Oh, well, is that all?" Cam rubbed her stomach. "Got any more food?"

Anya handed her a second bag with a knowing smirk. "If they catch us, they'll use their miasma to try and slow us down. You're not as helpless as a human, but you're still pretty young." Her grin widened into one of pride. "Though I have to say, that you could stand upright in front of the nox schism is pretty impressive."

"Okay," Cam said, putting down the pastry. "What's with you this morning? You're smiling at me like I'm your best friend, and you brought me *two* chocolate conchas *and* coffee." She narrowed her eyes. "Are you trying to get in my pants for real?"

Anya quirked a brow. "Would you be averse to that?"

"*Seriously*. Are you drunk or something?"

"Fine," Anya said, her smirk disappearing. "Turning you gave me a much-needed boost. But it also seems to have made us a little bit closer than I anticipated."

"How so?" Cam said, re-engaging with her concha with vigor.

"Well, I've got a pretty good idea about what you're feeling. That your favorite pastry is that thing. That you were having some pretty vivid dreams that made you happy." She looked out the window. "I didn't realize the maker connection was that… well, clear."

Cam stopped mid-chew. "You can read my mind?"

"Not explicitly," Anya said. "Thank God."

"Yeah, thank God," Cam said, squirming away from her. "I don't want you in my mind."

"And I don't want Bael in mine," Anya replied with her usual harshness. "*That*, Cam, is my concern. That, and he never told me anything about it. I have no idea how long this connection will last, or if mine endures with Bael with this level of intimacy. Until I know for sure, let's assume it does."

Cam nodded, leaning back in the seat and taking stock of herself. The initial euphoria had faded and Cam was feeling rather…normal. "Why don't I feel any different?"

"Like what? You aren't a lilin. It's not like everyone's going to want to fuck you all of a sudden."

"I beg to differ," Cam said, throwing her a haughty glance. "You seemed rather interested in my pants a few minutes ago."

She chuckled. "You won't feel different for a while. Athtar magic takes a while to settle in. But we don't have a lot of time to waste—and now that you're up, you need to go fetch us some supplies. We're in for a long journey."

While Anya stayed behind to watch the nox entrance, Cam found a nearby twenty-four-hour superstore to pick up the essentials. She'd left her grandmother's house with nothing but her weapons. So she stocked up on underwear, t-shirts, and an extra pair of pants, and got two backpacks that might be easier to carry than the two duffle bags. She also grabbed three bags' worth of non-perishable food.

When she returned to their meeting spot, Anya was in the same position, watching the nox entrance with a steely-eyed gaze. The purple bags beneath her eyes had all but disappeared.

"What did you buy?" Anya asked as Cam opened the trunk to reveal twenty bags. "We can't take all this."

"Well..." Cam said, fishing out the two backpacks she'd bought and handing Anya one. "It's better to have more than less."

Anya dug through the bags, finding the undergarments and packing them into one of the rucksacks, along with one of the water bottles. "That will do."

"What about all this food I bought?"

"We won't need it," Anya said. "What are you going to do with the car?"

Cam frowned. She didn't really want to leave her car in the middle of a demonic neighborhood.

"Maybe your grandmother can come get it," Anya offered. "Don't you have cousins here, too?"

Cam nodded and pulled out her phone, deciding to spare her grandmother the details of what she was doing. But she'd be the one to ask the least amount of questions.

"Be careful, my love," Juana said. "Use your talismans."

Cam looked inside the car to where her bracelet had been

since the night before. "I may not need them."

A sigh. "You may not need the athtar one, but you'll need the others."

"Wait…what?" Cam gaped at a nearby brick wall. "How did you figure *that* out?"

"It's what I would have done," Juana replied with a low chuckle. "Take care, my little neophyte. *This* I won't tell your mother about."

Cam thanked her, then hung up. She climbed into the passenger side, reaching down with delicate fingers to grab the bracelet. Even without her touching it, the athtar talisman pulsed with the promise of electric shock. Cam carefully unhooked the band and let the offending talisman slide to the ground then attached the other four to her wrist. Juana was probably right; Cam was a demon only hours old. She'd need all the help she could get.

She stared at the symbol, indecisive. Jack might need it when they rescued him; he'd have no protection on their journey home. So, with a grimace and a few pairs of underwear to shield her from the magic, she picked up the coin and wrapped it tightly, sticking it into the bottom of her bag.

Next, she strapped Jack's knives around her waist, and played around with the positioning of her macuahuitl on her back. With the straps of her backpack, it was difficult, but eventually, she found a spot for her cross-body holster that worked.

"Are you ready?" Cam asked.

Anya nodded, adjusting the weapons on her back. She handed Cam three of the five nox talismans. "You may need it more than I do."

Cam handed one back. "I already have one. Three and three. But hopefully we won't need them, right?"

With the coins clutched in their hands, they crossed the early morning streets toward the two nox statues staring them down. Unlike before, Cam barely felt their magic, although as they crawled down the long, dark staircase, it pressed against her mental and talisman barriers.

Anya pressed against the wall for the final few steps, inching closer to the opening and peering out. Heavy breathing echoed from the chamber. Cam looked over Anya's shoulder to where twenty noxes stood guard in front of a sleeping hellbeast.

With two short inhalations, the world slipped under Cam's feet, and she and Anya had moved further inside the room, hiding behind one of the large columns. After a moment, Anya leaned around the column and smirked. "They haven't noticed us yet. That's good."

"Where's the portal?"

Anya scanned the room then shook her head. "I don't see it."

"Maybe he's sleeping on it?" Cam asked. "Like Fluffy in that movie..."

"You're right," Anya said, squinting at the floor beneath the giant paws. "I can See it. Underneath the dog is another staircase. I'll bet that's where they've stashed the schism."

"How can you see it?" Cam asked.

"Athtar sight. You'll learn about that soon." She smiled. "I haven't been able to See this clearly in centuries. Guess more power is coming back."

"Good news all around," Cam said. "But how does that help us get to the portal?"

"If I can See it, I can get there," Anya said, taking Cam's hand. Her eyes turned pitch black, and the world slowed once more. Again, Cam's vision shifted and the dim lights of the room winked out. The air became musty and cramped, and the ceiling scraped the top of Cam's head.

"Careful," Anya said, pressing her hand to the crown of Cam's head.

"Don't worry, I won't bump my head, Mom," Cam said. But as soon as she removed Anya's hand, her head cracked against the wood.

"It wasn't that," Anya said, as the sound of a large paw scraping against the wooden door echoed above them. "I don't want to wake anyone up."

"Right," Cam said with a brisk nod. "So...where's this schism?"

"C'mon." Anya took Cam's hand and pressed it against a cool stone wall. "For balance."

"Don't you need to balance?" Cam asked, carefully moving down the stairs.

"I can see," Anya said, placing Cam's other hand on her shoulder. "Let's go. It should be down here. I can feel the magic getting stronger."

"Wow," Cam breathed as they came into the light at the bottom of the stairs. It was another antechamber, this one much smaller. On the other end of the room was the nox schism; a black hole-like void that led nowhere. It was smaller than the portal that had formed in Atlanta, or even the one Cam had seen in Los Angeles during the previous Demon Spring. The smell of ions and electricity was the same, though, as was the way the hair on Cam's arms stood up.

"Wait," Anya said, throwing her hand in front of Cam. "Something's coming."

Indeed, something was walking out of the darkness, rippling the blackness like water. Cam's heart thudded in her chest—was it Bael? Lotan? Some other devil?

"Let me handle this," Anya said, sliding her backpack off and handing it to Cam. As she pulled her swords from their sheathes on her back, the man fully materialized.

There was something familiar about him, but Cam couldn't put her finger on it. Like all the other noxes, he had deep brown skin, but wore his black hair in a low pony at the nape of his neck. Unlike Levi or Oce, this nox's eyes were cold and calculating.

"Cerberus," Anya said, holding out her sword. "I don't want to fight you. Let us pass."

"If that's Cerberus, who's the dog upstairs?" Cam asked.

"A decoy, of course," he said. "I never sleep. I was given the solemn duty to protect this schism by Belu Xo," he said. "And I'll protect it with my life."

"We're not trying to destroy it," Cam said. "We just want to pass."

"Belu Xo created this portal when she gave birth to her son," Cerberus said. "I refuse to sully it with the presence of her murderer."

"Cerberus, move aside."

Cam jumped at the voice behind them, as Oce moved into the light. Cam hadn't even heard her coming. She wore a sword low around her hip, but by the power emanating from her body, Cam was fairly sure she didn't need it. Anya had been right—she was formidable.

"Talismans, Cam," Anya said before looking at Oce. "What are you doing here?"

"I thought I would lend another hand," Oce said with a smile. "Cerberus, do as I say. Step aside and let them pass."

"You have no authority here," he growled.

"I have authority bestowed upon me by Lotan himself," Oce said, stepping forward. "Let them pass or I'll make you."

The man transformed into the hellbeast Cam was more accustomed to, growing so large his back scraped the ceiling of the room. A sliver of fear—helped by the nox magic—lodged itself in Cam's mind, but her training kicked in. She inhaled and exhaled, keeping the talismans against her skin.

"I don't wish to embarrass you," Oce said, staring up at Cerberus. "This is your last chance."

"C'mon," Anya said, grabbing Cam by the hand. "We don't want to be around when this gets ugly."

"Wait, we're just going to leave Oce?"

Anya paused, just momentarily. Then she looked at Oce. "In the car, the duffle bag. You will find Sharur. I hope it will be adequate payment for this."

Oce dipped her head once.

"*No!*"

Cerberus' giant paw flew toward them, then was batted away by an even bigger paw. Oce had transformed into a creature so large her head scraped against the ceiling. With a mighty roar, she pinned Cerberus to the ground.

Cam's words died in her throat as Anya shoved her into the schism, and everything went dark.

CHAPTER ELEVEN

Footsteps jerked Jack out of a light snooze. He refused to make himself comfortable in the bed, opting instead to perch on the high-backed, velvet-covered chair. Clenching his jaw, he readied himself for another onslaught from his late wife.

Instead, a rather young-looking kappa appeared in the doorway, her eyes focused on the ground and a long clothes bag resting on her arm.

"Who are you?" Jack asked.

"King Bael has requested your presence for dinner," she said quietly. "He has sent me to ready you."

"Ready me?"

She nodded. "He wishes you bathed and presentable." She chanced a look up at him. "I am to shave your face as well."

Jack scratched his cheek. He hadn't really been in the mood to keep himself presentable, although he had noted Bael's use of indoor plumbing when he'd had to use the facilities, and seen a large golden tub waiting for him.

"I'm pretty sure I can handle shaving myself."

"King Bael doesn't wish to give you a weapon," she said.

"I'm sure he doesn't." He pushed himself out of the chair. "Shave if you must, but I'll take care of the rest." He approached the kappa, who actually looked nervous to be in his presence. Gently, he took what he assumed was a suit from her arms. "Thank you."

She nodded once, then slipped through the door, the lock clicking behind her.

"Fair enough," he said, putting the suit on the bed and heading toward the bathroom.

His shower helped clarify his thoughts. This would be his first time outside of this room, and if he ever wanted to get out of here, he would need to understand the layout of the castle. Although without any talismans to help him see past the athtar magic, which skewed perceptions and distance, having a plan might not be all that helpful.

When he emerged from the bathroom with a towel around his waist, the kappa was waiting with a bowl of steaming water, soap, and an old-fashioned straight razor.

"So Bael hasn't figured out how to use electric razors yet?" Jack asked, sitting down in the chair before her.

"Please don't talk. I don't want to cut you," she replied, gently pushing him back. She worked quickly and expertly, lathering Jack's patchy cheeks with warm, sweet-smelling soap then slowly dragging the razor along his skin. It was clear she'd done this a few times.

As she gently rubbed lotion into his skin, Jack had to ask, "Do you do this for Bael?"

She nodded. "I am King Bael's personal caretaker."

"How's that working out for you?"

"I'm sorry?" She looked taken aback.

"Is he as big of a jackass as Anya said he was?"

Her brown eyes grew stormy. "He is a wise and fair belu, human. You would take care not to insult him. He is bringing you to dine with him personally. He's sent his personal valet to tend to your needs—"

"He's torturing me with visions of my dead wife," Jack replied bluntly. "And he's trapped me in the Underworld."

"King Bael has his reasons," she said, with the same downcast look Anya wore when she spoke of him.

"Mm-hm," Jack said, rubbing his face and marveling at the softness of his skin. "Thank you for helping me. I'd give you a tip, but I don't have any money."

She furrowed her brow. "I don't understand. A tip about what?"

"Never mind."

Bael's valet, who declined to give her name, helped Jack get into his tuxedo, tying the black tie and buttoning the cufflinks. But once he was dressed, she hurried to the door, bowed, and promised someone else would be along to fetch him.

So Jack waited, careful not to wrinkle his pants or jacket.

The door opened, and in walked none other than the King of the Underworld.

"Jackson," Bael said, as if they were old friends. "You're looking well. I'm glad I sent Hyun to tend to you. I'd hate you to look unpresentable this evening."

Jack chose his words carefully. If he wanted any chance of escape, he needed to first get out of the room. It was best not to piss Bael off. Yet. "Thank you. She's quite good."

"I only employ the best," he said, gesturing to the door. "Shall we? I have an exquisite wine from the Bordeaux valley that I would love to share with someone special."

"By all means," Jack replied, walking to join him.

But before Jack could blink, they were in a dining room.

So much for learning the lay of the land.

"It's so much faster to move this way," Bael said with a knowing smirk. "I know you tasted some of the athtar magic with Anat. Poor thing is a shadow of herself, you know. Surprised you found her attractive at all."

Jack bit his tongue, the pain reminding him to remain passive. "It's been a while since she's been to the Underworld."

Bael, clearly annoyed he hadn't gotten a better response, walked to the head of the table. "Gita, please inform the guests that we are ready to dine."

An Indonesian girl, looking younger than any other athtar Jack had seen, appeared out of thin air and nodded at Bael as if he were the most amazing thing she'd ever laid eyes on. Then she disappeared once more, and two giant doors at the front of the room opened. A crowd of finely-dressed elokos, kappas, and lilins wandered in. The men, despite their magical deformities, wore suits not unlike Jack's, and the women wore long dresses that would've looked more at home in Paris or Milan. They all spoke with an ease and comfort Jack hadn't seen from the belus the last time he'd had dinner in the Underworld. Perhaps the belus were just smarter or maybe Bael hadn't yet shown his darker side to these demons.

"My friends," Bael exclaimed, gripping Jack's shoulder and arm. "I'd like to introduce you to our new guest. Jackson Grenard, of the Grenard family of humans."

The audience clapped quaintly, like he was some curiosity.

"Please, please, I know we're all starved. Take your seats, and we'll begin our feast." Bael smiled at Jack and half-walked, half-dragged him down a few place settings on the table. "Jackson, I've taken great care to seat you next to someone you know." He nodded to a woman walking toward them wearing a long, silvery dress open to her navel.

"Angela?"

The Atlanta lord's second, Angela had been Jack's contact during his short stint in the city. Then, she'd been on top of the world, handling Nunzia's issues with aplomb, and trying to bed Jack in the process. Now, she wore a smile of a women unsure of her place.

"It's nice to see you again," she said quietly.

"Angela has been helping me sort through the mess Nunzia

left in Atlanta," Bael said, leaving Jack's side to take Angela's. Jack couldn't help but notice the way he leaned into her, and the way she stood awkwardly next to him.

"I see," Jack replied, and allowed himself one quirk of the brow.

Bael chuckled as he slung his arm around her waist. "Well, I suppose it's pretty well-known now. Angela has also been there for me as I work through the pain of losing Anat." He turned to her, stroking her cheek and staring into her eyes. "I am most in love with you, Angela."

"And I you, my king," she said.

Again, Jack bit his tongue. His very presence in the Underworld meant Bael was *not* over Anya. And from Angela's expression, she looked more a hostage than a willing participant. But what could she to do? The lilin belu was one of Bael's allies. Whatever he wanted, he probably got.

"My love," Bael said, sliding his other hand to rest on her hip. "Will you keep our guest company while I entertain the rest?"

"Of course," she said.

He captured her lips in a kiss that left Jack's stomach unsettled. "Thank you, my lady."

Jack stood awkwardly as Bael walked away, clearly thinking he'd put on a masterful show for Jack. Angela gestured to the two seats and Jack stepped forward to pull out her chair.

"You are a lady, after all," he said dryly.

"Thank you," she murmured, taking the seat.

Jack joined her and took the opportunity for a quick chat while the rest of the guests were milling around. "Good to know I'm not the only prisoner here," he murmured. "What are you doing here?"

Angela cast a look toward Bael, then back down at her plate.

A vague memory crossed Jack's recollection, from when he'd returned from the Underworld the first time. "Bael said he was going to make you a lord, didn't he? If you'd go down to the Underworld."

She glanced at Bael again, then nodded briefly. "I'm doing what I must to keep my flock together."

"Know any good escape routes then?" Jack asked.

"It's best to stay put," she whispered. "You shouldn't make him angry."

"I can't imagine a worse fate than the one I already have," Jack said. "He's sent a demon dressed up as my late wife to visit me every couple of days."

Angela's mouth dropped, but she quickly schooled her expression. "Have patience, Jack. As hard as it may be."

Whatever else she wanted to share with him was lost when the seats around them scraped against the floor and a collection of elokos, kappas, and lilins took their seats.

"What news from the noxlands, Lazlo?" Bael asked, sipping his wine.

Jack turned to a human-looking man with jet black hair, pale skin, and the signature athtar smirk. "Lotan continues to lead in absentia. His generals have begun to question his abilities and more and more noxes are looking to you, my liege, for guidance."

"That poor boy," Bael said, tutting. "I should offer to mentor him in the finer arts of leadership."

It took everything in Jack not to spit his wine across the table.

"It seems to me we may have no other choice but to move up our reclamation of the noxlands."

"My lord, it would be so easy for you to kill Lotan," croaked a kappa.

"Ah, it would take me but a moment," Bael said with a patronizing smile. "But what you may not know is the belu and their lands are inexorably tied. Anat found that out when she killed the traitors Mot and Xo. If not for their son's existence, the noxlands would have collapsed in on itself almost immediately."

Silence fell at the table, as this was clearly news to everyone except Bael.

"So we must continue to work with the young prince," Bael said, patting his napkin against his lips like it was no big deal. "I'm not willing to risk my own life, nor the lives of my fellow athtars, by needlessly putting myself in harm's way." His eyes bored into Jack's. "As most everyone knows, killing me would also require the sacrifice of the killer herself. Because if I die, so dies Ath-kur and everyone in it."

"Herself?" asked Lazlo.

"Or himself," Bael said with a charming smile directed at

Jack. "Whoever."

CHAPTER TWELVE

Traveling to the demon world was like the world's worst flight, except there was no plane and it was all free-fall. But almost as soon as it began, it ended with a loud *pop* in her ears, and a face full of something soft and verdant-smelling. Cam opened one eye, and where she expected to see green she saw… the most vibrant purple she'd ever laid eyes on.

"W-what the…" Even her voice sounded strange. With great effort, she pushed herself onto her back, shock washing over her. The trees were black, their leaves the same bright purple as the moss under her fingertips. It was as if everything had gone through an inverse color filter. Even the sky was an orangish hue, although the moon, at least, looked somewhat familiar. She'd never actually considered what the Underworld would be like— or if she did, she pictured something that looked like earth. But the biodiversity in this jungle was astonishing—rivaling that of the Amazon.

"You all right?" Anya asked from a few feet away. She had a bright orange leaf stuck in her hair but otherwise looked intact.

"This place is trippy." Cam ran her hands over the moss, hoping it wasn't poisonous. "Where are we?"

"The noxlands." Anya hopped to her feet, but swayed a little as she righted herself. "If I never make that jump again, it'll be too soon. But fair warning: it's worse going the other way."

"I'll keep that in mind."

Cam took the outstretched hand and stood, brushing her pants off and making sure her macuahuitl and her backpack full of supplies were there. Her metal water bottle had a shiny new dent in it, but other than that, everything seemed in order. Even her athtar talisman was still lodged in the bottom of her backpack. She was starting to regret leaving all their food, though. The conchas sat uncomfortably in her stomach, reminding her she'd only had sugar to eat this morning.

A bright red bird squawked somewhere above her head and Cam jumped out of her skin as it took flight, revealing a rainbow of under feathers.

"So…there's more than just you guys here?" she asked.

"It wasn't just the six belus who landed here, yes," Anya said, watching the bird circle above their heads. "Most of the creatures here are beasts. At least, they didn't offer much in the way of conversation."

In one fluid movement, she pulled her sword and flung it at the bird, but it missed. The bird squawked and flew higher, disappearing into the purple sky.

"Shit," Anya said, jogging into the brush to retrieve her sword.

"What was that?" Cam asked, rubbing her stomach. "Dinner?"

Anya shook her head. "Maybe nothing. Maybe a sentinel. Either way, we should get moving."

The pace was brisk, but the queasy feeling in Cam's stomach subsided after a while. Anya led the way, hacking and slicing her way through the underbrush. But Cam hadn't seen any sign of a directional marker—it was daylight, so there were no stars to navigate by, and there didn't seem to be anything different about the trees.

She sat on her question for as long as she could, until finally, she couldn't stand it.

"Do you know where you're going?"

Anya paused, only briefly, then slashed through the tree branch in her way. "Yes."

"Okay, but…" She winced as the metal sang through bark. "How?"

"I just do."

"That isn't an answer."

Anya muttered something inaudible, but Cam was sure it was foul and about her. Still, she wasn't going to let her pride get in the way.

"Okay, I understand that you don't want to use your magic," Cam said. "But can I use mine already? Maybe I can help expedite this process."

"It's inadvisable to use your magic just yet. There's a reason we don't spawn often, and it's not just because Bael wants to maintain a high level of quality. Young athtars need time to mature. Bael usually waits until the last athtar has grown into full maturity before turning another."

"Uh-huh," Cam said. "Or maybe he's intentionally not giving them enough juice so they'll be dependent on him until he's wormed into their minds and fucked them up."

Anya slowed to a stop and turned to Cam. "It doesn't work like that."

Cam shrugged, unconvinced. "So tell me something else: I haven't really been feeling the nox magic since we got here. It was a lot stronger in the human world, right?"

"The magic was used as a deterrent, I'm sure," she said. "You're right. Here it's less…potent. And besides that, you're getting used to it—and getting stronger."

"But I'm still a brand new demon, as you've pointed out."

"A neophyte athtar is still stronger than a three hundred year old kappa," Anya said. "And no, that's not something Bael told me, it's something I witnessed. It probably has something to do with the dilution of the magic. There's only been a handful of athtar compared to the rest of them. And they're all seconds to Bael."

"Which is another problem we'll have to deal with," Cam said.

"The main problem is this connection. I don't know if Bael

and I share it, but I assume we do. Therefore, it'll be impossible to sneak in anywhere. So we'll have to account for that. And the four hundred and sixty-one athtars he has at his disposal."

"Oh, fantastic," Cam said. "So how are you planning to deal with all that?"

"Sometimes it's best to adapt to the situation as it arises."

"You and Jack," Cam said, putting her macuahuitl by her side. "First thing we should do is map out the castle. Find any entrances and exits. Then we need to take stock of our allies and assets—"

"We have no allies. Everyone is either with Bael or the noxes, and neither one is on our side."

"Fine, Negative Nancy," Cam said, pulling her hair back into a bun. "Let's just talk assets, then. What do we have?"

"We have one neophyte and one athtar who's at maybe five percent of her full strength."

"Five percent?" Cam said. "I thought you said you were feeling better?"

"Five percent *is* better."

Cam released a breath and counted to ten.

"Look," Anya said, putting her swords in their sheaths. "Right now, our first priority is getting the hell out of the noxlands. I doubt they'll be too happy with us sneaking past their guards and using their gateway. And if Lotan finds out about me, he'll have his guard dogs on the prowl. The sooner we get out of this jungle, the better."

"Which, again, I ask—"

Anya released a frustrated growl. "It doesn't matter where we go as long as we go in a direction. The land will end eventually."

Cam opened and closed her mouth. "W...what?"

"Here," Anya said, grabbing a stick from a nearby tree. She drew a large circle then made several lines, divvying it up into five sections. "This isn't exact, but nobody's really ever mapped the entire world." She placed an x in the section closest to her. "Let's call this the noxlands. It's a thick jungle here, and a river separates them from the Kappanchi—that's the kappas. There, obviously, is mostly marsh and swamp, so we don't want to go that way. On the other side of the noxland jungle is a plain of dry grasses. That's the Elonsi where the elokos live. It ends in a mountain range here." She pointed at the line between the next two sections. "That's Ath-kur."

"Why don't we just go straight north and cross into Ath-kur?" Cam asked, pointing at the intersection of all the slices of the circle.

"Because that's the Nullius," Anya said. "It's a plane of nothingness. Some of the lesser demons believe it's where the belus were first dropped on this land. Even Bael won't cross into it."

"Why?"

"I think he's afraid to," Anya said. "The other belus say it strips them of their magic. None of them have ever tried it, though, so we can't say for sure."

"That doesn't mean *we* can't go that way..."

Anya stuck the branch in the center. "We go through

Elonsi."

As if that was answer enough for Cam. "So, you're going to intentionally go out of the way just because you're a little scared of—"

"That place is sacred. No demon sets foot there. End of story."

And with that, Anya began cutting her way through the jungle again.

"End of story," Cam said, mockingly. "Damned stubborn demon." Realizing she was being left behind, she hurried along after Anya. "Okay, maybe you know where you're going. How do you know you're not walking right into Lotan's castle or whatever?"

Anya glanced at the sky and shook her head. "Has anyone ever told you how obnoxious you are?"

"Every person in every group project since kindergarten," Cam replied without missing a beat. "But they all thanked me in the end, when we didn't fail miserably. And if there were a pack of hellhounds hunting us, you're giving them a large path right to us."

"What are you talking about?" Anya asked, putting down her sword.

"Look." Cam pointed behind her to the wreckage. "It's not like you're being subtle here."

"I'm aware of that," Anya said. "But I also know that as soon as we get out of this jungle, the trail will go cold. So, if someone would quit arguing with me and just *walk*, we could get there a lot faster."

"I'm still not convinced that just blindly walking through the jungle is the best idea," Cam said, folding her arms across her chest.

"I'm not…" Anya released a growl of frustration and started hacking. "*For the last time,* I know where I'm going."

"*How?*"

"Fine, you miserable little shit," Anya said, grabbing Cam by the shoulder and lurching her forward. "Look at the ground."

Cam blinked once, twice, not sure what she was looking at. "Uh…"

"Do you see this crack?" Anya said, running her sword along a faint line on the ground.

"Barely."

"It's growing larger the further we walk. That is telling me we're going the right way."

"Why?" Cam said. "What is it?"

Anya exhaled, continuing her assault on the leaves. "When I killed the belu noxes, the noxlands fractured."

"F…fractured?" Cam said.

"Relax, you're in no danger," Anya said, not bothering to turn around. "More than you were before, in any case."

"Funny."

"The belus have a deep connection to the land," Anya said. "They're the main conduit for the magic that surrounds us."

"I thought they were the magic," Cam said. "They're the sin?"

"There's a bit of debate on that. Regardless, if you kill a belu, that connection is severed, and things tend to go sideways."

"So if you killed the belus, how come the noxlands are still here?"

"Their son," Anya said. "He was born of two belus, so he was able to maintain the connection." She tapped her sword against the ground. "This is the result of that transition from parents to son."

"Uh-huh," Cam said. "So…what's going to happen when we kill Bael?"

"Presumably the same thing. Ath-kur will cease to exist."

Cam stopped short. "And *when* were you going to tell me that?"

"When it became something you needed to know," Anya said.

"Any other tidbits of information you're keeping from me until then?" Cam asked.

"When you need to know, I'll tell you."

"Go fuck yourself, Colibrí."

The crack, which had been almost imperceptible, was now two feet wide. Anya kept to the left side of it, continuing to swing wildly. The long circle of sweat on her back was her only sign of exhaustion.

Cam, on the other hand, was a dead girl walking. The humidity pressed in on her, and her earlier use of magic had caught up to her some time ago.

"I can't, Anya," Cam said, sinking onto a nearby log. "I'm exhausted. I'm thirsty. I need a break. How much longer are you expecting to be in this God-forsaken hellhole?"

She pointed her sword at the ground. "This thing will need to become a canyon."

"Yeah, I'm not moving." Cam folded her arms across her chest. "Not until I get a breather."

"I suppose we could stop for a moment," Anya said, glancing up. "Are we out of water?"

"Yeah, like three hours ago." She wiped her sweaty brow. "Hope that little trickle turns into a river quick."

Anya sighed and put her hands on her hips for a moment. Then she walked up to one of the nearby trees and tossed her sword in the air. It sliced through something in the canopy, and Anya caught both her weapon and a large coconut-looking gourd with yellow and green stripes. She placed it onto the ground and used her sword to cut a hole in the top of it.

"Here," she said, handing the gourd to Cam. "It'll tide you over."

"That was pretty impressive," Cam said, taking a swig and regretting it immediately. It tasted like lemon-lime soda concentrate. "You're a regular pioneer woman over here."

"There were a few years where it was just us. Bael and me," Anya said, taking the fruit and sipping it. She didn't seem as bothered by the taste, but handed it back to her. "We had to learn how to be self-sufficient."

"Yeah, so..." Cam wiped her mouth. "What do demons eat

down here? Do you hunt? Fish? Eat each other?"

"Only our neophytes when they get on our nerves," Anya said with a smirk. When Cam elbowed her, she relented. "When the originals were banished, so were some livestock. Suppose God didn't want them to starve. But they've been transformed by the miasma here. Since demons have been coming and going, they've been bringing non-magical animals, too. So yes, there are demonic birds but also chickens and cows."

"Won't they turn into demons?"

"In about three thousand years," Anya said standing. "C'mon, we need to get moving."

"How are *you* not tired?" Cam said, wishing she had a toothbrush to wash the sugar out of her mouth.

Anya wiped her brow and scanned the trees. "Probably because I've got a minion standing right here."

"You did *not* just call me your minion."

"Well," Anya said, taking the gourd and sipping it. "I don't have a name that's not spawn. So I'm trying out new ones."

"Cam works."

"What is it you call me?" Anya asked. "Colibrí?"

She nodded. "Hummingbird. Cause you're small and speedy."

"That doesn't work," Anya said, handing the gourd back to Cam. "I guess I could call you a polluelo."

Fledgling. Cam snorted. "If you have to call me something, that works, I suppose. There really aren't any athtar thirds other than me?"

"Expressly forbidden," Anya said, a sad look crossing her face. "I had to enforce it a few times."

Cam passed the fruit back, unsure what to say to that. Instead, she said, "Thanks for letting me sit for a while."

Anya's head snapped up, her brow furrowing in concentration. Cam reached for her club, fear sliding up from her fingertips when a chorus of growls emanated from the forest.

Anya stood and pulled her swords out, readying them for the unseen foe. "Come out. I know you're there."

Yellow eyes blinked into existence around the edges of the clearing. They were surrounded.

"Anya…" Cam whispered. "Now might be a good time to do that stop-time thing you do."

Anya twisted her swords. "We're not in Ath-kur yet. I don't want to waste my strength on these mongrels."

"I hope it won't come to that, Lady Anat," growled a feminine voice in the center. The voice was the only thing distinctly female about her. She prowled forward with long legs and yellow eyes. "We are merely escorts, sent by Lord Lotan himself."

"I didn't receive an invitation," Anya replied with a narrowed gaze. "And I've made other plans."

The hellbeasts laughed, some dissolving into loud barking and howling. "You were invited the moment you set foot on our lands. The very moment you used our portal that the great belus Mot and Xo created with their magic. It would be rude not to show your gratitude to our fair lord."

"It would also be rude to slice every one of your heads off," Anya replied.

"Anya, don't antagonize them," Cam snapped. "We're sorry we're trespassing. We're leaving as soon as we get out of this jungle."

The barking returned, and Anya sighed.

"You'll be walking for the next three weeks," said the first voice as she entered the clearing.

"Three weeks?" Cam said, putting her hand on her hips and looking at Anya. "You were going to make me walk for *three weeks*? Was that one of the things you were going to tell me when I needed to know?"

Anya pursed her lips. "I'm athtar. Distance means nothing to me. I can cross it in a mere second."

"Then, by all means, Lady," the nox said, teeth gleaming. "Show us your power."

Anya stood deathly still, staring at the nox as if she could set it on fire with her gaze. But she didn't use her magic, or even attempt it. For all her talk of strength, Anya was still very, very weak, it seemed.

"I'll offer you an alternative," the woman purred. "Lord Lotan offers his assistance to get you to the Elonsi, if you'll meet with him at his castle."

"Not a chance," Anya said. "I'll take the three weeks."

Cam scoffed. "Anya, don't be a brat. We'd be glad to go with you."

Anya's expression melted into one of horror and rage. "Are

you *kidding* me? What about Jack?"

"Yeah, I am thinking about Jack," Cam snapped, adjusting her backpack. "Because if it takes us three damned weeks to get across the noxlands, that's three damned weeks he's stuck with your ex-boyfriend. So in my view, I'm taking the quicker route."

Anya just stuttered.

"So how are we going to do this?" Cam said, turning to the noxes. "Do we ride or walk or what?"

"You may ride one of us," the female nox said, nodding to another standing nearby. "I'll carry the Lady."

"I would rather eat my sword than ride one of you mongrels," Anya snarled.

"Then start eating," Cam said, climbing up on top of the other nox and giving her a look. "You're weak, I'm tired as hell, and the only thing keeping us from a nice warm bed and a shower is your damned ego. See you later."

CHAPTER THIRTEEN

It was an odd procession, Cam and Anya riding two horse-sized, dog-faced hellbeasts and flanked by at least ten others. But one thing was for sure—they were a lot faster than Cam and Anya walking by themselves. Their paws thundered on the ground, a loud echoing in the clearing that reminded Cam of a stampede of horses. They knew this jungle better than Anya, because they cut nothing while still managing to avoid every branch and tree trunk, even as the sun began to set around them.

Cam's steed had said nothing to her, so she didn't know if it was male or female. Anya was riding the nox who'd spoken to them, and she looked absolutely furious to be doing so. She'd argued with Cam for another five minutes before Cam told the noxes to leave her. Begrudgingly, she'd joined them. But Cam was sure she'd hear about it when they finally got to the nox castle.

Anya's nox opened her throat and howled so loudly that Cam almost lost her balance covering her ears. Once she regained it, she spotted lights in the distance. Out of the thick foliage, the castle emerged. It was made of the same black stone that had marked the nox entrance back in the human realm. A long set of steps ended in a cube-shaped building at the top, flanked by two torches that burned brightly.

"Wow," Cam breathed. She could've sworn the nox chuckled under her fingertips.

The procession led them up the flight of stairs, big paws climbing with ease, but Cam struggled to keep her seat on the beast. Then, the two noxes with Cam and Anya stopped in a large room with a shiny, jet black floor.

The nox carrying Anya bucked, sending Anya flying to the ground with an ungraceful thump. The nox chuckled and scampered from the room.

Cam gripped the fur of her nox, praying she wasn't about to get the same treatment, but he knelt gently, allowing her the time to slide off.

"Uh… thank you," she said, unsure if she should pet the beast or what.

It nodded and quietly padded to the other side of the room, presumably to watch them.

"I *hate* noxes," Anya grumbled to the room—empty except for them and the single nox—as she jumped to her feet. "Where the hell is this stupid nox prince anyway?"

"Probably going to make us wait for him," Cam said,

craning her neck to take in the room. Thick square columns held up the stone ceiling, with a single torch between each one. At the front of the room was a single golden seat, behind which were two carved statues. If Cam had to guess—Mot and Xo, keeping watch over their son.

"Ridiculous," Anya said, looking at the statues. "Gaudy. This was a mistake coming here."

Cam reached into her pocket for the talismans. "Do you think he wants to fuck with us? Or do you think he actually wants to talk about something?"

"I wouldn't worry yourself. I'll see what the *boy* wants," Anya said, loudly enough to earn a growl from the nox. "Then we'll be on our way."

"Boy?" The nox stood from his haunches and walked forward. The transformation was a fluid movement, like water pouring out of a cup. When it stopped, a man stood where the beast had been.

Levi from Cerberus' lair. "So nice to see you two ladies again."

Anya tutted, but Cam went stick straight. Something about knowing she'd been bareback on such a handsome creature left her a little red in the face. As if he knew what she was thinking, he winked at Cam, and she could've just dissolved into a puddle.

Especially when the handsome man that she'd ridden for a few hours walked to the throne at the front of the room and sat down.

"Oh fuck me," Anya growled as he settled in. "I knew it was

you. Got the same self-satisfied smirk as your mother."

"I don't believe we've ever been formally introduced," he said, laying his hands on the arm rests. "Lotan. Prince of the Noxes. Son of Mot and Xo, who you so mercilessly slaughtered in their sleep." He spoke evenly, but there was a sharp edge to his words.

"Your father killed my daughter," Anya snarled back.

"Ah, we've been over this, my lady," Lotan said with an exasperated sigh. "My parents were incapable of such atrocities. Bael, on the other hand—"

Anya pulled her swords. "Shall I finish what I started? You seem determined to bring me to it."

Lotan smiled, as if challenging her. "And here I thought you were past your bloodthirsty ways."

The tip of her sword dipped. "What do you know of that?"

"I know a lot about that," Lotan said, pushing himself to stand. "Which is why I'm willing to put aside our grievances about my parents and your daughter for the moment. It's clear we are at an impasse, and there's no use in fighting old battles when there are new ones to wage."

There was no fear on his handsome face, but the challenge was gone. After an eternity, Anya sheathed her swords.

"What do you want, prince?"

"Lotan, please. We're on informal terms, are we not?" Lotan said, turning his brilliant smile to Cam.

She swallowed, wondering if he was referring to the hours she'd spent with her crotch pressed against his back. Probably better not to ask.

"Does Cerberus know who you really are?" Anya asked, folding her arms across her chest. "I can only assume Oce does."

"Cerberus? Of course," Lotan said with a chuckle. "The rest of La Madriguera, however, do not. And I've asked Cerberus to keep it that way. People are much quicker to spill secrets when they think you're one of them." His gaze slid to Cam for a brief second before turning back to Anya. "And I wanted to know what your mission was. I had a feeling you might've hidden it from me if you'd known my real identity."

"Nope," Anya said. "Don't care what you think."

"I'm sure," Lotan said with an unflappable smile.

"Anya, don't be a shit," Cam said with a sigh. "If he wants to help us, let him."

"Forgive me," Lotan said, turning toward Cam fully and offering his hand. "I don't believe we've met formally either. And, pardon my coarseness, but...weren't you human the last time we spoke?"

Cam took his hand, forcing herself *not* to be a complete tongue-tied idiot. He was just handsome, no need to turn into a sniveling idiot. "Agent Camilla Macarro. US Division, Atlanta Office."

"Agent Macarro," Lotan said, her name rolling off his tongue like butter on a hot roll.

"Bael took my partner Jack," she continued with a steely-eyed professionalism she certainly didn't feel. "And we're going to get him back. We don't have a lot of time to be dicking around. Tell us why you brought us here or how you're going to help us and let us get on with it."

"You're either very brave or very stupid," Anya muttered beside her.

Lotan had an amused smile on his face, his dark eyes alight. Cam fidgeted under his gaze, although it was less because of what she'd said, and more about the way her heart skipped when a black curl fell onto his forehead. So much for professionalism.

"I understand your mission, Lady…Cam, is it?"

"Lady is a stretch." Cam bristled. "Agent Macarro works."

"You aren't an agent anymore," Anya muttered.

"Very well, *Agent Macarro*." He winked. "You are correct that your mission is a very important one. I want to help."

"Really," Anya said with a quirked brow. "So concerned about a human, are you?"

"I'm concerned about all of demonkind and all of humanity," Lotan replied, finally tearing his attention away from Cam. "Which is why I think if you go straight to Ath-kur now, you will fail."

Anya clicked her tongue. "Oh?" She reached behind her to draw her sword again. "Care to test that theory?"

"My lady, you are without equal in swordplay," Lotan said, holding up his hands in surrender. Not that he could fight against her—he wasn't armed. "I'm talking about a different type of strength. You lack the mental strength to kill Bael. And for good reason." He actually looked sorry for her. "It is a lot to ask of anyone, to slay their own lover."

Cam expected Anya to start swinging her sword, but she didn't. In fact, she released her grip.

"Unfortunately, you're the only one who *can* slay him," Lotan said, as easily as if they were discussing the weather. "So that's where I offer my assistance. While you've been away doing whatever it is you've been doing, cursed or something, there's been a shift in the Underworld," Lotan said. "The other belus are starting to chafe under Bael's iron-fisted rule. After all, as you know, platitudes and small trinkets of affection only go so far when you're being beaten down by the hand that gives them to you."

"Waaaait a second," Cam said with a nervous laugh. "What the hell are you saying? We're just here to get Jack back. Not get involved in some intra-demonic war."

"I'm *not* getting involved, don't worry," Anya said firmly. "We will retrieve the human and be on our way."

"And tell me, lady, what will you do once you have your human back?" Lotan asked, resting his hands on his hips. "Do you believe Bael will give up in bringing you back into the fold? Do you think he wouldn't find you wherever you hid? He is very persistent, as I'm sure you remember."

"It's none of your business what I plan to do," Anya said, although the pink on her cheeks conveyed the lack of said plan. "I'm not going to be *your* weapon. How convenient that you wish to dethrone Bael. Who else would replace him as the King of the Demons but yourself?"

Lotan smiled. "I don't want power. What I want is for my

family to be able to roam this world and the humans' without fearing Bael will punish them for it."

"Yeah, no way in *hell* that's gonna happen," Cam snapped. "If Bael goes, the humans won't have to bow down to him anymore. If you think your noxes will be able to wreak havoc on my world, you have another thing coming."

The belu nox just laughed, as if everything about Cam was amusing to him. She wasn't sure if she found that attractive or annoying. Perhaps both. "I know this is quite a lot to ask of you, especially after you've been traveling for so long. I'm sure you both would like to freshen up and have a meal. I find everything is much easier to discuss on a full stomach."

"We really have to be getting on our way," Anya said, inching toward the door. "Your nox said we had to meet with you. That was it."

Cam could've punched her. She was starving.

"Indeed she did," Lotan said. "And I'm a man of my word. If you wish to leave now, you may. But if, as I suspect, you'd prefer to have a warm, safe place to bed for the night, I'll have my noxes take you to the border of the noxlands in the morning. Otherwise, it would take you a week, maybe two." A cat-like grin appeared on his face. "If you even knew where you were going."

Cam wracked her brain for everything she'd ever learned about noxes. With kappas, one had to be careful when striking deals, because there was always a catch. But noxes weren't known for underhanded dealings. Scaring the piss out of people worked just fine.

Anya seemed to have a similar train of thought, her lips pursed in deep thought. Finally, she threw back her shoulders. "One evening, Lotan."

<hr>

Cam had taken up Lotan's offer to bathe and freshen up, surprised to see running water in the bathrooms but grateful it was hot. Her limbs ached under the scalding water, and she nearly fell asleep in the tub. She might have, if not for Anya barging in, still wearing her clothes.

"Uh, excuse me," Cam said, crossing her arms across her chest.

"I don't like this," Anya said, pacing the room and leaving muddy footprints on the pristine tile floor. "What is he planning? Demonic war? Is he *insane*? He must be, if he thinks I'm enough to defeat Bael."

"Uh-huh," Cam said, reaching for the fluffy white towel near the bathtub. Then, deciding if Anya didn't care, she wouldn't either, Cam stood and toweled off. "So...demons have indoor plumbing? What other human inventions are down here?"

"Oh, who remembers?" Anya said.

Cam wrapped the towel around herself and padded out into the main room. Someone had left a simple green dress for her. She didn't want to know how they knew her size, but she was glad to have something that wasn't covered in sweat. Shimmying into the green dress, she caught Anya's look of disgust.

"What?"

"I can't believe you're going along with all this," she said, rolling her eyes.

"Can you, I don't know, take a chill pill for a night?" Cam said. "You don't like these guys, I get it. But it can't hurt to be cordial with them. They did let us use their schism. And maybe —just maybe—Lotan might have something to offer that's worth listening to."

"I sincerely doubt that," Anya said, but her shoulders relaxed and for the first time, she looked tired. "Fine. I'll eat and rest tonight. But don't expect me to be nice."

"I never do," Cam said with a happy smile.

CHAPTER FOURTEEN

Cam hadn't realized just how hungry she was until she walked into the large dining room. Much like the rest of the castle, it was crafted in black stone with black columns. But the long table was loaded down with more food than Cam had ever seen. Roasted bird-like beasts sat surrounded by succulent fruit in every color of the rainbow. Chocolate drizzled delicacies rested on the end of the table. It was a feast fit for a king—or a prince, she supposed.

"I'm so glad you decided to join me," Lotan said, standing from his seat at the head of the table. He'd changed into a loose white shirt, open at the neck, and black pants. Somehow, he managed to look both powerful and somewhat embarrassed.

"I apologize for all the food," he said, gesturing to the table. "It's been some time since I've been back to the castle, and the staff has decided to go all out."

"I'm sure," Anya muttered.

"This is pretty impressive," Cam said, counting the number of seats around the table. "Are we expecting anyone else?"

"Just one more..." Lotan said as the door opened behind him. "Ah, right on time."

Oce strolled into the room, a smile on her catlike face. She wore no weapons, and her slinky black dress moved like water against her body. She paused to press a sisterly kiss on Lotan's cheek before smiling at Anya, who seemed torn between glowering and happiness.

"I take it Cerberus wasn't too much trouble," Anya finally said.

"Cerberus?" Lotan asked with a frown on his face. "I thought I gave the order to let them pass?"

"I had to enforce it," Oce said, walking to the table. "It's been handled, my prince. Do not worry yourself." Her gaze turned to Anya. "I retrieved your sword, Lady, if you would like to carry it with you."

"I don't think so," Anya said. "It was payment for the help you provided."

"No payment necessary," Lotan said. "After all, Cerberus had failed to follow orders, so—"

"Keep it," Anya said.

Cam wasn't quite following the conversation, as her stomach was starting to eat itself from the inside out. And it chose that exact moment to growl loudly.

"Enough discussion. I think we should eat," Lotan said with

a chuckle. He pulled out a chair across from him, and smiled at Cam. "Please, Agent Macarro, have a seat."

"Well, it would be rude not to," Cam said to Anya's dry glare. She perched on the seat and let Lotan slide it to the table. "Thank you."

"You're—" Lotan frowned when Anya loudly pulled her chair out, sat down, and scooted to the table. "Welcome."

"Ignore her," Cam said with a wave of her hand.

"I plan to," he said with a wink. "Wine?" He plucked a glass carafe off the table and tipped it into a nearby wine glass. "There's a vineyard here in the noxlands, but you really can't beat a vintage merlot. Wouldn't you agree, Lady Anat?"

"I'm partial to cabernet franc," Anya said as he poured wine into her and Oce's glasses.

"I'm partial to wine, period," Cam said, swiping hers from the table. "Cheers."

Lotan and Oce lifted their goblets, but Anya hadn't lifted a finger. The wine was like velvet on Cam's tongue, probably the most delicious vintage she'd had in her life. Then again, she mostly drank boxed wine for expediency's sake.

"Now, please, eat," Lotan said.

Cam didn't need to be told twice. She helped herself to as much as she could fit on her plate. Then, when that was gone, she took second helpings of the potatoes and fruit relish, and bread so fresh it must've just come out of the oven. And just when she thought herself stuffed, Lotan passed her a plate of dark chocolate bark flecked with berries.

"This wasn't what I was expecting," Cam said, nibbling on the chocolate so her stomach wouldn't burst. It was perfect with the wine, which had relaxed the tension in her shoulders and left her feeling quite content.

"What?" Lotan asked.

"I mean, all this," Cam said, looking up. "When I learned about the Underworld at the Academy, we didn't really have a lot of information about how the belus lived."

"The Academy?" he asked.

"The Academy for Demon Management in Denver," Cam said.

"She's a formidable human," Oce said, swirling the remnants of her wine in her glass. "Your partner Jack was highly complimentary of you."

Cam's face burned. "Yeah, well…"

"Tell me everything there is to know about you, Cam," Lotan said, leaning across the table.

Cam nearly choked on the chocolate as Oce tutted. "W-what?"

"Lotan," Oce said. "You shouldn't ask such direct questions."

"I can't help it, I'm fascinated," he said, taking another sip of his wine without breaking his stare. "What kind of woman forces the Lady of Destruction to transform her so she can go on an ill-advised rescue mission?" He chuckled. "This Jack must be some kind of man to be so loved by two women."

"I love Jack, but she's the one with the romantic angle,"

Cam said, looking at Anya, who had eaten, but hadn't touched her wine nor the chocolate sitting in the center of the table. She didn't look pleased to be having this conversation either.

"So," Lotan leaned on his hand with a charming smile, "you aren't in love with this Jack?"

Holy shit, is he hitting on me? Cam was, for once, lost for words.

"They are partners," Anya said, with a curious look across the table. "And my feelings about Jack are not intended for public discussion."

"And a Division agent as well," Lotan said, taking another piece of chocolate from the stack and ignoring Anya completely. "Yet, here you are, now transformed—willingly, I assume—into a very rare athtar third."

"Is there a point to this prattling?" Anya interjected with a sharp look. "You invited us to dinner, not an interrogation."

"Calm yourself, Lady," Lotan said. "I want to get to know your charming compatriot a little more."

"Why? So you can learn more about her talismans?"

"Can't I just find the woman fascinating?"

Anya's eyes narrowed. "No. You can't."

"Perhaps it would be better, Prince Lotan, if you and Agent Macarro went for a stroll," Oce said. "Anat and I have some catching up to do."

Cam wasn't sure if that was true, or if Oce was simply trying to separate Lotan and Anya. Either way, she could probably do with a walk before going to bed.

"Yeah, let's go," she said. "Anya, are you going to be okay?"

"Fine," she snapped. "Go."

Lotan stood probably about six four or six five, Cam decided, as she walked next to him. His cologne wafted toward her nose—something out of a designer's studio, probably. Lotan seemed a man who enjoyed the finer things the human world had to offer. She wondered if he was human under his…

Those kinds of thoughts needed to stop.

"So that was pretty shitty of you," Cam said, needing to break up the conversation in her head. "Not telling us who you were. Where'd Levi come from?"

"Ah, well." Lotan ran a hand through his curls. "In some circles, the humans call me Leviathan. I rather liked that, so I thought it would be a fun moniker to use in the human world."

Cam stopped. "How the hell do you get sea monster from nox prince?"

"Well," Lotan said with a chuckle, "the sea monster bit is rather new. It used to be that I was a snake, the devil, a monster. Which, I assume, was spread by Bael to make humans fear us more than they do." He shrugged. "No one in Europe had even seen a nox until the fifteenth century when my parents made the schism, so they had fun making up all kinds of different variations."

"So why did you want to talk with me?" she asked, closing her hand around the talismans in her pocket. "You…aren't interested in the talismans, right?"

"Eventually, I'd love to discuss them with you. But for now we'll put them aside," he said, turning to look at her with a sly smile. "You see, every demon I've ever met became that way because they wanted to become a demon. You, on the other hand, became a demon to save someone else. You're a rarity."

"And, let me guess, you like to collect rare things?" Cam said with a heavy eye roll.

"No," he said. "I'm the only one like me, so I like finding unique people. It makes me feel a little less lonely."

That was an admission she wasn't expecting. "What do you mean, you're the only one like you?"

"I am the only demon borne of two belus." He tilted his head. "Even Lady Anat's child was different, because she wasn't belu. I'm the only one who'll ever be."

"And how, *exactly*, did that happen?" Cam asked.

Lotan turned to her fully, his thick lips curling into a provocative smile. "Would you like a demonstration?"

Cam would've bolted to the other room if her legs had been working. "I mean, how does a demon procreate? And not the sex part. I know how that works. I've done—" *Shut up, shut up, shut up, Cam.*

He laughed, a throaty sound that sent warmth straight down to her stomach. "The truth is, Lady Cam, that I have no idea how my parents were able to create a demon child—or even create the schism. Sadly, I never got around to asking them. I was only a child myself when they died. There are so many things I wish I could talk to them about."

"And yet…you've let their murderer come to to your table and eat your food." She narrowed her eyes. "You're either an incredibly forgiving person or have an ulterior motive."

"Maybe a little of both," he admitted a little sheepishly.

She would've responded, but they came to the most breathtaking sight she'd ever seen. The moon overhead cast an ethereal glow on a waterfall cascading a rocky face into a river and the dark foliage.

"I can't believe this all exists," Cam said. "I wish I'd brought my camera so I could document it all. They'd be studying this for centuries back at ICDM."

"This was my father's favorite spot," Lotan said. "He'd bring me here at night and tell me stories of the time before Bael brought more demons. When it was just him and my mother alone in their corner of the world."

"That sounds lonely," Cam said.

"Does it?" Lotan asked, keeping his gaze on the waterfall. "It sounds quite easy to me. No need to worry about political battles or pleasing anyone. To have one person to be concerned for, instead of thousands."

Cam had to admit that did sound like a lot less stress.

"How much do you know about when the first demons arrived in this world?" Lotan asked.

"Depends on who you ask," Cam said with a chuckle. "My grandmother says God banished the most evil humans to the Underworld for their sins. The evil in their hearts changed the world, turning it into the magical cesspool it is today—no offense, of course."

"Of course," Lotan said, the amused smile still sitting on the edges of his mouth.

"My great-aunt and others with more scientific minds believe there was seismic activity, the first breach between this world and ours, and a small group of humans fell through. The survivors are the belus."

Lotan leaned in so close Cam could count each one of his black eyelashes. "Your grandmother was correct."

"O-oh good," Cam said, suddenly unable to breathe.

He turned back to the overhang, inhaling the night air. "When I was a babe, my father took me on his knee and told me about the day he and my mother arrived in this world. They'd been living in a village in what you humans now call Central America. God arrived to take my mother to the Underworld. She would be a martyr, suffering for all eternity for the sin of anger. It was a great honor, so God said, to be given this great power."

"Sounds like kind of a cop out," Cam said.

"My mother was of the same opinion, especially when she learned she would leave my father behind in the human world. There are some who would say my mother's anger wasn't anger at all, but passion. And much of that passion was for my father. They worshiped each other. So how could she rejoice in everlasting life if my father wouldn't be in it?" He smiled. "So God relented, and allowed my father to join her as an act of mercy."

"That's beautiful," Cam said quietly. They had been together forever until Anat came along. "So while we're telling truths here, why do you want to know about my talismans?"

"If your lady is successful, Bael will be gone. The humans will realize their master no longer has dominion over them, and I'm afraid the pendulum will swing in the other direction. They may be more willing to take revenge against their former overlords. I don't want my noxes to be caught unawares—especially the innocent ones."

Cam snorted. "Are there innocent noxes?"

He was quiet for a moment, then asked softly, "Did a nox really kill your sister in cold blood?" His gaze once more captured her in its snare, but this time, there was a bit of desperation in his eyes. Almost like he was begging her to admit it was a lie.

"Yes," Cam said, turning away from him.

"Why?" he asked softly.

"Jack and I had been closing in on getting real, hard evidence on the nox lord in Washington," Cam said. "It's hard to catch demon lords in enough shit to bring charges against them. It's harder still to make them stick. The Division does a good job of kowtowing to the lords." She sighed, rubbing her forehead. "All of them, apparently."

"And this nox demon thought you were going to convict him?"

"That, or maybe he was just tired of us showing up at his hotel every few days," Cam said with a sad laugh. "All I know is

I get this call from Jack, and I can't even..." She swallowed, the memory rising in her mind. "I couldn't even understand him. But I'll never forget walking into that house, seeing him cradling her in his arms and begging her to wake up."

A warm hand covered hers. Lotan's brows were knitted together, his eyes full of sincere regret. "Cam, I am truly sorry."

"It's fine," she said, removing her hand from his. "I mean, it's not fine. But it's not like... Well, I guess you could have stopped it, actually." She brushed away a tear before it fell.

"I could have, and I should have," Lotan said. "There are some lines of noxes who are more loyal than others. The ones who bow to me are forbidden from transforming humans unwillingly—and absolutely forbidden to kill. Others ally themselves with Bael's rule of law."

She squinted at him. "Are you sure you aren't telling me all this so we'll side with you? How do I know you won't renege on all this when Bael's dead?"

He smiled. "I like you, Cam. You aren't afraid to say what you feel."

"I've been told that before," she said, her confidence evaporating.

"I'm not going to try to sway you with pretty words and trinkets like some other belus," Lotan said. "But I gave my word to you and your maker I would take you to the edge of the noxlands if you stayed one night. Perhaps if we begin building the trust there..."

"I'll trust you when I have Jack back in sight," Cam said.

"Until then, we have to stay focused."

He nodded and offered something of a resigned smile. "Then I shall do what I can to assist you in completing your mission."

CHAPTER FIFTEEN

Anya watched the door close behind Lotan and Cam, uncomfortable with them being alone together, but also grateful to have a break. How much of a break was debatable, since every single fluctuation in Cam's mood was broadcast over their connection. It was one thing to have her in the room—it was quite another to get a ringside seat to every nervous heartbeat.

"You look perplexed," Oce said, placing her fork down on the table. "Care to share what the hell is going on with you lately? Cavorting with humans? Asking Bael to leave you? Transforming a third?" She tilted her head. "Has the lack of magic caused some temporary insanity?"

"Perhaps," Anya said, finally swiping her glass off the table and gulping down as much as she could. "This demon connection thing takes some getting used to."

"Meh," Oce said, reaching for the plate of chocolate and

handing it to Anya. "That's why I never spawned. I have enough trouble keeping my own thoughts straight." She picked up her glass. "And you didn't answer my question. What's going on with you?"

"I don't know," Anya said, nibbling on the dark chocolate. "When I have Jack back, I'll have a better answer."

"If you're going to face Bael, you should take Sharur," Oce said. "And the rest of the weapons I made for you. I can't believe you just *left* them in a car." She tutted and shook her head. "No way to treat a gift."

"They weren't gifts," Anya said. "They were paid for. Sharur was payment for helping us. You should take it."

"When are you going to quit this idiocy of keeping our relationship businesslike?" Oce asked, reaching a hand across the table. "We've been friends for a long time, Anat. Despite what you say. You can get swords from anyone. You kept coming to me."

Oce's piercing gaze and Cam's teenage nervousness were too much for Anya. She abruptly stood and tossed her napkin on the table. "I think I'm going to bed. Excuse me."

The nox pouted as Anya walked out of the room. But it was for the best. Oce had always tried to be friendlier than Anya liked. Even being on the outs with Bael, Anya was leery about getting too close with anyone. Not after what had happened to Ayumi. Bael was well-versed in finding Anya's pressure points and using them against her, Jack being the most recent example.

Still, Oce allowed Anya to push her away in ways Jack or

even Cam hadn't yet. Perhaps it was because she'd been witness to Bael's whims and seen firsthand what the humans (or former humans) hadn't.

Mot and Xo had always been spoken about in Mount Zephon, but Anya had never met them. Bael was somewhat obsessed, complaining often to Anya that it was unfair Xo had been allowed to bring her husband with her, while Bael was alone. Anya had consoled him; she was there now, what did it matter?

Because, he would say, with something of a mean glint in his eye, unlike Anat, Xo was touched by God. And that made the Belu Nox better.

Anya tried not to let Bael's words get to her. She trained hard with a sword, becoming a fierce warrior who earned a reputation during Demon Springs. Her body count, which had once been an albatross, was becoming a point of pride. She wanted to earn her place by Bael's side, and to be worthy of being his Lady of the Mountain. Then, perhaps, he might forget about competing with the noxes.

Still, his jealousy persisted.

"I want to go to the noxlands," he announced one day, toward the end of a bloody Demon Spring. "I don't think the noxes understand what I offer. I want to show them."

"If you say so." It was her standard answer to most things. Bael's anger had become quicker the more power he amassed, and she'd borne the brunt of it. His words could slice a hole in her heart faster than her sharpest sword. But then he'd apologize, swear he'd never do it again, and things would return to normal.

Bael was in a good mood, though, as they gathered their best athtars and a group of humans who had yet to be claimed by any demon and made the trek in one of the carriages. Elonsi was comprised of vast tracks of grassy plains, but in the distance, a lush, purple forest loomed. The noxlands. The trees were so thick the carriage could go no further, so Anya and Bael had to walk on foot.

Unlike the sprawling monstrosity the nox prince lived in, the belu noxes' home was a simple hut, made from the trees and leaves of the forest. They wore raggedy clothes, had a small fire to cook on. It reminded Anya of the years she and Bael had been alone in his formerly small home. Before the neophytes had arrived and built him a fortress at Mount Zephon.

"My friends," Bael announced, stepping into the clearing.

"Friend is a strong word," Xo said. She was a stunning beauty, with dark brown skin and shiny black hair that curled down her back. Her dark eyes bore a fierceness befitting the demon of anger. "Mot. We have a guest."

Her husband shared her coloring, though his shoulders were broad and muscular, perhaps from years of having to hunt and fend for himself in the jungle. But unlike his wife, he gave off an easy air, as if he were a man content with life.

"Bael," he said. "To what do we owe the pleasure?"

"Since you've neglected to answer my invitations to dine with me, I thought I might invite myself to your table." He glanced at the fire. "Or whatever you eat on."

Xo rolled her eyes and disappeared into the hut.

"We have received your notes," Mot said evenly. "But we're uninterested. Life is good."

"Is it?" Bael said, looking at the door Xo had disappeared through. "Your wife seems to think otherwise."

"My wife adores our life so much she abhors interruptions to it."

Anya had to fight to keep a smile off her face. She didn't want to make Bael angrier by taking their side. But she could empathize. They had shown up uninvited.

"My good man," Bael said, taking a seat on an overturned log. "You're living in squalor. It's been centuries since I've hunted my own food. I can't even remember how to start a fire."

"I'd be glad to teach you."

"I don't want to learn. What I'd like is to help you. I have a hundred humans on the edge of the forest just waiting for a master. I would be glad to give them to you."

"What is your price for such generosity?" Mot asked evenly.

Bael shrugged. "Can't it simply be a gift from the King of the Underworld?"

"How kind," Mot said, rising from his seat. "Just one problem: The Underworld includes the noxlands. And you are not king here."

Anya swallowed, bracing herself for Bael's anger. But her king kept his cool, rising smoothly from his seat and brushing the dirt from his pants.

"As you wish, Lord Mot." He snapped his fingers and Lazlo appeared in the clearing, a human woman gripped between his hands. "As a peace offering, I'll leave this human with you."

"I told you," Mot said. "I don't want her."

"Very well." Bael snapped his fingers. "Anat, will you dispose of her?"

She jumped. "What?"

"If Mot doesn't want my gift, dispose of it. And the other hundred. Just kill them all."

"Why don't we give them to Freyja or Mizuchi?" she said, a cold sweat breaking out on the back of her neck.

"Because they were a gift for Mot, and it would be rude to give them to someone else," Bael said, looking at his hands. "We'll get more next time."

"You would kill a hundred humans as if they meant nothing to you?" Xo said, appearing in the doorway again.

"Why not? They're just men. Unwashed, filthy creatures," Bael said. "I can find a thousand more in the human realm. And they'll be grateful to have a moment in my presence. I'm a *god* to them."

"You think you're God," Xo said, narrowing her eyes as they turned yellow and her teeth elongated. "But you were once a man, same as them. You're no better, Bael. Just a man with an inflated sense of self."

Anya forgot to breathe, sure now that blows were coming.

"Anat," Bael barked. "Kill the woman."

"We'll take her," Xo said. "And the rest."

Bael smiled. "I knew you would come around, Lady Xo."

"*Belu* Xo," she said, raising her head higher. "And if you set foot in the noxlands again, I'll rip your tongue from your pretty mouth and feed it to the humans."

"So that went pretty well?" Anya said, once they were back at the castle.

"I would hardly call that pretty well, Anat," Bael said, staring at the alcohol in his glass goblet. "I was humiliated in front of them."

"I don't think you were humiliated," she said, running a stone down the length of her sword. "They took the humans, just as you asked."

"They took the humans to save their lives, not because I wanted them to, you simple woman," Bael said, slamming the goblet onto the table.

Anya turned to her sword. "What does it matter why they took them?"

"Because I want them to *bow* to me," Bael said, standing. "Do you not understand what I'm trying to accomplish here? Are you that incompetent?"

She didn't answer, quietly running the whetstone along the blade.

"And that Xo, walking away from me as if she could. *Belu.* As if she were in charge of anything," Bael said, pacing the room. "As if she had the *right* to speak to me in such a way."

Nodding, she completed another iteration on the stone.

"And that husband of hers. Does he not understand that I am a god? I am to be *revered.* I am to be *worshiped.*"

The sparks on the stone were mesmerizing, and kept her focus off from Bael's screaming.

But the man stood before her, his face wild with anger.

"Stop sharpening your damned sword and listen to me!"

The back of his hand connected with her cheek and she fell backward, landing hard on the ground as the sword clattered to the floor beside her. Bael had yelled, but he'd never *hit* her before. She held her cheek, stunned and scared to move.

"Anat!" he gasped, joining her on the floor. "My sweet lady, I'm so sorry. I didn't mean to."

Numbly, she nodded.

"Look at me, my love," Bael said, slowly removing her hand from her cheek. "My lady, my light, my everything. I'm sorry. I'm so sorry."

Tears had gathered in her eyes, falling down her stinging cheek. Bael wiped them away, cooing to her and whispering his apologies. He swept her into his arms, holding her to him as though she were a piece of breakable glass. Slowly, she came back to herself, returning his embrace weakly.

"Please, tell me you forgive me," Bael said, rocking her. "Please, I couldn't live with myself if you hated me. Tell me you forgive me, my love. It was an accident. I swear to you, I swear on everything I am and everything I have, it will never happen again. Just please...please forgive me."

"I forgive you," she whispered. And she did, because what

other option was there?

⊷⟡⊶

It would be several more centuries before Anya became reacquainted with the woman Xo had spared, and several more before Anya would develop somewhat of a fondness for her. But by then, Anya had learned what happened when Bael felt threatened. So she kept the weapons master at arm's length for her own safety. She kept everyone at arm's length for her own sanity.

A soft knock at the door pulled her from her thoughts. Cam was on the other side. Their connection was so clear—and it made Anya wonder how Bael could stand to hurt her if theirs was as strong. Wiping her face, Anya schooled her features before opening the door.

"Hey," Cam said, indecision plain on her face. "Um. Just wanted to check on you."

Anya was grateful the connection was a one-way street, for she desperately wanted Cam to come inside and stay with her until she fell asleep. But her pride wouldn't let her.

"I'm fine. Get some rest."

CHAPTER SIXTEEN

Jack hadn't been invited to dinner in three days. Perhaps Bael had realized that giving him access to potential allies was dangerous, or maybe he just wasn't having any parties. Instead, Sara had been tending to him, bringing him breakfast, lunch, and dinner. The exposure was helping his reaction; he no longer dreaded the sound of the jiggling handle. But seeing her, or whatever demon had been glamoured to look like her, would never not take his breath away.

Between her visits, Jack would brainstorm escape ideas.

There were two egresses in the room: a window and a door. The window wasn't an option; Jack was at least four hundred feet in the air—maybe. He couldn't trust his own eyes when it came to athtar magic, but he had a pretty good idea that he was too far up to attempt an escape that way.

The door was locked from the outside, and although Jack

had learned to pick a lock in his more youthful days, he lacked any supplies to do so. Breaking the door off its hinges was another option, but the sound might attract guards. The only time it opened was when the demon masquerading as Sara walked into the room. She carried a key around her wrist. And that key was how Jack was going to get out of there.

Once he was out of the room, he had no idea what was next. He might starve to death wandering the halls of the castle, or he might get caught immediately. But he'd just keep trying until he was successful. Until he got home.

He glanced at the door when he heard soft footfalls. His pulse quickened, and he took three deep breaths to remain impassive. If the demon thought he was up to something, she wouldn't let him get close. He had to play this right.

She walked in with a tray of food, wearing a dress that showed her cleavage. Jack let his gaze linger there long enough for her to notice.

"Do you like the dress?" she asked, placing the food on the table.

"It's nice," Jack said, careful to keep the disgust in his voice. Slow and steady wins the race. "What's for lunch? More guilt?"

"A roast chicken," she said with a sad look. "I thought we could eat together today, unless you're going to be ugly."

Jack pushed himself to stand. This was her usual line, and even if Jack *was* ugly, she'd stay. In fact, the meaner he was, the more she wanted to stay.

"Do what you want," he huffed, sitting down at the table.

Despite being a prisoner, he had been eating whatever was in front of him, and did so again this time. As usual, the food was delicious—rich and succulent chicken with herbed, salted potatoes and asparagus. "So where's all this food come from?"

"Hm?" She looked honestly surprised. "What do you mean?"

"Does Bael have chickens and a garden somewhere? Doesn't look like you guys can run up to the Wegmans when you want."

The demon looked confused for a moment, which actually made Jack chuckle. Wegmans had been Sara's favorite grocery store—so much so that she joked about marrying it instead of Jack. To her credit, the demon-dressed-as-Sara didn't ask him to clarify.

"Why so interested?" she said instead, taking his hand. "Are you finally becoming more comfortable here?"

"Just curious what I'm eating," Jack said, pulling his hand away from hers.

As predicted, her surprised gaze became more determined. "Jack, I don't understand why you're being so mean to me. I didn't do anything wrong." She inched closer to him. "I just want us to be together again. Have you really fallen out of love with me?"

Stay strong, Jack. The chicken turned to ash in his mouth, but he swallowed it regardless. "I'll always love my wife."

"Then why are you resisting me?" she said, moving her hand to his knee. "Jackie, I've missed you so much. Why can't things just go back to the way they were? Before that awful woman came between us?"

He didn't remove her hand, carefully gauging her reaction. "Anat didn't come between us. You died."

"I'm here, Jack. Can't you see me?" With her other hand, she gently pulled his face toward her. "Can't you feel my touch?"

He let her kiss him, screaming in his mind as her lips slid against his. This was a dangerous game; one small slip-up and he'd believe what she was saying. Confident that he retained the upper hand, he kissed her back, opening her mouth with his tongue and tasting her. She moaned in relief, clutching his shirt and pulling herself onto his lap.

The key tied around her wrist pressed against his chest, and he focused on that instead of the way her hips moved against his. He cracked open an eye to look at her. She was all-in, the smell of sex and flowers filling the air. He couldn't help his biological reaction to it, but that just made her think he was hers.

"Jack," she whispered, "I want you. I want you so badly."

He grasped her wrists, a move that she took as sexual, but one that he used to find the knot of the key on her wrist. Without a word, he stood with her and guided her back toward the bed, all the while working on the knot while she pumped him full of lilin magic. The back of her knees reached the bed and she fell backward with Jack. His hips pressed against hers, he kissed her soundly to keep her distracted from his fingers against her wrist.

Trailing kisses and sneaking glances at his fingers, he pressed his face into her cleavage, watching her close her eyes and arch her back.

That was when the key came loose.

Before she could react, he grabbed it and dashed toward the door, ramming it in the holder and bolting as fast as he could. Her screams echoed after him in the distance, and he grinned to himself as he pressed himself against a wall to catch his breath. He'd outsmarted Bael *and* withstood lilin magic.

Not too shabby.

He craned his neck around the corner and listened for the sound of guards rushing to him. So far, so good, but athtars didn't play by the rules. Any moment now, they'd be on him. Until that happened, he'd get as far as he could.

His room was on a long hallway, one that he vaguely recognized from the last time he was there. From what he remembered of the castle from the outside, there were stretches of windows and porticos built into the mountain. How many levels, how many winding hallways, he had no idea.

Beyond the sound of his heartbeat, he heard footsteps and waited, pressing himself into a dark corner. He was fairly sure the athtars just zipped from place to place, so it was probably a servant of some kind. An eloko, a dwarf-like creature with a potbelly and long green hair, shuffled by with a sword in his hand.

Jack didn't breathe, remembering what Anya had said about elokos having heightened hearing.

The eloko suddenly stopped, as if frozen in time. The rise and fall of his chest slowed to almost imperceptible movements, his lids falling slowly mid-blink.

"Ah, poor devil," came a soft voice behind Jack. "He'll probably die of thirst in there."

Dread slid down Jack's spine like ice water. The man who stood next to him had appeared without any sound, and emanated almost the same amount of power Bael did. Jack recognized him as one of the men who'd attended Bael's fancy dinner party, but that didn't make him feel any better.

"What do you mean?" Jack asked, buying himself sometime to figure out his next steps.

"Our fair belu has laid these traps around the castle," the athtar said, stroking the kappa's scaly skin. "To him, he's walking down an impossibly long hall that he will never reach the end of. Days will pass, maybe even weeks if he's willing to drink the water on top of his head. But here in the normal time…"

Before Jack's eyes, the kappa's skin grew dry, flaky. And like watching a flower bloom in high speed, the kappa shriveled into nothing but a skeleton, which turned in moments to dust.

The man knelt next to the pile on the floor and blew it away.

"Our belu is a magnificent creature," he said, standing again. "He has been touched by God. Unlike the other lesser creatures, God didn't just give him power. He made him in His own image."

Jack unstuck his tongue from the roof of his mouth. That was a new one. "I'm sure He did."

"After all, Belu Athtar was the one who could make the schism to the human world. He brought God's power to the humans. He made the world great." The man tilted his head at Jack, his brown eyes piercing. "And you would throw all that away?"

"That was the plan."

Pain unlike any Jack had experienced exploded from every part of his body, as if he was being torn apart and smashed together at once. Blackness edged the rim of his consciousness, but the torture would not let him submit to it. He would experience every agonizing nanosecond of this.

Then it stopped, leaving him heaving and trembling in a bright room. He thought he might be dead, except that his body still shuddered from the ghosts of pain.

"Jackson, I'm so very disappointed in you."

A hand rested on Jack's sweaty, tear-soaked cheek. He weakly opened his eyes, looking into the belu athtar's.

"Your wife is upset that you tricked her," Bael continued, gently stroking Jack's cheek. "She thought you were getting somewhere. All she wants is for you to honor your marriage vows. And you do this." The stroke turned into a pat and Bael left him.

With strength he hadn't known he'd possessed, Jack turned himself onto his stomach and pushed himself onto his hands. He was in Bael's throne room. Demons lined the walls—mostly elokos carrying similar swords to the one he'd seen earlier. They almost looked like an army.

"Well?" Bael said from his throne. "What do you have to say for yourself, Jackson?"

"Worth it," he replied with a smile. There was blood in his mouth, and he spat it out, wondering if he'd bitten his tongue, or if he was just being put back together.

"Are you not comfortable in your new home?" Bael asked. "Do you not have everything you need?"

"A few less visits by my late wife would be nice," Jack said with a grimace.

"Those were a gift, my friend. Your wife's passing was an atrocity, and from what your superiors have told my informants, it affected you greatly. I'm simply trying to offer peace by giving her back to you."

"She's *dead*, you son of a bitch," he growled. "And you're fucking twisted."

Bael shrugged. "I am kind. Lazlo, my dear athtar, developed a unique brand of torture using the power of time. You should be thanking me for making it stop."

The aforementioned Lazlo stood next to Bael, looking much like a prized cockateel.

"Huh," Jack said, pushing himself to stand. His legs were jelly, but he found strength in his own lack of shits given. "Didn't there used to be a second chair there?"

The anger that fired on Lazlo's face was immediate, but Bael held up his hand. "Don't be so easily baited, Lazlo. It's one of your lesser qualities." He looked at Jack with an unmistakable grimace. "Anat's chair has been removed because Anat is no longer part of our family. She gave up that right when she—"

"What? Told you to get lost?" Jack said. "Or was it when she stayed with *me*? A lowly human."

"It doesn't matter," Bael said, but the color had risen in his cheeks. "Anat is as good as dead. She will not survive much longer without the magic of Ath-kur, and she knows better than to set foot in my lands. There is no place for her, and she will perish."

"The other lands will not sustain her either, even as she allies herself with the traitorous noxes," Lazlo said with a smug expression.

"The noxes?" A flicker of hope ignited in Jack's mind. Did that mean Anya was in the Underworld?

"Lazlo, dear," Bael said with clipped words.

Something unsaid passed between them, but that was all the confirmation Jack needed.

Jack chuckled. "Sounds like you fucked up, Lazlo."

As the next few painful moments passed in an eternity, the only thing that kept Jack from falling into a pit of despair was the knowledge that Anya was coming for him. And he just needed to stay alive and sane long enough until she arrived.

CHAPTER SEVENTEEN

Cam slept like a baby, waking up refreshed and ready to continue their journey. A breakfast of fresh fruits and dark coffee arrived almost as soon as she put her feet on the ground, and once she'd had her fill, two noxes escorted her through the castle down the stairs. Lotan was waiting with a carriage pulled by a gorgeous white horse. But as Cam drew closer, its more unique features came into view, namely, the white scales and orange hair.

"What is…that?" Cam asked, keeping her distance from the creature.

"A kelpie," Lotan said, petting the animal on the shoulder. "They're more prevalent in Kappanchi in the marshes and bogs. But he's the quickest beast in the Underworld. On loan from Mizuchi himself."

"It looks dangerous," Cam said as the beast flashed a row of sharp teeth.

"Come pet him," Lotan said. "I promise he won't bite."

Cam inched closer, keeping her fingers and other bitable appendages against her body. The kelpie turned its head and flared its nostrils at her and Cam jumped back.

"Oh stop," Lotan said, patting the beast. "Don't be difficult."

The kelpie turned to Cam and bowed his head. Feeling a little better, Cam tentatively scratched the velvety, warm nose. The kelpie nudged her hand when she stopped, so she kept scratching.

"That means he likes you," Lotan said.

"So you're going to be driving this thing to Elonsi?" Cam asked. "Right?"

"Sadly, no," Lotan said. "Some nox business has come up and I must stay here. I trust that Wihwin here will get you to your destination safely. And besides that, I have a feeling Mother Athtar would be averse to spending any more time in close quarters with me."

"Hmph. At least you aren't stupid." Anya stood at the top of the stairs, Oce following right behind her.

"My lady, be nice," Oce tutted. "And I wish you'd reconsider taking your weapons bag."

Anya tossed her double swords and backpack in the carriage. "I told you. Sharur is yours."

"And the rest of the weapons I made you?" Oce asked.

Anya paused then climbed into the carriage. "Keep them.

They were paid for, and they're mine to do with what I please. So take them back as additional payment."

Oce sighed and shook her head at Cam. "You are a better soul than I to put up with her."

"Well, she's kind of my ticket into Ath-kur, so I don't have a choice," Cam said. "And for some reason, my best friend likes her."

"Let's *go*, Cam."

Lotan smiled and took Cam's hand. "I wish you two the best of luck. I hope this isn't the last I see of you."

"It's really up to La Colibrí if she wants to kill Bael," Cam said, warming at his touch.

"Well, that aside," Lotan said, tilting his head and smiling. "I hope we can continue the conversation we started last night."

"*Hurry up.*"

"Coming, Mother," Cam said with a smile to the prince as he helped her into the carriage. Inside was the same high-quality velvet and silk as the castle, and a comfortable, plush seat that enveloped Cam as she sank into it.

The carriage rocked forward, and Anya released a breath, looking pleased to be finally on their way. "Well, it's not the fastest way, but it'll do."

"You're awfully ungrateful, considering how last night could've gone," Cam replied. "You did kill his parents."

"They did kill my child," she replied with a glare. "And if you ask me, it went poorly. The boy has some pretty lofty ideas if he wants to engage in all-out war with Bael and the athtars. I won't be his weapon."

"I wouldn't think of it as being a weapon. More allies to the same goal," Cam said.

Another *hmph* from Anya. "You like him."

"W-what?" Cam blinked wildly. "Why do you say that?"

"I felt your heart pounding the whole time you were with him," she said casually. "And at dinner."

"Is that..." Cam chewed her lip. "Against the rules or whatever?"

Anya shrugged and sat back. "I've slept with lilins before. I just personally don't like noxes. You feel differently."

"I didn't sleep with him, if that's what you're asking," Cam said.

"Not saying you did." She paused. "But you should consider it. You're wound up way too tight."

"I wonder why," Cam said with an eyeroll. "My partner's been too busy chasing you all over creation, and your other boyfriend's been kidnapping him every few weeks. I'm a little stressed." She allowed disappointment to creep into her infatuation, like oil into white paint. "And I'm sure he was only flirting with me to get to you."

Anya's gaze blinked to her then back out to the landscape. "I don't think that's entirely true."

"Yeah, like a nox prince was actually into me," Cam said with a shake of her head. "Of all the thousands of women—demon and human—he's dealt with over his lifespan."

"You've dealt with hundreds of men in your lifetime," Anya

said. "Attraction doesn't work like that. If you mix with someone, it happens."

"Right, but he was still trying to get to you through me."

"The prince seems to know me pretty well," Anya said with a cool tone. "And he would know that there's no one on this plane or the next who could convince me to do something I don't want to do."

"Except Bael," Cam said with a knowing look.

The glaring response sent shivers down Cam's spine and the conversation went quiet for a moment.

"So…if you didn't think he was trying to get to you through me," Cam started slowly. "Why were you so pissy?"

"I'm worried he has some ulterior motive," Anya said, shifting in her seat. "There's something to his interest. Maybe he wants to know more about the talismans, so he's buttering you up to get them."

"Yeah, that's one theory," Cam said. "Or maybe you're just projecting. Not every guy is Bael, just like not every belu is Bael." She nudged Anya with her foot. "Does this mean you're looking out for me?"

Anya's frosty expression warmed. "Of course I'm looking out for you. Until Jack gets back, I think he'd want me to. Especially when it comes to a manipulative demon like Lotan."

"Wow," Cam said with a throaty chuckle. "So the mom comment wasn't far off, was it?"

"It was so far off, it was still in Mexico," Anya replied, although there was a ghost of a smile on her lips. "But if you decide to roll around with the nox, I won't stop you. As long as you know what you're getting into. Noxes aren't lilins, but from what I've heard, they're attentive lovers."

Cam's face turned bright red. "I don't have time for a sexual escapade anyway. So it's good that we're moving on."

Anya looked like she wanted to say something else, but instead said, "I'm going to sleep."

Cam couldn't sleep, not when the world was morphing before her eyes. Where thick, lush jungle had touched the edge of the window, now the trees had grown sparser, revealing low grasses and rivers. Time passed imperceptibly, although Anya did bark at the kelpie every few hours to stop so she and Cam could stretch their legs and relieve themselves. Cam was grateful they were the only two people around as she ungracefully squatted in the forest.

But when the sun was low in the sky, the kelpie halted of their own volition.

Anya cracked open an eye. "This is it?"

"Looks like it," Cam said, opening the door and stepping out. Immediately, her foot sank two inches into sludge. "Uh... Anya?"

"What?" said the other woman with a hearty yawn.

"Did you tell Lotan which way you wanted to go?"

"Of course, I wanted..." The words died in her mouth as she joined Cam outside the carriage. "Son of a bitch."

Their new environment reminded Cam strongly of the

Louisiana swamps, which was probably why the kappa Wani had lived there for so long. The short trees rose from blue water and there were small patches of land between much larger bodies of water.

This was definitely Kappanchi.

"Goddamned nox prince," Anya muttered, pulling her leg out of the muck. "I wanted to go to *Elonsi*!"

The kelpie looked at her, uninterested, then took off in the other direction, spraying Anya with mud. She let out a feral scream and kicked the ground. "*Go fuck yourself, Lotan!*"

Cam did her best not to laugh and gathered one of the two rucksacks Lotan had sent with them. "Are we going to try to go back into the noxlands?"

"No," Anya grunted, snapping up the other. "It would take us longer to go back. And through that jungle? No way. If we keep going in this direction, we'll pass through Liley then cross the mountains into Ath-kur." She glared over her shoulder. "If we'd gone into Elonsi *like I asked*, we'd have been in Ath-kur in a few days. Now? With this swampy mess?" She growled.

"Why did he bring us this way?" Cam asked, careful not to show preference.

"Because he's a Goddamned prick, that's why."

Cam swallowed. He was coy, slick, and handsome as the devil, but he'd also seemed genuinely concerned about helping them. "Any other reason?"

Anya stopped fighting with her leg and glared at Cam. "Do *not* take his side. He's screwed us because we didn't agree to play his little damned game."

"And why aren't we?" Cam asked.

"Oh, what? He flashes his pretty brown eyes and suddenly you think he's a genius?" A loud sucking sound followed her extricating her leg from the goop, but it only sank back in when she put it down.

"I don't think he's a genius, but I also don't see why he'd intentionally not do what you asked him," Cam said. "Are the kappas part of his plan, perhaps?"

"Whether they are or they aren't, he should've done as I asked," Anya said.

"Maybe we should try to head up to the Nullius," Cam said. "If we're close to the border, we could keep walking along the edge until we—"

"Cam, what did I say about the Nullius?" Anya barked. "Let's go."

They slowly made their way through the muck and mush, Cam's quads burning with each movement. She was starting to agree that Lotan could've left them with something to navigate the swamp, because they were making precious little progress. Littler still when the sun—already low in the sky—disappeared completely, as did their light.

"I can't see shit," Cam said. "Can you?"

"Yes," came the grunting reply. "But perhaps we should find a place to camp for the night."

"And how," Cam asked, yanking her leg out of another sinkhole, "are we supposed to do that? I don't see any Air BnBs around here."

"Well, Cam," Anya placed a hand on Cam's shoulder, "how would you like to learn something about being an athtar?"

"Like...what?"

"Like using your magic to transport the two of us to somewhere a bit firmer."

Cam shimmied out from under her hand. "Why didn't you suggest that sooner?"

"Because you're still a neophyte and using magic could be dangerous."

"So why are you suggesting it now?"

"Because there are things in the Kappanchi swamp that could eat us both, and I don't feel like waking them up. Quit arguing with me and just listen so you don't get us both *killed*."

Cam clammed up, mostly in protest. She hated creepy crawlies.

"Now then: how strong is your magic?" Anya asked.

"I have no idea," Cam said, looking down at her body. "How do I tell?"

"Do you feel like you're about to fall asleep or die?"

"...Not particularly."

Anya nodded. "Then it'll be fine. Close your eyes and use your Sight to locate a somewhat shaded tree."

"How am I supposed to see if I'm closing my eyes?"

"You don't look with your physical eyes," Anya said. "Your Sight. It's how an athtar travels to places unknown." A rumbling echoed in the distance. "Hurry up. We're sitting ducks out here."

Cam closed her eyes and concentrated on…well, she wasn't sure what she was supposed to be concentrating on. In the space between her ears, she sought out that unfamiliar part of her that Anya had breathed down her throat. It had become unnoticeable over the past few days, but now stirred in her chest. Conscious of Anya's annoyed sighing, Cam asked the magic to let her See.

A vision entered her mind. She was flying through the world, seeing everything from every angle, taking in so much that she barely had time to absorb any of it. Then, in the distance, she found a tree—a nobbly, black-leafed thing rising up out of the muck on a small hill. The magic tingled against her chest, and she grabbed Anya by the arm as the world shifted beneath her feet. The mushy earth dried, and the air changed slightly. It was colder, smelling of impending snow.

"Good work."

Cam cracked open an eye then the other. The reeds and swamp were still there, but mountains rose in the distance, and there were pockets of dry land with brown moss and short trees, one of which they were standing under. It resembled a pine, except the needles were black.

"You went the right way, too," Anya said, pulling off the rucksack and digging through it. "We're getting close to Liley. Maybe five more days of travel." She squinted at Cam. "How do you feel?"

"Honestly?" Cam looked down at her body. "Not that bad at all. Is that normal?"

Anya shook her head. "We aren't in Ath-kur, but there's still magic here to draw from. That distance might've killed you in the human realm." She pulled a blanket from her bag and laid it on the mossy ground then found another and used it to cover herself up. Then, without another word, she rolled over and shut her eyes.

Cam, on the other hand, didn't like being exposed. She'd never liked camping. Sleeping under the stars in Texas just meant more opportunities for bugs and critters to crawl up in her business. At the very least, she wanted something over her head.

Looking up at the black tree hanging over her, she decided to do something about her situation. She walked to the tree, scanning the dark branches for something that might work. With a grunt, she wrapped her arms around the tree and found a foothold against the bark. With slow, methodical movements, she shimmied her way up to the nearest, lowest branch.

"What are you doing?" Anya asked from the ground.

"Camping," Cam said, sitting on the nearest branch and looking for another she could snap off. She wrapped her hands on the branch just to the left of her and yanked.

"Wait, don't!"

The branch moved underneath Cam's body, and before she knew what was happening, she was flying through the air then she landed with a loud *squilch* face-down in the mud. Shaking herself, she pushed herself onto her back to look behind her.

Just in time to watch the black tree march away, its roots

serving as makeshift legs.

"Well, there goes our shelter," Anya said with a frown.

"Wh…at the actual *fuck* just happened?" Cam screamed, mud sliding into her eye. "Was that… what the… *What the what?*"

Anya left the small, tree-less mound, walking to Cam with an amused smile on her face. "You might want to be careful about which plants you attack."

"*Are you kidding me? You just hacked your way through the Goddamn nox jungle!*"

"Yeah, because noxland plants aren't sentient. Plants in Kappanchi are."

"Oh, well, I'm *so* sorry," Cam said, wiping the disgusting dirt off her face. "I obviously missed that lesson at the Academy."

"Come on," Anya said, holding out a hand. "There's no use sitting in the mud."

Cam ignored her hand and stood, pining for the indoor plumbing and amenities of Lotan's castle. Maybe that was his plan—hope they'd get so miserable in the swamps that Anya would turn around.

Anya laughed. "Not so in love with the nox prince now, are we?"

"This lack of privacy thing sucks, by the way."

"You can say that again."

When Cam awoke the next morning, she was still covered in

mud—which had now dried and caked in her hair and clothes. Anya didn't bother to ask how she was feeling, but did fork over a turnip-looking vegetable for breakfast. Cam chewed on it, wondering if the mud taste was from the root or from her face. It was unsatisfying but it staved off the low blood sugar, and they got to walking.

"When you've fully recovered from yesterday's magic, we can try more," Anya said. "But I'd prefer to save it. I don't know what we'll find in Ath-kur."

Cam looked behind her as a dark cloud formed in the distance. "Well, if it starts raining, I'm booking it."

"It's just water. It won't hurt you," Anya said. "And it might do you some good to get cleaned up."

"Speak for yourself," Cam said, kicking a glob of mud in her direction.

The rain began shortly after that, although it wasn't enough to clean the mud from Cam's body and hair, but just enough to set her teeth chattering. She was almost hoping for a deluge to get it over with, but the steady sprinkle continued for the rest of the morning.

"So tell me this, how did all this world come to be?" Cam asked, after they'd stopped for lunch—more turnips. "Is it a coincidence that the noxlands looks like a Costa Rican rainforest?"

Anya shook her head. "From what I've heard, when God left the belus in this world, He crafted their new homes to be similar to the ones they'd left," she said. "Kappanchi resembles the marshlands where Mizuchi lived in Japan. I think it's somewhere in the center of the main island. The noxes were from—"

"Central America, yeah," Cam said. "And Bael?"

She kept a soft smile on her face. "He never said. I guessed, perhaps because he arrived near my village in Syria, that he might've been from there originally."

"Why didn't he tell you about it?"

"He didn't like to talk about when God chose him to bear the sin of pride," Anya said. "He preferred to talk about when he breaking the barrier between the worlds—finding his own humans, turning them into demons."

"So he considers himself a god then?" Cam shook her head. "Typical."

"He did sometimes get a little too wound up in his own grand visions of himself," Anya said, although it was very quiet.

"Hey!" Cam said, slapping Anya on the back. "That was positively derogatory, coming from you. There's hope for you yet, Colibrí!"

Anya stopped short, her shoulders going stick straight. "Do you see that?"

"See what?"

"Something's coming," Anya said, nodding to the distance, where a small object was quickly approaching. Cam squinted—it was a box of some sort, drawn by two blue, dragon-looking serpents who squiggled through the mud like copperhead snakes the size of horses. Cam, never the biggest fan of snakes, shivered and gripped her club.

"That's not Bael, is it?" she asked.

"No," Anya said, lowering her sword slightly.

The box, which now was very clearly a carriage, came to a skidding halt in front of them, although unlike when the kelpie left, the mud was kept to a minimum. The door handle jiggled then the door swung open. And out walked the ugliest creature Cam had ever laid eyes on.

CHAPTER EIGHTEEN

"Mizuchi," Anya said, lowering her sword completely. "What the hell are you doing out here?"

"Hunting for a pair of wayward travelers," the frog-man said. He was like a cross between a turtle and human, with a wide pink mouth and a decidedly green appearance. His froggish legs ended in webbed feet, and his long black hair was tied in a low knot behind his bulbous head. His red eyes gleamed in the light, looking somewhat amused to see the two of them.

Cam openly gaped, tilting her head to the side.

"Cam, don't be rude," Anya snapped. "And why, pray tell, are you hunting for us?"

"As it happens, my lady, I'm on my way to the Liley. I heard you were on your way to Ath-kur and thought you might want to expedite your journey."

Anya clicked her tongue. "At what cost?"

"A discussion of your journeys these past hundred and thirty years," Mizuchi said, dipping his head. Water splashed out onto the mud below. Cam had learned at the Academy that this meant a kappa demon was giving his word. But she still wasn't sure she trusted him not to eat her.

"Cam, let's go," Anya said, putting her sword back in its sheath.

Even though they were both covered in brown mud (Cam more than Anya), they climbed into the fancy carriage, sitting opposite the kappa belu. Cam still didn't fully believe this monster was real, from his scaly skin to the way his tongue moved in his mouth.

Anya elbowed her roughly. "Knock it off."

"It's quite all right, Lady Anat," Mizuchi said with a hearty chuckle. "I've heard all about your spirited partner. Tell me, Lady Macarro—"

"Agent," Cam said, wiping the drying mud from her cheek. "Agent Macarro is fine."

"Agent, my apologies. How did you come to have so much mud on you?"

Anya cleared her throat. "She tried to take a branch from a numachi tree."

"Ah, yes," Mizuchi said with a wide smile. "Best not to disturb the tree spirits."

"Wish someone had told me that," Cam said with a dirty glare.

"You should've asked," Anya said with the ghost of a smile.

"I did ask that we *not* wander into the swamp," Cam said. "I wanted to go up through the Nullius. But no, you're a damned chicken."

"My lady is right not to venture that way," Mizuchi said. "The Nullius is a land no demon enters."

Cam huffed. "What's so damned terrifying about it? It's where you landed, right?"

"That is the theory," Mizuchi said. "But many of us have very little memory of that day. Even Bael, I believe, cannot clearly recall the circumstances. He will tell you otherwise, though." He looked at Anya. "And how have you been, my lady? You look better than the last time I saw you."

"I think you know the answer to that question," she replied tightly.

"Don't be reticent. We had an agreement," he said, although there was little concern in his voice. To Cam, he seemed to already know everything about Anya. Perhaps he just wanted her to talk about it.

"*Fine,*" she said, wrenching her gaze away from the scene outside. "I thought I was cursed. Turns out I wasn't. I'm returning to Ath-kur to fetch a human. There isn't much more to tell."

Mizuchi bristled. "There's plenty more. This curse, I heard tale of it, but never quite got the story right. I'd love to hear the details."

Anya pursed her lips, but exhaled a breath. "It was in New Orleans. A group of witches or...something put this curse on me. I believed them that I had to repent for every soul I'd killed."

"How many was that?" Mizuchi asked.

"Ten thousand, seven hundred, and forty-two."

Cam whistled. "Really?"

"It was over a long span of time," Anya said, looking out the window.

The kappa clasped his green hands over his belly. "Was it simply humans you were repenting for, or others?"

Her neutral expression turned icy. "Unfair question, Belu Kappa."

"I am simply asking you to fulfill the bargain we made."

Cam was again lost, but tried to keep up anyway. "What happens if you don't fulfill a bargain with a kappa?"

"The kappa will get angry," Anya said. "It's inadvisable to make him that way."

"I could never be angry with you, my lady," he tutted.

"Of course," she said with narrowing eyes. "Not while you're trying to guilt me into suicide. You'll wait until after Bael has lopped my head off to be angry with me."

Mizuchi's thin lips turned downward. "Did you allow the nox prince to tell you any of his plan?"

"I don't need to hear his plan. It's ludicrous," Anya said. "He miscalculated how weak I've become. I haven't been to Ath-kur in almost a century and a half. I'm barely able to use magic without falling over. Killing Bael? I won't even be able to lift my sword against him."

"Bael is weak," Mizuchi said. "He's overextended himself by leaving the schism open for as long as he did."

"It wasn't open that long," Anya said, but there was less certainty in her voice now. "And it's been closed for a few days. I'm sure he's recovered."

"My lady, now you're just being unreasonable. Historically, Bael needs a year or two without any activity to fully recover."

Anya pursed her lips. "And how did you come by that information? He keeps that closely guarded."

"Not closely enough, it seems," Mizuchi said. "The kappas in his castle aren't as loyal to him as he believes. Nor, I assume, are they as loyal to me as I think."

Cam was starting to get a neck crick from watching their conversation. "Bael's weak right now? This might be the best time to strike."

"Weak-*er* than normal," Anya said. "But still capable of killing everything if he wanted to."

"As are you, my lady," Mizuchi said. "I only wish you would see it for yourself."

"I have one mission, and one mission alone: Finding Jack and getting him back to the human realm where he'll be safe. Whatever other plots you and Lotan have concocted, leave me out of them. I want no part."

"Ah, well, I did try," Mizuchi said. "I'll get you to Liley, although I'll say Freyja will be upset to know you did not stop in to see her."

"Meeting Freyja is not part of our agreement, Mizuchi."

"True, true," he said. "But I apologize. I do have one stop to make before we reach Liley. I'm sure Lady Macarro would be happy to use Tabiko's facilities."

Anya shifted beside Cam. "Tabiko?"

"Yes, my lady. I promise, it will be a short visit," Mizuchi said. "Unless, of course, the weather continues to turn bad. Then we may stay the evening. If that's acceptable to you."

"I suppose that will be fine. We can't travel in the rain either." But Anya's face told a different story. She actually looked nervous. Whatever the issue was with this Tabiko person, Cam would find out soon enough.

The ride was silent after that, so Cam watched the world outside the window. The rain was really coming down now, splattering against the mud and the carriage side. The serpents pulling the carriage had taken a turn down a small river growing wider and wider. Mangrove-looking black trees dug their fingers into the murky brown water, growing together in a canopy of purple-leaves.

Eventually the rain stopped, but the sky remained gray. The serpents came to a halt in front of a small wooden house, barely visible amongst the trees. Smoke wafted out of a chimney on top, and a woman stood outside, hanging her wash on the line. She pinned the last of what was in her hand, wiped her hands on her apron, and walked to the edge of the river to greet them.

Anya looked visibly uncomfortable as she followed Mizuchi out of the carriage. The woman was of similar froggishness to Mizuchi, although her face was more feminine, it was also sharper. Whatever had transpired between this Tabiko and Anya had clearly not been resolved.

But the kappa turned to Mizuchi and softened. "Belu Kappa," she said with a bow, splashing all the water from her head. Mizuchi approached her with a pitcher of water he'd retrieved from inside the carriage, and carefully refilled the reservoir.

"My dear Tabiko," he said. "You remember Lady Anat? And this is her partner, Agent Camilla Macarro, of the humans' demonic management agency."

Tabiko's gaze lingered on Anya for longer than was necessary and to Cam's surprise, Anya averted her gaze. As if she were ashamed of something.

"It is my pleasure to welcome you into my home," the female kappa said after a moment. She looked to Cam then blinked a few times. "Please, make yourself comfortable with the bath out back."

"Is it that obvious?" Cam grumbled, looking down at herself. The brown mud coated her from shoes to tits. Perhaps a bath was in order.

"Tabiko, please take care of Agent Macarro," Mizuchi said. "I'll play host to Lady Anat until you return."

Tabiko beckoned Cam and she followed. The woman's air was chilly, even toward Cam, who decided against making small talk. The kappa led her to a hut with a pool sunk into the ground, steaming with hot water. Cam could have kissed her.

"I'll retrieve fresh clothes," Tabiko said, without making eye contact with Cam. "Please leave your things by the door so I can launder them."

"Oh, you don't have to," Cam said. But then she realized there probably wasn't a laundromat here in the Underworld. "I mean…if you want to, that would be great."

"Lord Mizuchi has brought you as his guests. It would be rude not to treat you with the utmost respect."

The words were kind, but the tone wasn't. Tabiko did not want them there, but was putting up with them for Mizuchi's sake.

"Thank you," Cam said as the door closed behind her. She peeled her mud-caked clothes from her body and sank into the warm water, releasing a loud sigh of relief.

Anya's voice wafted through the thin walls, breaking Cam from her reverie. She waded to the other side of the pool, cracking the door open just a hair. Anya and Mizuchi stood in the center of the courtyard.

"…one night. Better to travel in the day," Mizuchi said.

"I suppose," Anya said with a frown on her face. She inhaled deeply and crossed her arms over her chest, staring at the ground. "While we're here, I wanted to apologize. For…Wani."

Mizuchi nodded, a bit sadly. "He was a good demon. But I've heard conflicting reports if it was by your sword or not."

"It wasn't," Anya said, looking at her mud caked boots. "But it might as well have been."

"If you feel that strongly, you know how to make it right," Mizuchi said, a little sadly. "Just as you knew how to make it right with Tabiko. It's not too late to repent for Ayumi's death."

Anya turned away and Cam quickly slid the door shut. She waded back to the other side of the pool then sank down to her chin.

The door slid open and Anya appeared, an annoyed look on her face. "Don't bother. I know you were listening."

"So?" Cam asked as Anya disrobed. "Care to share?"

Anya stepped into the pool and sighed, closing her eyes. "Do I have a choice?"

"I mean, you always have a choice," Cam said, making waves with her hands. "I'm just going to bother you until you spill the beans, though. Who's Ayumi?"

"She was a friend of mine," she murmured. "A long time ago."

An uneasy knowing crept into Cam's mind. "Bael doesn't seem like the kind of guy who'd let you have friends."

Anya's eyes opened to the ceiling. "He made me kill her."

Cam's jaw fell, splashing hot water into her mouth. She spat it out and shook her head. "Are you *kidding* me? How the hell did he make you do that?"

"It was either her or a thousand human children," Anya said, numbly brushing her fingers against the water. Then she sank her hand underneath. "Bael killed them anyway."

Cam swore something filthy in Spanish, for there was nothing in English to convey the depths of her disgust. "And Tabiko?"

"Tabiko is…was her wife," Anya said. "They'd become

demons together, and Mizuchi sent them to work in Bael's castle."

"That explains the cold reception," Cam said with a humorless chuckle.

"Tabiko never liked me anyway," Anya said with a small smile. "She thought it was dangerous for Ayumi to become friends with me in the first place." Her smile faded. "Guess she was right."

"And you think bringing us here is Mizuchi trying to convince you to join with Lotan, huh?" Cam said. "Looks like it's working."

"I can be sorry for the death of someone, that doesn't mean I'm able to do what the nox prince is asking," Anya said. "Or that I believe their plan is worth accomplishing. Bael is simply too powerful."

"So you'd rather just not try than try and fail?" Cam asked. "What about Jack?"

"You will get him to safety, as was our agreement."

"Anya," Cam said with a sigh. "I'm talking about you and him. Don't you care for him? Don't you want to have a life together?"

Anya stared at the bottom of the pool, falling back into her pensive look.

"I know you do," Cam answered for her. "Because you wouldn't be here, running through the Underworld, trying to save him with me. You're just afraid to say it out loud." She chuckled, darkly. "I see why."

"I want to so badly," Anya said. "But I don't know if my heart could handle it if Bael did to Jack what I did to Ayumi."

"What *Bael* did to Ayumi," Cam corrected.

"It was my sword, my actions," Anya said. "I am responsible for letting him manipulate me."

"Well, the first step is admitting it," Cam said. "And the next step is slicing his lying head off so he can never do it again."

CHAPTER NINETEEN

Later that evening, Anya lay wide awake in a room Tabiko had made up for them while Cam snored lightly next to her. Anya's polluelo seemed to be able to fall asleep anywhere. Even while she was dreaming, their connection remained active. Anya actually didn't mind it as much anymore. It was a welcome distraction from everything else on her mind.

Tabiko had looked exactly the same. Same piercing eyes, same disgust on her face. Mizuchi was trying to manipulate Anya so she'd listen to the belus. She wanted to hate him for it, to rise above his machinations. But there she was, walking along the path Mizuchi wanted her to. Remembering the first time Bael had become a monster in her eyes. The first time she'd ever really feared him.

It had been several years since Bael had lost his temper and hit her again. Then again, Anya had become accustomed to managing his moods, diffusing the situation before it escalated. So things were good.

She continued working on her swordsmanship, spending her days training with blades of all kinds. Bael encouraged, but seldom joined her in the training room. It was usually up to some poor kappa or lilin to bear the brunt of her daily regimens. Then, as more athtars joined their ranks, Anya began to train them as well. She'd perfected the marriage of athtar speed and swordsmanship, and took great pride in showing the neophytes how to do it. No one, of course, was as good as she.

Bael, too, had grown powerful amongst the belus. Although he continued to bring thousands of humans to the other belus, he'd only transform one athtar per Demon Spring. When Anya asked him why he chose the imbalance, his answer was always the same:

"I can stop time. Their armies live as long as I allow them to," he'd say with a smile. "And they would never be able to rebuild without my strength."

Slowly, as the demons left behind between breaches reached further into the human realm, the other belus began to know things that Bael didn't. Languages flourished among the servants in the castle, and, although Bael paid little attention to them, Anya found it fascinating.

One of the girls with this particular talent was the handmaiden who washed Anya's clothes. She was kappa, still looking mostly human. She brought with her a kind, quiet energy that put Anya at ease, even when Bael was in one of his angry moods.

The first time Anya had an extended conversation with the woman was right after a Demon Spring. Bael was always exhausted and weak after spending a fortnight in the human realm, and it left him with a shorter temper than usual. Anya couldn't even remember what had set him off, but he'd struck her in the face, and she'd run off to her bedroom to hide until the bruises and his anger faded.

There, the kappa had been in the middle of changing her sheets. She took one look at Anya, then bowed, begging Anya's forgiveness as she darted from the room. Anya had thought the woman was apologizing for seeing her in a vulnerable moment, but she'd returned a moment later with a salve.

"Put it on your eye," she said, handing Anya a cloth with a sweet-smelling lotion. "It will help with the swelling."

"What will help with the pain?" Anya asked, but could no longer keep her emotions inside. She let the words flow from the place she'd kept them locked away while tears leaked down her face. The kappa didn't leave, but sat down and listened to her speak about how much she both feared and loved her king. There had been no solutions offered or judgment, just quiet nodding and a soft hand over hers. And when Anya had cried her last tear and gone back to Bael's bedchambers, she'd felt better for confiding in someone.

For the next few weeks, the girl had kept to herself when she tended to Anya. It was as if she knew that seeing the Lady of the Mountain so weak was a private affair, and speaking of it would only ruin the mystery. So Anya broke the ice.

"That lotion you made me," she said. "Can you show me how to make it?"

Anya learned the name of the potion, and how to find the plants in the swamps of Kappanchi. Along the way, she also learned the girl's—Ayumi's—language. It wasn't one Anya knew, as Bael hadn't transitioned anyone who spoke it. It was a fun exercise—like learning how to use a new kind of weapon. After several weeks, Anya was speaking it as well as Ayumi and her wife, Tabiko.

There was something freeing about speaking in a language only a few understood—in a language Bael didn't understand. Anya could confide her fears and secrets without the fear of being overheard. It wasn't that she wanted to keep secrets from her king. But he was so prone to overreaction.

She was careful to keep her newfound talents from Bael, but eventually, as with everything, he began to notice the phrases and words she'd let slip.

"What is that you're saying?" Bael asked with a curious look.

"Oh," Anya said, a blush rising to her cheeks. "It's one of the human languages."

"And how, my lady, did you come across that language?" Bael asked with that smile that boded nothing good. "I don't think any of our athtars speak it."

Anya felt like she was in trouble, although she'd no idea why.

"One of the kappa servants taught it to me."

"Oh," was all he said. And it was enough to plant a seed of doubt in Anya's mind.

The questions started very subtly. During the course of their daily conversations about athtars and their demonic concerns, Bael would slip in questions about Ayumi. Asking if Anya had asked the servant for her opinion. Anya's response was, "Of course not. Why would I?"

Then the questions grew into accusations.

"I don't even understand why you're talking to her in the first place!" Bael would cry. "Am I not enough for you?"

Anya could say nothing to appease him. It didn't matter that Ayumi and Tabiko had been lovers for centuries, and Anya's heart had been Bael's for even longer. Bael was inconsolable, jealous, and dangerous.

But Anya hadn't realized how dangerous until the next Demon Spring, when she arrived in the human world to see a group of children assembled—and Ayumi, bound and gagged and teary-eyed.

"What is she doing here?" Anya asked, her voice sounding odd in her ears.

"I have been most angry with you, Anat," Bael said. "You've betrayed me, laid with another, and given your heart to her. This is how you repay the gifts I've given you? This is how you treat the love I have for you?"

"Bael, I didn't do anything with her! I don't love her, I love you!" Anya cried, sensing that something truly horrible was about to happen. "I swear to you!"

"Then prove it," Bael said, his eyes cruel and merciless. "Prove to me you love me more than her. Kill her."

Something slid out of place in Anya's mind. "What did you say?"

"I told you: Kill the bitch or I'll know you don't love me," Bael said. Then he glanced at the children who'd been assembled, many of them screaming in fear. "And if you don't love me, then I'll just have to take my pain out on these children."

"Bael, you can't…you can't be serious…" He was insane. Anya had seen him be cruel, but this? This was beyond cruel.

"It's your choice, Anat," he said, his voice as even and emotionless as ever. "You can either kill Ayumi, or you can kill all these humans."

Anya looked at the babies, horrified. "They're children, Bael."

"They're human," he spat. "I don't care how old they are. The vermin will simply make more." His gaze settled on Anya once more. "Now make your decision or I'll make it for you."

A little girl nearby rushed forward, pleading with Anya to save her. She was too thin, and reminded Anya of the little girls she'd seen in her village centuries ago. Reminded Anya that she, too, was once a little girl like that.

But the alternative…

Anya swallowed hard and turned to Ayumi. She was her friend—her only friend. Anya should've known better.

Should've known that Bael wouldn't approve. She had known, and she'd done it anyway. If there was anyone to blame for this…it was Anya herself.

Anya pulled her sword, the metal feeling strange in her hands as she trudged the impossibly long distance to her dear friend.

"I'm sorry," Anya said, unable to shed a tear. Not feeling worthy to. "I'm so sorry."

"Do it," Ayumi whispered. "I am ready."

"Please forgive me," Anya whispered in the language she would never speak again. And as her sword fell against Ayumi's bowed neck, she heard a scream that sounded like her heart breaking.

Shaking, she turned away from the scene to another horrifying one. Every last child was dead, including the little girl who'd pleaded for her life.

"I had to know, Anat," Bael said, throwing away his bloody sword. "I had to know that you still loved me. You brought this on yourself. If you hadn't befriended her, I never would have doubted you."

His words fell flat, her heart too broken to process his hatred and disdain for her. But nothing prepared her for Tabiko's wrath when she returned to Ath-kur.

"Ayumi felt pity for you," Tabiko screamed, not caring that Bael and the other athtars were watching the scene. "She thought you the loneliest woman in the world, living as you were in fear of the belu athtar. She was a kind person, giving. You did not deserve her friendship. You didn't deserve to take her life. Not when you still love that monster. How can you love someone like that?"

Tabiko's voice echoed in Anya's ear as she wiped away a tear. It had been centuries since that day, but the memories were as sharp as the pain in her chest.

She sat up, knowing she wasn't going to get much sleep. So she decided to take a walk, tossing the covers off her and strolling the grounds. Mizuchi's two snake demons, the nureonna, were also awake, splashing in a small pond in the center of the houses lit by blue algae. They'd dip their blue heads into the water and come up with a wriggling fish between their teeth, swallowing it in one gulp.

Anya sat down next to the pond, taking off her shoes and dipping her toes into the water. One of the nureonna slithered over to her, nudging her with its foot. She petted it on the snout and shrugged.

"I have nothing for you," she whispered. "I'm sorry."

The nureonna moved back to its brethren, sliding around a statue in the center of the pond. Anya squinted to read the writing in the dark, then her heart stopped.

The statue was a memorial to Ayumi.

"Beautiful, isn't it?" Mizuchi said behind her. "Tabiko sculpted it herself."

Anya nodded, pressing a hand to her chest to massage away the pressure. "It's pretty."

"I am sorry for Tabiko's frosty reception."

"She has every right to hate me," Anya said firmly. "I hate myself for what I did."

Mizuchi tutted to himself as he took a seat beside her. "Something on your mind, my lady?"

"Lots of things," she said, kicking her feet. "Mainly the many excuses I've made over the years for the things I've done to hurt people."

"Some of those excuses were good ones."

"Not many."

"Well, my lady, what do you plan to do about it?" Mizuchi asked. "Will you pick up your sword to our cause?"

"You are the smartest demon I've ever met," Anya said. "Do you think there's any chance of success?"

"Hope is a powerful motivator," Mizuchi said. "It can make the impossible possible."

"Stop talking in riddles and answer me."

"I don't believe it matters if we have a chance. What matters is what we think is right. I wouldn't be here, risking my life and my spawn, if I didn't believe this was the right place to be." He procured some dried fish from his pocket and tossed it into the waiting mouth of his nureonna. "You have always been a woman who calculates risk. You've had to be, with a lover such as Bael. I've watched you weigh decisions for centuries. Almost always, you chose the path of least resistance."

"So I'm a coward," she said. The moniker certainly fit.

"Self-preservationist is the term I'd use," Mizuchi replied with a wink.

"Selfish coward, then."

"It sounds to me," Mizuchi said after a long silence, "as though you are looking for redemption. It's why those humans were so successful in making you believe you were cursed. You didn't need a charm to remind you of those you've killed. You carry it with you every day. By believing in the curse, it absolved you of responsibility. You could be redeemed without having to face the truth that you needed redeeming. And I believe you're still seeking that easy solution." He turned to her, his large eyes growing sad. "But just as you knew the curse wasn't real, you know that rescuing Jack will be a temporary solution to a much larger problem."

"But at least he'll be safe."

"For how much longer?" Mizuchi asked. "Bael has already proven his reach is far into the human world. The human committed the ultimate sin of turning the Lady of the Mountain's heart against Bael. The King of the Underworld won't let that stand."

"Jack didn't do anything," Anya said. "It was my choice to fall for him. It should be my consequence to pay."

"Unfortunately, that isn't how Bael's mind operates. The only way to keep your Jack safe is to make sure Bael can never hurt him again. Even if you returned to his side, even if you promised fealty and love forever. Even if you told Bael to kill you instead. He would kill the human, just to satisfy his own pride. You must know that."

She did know that, but it didn't mean she accepted it. "What

Lotan wants me to do…even if I could stomach the act, I'm no match for Bael in power or strength."

"But at least you would die in pursuit of something greater than yourself. And what greater act of redemption could there be?"

CHAPTER TWENTY

Cam had slept well on the makeshift bed, but Anya looked exhausted and miserable the next morning. Mizuchi stood in front of his carriage, feeding fishes to his two demons. Cam watched them warily from a distance—they seemed friendly, but they could still take off her arm.

"Tabiko will be joining us on this last leg," Mizuchi announced, as the kappa demon appeared next to him in traveling clothes. "I'll need an attendant while at Freyja's Kastali, and she has graciously agreed to step in."

She glared at Anya, as if daring her to say something, but Anya kept her mouth closed.

The carriage was a bit more stuffed with four, as Mizuchi took an entire side of the carriage, so Cam, Tabiko, and Anya squeezed in on the other side. Cam sat in the center, feeling she would be an adequate buffer to the animosity between them. Or rather, Tabiko's animosity and Anya's guilty reception of it. Drawn by the two blue serpents, they continued on their way down the river, which had grown wider and the air chillier. Soon they were skimming along the beach of a bay, and small snowflakes had begun to fall.

"Are we in Liley yet?" Cam asked, craning her neck to get a good look.

"Yes," Mizuchi said. "We should be arriving at Freyja's Kastali within the hour. My nureonna don't do well with the cold, but she'll have a warm bath ready when we arrive. A wonderful host, that Freyja."

Cam blinked and turned to Anya. "Wait a minute, I thought we weren't going to Freyja's? I thought we were just being dropped off at the border?"

Anya shared a look with Mizuchi. "There will be a meeting tomorrow with the belus regarding the nox prince's plan. I have decided to attend."

"Wait, *what?*" Cam gaped, spinning in her admittedly cramped seat. "Why?"

"Because it is what I've decided to do."

Cam caught a look of triumph from Mizuchi, who winked at her with his wet, bulging eyes. "Freyja will be most pleased to see you, Lady Anat."

"But what about Jack?" Cam said. "I thought—"

"I believe that partnering with the noxes and others might improve our chances of success," she said, her tone warming slightly. "I promise you, Jack remains at the forefront of my mind. As soon as I believe we can get him out safely—and keep him that way—we will."

Cam was torn—on the one hand, yes, maximizing success was important. But on the other, it was yet another layover, another night before they could get to Jack.

Anya rested her hand on top of Cam's. "We won't stay longer than we need to."

"Have I mentioned how much I really dislike this connection?" Cam grumbled, wrenching her hand away.

In the window beyond Mizuchi's head, Cam spotted the castle rising in the distance, a black monstrosity with spires reaching to the sky like an evil queen's castle in a fairy tale. White lights dotted the facade—presumably windows. From afar, they seemed like pinpricks, but as they drew closer, the size of the castle became apparent. Where Lotan's castle had been nestled into the jungle, masking its breadth, there was no hiding the magnitude of Kastali.

"What is it with you demons and your castles?" Cam asked.

"Freyja wanted to have plenty of room to house her spawn," Anya said. "And whomever else she wanted nearby."

"So is this place like a constant orgy or is there some semblance of decency?" Cam asked. There certainly hadn't been any stirrings of the lust that usually came with lilin demons; then again, her nose was frozen from the cold, wet air, so she was more concerned about frostbite.

"Little bit of both," Anya said. "I'm sure things may be more somber though, with all this talk of war."

The snow had begun to fall in earnest, fluffy white puffs that landed and melted against the gray water the nureonna slithered over. The castle was now so large outside the front window, Cam could no longer see the top. The snake demons slowed as they arrived at the castle.

"Hold on," Mizuchi said, grasping the edge of the carriage.

"Wha—" The carriage jostled, throwing Cam nearly into Anya's lap and Anya onto the floor. Only Tabiko and Mizuchi remained upright, as Tabiko made quick work of unlatching the carriage door and stepping out. Cam ambled out behind her, still seeing stars from the rough entry. The two serpent demons had slithered right up on top of the black rock at the foot of the castle. Why they didn't use the docks nearby, Cam had no clue. They shivered in the frigid air; perhaps they just wanted to get out of the water.

"Anat, my love!"

Freyja appeared in the doorway to the castle. She was the most beautiful woman Cam had ever seen. Porcelain skin, long, yellow hair, piercing blue eyes and long pointy ears. She wore a fur coat that was open down to her naval, which rather defeated the purpose of it, and fur-lined boots that clacked against the dock.

She gathered Anya in her arms then pressed a kiss to her lips. "It has been too long."

"Same," Anya said. "Freyja, this is Cam."

Freya turned and offered a kind, loving smile. And before Cam could stop her, the lilin had taken her by the face and kissed her soundly. Cam froze, unsure what to do or how to react.

"Freyja, Cam isn't used to your greeting," Anya said with a little chuckle. "A handshake will suffice."

"Not in my kingdom, love," Freyja said with a frown and a loving stroke of Cam's cheek. "We shall melt your little heart of ice, young athtar."

"Uh… nice to meet you, too," Cam said.

"Mizuchi!" Freyja said with an equally happy smile. As before, she kissed the kappa on his greenish-pink lips, then did the same with Tabiko. Neither seemed to mind or be surprised by the greeting, as Cam had been. Perhaps the lilin belu really did just make out with everyone she met. She was surprised Freyja didn't stick her tongue down the serpents' throats, although she did stroke them lovingly.

"Your pets are probably freezing," she said. "Take them inside where there's a lovely pool for them. Tabiko, would you care to join us for dinner?"

"No, m'lady," she said with a glance at Anya. "I'll assist Belu Kappa with the nureonna."

"As you wish," Freyja said. "I'll have two dinner plates sent down as soon as you want them."

With the kappas taken care of, Freyja turned and looped her arms through Cam and Anya's. "I have planned a marvelous feast for you, my love."

Cam definitely preferred staying in demonic castles to

camping. She flung herself onto the cushiony, downy bed with thick, velvet blankets and sighed happily. The castle was almost as cold as the outside, but the roaring fires in every room dispelled the frost admirably. She was also probably feeling a little giddy from all the magic.

"Get nice and comfortable," Freyja said with a grin before looking at Anya. "You look like a tiger trapped in a cage, Anat. Come sit at my feet and let me brush your hair."

Anya frowned, resembling a petulant toddler. "No."

"Come. Here." Freyja took a seat on a plush red chair. "You are here until tomorrow at least, and you're wearing a hole in my carpet."

With an angry sigh, Anya stomped across the room and sat down on the floor in front of Freyja. "Isn't that better?" the belu cooed, procuring a brush out of nowhere and untangling the rubber band around Anya's hair. Once the mound of curly black hair was down, Freyja gently ran the brush through the strands, her touch gentle and motherly.

"Take care, little athtar spawn, or you'll be next," Freyja said to Cam.

"Polluelo," Anya said with a look. "I hate that word *spawn*."

"You always were very particular," Freyja said, with a little chuckle. "Now, tell me of this Jack you are off to rescue."

Anya looked at Cam then down at the ground. "Nothing to tell."

"Nonsense," Freyja said, gathering locks of Anya's hair to detangle. "I hear you're fond of him. The first human ever to earn such a prestigious title in your heart. He must be special."

Cam got a whiff of pheromones, and calming, lovely thoughts crowded out all the anxiety she'd been nursing for weeks. She reached for the talismans around her wrist, but then decided against it. After all, there was nothing really to worry about. Freyja was a gorgeous, soft, beautiful creature with skin that begged to be touched. Anya's frown had melted away. She leaned into the lilin's knees as she allowed her hair to be played with.

"Tell me," Freyja cooed, running her fingers through Anya's hair. "Tell me all about this man."

"He's Jack," she whispered, closing her eyes as a lovesick smile spread across her face. "When I first met him, he was a shadow—barely alive. But he thought I was worth saving. He gave up everything…even his best friend, his family." She closed her eyes. "Just for me. To save me. When I needed his help, he gave it freely. He never asked for anything in return."

"Do you love him?" Freyja asked.

Anya's cloudy eyes blinked once, twice, then filled with fury as she jumped to her feet. "Fuck you, Freyja. Turn it off."

"What?" Freyja said with an innocent shrug. "What did I do?"

Suddenly, the smell of flowers disappeared, and Cam was left with an uncomfortable feeling in her lower abdomen.

"You were pumping me for information," Anya said, her face the reddest Cam had ever seen it. "That's not fair."

"Why are you so upset with me?" Freyja asked, sitting back.

"You would waste no time in telling me the depths of love you carry for Bael, so I know it's within you to be poetic. Why are you afraid to share about this man?"

"Because if Bael knows how I really feel, he'll kill him," Anya snapped, rubbing her chest. "This connection between maker and demon—"

"Your love is there whether you hide it or not," Freyja said gently. "There are no secrets. Bael already knows the extent of your love. That is why he has done what he's done."

Cam nodded, but Anya seemed to read something more in Freyja's words. "What's he done?"

"Taking Jack, of course," Freyja said, almost too quickly.

"No, Freyja," Anya said, walking forward. "What is Bael doing to Jack? What has he done?"

The lilin demon lost her softness as her face became heavy. "One of his lilin servants is tending to him glamoured as his late wife."

Cam sat up, slowly processing what she'd just heard. It didn't make any sense to her at first, because the idea was so horrifically disgusting that she'd never thought any creature capable of such a thing. In the back of her mind, she'd been nursing a fear that the worst had happened; that they'd get to Ath-kur and find Jack's dead body.

But perhaps this…this was worse than even she could've imagined.

"Are you….*serious*?" she spat out finally. "He's…"

"He's doing well," Freyja said, holding up her hands. "My

spy reported he went to dinner with Bael and his inner circle and seemed in good spirits despite everything."

Cam's stomach had risen to her throat and she looked at Anya, desperate. "We have to get him out. *Now.*"

"Now, darling," Freyja said. "It is as I said. If you go in alone, things will assuredly get worse."

"What's worse than seeing the *ghost of my dead sister*?" Cam cried, her voice growing higher as her pulse quickened. "Jack barely survived her death! How the hell is he supposed to survive this?"

"Jack is stronger than you think—" Anya started.

"Nuh-uh," Cam said, anger surging through her as she stood upright, marching toward Anya with her fists balled. "You do *not* get to talk about him like you know him. You don't get to act like you two have this great connection because you fucked once and spent a few weeks together. *I* am the one who had to pick up the pieces. *I* am the one who had to be strong for the both of us. You—"

"Cam," Freyja whispered.

The smell of flowers and sex drew tears to Cam's eyes as she sank back down on the bed. "I mean, who…who *does* that? Who is so fucked up in the head that he thinks it's normal to send a demon dressed like somebody's dead wife?" She turned to Anya, incredulous. "And how the hell can you *love* someone like that? How can you keep making excuses for him?"

Anya had no response but to look at the floor.

"Why don't I take your polluelo and go for a walk," Freyja

said, swinging her arm around Cam. "Anat, my sweet love, please continue to make yourself at home, as I know you will."

⸻ ⟨⟩ ⸻

"Ssh, my love," Freyja said, nestling Cam tighter against her as they walked down the hall. "You're shaking. Are you cold?"

Cam didn't know if she was cold, disgusted, angry, or all of the above. In her mind, all she heard was every excuse Anya had ever made for Bael and the sound of Jack's voice when he'd called her on that painful night three years ago. They pounded with her pulse and the heaving of her chest until she was dizzy with rage.

"Astrid, dearest, please fetch a bottle of our strongest wine," Freyja said to a lilin walking by. "Bring it to my chambers."

"Oh great, now are you gonna sleep with me?" Cam said, wiping a tear from her cheek.

"Only if you want it," Freyja said with a hearty smile.

"I don't," Cam said, letting tears fall freely now. "I want my best friend back. He was almost who he used to be. He was almost there. And *she* went and fucked it all up. If it wasn't for *her*, we wouldn't even *be* here! A damned demon and miserable and Jack being tortured. And…" Cam's words ended in sobs.

And despite being veritable strangers, she let Freyja hold her as she bawled into the belu lilin's shoulder.

"Let it out, my love," Freyja said, patting her on the back. "You've been holding this in for quite some time, haven't you?" She stepped back and wore a look of pity. "Do you want to get that drink now?"

Cam sniffed loudly, rubbed her face, and nodded.

Freyja took her by the arm and guided her the rest of the way to her bedchambers. The room was befitting for the goddess of lust, with red drapes canvassing a bed larger than any Cam had ever seen—like two king-sized mattresses had been shoved together.

"How many people can you fit on that bed?" Cam found herself asking as she sniffed.

Freyja chuckled. "Twenty-seven is my current record. But I prefer just two most nights."

Cam nodded, again wondering if she would be the second in that number.

"Everyone who comes to my bed does so willingly," Freyja said, walking to the table where a bottle and two glasses had been placed. "Even Bael, although it's been centuries since he's allowed himself to be vulnerable with me."

"What do you mean?" Cam said, accepting the glass.

"Bael doesn't like not to be in control," she said. "Here, he is too quickly under my spell if I allow it. I remind him of the human he once was."

"So you've slept with him?" Cam said with a bit of a grimace as she tossed her head back and downed half the glass.

"Careful, that vintage has been infused with lilin magic," Freyja said, lowering Cam's glass with her finger. "Designed to relax in small doses."

"Answer my question," Cam said, although she was feeling much better.

"I was Bael's lover before Anya," Freyja said. "But it was a match of mutual benefit, not the one-sided, master-servant relationship he has with Anat. I freely shared my gifts with Bael, Mizuchi, Biloko, and even paid a visit or two to the noxes, before their passing." She tapped a finger against her chin with a sad smile. "Although I could do nothing for them. Theirs was a love deeper than any magic I possess."

"Bael was okay with you sleeping around?" Cam asked. "He seems the jealous kind."

"Bael wanted what Xo and Mot had," Freyja said. "That was something I couldn't give him, so he sought it elsewhere. And that's how he came to find Anat, precious girl that she was. But she wasn't Xo, who had been touched by God Himself. And that is the beginning and the end of why their relationship never worked."

"Sounds like it never worked because Bael is a fucking pig," Cam said.

Freyja giggled. "Well, that too. When she first arrived at my castle, Anat was a young girl trapped in a woman's body. Scared, out of her element, and grateful that someone like Bael had seen potential in her. Over the centuries, he took that gratitude and twisted it into this horrific thing he calls love. Although she puts on a brave face, I still see that scared little girl who was trying so hard. Who was so scared her savior would abandon her if she made one wrong step." She tilted her head and swirled her wine around in her glass. "I suppose that's why she was so taken aback by your Jack. She's a woman who yearns for love, yet knows nothing of it. And to someone who's felt love's sweet embrace, her behavior can seem unbelievable."

"That's a really sad story," Cam said. "But it doesn't excuse her excusing Bael."

Freyja covered her hands. "This hurt you feel, it's caused by Bael. Not by Anat. Try to be gentle with her. After all, she's here. She's trying to get there. We just need to help her along."

Cam stared at the red wine in her glass. "I'm tired of helping people along. I want to be helped for once."

"Then drink up," Freyja said, filling her glass.

"I'm sorry," Cam said, readily accepting it. "For crying and getting drunk like an idiot."

"My lovely Cam," Freyja said, pouring herself a glass. "There are no apologies for love in this realm. In fact, I encourage it wherever possible."

CHAPTER TWENTY-ONE

As hard as he tried, Jack still couldn't shake the trepidation when the lock clicked on his door. He now had three choices—food, Sara, or more torture from Lazlo. The latter had only happened twice now, but it had left a lasting impression.

But he still hadn't given up. He was going to get out of this. Lazlo had let something slip he wasn't supposed to. Anya was coming for him. Until he heard otherwise, he was going to cling to that little bit of hope.

The door handle jiggled and Jack prepared himself. Door number one opened to reveal a kappa servant sans food but with another tuxedo. Hyun was behind her, along with another human-looking Indonesian athtar Jack had seen briefly. She wore her long black hair in a braid down her back, and walked into the room as if she were the queen of England, a sword hanging from her hip. Had she been human, Jack would've pegged her at eighteen.

"I'm here to make sure you don't give Hyun any trouble," she said with a steely glare.

"Wouldn't dream of it," Jack said, dutifully sitting down on the chair the kappa had motioned to. "And you are?"

"Gita," she replied with a look out the window, as if checking for escape routes.

"I haven't tried to escape again," Jack said, leaning back as Hyun lathered his face with warm soap. "Although there's a shiv under my mattress."

Gita was there in the blink of an eye, flipping the mattress over. "Where is it?"

"It was a joke," Jack said.

"Don't talk," Hyun ordered softly. "I don't want to cut you."

That makes one of you. Jack opted to remain quiet while Gita rifled through the rest of his things, looking for weapons. When Hyun was rinsing off the blade, he asked, "Are you really that concerned or are you just showing off?"

Gita's eyes flashed, so it was probably the latter.

"I do not understand what she sees in you," Gita said with a glare.

"Who?" Jack said, tilting his head back. "Anya?"

"Anat is her name, you filthy creature," Gita snarled. Beyond her haughty anger was something more—almost disappointment.

So Jack poked the bear. "Were you close to her?"

"As close as anyone could be to the Lady of Destruction," Gita said, placing a hand on the long dagger at her belt. "She taught me a few things. Her betrayal was unfortunate."

Jack had been around athtars long enough to read between the lines. Anat must've been this girl's idol, perhaps taught her everything. The question was: did she simply worship Anya, or did she want to take her place?

"It must've been hard to see Bael continue to lust after her," he said, as the blade swept down his neck. "Especially after she left."

"Bael will eventually see," she said, pacing the room. "Anat will soon be dead and I'll assume her spot."

Like clockwork. "Bael has chosen you, then?"

"Of course he has," she said. "I am the Badai. The storm. I wreak havoc across humanity. They will tremble at my feet."

Hyun placed a warm towel against Jack's skin, so he bit down his commentary on athtars and their egos. But Gita was primed for information sharing, so Jack carefully formulated his next question.

"Are you planning on killing Anat?"

"No, sadly," she said. "Bael has requested that privilege himself. He wishes to give her an honorable death by his sword. I would behead her and feed her corpse to the animals for what she's done."

"Seems harsh," Jack said. "You must've really looked up to her."

Gita's eyes widened, then narrowed. "Enough talking. Bael is waiting. Hurry up, you idiotic kappa."

Hyun nodded and hurried to the bed where she'd laid out the tuxedo. Jack undressed in plain view of Gita, who of course made commentary about how his physique paled in comparison to Bael's.

"So you've seen his entire body then?" Jack asked, putting on the pants.

Gita's lip twitched. "I have seen enough."

In his mind, Jack slid her from "fuck buddy" to "girl with a crush." He was genuinely curious if Bael had slept with any of the athtars, or if he only used Anya for that.

Once he was dressed, Gita grabbed him roughly by the arm and in one breath, they stood in Bael's throne room.

"Ah, Jackson," Bael said, sitting on his golden throne, with a thoughtful look on his face. "So kind of you to join us. Thank you, Gita, for retrieving him."

"Of course, Belu Athtar." She bowed at the hip, then straightened. "Is there anything—"

"Dismissed," he said, getting off the chair.

Jack caught the ghost of a frown before the girl disappeared. Definitely one-sided then.

"To what do I owe the pleasure?" Jack asked.

"You have been well behaved, so I'll reward you for it," Bael said, sliding his arm around Jack's shoulder. "And I have a *very* pleasant reward in store for you tonight."

He led Jack through the double doors to the grand dining room which had been set for three. Angela was there, dressed in a sexy white gown that left little to the imagination, and so was Sara, who looked much more chaste in a slim green dress that came to her knee. Jack counted five place settings, however.

"My dear," Bael said, releasing Jack to kiss Angela on the cheek. "And my lovely Sara, you're looking well."

"Thank you, my king," she said with a bow of the head. "Jack, don't you think I look nice?"

Sensing he'd better play along, Jack nodded. "You do."

Bael's smile widened and he walked to the table, holding out the seat next to the head. Angela dutifully sat and he pushed her in.

"Jack," Sara said with an annoyed sigh.

Hating himself every step of the way, Jack went to the table and held out the chair for Sara, before taking the one next to her.

"Is our final guest on his way?" Bael asked, sliding a hand across Angela's shoulder.

"Yes, my lord," she said. "Gita, dear."

The athtar appeared in the center of the room, a fiery look on her face. "*Yes*, my lady," she ground out.

"Please see our final guest in," Angela said, ignoring the way the athtar's fists were clenched at her sides.

The athtar disappeared again, and Bael chuckled, placing his other hand on Angela's shoulder. "Worry not, my love. Gita is a jealous woman. But I only have eyes for you."

And Anat. Jack sipped his wine.

The doors opened once more and a man waddled into the room. His brown skin descended over a pot belly and his green hair swung low against his ears. Complete with a bulbous nose and green beard, Biloko was every bit the storybook dwarf.

"Biloko," Bael said. "Come, come. We're glad to have you."

The dwarf sat next to Jack, who began to hear the faint clanging of bells. How he wished for his talismans now. Instead, he focused on the fork on the table, using it as a reminder of where he was. And who he was with.

"Biloko, you remember Jackson Grenard," Bael said, finally taking a seat at the head of the table. "Jackson, the belu eloko."

Jack nodded. "Nice to see you again."

The dwarf looked even stranger up close. He almost reminded Jack of his childhood, playing with a boy down the street named Tommy who had fire-red hair. They would go into a nearby creek with their toys and play—

Jack took hold of the fork, the cool metal returning him to the room. That was too close.

"...my only ally left, it seems," Bael said. "Freyja and Mizuchi have left us."

"No," Angela said with a hand over her mouth. "Belu Athtar, say it isn't so. She would never betray you."

"She has, my love," Bael said. "It's a good thing your maker has perished, or else I might worry about you."

"Never," she said, taking his hand. "It is you I swear fealty to. Always."

"I fear they are gathering strength," Bael said. "We must do what we can to protect Ath-kur and Elonsi. Biloko, tell me what you've been able to gather."

"We're at seven thousand," he said. "I've arrived with another contingent of fifteen hundred. With your guidance, I was able to find more willing soldiers from the topside."

"Outstan—" Bael caught Jack's gaze and a look of annoyance flitted across his face. "Ah, it seems you've returned to us, Jackson."

"What?" He hadn't been out that long, had he?

"Biloko doesn't know his own strength sometimes," Bael said. "We must be gentle with the human."

"Poor baby," Sara said, stroking his hand.

"Do you like my gift to you, Jack?" Bael said, picking up his glass. "A double date, if you will. Not many humans get the chance to dine with me. Nor are many brought back from the dead. Tell me, have you re-consummated your marriage yet?"

"No," Sara said, removing her hand. "Jack won't touch me."

"Jackson, really," Bael said, tilting his glass toward Sara. "With a wife such as this, how could you stand to keep your hands off her?"

"One problem," Jack ground out. "She's not my wife."

The smell of flowers had infiltrated his senses, but instead of making him horny, it upset his stomach. Caught between Biloko's bells and the lilin's pheromones, his mind was stretching in two different directions.

"Jackson, I thought we were over this?" Bael said. "I went to the afterlife. I found your wife. I brought her here as a gift for you."

"Bull. Shit." Jack glared. "You aren't God. You can't just do something like that."

Bael smiled, sitting back. "Are you so certain of who I am? What's to say I'm not God? What's to say I didn't come from the heavens and grant powers to all the other belus?" He sat back. "Were you there?"

"No," Jack said, looking at Biloko. "But he was."

"I do not recall the day I arrived in the Underworld," the eloko said. "King Bael has the power to cross worlds, the same way God crossed to the human world to find us—"

"Find you," Bael said with a glare.

"King Bael," Biloko said with a small chuckle. "Are you suggesting that you were not a human brought here?"

"I am God," he said, standing. "If I say I can bring a human back from the dead, I can very well do it. Do you wish to see the extent of my power, Lord Biloko?"

"N-no," Biloko said, shrinking back into himself. "You are most powerful. If you say it, then it is true."

Jack found himself chuckling.

"Do you find something amusing, Jackson?" Bael asked, his gaze dangerously void of any emotion.

"You," Jack said, picking up his wine. "I find you and your bullshit highly amusing."

The room went deathly silent, and even Jack began to wonder if pissing Bael off was a smart thing to do. Especially when Bael straightened with a smile.

"Lazlo, dear," he called to the air.

The athtar appeared, looking murderous.

"Please take Jackson back to his room," Bael said. "I feel he's quite finished with this meal."

CHAPTER TWENTY-TWO

When Cam awoke the next morning, she was greeted by the feeling of a screwdriver above her left temple.

"This will help," Anya said, pressing a cool glass into Cam's hand. Then, she added softly, "Good morning."

"Is it?" Cam said, sitting up and gingerly drinking the perfumed drink. "What's this?"

"The lilins use it as a tonic," she said, staring at the ground. "Did you have a good night with Freyja?"

Cam glanced down at her clothes—still on. She was also back in the room Freyja had settled them into the night before. "Do I get a prize for going to the lilin belu's bed and not having sex with her?"

"It happens more than you think," Anya said with a smile. "Freyja is a big proponent of consent."

"Don't tell that to her lilins in Atlanta," Cam said, pressing the glass to her temple.

"The topside lilins are allied with Bael," Anya said. "Freyja is limited in what she can do to control them. And between us, there are so many lilins out there that Freyja has a hard time keeping track of them. But she loves them all, and would make every human a demon if she could."

"I'm sure she would," Cam said, putting down her drink. "Sorry for yelling at you last night."

Anya stared at the bedsheets. "She told me more about Jack. I know it sounds horrible what Bael is doing—and it is—but as far as her spy says, Jack seems…well, he seems to be taking it in stride. He's not broken, I guess is what I'm trying to say. That doesn't make it better but…"

"As long as Jack is still Jack," Cam said. "But how long until Bael decides to break him?"

"I don't know. Bael can play a very long game if he wants. Freyja gets reports from her spy weekly, so…"

The door flung open, effectively ending their conversation as Freyja breezed in, this time wearing a blue silk robe open to her navel. She marched to the windows, pushing them open to allow the morning light to shine into the dark room. With a harrumph, she pressed a hand to her hip and glanced over her shoulder.

"Anat, come look at this."

Anya slipped off the bed and Cam followed, albeit much slower. The bright blue bay stretched from the castle to shores farther away. Dotting the surface, twenty or so ships with billowing sails rode the breeze toward them.

"Is that Bael?" Cam asked, fear spiking in her chest.

"If it were Bael, he'd just appear," Anya said. "It's the noxes, I believe."

"Lotan flouts Bael's authority," Freyja said with a shake of her head. "I told him to come inconspicuously and he does this. An entire armada. I doubt Bael could've missed such a scene."

"I would be surprised if he didn't already know," Anya said quietly. "He sees more than you think. He just doesn't always act on it."

"Perhaps you're right," Freyja said. "It is in our favor that he simply believes himself invincible."

The ships, which had been black dots in the distance, were monstrosities, towering a full fifty feet in the air from water to mast. The noxes inside wore leather outfits to protect them from the cold, although some had given up and wore their hellbeast form. Lotan, wearing a modern leather jacket that set off his brown eyes, strolled off the nearest ship, flanked by several of his warriors. They were a fearsome bunch, or maybe that was just their miasma mixing with the lusty pheromones.

Freyja didn't seem bothered by it as she practically flung herself at him. "My darling Lotan," she said with breathy excitement. They shared an intimate kiss that Cam might've thought meant more had the lilin not turned to the rest of his gathered forces and done the same to them.

Lotan locked eyes with Cam and his smile grew. "Agent Macarro, I told you I'd be seeing you again."

Cam forced a non-emotional look onto her face, but she was sure Anya felt the heart-skip. "Nice to see you, too."

"Where's Mizuchi? You didn't throw him into the ocean, did you, Anat?" Lotan asked.

"He is tending to his lovely pets," Freyja said with a sigh after she'd finished making out with the last nox. "He does dote on them so. I just adore him."

Anya had ignored Lotan's jab in favor of scanning the noxes who'd arrived. "Is Oce here?"

"No, but she sends her regards. She has offered to keep the castle secure in my absence." He motioned to a rather severe-looking woman beside him with short-cropped hair and tattoos crawling up her bare arms. "This is Izel. She was my mother's favorite second, and my best strategic planner."

"It is a pleasure," she said, more to Cam than to Anya.

"You sound familiar," Cam said, eyeing her.

"I carried Lady Anat to the castle," she said with a smirk to Anya. "The prince wanted to make sure there were no problems."

"I suppose if we're all here, we should find Mizuchi and get down to business, hm?" Lotan said, cutting off what was probably going to be another pissing match between Anya and the noxes.

"Yes, before Bael kills us all," Anya drawled.

"Ah, well, I can see not much has changed since we last talked," Lotan said to Cam.

"You'd be surprised," Cam said. "I just think she doesn't like you that much."

"Lucky for me, I don't care what *she* thinks," he replied with a cat-like grin. Cam forced herself not to read too much into that statement.

Freyja led them into a large room with a circular table in the center. Anya took a seat next to the most ornate chair, and Cam sat next to her. Lotan and Izel took the next to chairs, and Freyja sat down at the far end. The final two chairs were occupied by Mizuchi and Tabiko, as they came in shortly thereafter.

"This is a fine assembly," Freyja said, placing her long fingers on the arm of her chair.

"Sure, let's just invite Bael and Biloko while we're at it," Anya said, glancing around. "Have an old fashioned belu meeting. Bring a couple humans for divvying up, too."

"I know this may come as a surprise to you," Lotan said. "But not everything in the Underworld is known or controlled by Bael. Much, in fact, happens without him being the wiser. Freyja has protections in place here. He dares not cross into Liley or this castle without her approval."

"Indeed," Freyja said, patting Anya's hand. "Now, Lotan, tell us the latest on your grand plan."

"Yes, so I can tell you how it will fail."

"Anya," Cam snapped. "Knock it off."

Lotan smirked, then cleared his throat. "The basic premise is simple: We will go to war with Bael. The lilins, kappas, noxes, and whomever else we can recruit to our side against the elokos and—"

"And the athtars, who can stop time," Anya interrupted. "And Bael, who is stronger than everyone in this room combined."

"Not at the moment," Freyja said. "After all, the schism was open for twice as long as usual. It takes a lot out of Bael to keep it open for even the normal duration."

"But his athtar army, I can assure you, are at their full strength," Anya said.

"How many are there?" Cam asked.

"Four hundred and sixty-two," Mizuchi said.

"Sixty-one," Anya corrected quietly. "Ekur was killed recently."

"Well, that's excellent," Lotan said, with a hearty chuckle, which was silenced by a frigid look from Anya. "I meant for our cause."

"I'm sure," Anya said.

"Okay, everyone just calm down," Cam said, leaning forward. "Lotan, tell us your plan. Without the commentary."

"As I said," Lotan said, with a look at Anya, "Bael is weakened, but Lady Anat is correct—his army is at full strength. While we have plenty of strong noxes, kappas, and lilins, we don't have enough to fight against even the four hundred athtars —"

"Four hundred and sixty-one," Anya said.

"Quiet, Anya," Cam snapped then looked at Lotan. "Continue."

Lotan once again paused, gathering his thoughts, then spoke. "What we *lack*, as the lady has been so kind to point out, is the ability to fight those athtars with our entire army. I'm not willing to put my noxes in a situation where they will die—unless there's a viable path to overall victory. And that's why I was thinking…we could take a trip to the Nullius."

Cam sat back in surprise, but Anya barked, "Are you *insane?*"

"Possibly," Lotan said. "The fact of the matter is, there's clearly something in that world that affects magic. What we'd like to do is to send a volunteer there to retrieve some stones. We've been bringing pieces of the noxland to the human world, and the magic goes with it. Maybe if we can bring back some of the Nullius, that magic can come with it, too."

Anya looked at the other two belus. "Are you two seriously considering this lunacy?"

"It isn't entirely crazy," Freyja began quietly. "Something has to give, Anat. We can't keep living under Bael like this. This is the most legitimate plan we've heard so far."

"Then obviously your plans are—"

"I'll go," Cam said.

Anya swiveled her head around so fast Cam heard it crack. "Are *you* insane? There's no way I'm letting you go there by yourself."

"Well, I mean, it's like you said—it strips magic, right? The worst that will happen to me is I revert to human, which I want to do anyway," Cam said with a shrug. "Besides, you aren't *letting* me do anything."

Lotan cleared his throat. "I appreciate your bravery, but… reverting to human might not be the worst thing to happen to you."

"What else could happen?" Cam asked, losing a bit of her moxie.

"The truth is, Agent Macarro, none of us know exactly what would become of any of us," Mizuchi said. "I've experimented with myself and some willing kappas of like-mindedness. Most of them turned before they reached the border, citing illness and fear of something unknown stopping them. I would have continued by myself, but I feared the destruction of Kappanchi and all the creatures that depend on me. We felt the demonic energy leeching from our bodies when we ventured too close. But if we set foot on the land, would our skin be ripped from our bones?"

Cam swallowed, but kept herself together. "Well, if my skin starts peeling, I'll turn around. How about that?"

"This isn't a joke, Cam," Anya said with more than a little heat. "We'll find some other solution to this athtar problem that doesn't involve you crossing into no man's land."

"And in the meantime, Jack continues to know what it's like to have his dead wife come back from the dead," Cam snapped. "We don't have time to come up with alternative solutions. So if you have one, spit it out."

Anya closed her mouth, her brows furrowed in anger, but

she said nothing.

"The Nullius is a day's trip on the water from here," Freyja said. "We should take a small contingent—"

"I'll take her myself," Anya said.

"We will go together," Lotan said.

Anya narrowed her eyes. "Is that wise, prince? You *are* the only thing keeping the noxlands together."

"And you are our only hope of defeating Bael," Lotan barked back, his gaze alighting with anger. "Which is the only reason I don't jump over this table and slice out your tongue." He smiled. "Then again, you don't need—"

"Lotan," Freyja snapped, her voice echoing in an almost ungodly sound. Cam shivered. "Enough, both of you. You may resume your mortal enmity once this war is over."

Mizuchi cleared his throat. "As long as the prince remains a safe distance away from the Nullius, there should be no harm."

Cam nodded. "Fine. Me, Lotan, and Anya. Anyone else want to join us on this crusade?"

"We will remain behind," Freyja said. "I'm expecting another report from my love inside Bael's castle soon. And it won't be good for Mizuchi to be seen, else we might raise more suspicion." She cleared her throat and looked at Lotan. "Which brings me to your little army, Lotan—"

"If you think Bael doesn't already know what we're up to, you're crazy," Lotan said.

"Thank you," Anya muttered under her breath.

"Good to know you both agree on something," Cam said

with a sigh.

"Agent Macarro." Lotan smiled as he jogged up to her after the meeting ended. "Might I have a word with you?"

"Sure," Cam said, but Anya threw a hand in front of Cam to stop her.

"What is it, nox?" Anya spat. "Don't think you can use the lilin miasma to get in her pants."

Lotan chuckled, and it made Cam squirm. "My lady, I don't need lilin magic to draw a woman into my bed."

"Then what do you want with her?" Anya asked. "We have to get ready to go to the Nullius, as per your dumbass plan."

"I wish to discuss something that has absolutely nothing to do with you, Anat," Lotan said. "Agent Macarro and I have prior business to resolve."

Anya kept her arm on Cam's. "Then show us both."

"Fine," Lotan said, waving his hand in the air to beckon them to follow. He led them down to the docks to the main ship he'd arrived on. With an order to remain on deck, he disappeared into the captain's quarters at the back of the ship.

"This had better be good," Anya said, crossing her arms.

Cam nodded, shivering in the cold air. "Wish I'd thought to bring my Division jacket. Didn't realize the Underworld was so damned cold."

Anya softened. "I'll get Freyja to find you some extra coats."

Lotan returned followed by a group of noxes—including one in shackles. It took Cam a few moments to run through her memory Rolodex of faces to recognize him, but once she did, her eyes widened and her jaw fell open.

Vicente, the nox demon lord of Washington, D.C., was a mere shadow of the demon that had terrorized Washington. When Cam had seen him in his downtown hotel, he'd been a king, surrounded by followers and worshippers angling for an audience with the man who controlled the capital city. Now, he looked neutered and concerned—especially when he saw Cam.

"This is the demon lord who had your sister killed, is it not?" Lotan asked, his voice carrying over the frigid wind.

"Y-yeah," Cam said, almost a little afraid of what admitting that would bring.

"What's your game, nox?" Anya snapped.

Lotan ignored Anya and turned to his captive. "Vicente, this former human is accusing you of an unjust killing of her sister," Lotan said, cocking his head to the right. "How do you respond?"

The nox cleared his throat and lifted his head. "I was under the impression that I was able to do what I want to the humans in my city."

Lotan smiled, exposing his bright teeth. "You sound like a nox who pledges allegiance to a different belu."

He might've been, but he was Lotan's captive at the moment. Wisely, he said, "Of course, my allegiance is to you, my liege."

"I'm sure it is," Lotan said. "Then why did you disobey a direct order from me?"

"My lord?"

"Two hundred years ago, when you left La Madriguera, you and the others promised to keep your dealings with the humans to a minimum. No killing, no forced transitions. And yet, I hear that you've been happily doing both." Lotan's eyes grew dark. "Is there something you wish to tell me?"

There obviously was, but in the face of the nox prince himself, the nox couldn't seem to bring himself to say it.

"Do you deny that you killed the human?"

"No, I don't."

"Very well." He turned around. "Agent Macarro, what do you think the punishment should be?"

"P-punishment?" cried Vicente.

Cam took a step back. "I don't..."

"This nox has overstepped his bounds. He's taken a life that wasn't his to take, for no other reason than you and your partner were making his life uncomfortable. What do you think the punishment should be?" Lotan put a hand on his sword. "Shall I take his life, too?"

Finally, reality snapped into focus, and a surge of anger roared through Cam. "You can't just *spring* something like that on me! I can't make a snap decision about someone else's life, even if he is a demon."

Anya smirked beside her. "Exactly."

"I would've thought you'd made up your mind about punishment," Lotan replied, looking honestly surprised. "You seem the sort of person who passes judgment quickly."

"Sure, in hypotheticals," Cam said.

"What was your hypothetical punishment then?"

"I..." Cam swallowed. Of course she'd come up with all manner of wish lists and revenge schemes after her sister died. But her parents had raised her with a sense of justice, and somehow, an eye for an eye didn't seem right.

"Why do you care?" Anya asked while Cam stuttered. "Why did you drag him down here in the first place? What's your angle?"

"I don't have to have an angle, Anat. I'm not Bael."

"Wait," Cam said before Anya flew off the handle again. "Can you demote him?"

"What?" Lotan asked.

"Like... can't you turn him into a fifth or something, instead of a lord?" Cam asked.

"I can do that," Lotan said with a nod.

"Good, do that," Cam said. "Then take away all his money, all his holdings. All his power. And then hand his ass over to the Division in D.C." She smirked. "There's enough evidence in the case file to have him executed."

"Very well," Lotan said. "Take him back to the noxlands and keep him under lock and key. When I return from battle, I'll do as Agent Macarro has asked."

"If you even survive," Anya said. "Why don't you do it now?"

"Because I'm not going back to the noxlands now, and I personally want to make sure it happens," Lotan said, his eyes narrowing. "I'm not sure I like your tone."

"Well, I'm not sure I like you using Sara's death as a bargaining chip," Anya shot back.

"How is this a bargaining chip?" Lotan said with a surprised laugh. "I'm trying to atone here—"

"Oh, *bullshit*. Don't pretend like this whole exercise wasn't a ploy to get her to give you the nox talismans."

"Agent Macarro can speak for herself," Lotan said.

"Yeah, *she* can," Cam interjected, coming between the two of them. "And I think you both need to take a chill pill. I'm not dragging you both to the Nullius if you're going to act like a bunch of children."

"You aren't dragging me anywhere—" Anya began, but Cam turned to her.

"You're being an ass, Colibrí. I can fight my own battles."

Lotan smirked in triumph, but Cam turned to him next.

"And you: I don't know why you decided to be so generous. While I appreciate it, I also am not one to be manipulated. Vicente gets the punishment, or he doesn't. But I'm not going to play into whatever game you've concocted. So both of you can knock it off."

CHAPTER TWENTY-THREE

The mood was decidedly frosty when Cam, Anya, and Lotan set out for the Nullius in one of Freyja's boats. Cam, curled into the fur coat Freyja had given her, stayed out of the line of fire. Lotan sat in the back, managing the rudder on the small skiff. Anya sat perched on the front of the boat, scanning the distance for any sign of trouble. Or maybe she just didn't want to be in close proximity to Lotan.

He was still a mystery to Cam. Vicente aside, why had he agreed to come with them to the Nullius? Especially if losing his powers could put all the noxes in danger? There was nothing really in it for him, unless there was an ulterior motive Cam wasn't seeing.

"Come to the happier end of the ship?" Lotan asked as Cam wandered down to join him. "It seems quite cloudy over there."

"Be nice," Cam said, sitting down. "So...why are you coming with us?"

"Because I'm offering my services," he said, not quite meeting her eyes.

"You also brought an army. Any one of them could have gone with us in your absence."

"Izel is a much better strategist than I. She and Mizuchi will come up with a fierce battle plan without my interference."

"Yeah, but—"

"You'll find, Agent Macarro, that I'm not the kind of leader to let others do the work for him," Lotan said. "I'd prefer to get my hands dirty."

"And how's that working out for you?" Cam asked, leaning against the hull of the ship.

His smile faltered. "Not that well, actually."

"Never does." She laughed when he chuckled. "I'm the same way. I want to be in charge, but I don't want others to do the work for me. I'd rather do it all."

"I don't want to be in charge," he admitted softly. "I never did."

"So again...why are you coming with us?" Cam asked. "Are you hoping you'll lose your demonic powers in the Nullius?"

"No, sadly, in order to protect my people, I have to keep a safe distance." He tilted his head. "Why are you so interested in hearing my reasons for joining you? I promise there's no sabotage involved."

"If you were planning sabotage, you wouldn't tell me about it."

"That is true," he said with a smile.

"And you also aren't answering my question."

"Also true," Lotan said, adjusting the rudder on the boat slightly. "Perhaps I'm not wholly trusting that the athtar will do what she says. Perhaps I just want to feel like I'm accomplishing something. Or," his gaze slid to her, "perhaps I simply want to spend a little more time with you, Agent Macarro."

Cam froze under his stare.

"Oi!" Anya barked from the front of the ship. "What are you doing to her?"

Cam wasn't sure which was worse: that Anya had felt the jolt, or that she'd announced it to Lotan. The nox's smile glistened in the darkness. "Nothing, Mother Athtar. We're having a conversation."

Anya glared at him but turned back around.

"I must say, I take it as a point of pride that I can elicit such nerves from someone so fearless," Lotan said with a wink to Cam.

"I'm not fearless by any stretch," Cam said, fighting the warmth on her face and grateful it was dark. "I'm the world's biggest chicken shit."

"I highly doubt that."

Cam wrapped the fur coat tighter around herself. "You'd be surprised."

"I'd say you've accomplished quite a lot for someone so chicken," Lotan said. "Convinced the Lady of Destruction to transform her. Traveled to the Underworld. Stood toe to toe with belus. Volunteered to go to the Nullius. Quite a list of achievements for someone who isn't so brave." He adjusted the rudder behind them. "And from what I hear from the noxes under Vicente, chicken shit is not an apt description of your job performance in D.C."

"That was then," Cam said. "Look, what you did with him…"

"It was a long time coming," he said quietly. "They've spent too much time getting comfortable under Bael's rule. Many of them swear allegiance to him over me." He tilted his head back to look at the stars. "After all, I am not the belu. God did not touch me Himself, and so I am a lesser demon. If I were a true belu, my flock wouldn't be revolting against me."

His disgust at himself was palpable, although Cam didn't think it was warranted. "One wayward nox doesn't mean you're a bad leader."

"It's not just one. I've been traveling the world, undercover as Levi. And I realized a few years ago I don't have the level of control I thought I had. I thought they feared me, but it turns out… you aren't the only human with grievances against the noxes."

Cam half-smiled. "I'm not human anymore."

"You're only temporarily athtar, as far as I'm concerned," Lotan said. "And your sister didn't deserve her death. I would like to make it right…or as right as can be. These noxes need to understand that their prince remains in command of them." He looked at her and his eyes grew soft. "And perhaps, I wanted to absolve myself of the guilt of causing you pain. Does seeing Vicente get justice give you closure?"

How she wished it did. "No," she murmured. "Sara's still gone. Nothing will ever make that better. But… it does mean he'll never be able to hurt another human. And maybe that's the best possible outcome."

"You and I are of similar minds, it seems," he said, looking up at the dark sky.

Cam furrowed her brow. "What do you mean?"

"Your maker was right about my ulterior motives," Lotan said. "I do want Bael dead for demonkind and humanity's sake, but I also…well, there's a part of me that believes it might help with my parents' deaths." He looked at the front of the ship. "And if Anat is successful—if Bael dies—his reign of terror will be over."

"So you don't blame her?" Cam asked. "For your parents?"

"She still raised her sword," Lotan said with a small growl. "She still let herself believe his lies. But Bael has many thousands of years' experience manipulating and controlling others. As much as I want to, I can't truly be angry with her. Perhaps when Bael is dead, I might find some wrath for her."

"Then what?"

"Then…who knows? Maybe she and I can pick up on our demonic war," Lotan said with a chuckle. "Maybe we'll all be dead. We'll cross that bridge when we get to it."

Cam snorted. "Maybe you can fight her for Bael's role."

"What? King of the demons?" He stretched his arms behind his back and shook his head. "I don't even want to be prince of the noxes. This role was given to me, and I don't want it. I've lived under one king for too long to want to be one myself. I don't have the temperament or ego. You've seen how well I fare with being a nox prince."

"Yeah, I guess it does take a lot of self-importance to want everyone to worship you," Cam said. "But what I don't get is if we're all at war with Bael—and Bael knows it—why doesn't he just stop time and kill everyone?"

"It's exactly as you said: he doesn't want everyone dead. He wants them to *love* him. Adoration is his addiction. Mizuchi and Freyja have play-acted their fealty for centuries, just to keep him from bothering them. Biloko still acts that way. My parents, on the other hand, never bended a knee to him, and he couldn't *stand* it. I won't either, and that's why he does what he does."

"What about Anya?"

"Oh, she's his obsession," Lotan said with a dark look. "In his mind, he believes he is the only man she could ever love. But at the same time, he lives in fear that she will fall out of love with him. Everything he has done to her is in service to either one. And she, poor devil, has been caught in the crossfire ever since."

The sun was high in the sky when discomfort became noticeable in Cam's stomach. It wasn't seasickness, but it left her unsettled. By the gray looks on Lotan and Anya's faces, it was a mutual discomfort. They'd been steadily approaching the beach ahead, the white sand as pristine and gorgeous as the Gulf of Mexico.

"We're getting close," Anya said, pinching the bridge of her nose. "Are you sure you're ready for this?"

"As ready as I'll ever be."

"Here is good," Lotan said, his words slurring slightly as he jerked the rudder toward the beach. The ship washed ashore with a soft *thump*, and a jolt of pain spiraled up Cam's legs and into her heart.

"Cam, this is a bad idea," Anya said.

"I feel fine," she lied, standing upright. "After all, my demon is just a few days old." It took her a moment to settle into the new feeling, but she licked her lips and tossed back her shoulders. "It's going to be fine."

"Here," Lotan said, handing her a rope. "Tie this around your waist. There's more below if we need it... One moment." He turned and vomited off the side of the boat.

"I'll try to be quick," Cam said, picking up the rope where he'd dropped it. She tied it around her waist and tried to hide the smile at Lotan's loud heaving. Somehow watching him do something so human made him less threatening.

"Once you get far enough inside, fill your bag with rocks and come back," Lotan said with a grimace as he wiped his mouth. "And please come back alive."

"Please," Anya said with emphasis. "If you feel like it's too much, tug on the rope and we'll pull you out."

"I will," Cam said.

"And be careful." Her voice was quiet, almost maternal in nature.

"I will, Mom." Cam inhaled deeply. "So, hey, if I die…"

"I'll tell him," Anya said with a nod. "And I'll get him back safely."

Cam took one step away from the boat, then another, and another, her pulse pounding in her ears. She understood why the demons were terrified of this place. The magic pumping against her heart began to send signals to her brain: *turn around, danger danger!* But Cam's still-human head kept her feet shuffling forward. The creature in her chest, if she could call it that, was simply renting space. And if it shriveled and died, she'd just tell Anya to make her one again.

She stumbled once, when the magic screamed in a voiceless, soundless echoes that left her ears ringing. Sweat beaded on her brow, but she kept walking. There was a canyon in her mind. On one side was the demon writhing in agony; on the other was her mission. As long as the demon stayed on its side, she could keep walking.

And walk she did, across an indeterminable desert plain with the sun beating down on her skin. She had no concept of time, and she'd long since given up counting her steps. The rope around her waist reminded her that she had a way back—the only thing keeping the terrified voices from taking over. Whether from thirst or the magic, or even just her own worries, she was having a hard time preventing a total panic attack.

"Okay, Macarro," she whispered to herself. "We're not going to let this get the best of us."

Lifting her arm, she poked at the skin. It remained reddish brown with sun and exertion, but wasn't peeling off.

"See?" she said, wiping her brow. "Just hysterical nonsense. There has to be a scientific explanation for all this. We have a mission to do, and we aren't going back to Lotan without something to show for it."

"After all, he *vomited* in front of me."

"He's still hot, though."

"So hot."

"Why am I talking to myself?"

Cam stopped in the middle of the desert and pinched the bridge of her nose. There would be no more conversations with herself; that was a sure sign she was losing it.

She adjusted the rope around her midsection and kept walking. Had Lotan brought enough? Would she turn around and find herself at the end and no idea how to get back? Or, alternatively, would she keep walking until she reached one of the demonic lands? It would be just her luck that she ended up in Ath-kur or something. Bael might save them all the trouble and—

"Stop. Thinking."

She placed her hand on her forehead to shield her gaze from the sun and squinted. Something shimmered in the distance, though she couldn't tell what it was. That something turned out to be a crater. It was massive, like one of those in the desert in Arizona where an asteroid had fallen to Earth. Cam sat on the edge of it, letting her feet dangle. The more she stared at it, the more she saw ridges and bumps, valleys and mountains that must've been eroded over thousands of years. So perhaps her meteor theory was bunk. Every meteor crater she'd seen was a perfect concave, even years after the impact.

So what was she looking at?

The rope pulled against her midsection, a reminder to get on with what she was here to do. The complexities of the crater could wait. Her mission called.

With great effort, Cam pushed herself back up and unsteadily rose to her feet. Disorientation clouded her judgment and uncomfortable pressure squeezed her stomach as she bent over and put rocks and sand into her backpack.

The rope tightened against her midsection again and she turned back the way she came.

"Follow the rope, Macarro," she muttered to herself, hoping she wasn't slurring as bad as she thought. She put one foot in front of the other, focusing on moving forward. Back to Colibrí, back to Jack. Back to Lotan.

The magical creature stirred against her heart. "So you're still there, huh?" Cam said with a chuckle. "Don't get comfortable. You're out as soon as this stupid thing is over with. Go find a new host."

She spotted figures in the distance, but couldn't make her feet move faster. In fact, they were slowing down.

The last thing she remembered was Lotan's beautiful face and Anya's worried one.

"Stay or go?"

What?

Cam was floating somewhere between here and there. There was a voice in her ear, buzzing like a mosquito she couldn't swat away. Her arms and legs were lead, but she didn't much feel like moving anyway. Not with the view. Stars and galaxies, the light and the dark, and everything in-between. It was the most beautiful and terrifying thing she'd ever seen, and yet she couldn't even summon the energy to cry.

"Stay or go?" The voice sounded like Sara's, or maybe Cam just wanted it to be. Somehow, she knew if she went with the voice, she would be reunited with her sister and everyone she'd lost.

But as much as she ached to hear her sister's laugh again, she had a job to do.

What kind of a question is that? Cam's voice floated around her mind. *Stay, obviously. Who the hell are you? Where the hell am I?*

The questions echoed into the ether, and the galaxies, light, darkness blended together as Cam lost consciousness again.

CHAPTER TWENTY-FOUR

Jack awoke to the sound of his alarm beeping. With his eyes closed, he felt around for the device and pushed the buttons then settled back on his pillow. Sunlight streamed against the bedroom floor. Another morning, another day at the office. He struggled to recall which case he was working on at the moment, or even what city he was in. Something didn't seem right.

But the smell of bacon drew him out of bed, as it did most every morning. Quietly, he padded down the wooden stairs on bare feet, walking into the small white kitchen where his wife was cooking breakfast. She was a vision in her black suit and purple button-down shirt. Her black hair was twisted in a bun behind her head, golden earrings dangling from her lobes.

"Making your favorite this morning, Jackie," she said, her voice stirring some deep longing in his heart. For some reason, he'd really missed her.

She was perfection, right down to the dimple on her cheek. He'd been just seventeen when he first really noticed her, the younger sister Cam was always showing him pictures of. Standing with her parents talking with Cam before a big weapons tournament. Jack had forgotten everything he knew about fighting and lost in the first round. But it had been worth it, to catch a few minutes alone with this beautiful girl.

Eventually, their talking turned to kissing, which turned into the deepest love Jack had ever felt for another human. When she walked down the aisle on their wedding day, he thought he might explode.

Unable to contain himself, he ventured into the kitchen and grabbed her from behind, kissing her soundly on the lips. She sighed against him, looping her fingers into his pajama bottoms and pulling him closer. When he tried to push her up on the countertop, she laughed and stopped him.

"Jackie, I have to go to work," she said. "And so do you."

"Right, right," he said, unable to shake the feeling of pure *relief* to have her in his arms. Still, he obliged, letting her return to cooking the eggs and bacon in the skillet. His knives sat on the cabinet, so he plucked them off the counter and put them on.

"Ooh, giving me a show, hm?" Sara asked. "You know how I love it when you use your knives."

Icy dread slid down his spine, but he had no idea why. Taking his knives, he walked into the living room and pushed the one chair out of the way. He unsheathed his weapons, the black plastic material feeling odd for some reason. Didn't he get new knives recently? For some reason, his skin was expecting leather instead—

The skillet clattered in the kitchen and Jack sprang to his feet. "Sara?"

"J-J-"

She screamed.

He rushed toward the kitchen, which now stretched into eternity. He ran and ran and ran, but he wasn't getting any closer. His palms sweated against his knives, his heart banged against his ribcage, and his mind went to all sorts of horrific scenarios when she screamed again.

"*Sara!*" he cried into the unending hall.

Finally, he saw her, lying on the floor. Covered in her own blood, staining the lilac shirt. Her mouth opened and closed as she struggled to breathe.

Standing above her was a nox hellbeast, mouth dripping with blood. His yellowish eyes turned on Jack, and he smiled. With a growl, he leaned down and clamped down on Sara's throat.

Jack screamed, but he couldn't move. There was nothing he could do but watch the monster rip her throat, listen to the gurgling sounds from her bloody, wet lips. Her gaze was locked on him, her eyes begging him to save her.

"S-Sara," he whispered.

With a final sigh, the last breath left her body. She was gone.

"No!" Jack struggled against whatever force was holding him in place, but it was too late. He was been too late. For all his training and ability and skills, he couldn't even save his own wife.

"Ah, Jackson," came Bael's soft voice. "I knew I could break you, given enough time."

Jack swallowed, finding himself against the wall, holding on for dear life. The image faded away, leaving nothing but the cold reality of his prison. And Bael, seated on a red velvet chair, with a glass of wine perched between his fingers.

"I only wish Anat was here to see you in this state," he said, placing his glass down on the table next to him and standing. "It's clear to me you're still in love with your wife."

"Of course I'm still in love with her, you fucking monster," Jack rasped. "She was my wife."

"Pity that Anat feels so strongly about you," Bael said. "It will pain me to tell her you don't feel the same."

"This may come as a surprise," Jack spat, heart pounding. "But it's possible to love two people at once. But since you've never loved a single thing other than yourself, I know that's difficult to understand."

Bael's eyes narrowed. "Are you insinuating I don't love Anat?"

"If you loved her, you wouldn't be doing this. You would have let her walk away." Jack wiped his cheeks. "The sad thing is *she* did love you. Probably still does. But you couldn't stop doing things like this—even when you had her at your feet. And that's why you'll lose her. One day, for good."

Bael chuckled. "What you forget, Jackson, is that I made her. So she'll be mine until death. And as for why I'm doing this, I just enjoy watching you break."

The room faded again as the sound of a beeping alarm filled Jack's ears.

CHAPTER TWENTY-FIVE

Cam awoke in a soft bed with a raging hangover-like headache. The conversation echoed in her head, sending chills down her spine. Had she been that close to death? Or had it just been the aftereffects of… Her eyes closed as her brain woke up to the reality of where she'd been.

"She's awake." Anya's voice was whisper-quiet, but still throbbed in Cam's mind. Before she could speak, cool metal touched her parched lips, and water rushed into her mouth. She drank as much as she could, which didn't appear to be very much. A warm hand rested on her forehead then, slid down to touch her cheek.

"Anya?" Cam croaked.

She appeared in Cam's line of sight, a worried crease between her brow. "How are you feeling?"

"Like I just had a rager," Cam rasped, rubbing her throat. Anya helped her to more water, which sat unhappily in her stomach. "How long was I out?"

"Long enough for our lady to work herself into a fret over your health," came Lotan's soothing voice. Cam turned her head, a rather difficult feat, as the bed dipped and a warm, large hand took hers. "We're glad to have you back among us."

"It was weird in there," Cam said.

"Once you've fully recovered, you can tell us everything," Anya said, forcing Cam to drink more. "I thought for sure you'd died."

"I think I did," Cam said, lifting a heavy hand to rub her forehead. "Someone kept asking me to stay or go."

Anya sucked in a breath but said nothing. Lotan asked, "What did you tell them?"

"Obviously, I needed to stay," Cam said. "I had things to do." She blinked. "I did imagine that, right?"

"It's a pretty common experience for demons on the verge of death, or when their makers have perished," Lotan said. "Those who stay remain demon. Sometimes they don't get the choice."

"Some demons think it's the voice of God," Anya said quietly.

"Oh, well," Cam said, sinking back into the pillows. Then, she cracked open an eye. "I am still a demon, right?"

"Yes," Anya said, rubbing her chest. "Although our

connection went quiet while you were in the Nullius. It's slowly reestablishing now." She squeezed Cam's hand. "I'm glad you made it back."

"Me too," Cam said. "What would've happened if I went with the voice? Would I have reverted to human? Or would I have just…died?"

"I'm glad we didn't find out," Anya said, standing. "Just stay in bed and get your energy back. I'm going to see about finding you something to eat."

And she hurried from the room before Cam could stop her.

"I never thought Colibrí would be the one taking care of me," Cam said with a soft chuckle.

"Lady Anat has many secrets," Lotan said, gently stroking Cam's palm. "One of those happens to be the amount of love she's capable of."

"Love is a strong word," Cam said, watching his thumb make circles on her hand.

"You didn't see her when you were gone, or the ration of shit she gave me about letting you go in there alone," Lotan replied with a shake of his head. "So… how was it?"

"There was a large crater," Cam said. "I think that's where the belus were left. Or it was some kind of asteroid."

Lotan pressed his hand against her forehead. "You must still be ill from your trip."

"I'm serious." A rush of hope flooded into her chest as she turned to him. "What about the stones I brought back? Did they do anything?"

Lotan forced a smile on his face. "We can talk about that when you've healed—"

"So no, then," Cam said, sinking back into the pillows. "I'm a big girl, Lotan. I can take disappointment."

He brushed a strand of hair from her forehead. "Whatever magic exists in that land apparently remains there. The stones offered nothing."

"I wish I could tell you I saw something else," Cam said with a frown. "The only thing I saw was that giant crater with ridges. Maybe *that's* something."

"Don't worry yourself," Lotan said. "Your recovery is most important right now. Mizuchi, Freyja, Anat and I'll—"

But something else clicked in Cam's mind. Something about the ridges on the crater, and how familiar they looked.

"Lotan, what if...what if that crater was a talisman?"

"What?"

"My talismans," Cam said, sitting up and swaying for a moment. "What if the Nullius' power comes from talisman magic? My grandmother says they were a gift from the same God who sent the demons to the Underworld." She chewed her lip. "I weaponized them by carving the symbol onto bullets. But what if they weren't just for shooting people? What if we could use them to recreate the Nullius?"

"Hm... Do you still have the athtar one?" Lotan asked.

"Yeah," she said, nodding to her bag in the corner. "It's in my bag."

Lotan went to her backpack and dug through her things.

Cam remembered that the talismans were stuffed in the middle of a pack of underwear just as Lotan pulled the wad of cloth out of the bag.

"What are…these?" he said with a devilish smile that said he knew *exactly* what he was holding up.

"I had to pad it with something," Cam said, her cheeks warming.

Lotan took his time removing each pair of underwear, opening them fully to their granny-panty-glory. Of course they were white. Of course they were huge. Cam wasn't about to traipse through the demonic underworld in a black lacy thong. She just never anticipated that the handsome nox prince would be pawing through them.

Finally, he revealed the small coin that had caused her so much pain.

"So, this is a talisman, hm?" he said, squinting at it. "Doesn't seem like much."

"Oh yeah?" Cam said. "Reach into my front pocket on the bag there."

Lotan did then cried out in pain, grasping his hand.

"Yeah, not so little, huh?" Cam said.

"I suppose that answers my question about taking those back to my topside noxes," Lotan said, sticking his finger in his mouth. When he pulled it out, it was bright red. "That burned. No wonder the Nullius is so potent, if this is what it's made of."

"Guess God doesn't want you to use those for evil," Cam said.

Lotan rejoined her on the bed and held the athtar talisman in his hand. "Does it hurt you to be this close to it?"

"No," she said. "But this is just one. And it's small. What if we had hundreds of them? We could give your nox army anti-athtar weapons. I bet you anything that with enough of them, we could knock their magic down a few pegs."

Lotan placed the talisman on the bedside table and laid his other hand on top of hers. "You seem quite certain of your plan, my lady."

"Maybe not certain," Cam said, her cheeks warming at his touch. "But I think it's better than what we had. In order to get to Bael, we have to get through his army." She chuckled. "Bael would be *pissed* if the demons used those talismans against him, too. Serves him right, the jackass."

"True," Lotan said with a smile. He leaned across the bed and placed a single kiss on her forehead. "Now, my brilliant strategist, you need to recover your strength. You've done enough for our cause for now."

Cam's heart thumped against her ribcage, and she heard herself saying, "I don't recall giving you permission to kiss me, Prince Lotan."

That earned a deep chuckle from the nox. "Oh, well, my sincere apologies, for I've kissed you several times, hoping it would wake up my sleeping princess."

"Wait…really?" She blanched.

His smile widened, and he brushed her hair behind her ear. "No, it was a joke. I believe your maker would have my head if I tried such a thing." But then he leaned down, his lips a hair's breadth from hers. "When I do kiss you, you will be awake for it. And you will remember every single second."

And with that, he winked and left her alone with her not-so-innocent thoughts.

Anya disagreed, but Cam was ready to be up and walking around by dinner that evening. She was growing tired of Anya's constant fussing and hovering. At least out of the bedroom, she could keep up to speed on what was happening with the battle planning effort.

"I don't think it's possible to carve the athtar talisman symbol into the ground," Mizuchi said, using a magnifying glass to examine Cam's athtar talisman. It made his already bulbous eyes even bigger.

"We could always do what we did before, and carve the marks into some bullets," Cam said. "That worked pretty well on Anya."

She nodded. "But how to get those bullets into the athtars is the question. The only way I was able to kill Ekur was to overpower his magic with my own. Stop time very briefly to shoot him."

"I wonder," Lotan said, playing with the lilin talisman between his fingers. "What if we were to shower the battlefield with talismans, so instead of one large symbol, there were a thousand smaller symbols."

"It's possible," Cam said.

"I'd like to test Agent Macarro's theory," Lotan said, rubbing his jaw. "Would the talismans be enough to mute an athtar's strength?" He turned to his left. "Izel, how long until you could make a hundred talismans?"

"We have already begun," she said. "Perhaps by this afternoon."

"Excellent—"

"And which athtar are you hoping to test this on?" Anya asked. "Cam is still weak from the trip to the Nullius."

"Then you'll make an apt substitute," Lotan said.

"Just because something works on me, doesn't mean it'll work on Bael," Anya said as the color rose in her cheeks.

"It's more the scale we're looking for," Mizuchi interjected. "We know that the talismans themselves are formidable weapons. What we don't know is whether a hundred talismans would have the same effect as the Nullius. That, my dear, you can tell us."

"Create some nox talismans and make Lotan test it," Anya said.

"We might as well create the athtar ones," Izel said. "As we'll be using them in battle. It will save time."

"This afternoon it is," Lotan said, standing. "I suppose we can use your courtyard, Belu Lilin?"

Anya's loud sighing and eye rolling had made it clear she wasn't onboard with the plan, but she'd been overruled. Cam retreated to her bedroom to spend more time recovering, but she had a bird's eye view of the preparations outside her window. Lotan and Izel stood in the center of the courtyard, pointing at different spots as they laid out the talismans. Freyja and Mizuchi looked on, offering commentary.

Eventually, Cam got bored of watching and ventured downstairs to see if it worked. She was already nursing a sick feeling in the bottom of her stomach, but the closer she came to the ground, the more pronounced it got. But she persevered through it; after all, she'd been able to walk through the Nullius.

She reached the courtyard, but as soon as she put one foot into the open area, a rush of violent sickness came over her. Her knees buckled and she fell backwards, right into the waiting arms of someone much taller.

"Well, I suppose that's a good sign," Lotan said, grinning from above her. "Perhaps you shouldn't be down here right now."

"Yeah," Cam said, letting him half-carry her to the step above. She plopped down on the stone ungracefully and pressed her hand to her lips to keep her stomach where it belonged. "This certainly sucks."

"You should return to bed," Lotan said, his brows knotting together.

"In a minute," Cam said. She wasn't sure she could stand at the moment, and she also wanted to see how Anya reacted to the magic. "Shouldn't this be enough, though? Me being sick?"

"There's a difference though," Lotan said. "You're still a young demon. We'll need to see how this magic affects an older, more mature demon. Even one that has been weakened."

Cam nodded, praying she wouldn't vomit in front of Lotan.

"There's are also a hundred talismans concentrated in this small space. I doubt we'll be able to have that coverage on the battlefield." His smile widened when he turned back to her. "We'll have to figure out how to make them so it doesn't affect you and Anat. Perhaps it would be better if you went back upstairs."

"I wanna watch," Cam insisted.

"Then go up a few flights," Lotan said, leaning down to take both her hands and pulling her upright. She leaned into his chest, grateful for the sturdy support under her cheek. His heartbeat was steady and strong, and she caught a whiff of some expensive cologne. She could honestly just fall asleep right there...

"What the hell are you doing with my polluelo?"

"Rest assured, Lady Anat," Lotan said, as he hooked one arm underneath Cam's knees and lifted her into his arms. She lazily mused that she'd been right about his ability to throw her over his shoulder. "I'm merely taking her to safety. When you're ready to begin the test, we can—"

"I can't," Anya murmured.

Cam cracked open an eye. "Why not?"

"I've been...trying," she admitted, looking at the ground. "But the talismans are too strong. My ability to stop time ends right about here." She slid her toe across the stone. "But I don't believe that's an indicator of how well this works. I think that's just a reflection on… on me."

Lotan was silent, his heartbeat filling Cam's ears with steady rhythm. "Then I offer my services to help you regain your strength."

"Uh-huh," Anya said, her embarrassment quickly fading to her usual hubris. "If I'm going to train, boy, it's not going to be with you."

"Then who?" Lotan asked. "Mizuchi? Freyja?"

"Freyja is a formidable warrior."

"She would take it too easy on you," Lotan said. "I, however, am nursing a grudge. It would not pain me to see you bleed a little."

"Hey," Cam said quietly, before Anya ratcheted up the argument. "Keep it civil."

"Bael will not keep it civil," Lotan said, adjusting Cam in his arms. "He'll do what it takes to win. Lucky for us, he includes reclaiming Anat as part of that victory. He won't want to use his sword against you, but if he feels he's losing, he will. He will do anything to win."

"I know," Anya said. "Believe me, I know."

"In order to defeat him, we have to get you into the same mindset," Lotan said. "You have to let go of whatever love you feel for him, or the hope that things won't end in bloodshed. You must want to win more than you want him alive." His hard gaze softened. "As hard as that may be."

Anya's lip twitched. "I'll prepare on my own. I don't need your help."

"You mean prepare for suicide," Lotan called as she began to walk away.

She stopped and looked over her shoulder. "It is what it is."

"You're acting like you don't have a choice in the matter," Lotan said. "You can choose to go out in submission, or you can go out fighting. If you opt for the latter, you'll have a higher chance of success. Maybe you won't survive, but your Jack might. Cam might. Train not for yourself, but for them, if that helps you swallow it."

"Anya," Cam said meekly, hoping her current condition would get past Anya's ego. "You should listen to him."

"Fine," Anya said with a heavy sigh. "I'll see if Freyja can provide a training room. But if you speak a word of this to any of your noxes—"

"Not a word to anyone," Lotan said. "Now, if you'll excuse me, I have a polluelo to put back in bed."

"Make sure you're just putting her there, and not joining her," Anya said with a glare.

CHAPTER TWENTY-SIX

The talismans had been removed from the courtyard—Cam didn't know how or to where, but she did feel a lot better when she finally awoke a few hours later. Anya had taken to hovering over her again, making her eat and drink water without much conversation. When Cam asked if she wanted to talk about training over dinner that night, Anya would shove food in her mouth and tell her to regain her strength.

In the morning, Anya had left a buffet of breakfast items for Cam, which she worked her way through with aplomb. Halfway through her third round of eggs, the door opened and Lotan walked in. Cam quickly wiped her face and hoped she didn't have jam all over it.

"Good to see you up and about," Lotan said, clearly amused.

"Anya helped with some of this," Cam said, pointing to the table where she'd plowed through enough food for four.

"Perhaps that explains her performance then," Lotan said, sliding down in the empty seat and helping himself to a biscuit.

"What happened?" Cam said, sipping her coffee. "Did you kill her?"

"No. But only barely. She's much worse than I thought," he said. "I tried to goad her into using more power, but even as she ranted and raged, it was barely anything." He ran a hand through his black curls. "I'm worried."

"Maybe it's mental," Cam said. "If she doesn't want to fight Bael, she's not going to really give it her all. They used to tell us back in the Academy that the best way to prevent demonic coercion is to not want to become a demon at all. Like, make it anathema in your mind."

Lotan quirked a smile. "Obviously didn't work in your case."

"I'm serious," Cam said. "The chick is obviously still attached to Bael. She doesn't want to kill him. And now, getting her ass handed to her a few times by you, that's got to be harmful to her psyche. Maybe she just needs a win to get back on the horse."

"I don't think we have time for that," Lotan said. "Every day we waste training Anat is another day Bael grows stronger."

And another day Jack remained in Bael's clutches. Cam swallowed her bite and wiped her face with her napkin. "I'll see what I can do to knock her out of her funk."

"How?" Lotan asked.

"I don't know," she said with a wince. "Maybe I'll just let her knock me around for a bit."

Lotan took her hand. "If you need a nurse, please let me know. I'd be happy to attend to you again."

Cam found Anya in a training room at the top of Kastali. By herself, Anya was a vision of deadly precision. Her swords were extensions of her arms, her movements controlled and fluid. The mask of concentration told a story of a woman who could walk through a battlefield and come out unscathed.

She caught Cam's gaze and stopped, dropping her arms to her side.

"What are you doing up here?"

"Wanted to check on you," Cam said, walking to the collection of swords laying near the wall. She picked up a broadsword—her second favorite weapon after her macuahuitl—and tested the weight.

"What are you doing?" Anya asked.

"Thought you and I could go for a round," Cam said. "It's been a few weeks since I've worked with a trainer. Feeling rusty."

"Then find someone else. Lotan, I'm sure, would be eager to be in close quarters with you."

Cam cleared her throat, recalling the prince's parting words. "Well, as nice as that might be, you're here. How about it?"

"I'm not in the mood," Anya said, lifting her sword again.

Cam knocked it with hers. "I'm not asking."

"Cam, I know what you're trying to do," Anya said, turning away from her. "Remember, I can—"

Cam poked her in the back with the sword.

"Cam," she said with a warning tone. "I said I'm not in the mood."

"Fine, then let's talk about whatever's wrong with you," she replied, putting her sword down. "Because Lotan said you're not getting any better."

"Lotan should shut his mouth if he knows what's good for him," Anya said with a glare. "I'm working on what I need to do, and I don't need any help from you. *Or* him."

"Well, okay. You said you defeated an athtar recently right?" Cam said. "How'd you do that?"

Anya paused, tossing her swords in the air and catching them. "I overpowered his magic, but only just. It was Jack who saved my ass. He thought to use the talisman and the gun, and I had just enough strength to do the deed. I won't get that close with Bael."

"You still overpowered his magic," Cam said.

"He was a neophyte."

"Still. Maybe we should pit you against someone less powerful. Why don't you try it against me?"

"I'll win."

"So? Let's try it," Cam said. "If I'm going into the castle, I should know how to defend myself against athtars anyway, right? Let's do both."

Anya pursed her lips, but nodded. "I suppose it's not the

worst idea. You've never been in a demon fight, have you?"

"I mean…"

"I meant when magic is involved," Anya said gently. "It's different. You've got the weapons to worry about, but also the magic. If you lose focus on the magic, you get stabbed. Lose focus on the weapon, you can get swept up in the magic, then stabbed. It's not a skill you can learn overnight, but…we can at least go over the basics."

Cam smiled. "Ready when you are."

"When you're a demon, magic doesn't affect you as much as it does a human," Anya began, gently placing her swords on a nearby table. "But since you're young, it still won't take much to sway you. I'm sure you learned defensive techniques at the Academy."

"Not against athtars," Cam said.

"Athtar magic is the hardest to fight against," Anya said. "For humans and lesser demons, it's almost impossible. But for another athtar, it's just a matter of pushing through with your own magic. Basically: They'll try to freeze your time, so you try to freeze them. Whoever wins…well, wins."

Cam nodded. "And how do I stop someone in time?"

Anya picked up a small dagger on the table, spun on her heel and flung it at Cam.

Cam screamed and held up her arms, ducking low. She waited for the sound of clanging, but it never came. She cracked open one eye, then the other, then straightened. The dagger was suspended in the air, crawling along its trajectory.

"Like that," Anya said.

"Is that usually how athtars learn to stop time?" Cam asked.

"Generally how I used to teach it." She chuckled and plucked the dagger out of the air. "It's not something you can explain. Danger comes, you react on instinct. Eventually you learn to manage those instincts."

"How do I do that?"

Anya picked up the dagger and flung it again.

They continued this exercise for what felt like an hour, until Cam finally began to get the feel for the magic that rose up from somewhere in the bottom of her chest. Anya seemed invigorated as she taught. Cam was hoping she'd take all this positive energy back to Lotan and actually put up a fight.

"All right," Anya announced after Cam successfully held an axe, a broadsword, and three daggers in the air. "Are you ready to try it against me?"

Cam nodded, shaking out her shoulders. "Take it easy on me, will you?"

Once more, everything slowed—even Cam's heartbeat. Her thoughts churned at the speed of sludge, and the act of blinking took five times as long.

Then it was over.

"That was a test," Anya said.

"How long was I out?"

"A breath," she replied. "Long enough for me to kill you."

"Right," Cam said, rubbing her neck. "How do I fight against that again?"

"Remember how it felt when that dagger was coming toward you? That instinct? Dredge up that feeling. Because an athtar who can overpower your magic will probably have a weapon in hand."

"R—" The words died on her tongue as the athtar magic surrounded her once again. This time, her eyes tracked slowly to Anya, who was a blur of movement. But the sword was clearly coming toward her.

She dug deep and just *pushed*, dredging the bottom of her well of fury, stubbornness, and disgust at everything that had happened in the past few weeks and channeling all of that into breaking free of Anya's magic.

The feeling intensified, and so did Cam's resolve. With everything she had, she braced herself against the magic and pushed hard. Something broke, and Cam's magic poured out of her, surrounding Anya and freezing her in place. With a gasp, Cam released her hold and stepped back.

"You...beat me..." Anya whispered, eyes wide. "That's impossible. I *made* you."

"Maybe I wanted it more than you did," Cam said, wiping her forehead and wishing she hadn't tried so hard. "C'mon, let's try it again."

"This doesn't make any sense," Anya huffed.

"It makes plenty of sense," Cam said. "You don't really want to fight. You can't be at your best if you aren't all in. You're still not furious at Bael. You need to channel all your anger."

"I don't need to channel anything. I need to think, and I

can't do that with your smug face staring at me all day."

"Whoa," Cam said, holding up her hands. "Take it down a notch. I'm just here to help."

"You're not *helping* at all. You're just making it worse." Anya held her hand against her forehead. "It's impossible that you can beat me. *Impossible*."

"Says who? Bael?" Cam said gently.

"Says me," Anya said, slumping on a chair. "Because if it's possible for you to overpower me, it's possible for me to overpower Bael."

Cam nodded her understanding and sat down next to Anya. "And you don't want to overpower him?"

"I just want him to stop all this nonsense," Anya said. "There's no reason we have to fight. No reason we have to go to war. No reason he has Jack."

"Yeah, there is," Cam said. "Because he's a lunatic. You can't reason with crazy, Anya. As much as you want to believe that he's better than he is, he's not. He's very clearly shown that to you a bunch of times. You've gotta start believing it."

Hurried footsteps echoed in the hallway, and the door flung open. Freyja ran in, her eyes wide.

"What is it?"

"Bael," she said. "Bael is here."

CHAPTER TWENTY-SEVEN

Cam raced for the door, but Anya was quicker, grabbing her and Freyja and using her magic to transport all of them to the front gates. There, Lotan and Mizuchi stood on the docks, a cold wind blowing. And on the other side, flanked by two athtars, was Bael. He was a handsome devil, but a devil nonetheless. His warning to Cam about slaughtering her family came back, and it was hard not to panic.

The athtar belu seemed unconcerned about the fear his appearance had caused, or he was relishing in it. "How very pleasant to see all of you assembled here in Freyja's castle," Bael said with deathly calm. His gaze settled on Anya, a smile curling on his lips. "And, my lady, you're looking well. I can see that spending time in the Underworld has given you that youthful glow again."

She swallowed. "Where is Jack?"

"He's fine," Bael said with a wave of his hand. "Worry not, my love. I'm keeping your human fed and happy."

"I hear happy is a bit of an overstatement," Cam snapped.

Bael's attention slid to her and his mouth opened in surprise. "Well, look at this. I didn't realize celebrations were in order. A new member of my growing family."

Cam took a step back. "It's temporary."

"Oh, I'm sure it will be," Bael said, turning his attention to Anya. "I hear you're planning to kill me, Anat. That's a true shame. You would kill me with the very gift I gave you."

"I don't have to," she said quietly. "Let Jack go—"

"Oh, you aren't in a position to demand from me, Anat," Bael said with an edge of harshness. "You should be begging forgiveness on bended knee for this...ridiculous show of betrayal. Allying yourself with the nox prince?" He shook his head. "After what they did to our daughter?"

"My parents were innocent of that crime," Lotan said, stepping forward. "And you know it."

A snarl would've been preferable to the easy smile Bael gave Lotan. "As you say, son of the God-touched. I've heard tales from your Madriguera that you are not as well-liked as you believe yourself to be. Many of your noxes are crying out for a true leader."

Nox miasma brushed against Cam's arms, sending chills

down her spine. Lotan's eyes had grown yellow again, his teeth looking more canine than human.

"Stay out of my nest," he growled.

"I haven't set foot in there," Bael said. "Your ineptitude has made you many enemies among your people. And sadly, it's going to cost you much more than your throne."

An athtar appeared behind him with a bag slung over his shoulder. He tossed it to the ground with a *thump*.

Cam's heart stopped in her chest and she prayed the athtar wouldn't open it.

Prayed it wouldn't be Jack.

The athtar removed the bag.

Cam only recognized Oce by the long black hair, for the rest of her had been so bruised and bloodied it was hard to tell she was even a person. Her clothes were tattered, shredded by knife and claw marks. And her eyes, half-open, stared at the room with a permanent plea to end the pain. Had the torture followed her into the afterlife?

Anya stared at the body, horror and shock etched on her face.

"You..." Lotan breathed. A low growl rumbled from the back of his throat. Freyja placed a hand on his shoulder, her gaze never moving from the body on the ground.

"Poor soul," Bael said, kneeling and gently pushing the matted hair from her bloody face. "It was simple for your governors to give her up. Many of these bruises were made by your own brethren. They wished to send you a message, Prince.

They've grown tired of your childishness."

Cam wanted so very much to snap back. But with Oce, vibrant, beautiful Oce now cold and bloody, she couldn't find her fire. She couldn't even find her tongue.

"Mizuchi, Freyja," Bael said, standing. "I've known this little war planning effort has been going on for some time. And while I find it to be in bad taste, I am nothing if not forgiving. Come back to my fold. Put aside this foolishness, and all will be forgotten and forgiven."

"I think I'll pass," Freyja said, with more fierceness than Cam had seen from her so far. "I prefer to rule over my own domain."

"Mizuchi?" Bael asked, although it seemed clear he knew what the kappa's answer would be.

"I'll remain here," he replied.

"Ah," Bael said softly. "So this is how it is, hm? After all that I've given you, all the gifts of spawn and power. All the times I let you sit at my table. The countries I let you conquer."

"Optimal word there is *let*," Cam said, feeling braver. "They're belus, same as you."

Bael smiled, and the hairs stuck up on her arm. "They are not the same as me, Camilla. For I am beyond anything they could comprehend. I can move the universe with a thought."

"So could my mother," Lotan snapped back. "You aren't special."

"So you say, so you say," Bael said with a shrug. "As a show of my graciousness, as long as you remain in your lands, the athtars will not come for you. But know this: If you as much as set one foot in Ath-kur, I'll take it as an act of war."

"Killing Oce was an act of war," Lotan murmured with clenched fists.

"Then rage against your own kind. I had nothing to do with this. I just brought her to you." Bael smiled, looking at Anat, who hadn't moved since she'd first laid eyes on Oce. "Anat, dear, if you decide the cost is too great, you will be welcome back by my side. I'll be waiting at my castle."

Then he was gone.

No one moved for minutes. Then Anya took a step then another then another, until she stood in front of the body. She fell to her knees clumsily, reaching a gentle hand out to the corpse and brushing away the hair. She sucked in a loud breath as she pulled something from the wounds in the chest.

Cam didn't need to see it close to know what it was. Jack's nox talisman.

"The noxes who allowed this to happen will pay dearly." Lotan's eyes were wet, his voice thick with emotion. "I'll rip them limb from limb."

Anya gathered the nox woman in her arms and held her close to her chest. Then, as if a dam had broken, she began to cry, softly at first, then loud wails of anguish as she crushed the body to her. The sound brought tears to Cam's eyes, but she didn't want to cry. Didn't feel as though she deserved to, not in the face of Anya's grief.

After a few moments, Anya stood with Oce in her arms, as if

she were a babe.

"Where are you taking her?" Lotan asked.

"I wish to give her a proper burial," Anya whispered. "Alone."

"She's part of my family," he said. "I should help."

"I'll help too," Cam said, stepping forward.

"Do what you wish," Anya said simply.

With Anya leading the way, the procession of belus, prince, and Cam walked the length of the castle to the other side, to a small cemetery. Freyja lovingly placed a hand on several as they walked by.

Anya walked the body around the small space, finally deciding on a particular twisted tree. One of Freyja's servants joined them with a shovel, which Anya took without a word.

As she dug in the cold earth, Cam, Mizuchi, and Lotan stood shoulder-to-shoulder on the side in reverent silence. There was no sound except the slice of the shovel and the movement of earth from one place to another, punctuated by the occasional sniff from Anya as tears leaked down her face, and—to Cam's surprise—the occasional hard swallow from Lotan. Cam quietly slipped her hand into his and squeezed. He met her gaze for a moment, then turned back to Anya.

It took the athtar little time to dig the grave, although she used no magic. Once the grim task was complete, she made no move to lower the body. She stared into the hole, gripping the shovel with dirty hands. As if unable to bring herself to complete what she'd started.

Lotan released Cam's grip and walked to stand next to Anya. "May I say a word?"

She nodded.

"Oce was more than a sister," he said quietly. "She cradled me in her arms and taught me how to use a sword. More than that, she instilled in me an appreciation for the beauty of humanity, and the true meaning of leadership. She was..." His voice broke. "She was Oce. And I'll forever be grateful for her presence in my life."

Mizuchi stood on the other side of Anya. "Oce would always bring tales of brilliant weapons masters and strategies. I'll always miss her keen eye."

"Oce was a nimble lover, and a much better friend," Freyja said. "She was a loyal asset to Xo and Mot, even after their deaths. She will be missed by all."

Cam swallowed. "I didn't know Oce very well, but..." She looked at the talismans around her wrists. "These talismans were a gift from the very god who banished the demons to the Underworld. She wanted to know more about them, so...I just hope that if you met God on the other side, He told you everything. I wish I could've had the chance."

Silence reigned once more, and Cam held her breath for Anya to speak. But the demon seemed too far gone, her eyes rimmed with red and her lips swollen.

"Let's go," Lotan said.

One by one, the belus nodded once to the grave in respect

then turned to leave. Lotan and Cam were the last, waiting at the courtyard entrance until Anya cradled the body and placed it in the grave. A heart-rending cry rose from her lips as she released the first shovel of dirt, and she fell to her knees, sobbing into her hands.

"No," Lotan said, as Cam moved to go to her. He slid his hand back into hers and they walked into the castle.

"They were good friends," Cam said, after a moment.

"No, they weren't," Lotan said with a sad smile. "Anat would never let them be. And that, I believe, is what she mourns."

"Freyja said Anya's a woman who's never known love," Cam replied. "Do you think that's true?"

"Bael is an evil creature," Lotan said with a numb look. "He's incapable of love. If he was, he wouldn't have done this. He wouldn't have killed Oce simply to hurt Anat." His voice was on the verge of breaking again, so he quieted.

Cam glanced down at their joined hands and placed her free one on his forearm. "I'm sorry."

"Me too," he said. "I don't doubt there are those in our den who gave her up. Loyalty is at a premium, it seems." He shook his head. "If I were a better belu—"

"Enough of that bullshit," Cam said, releasing him and facing him dead-on. "You're a damned nox prince. Own your title, even if you don't want it. The only person responsible for Oce's death is *Bael*, and if you start blaming yourself, you're letting him win. Keep focused on the asshole responsible. Don't be Anya."

His mouth fell open in surprise, and Cam was *sure* she'd overstepped her bounds. After a tense few moments, he licked his lips and shook his head in disbelief.

"Right, of course," Lotan said with a soft chuckle. "I'd rather be a Cam than an Anya." He tilted his head at her. "Are we past Agent Macarro yet? May I call you Cam?"

She smiled, relieved that he hadn't yet tired of her brusqueness. "Yeah, I suppose we are."

"You are…a very remarkable woman, Cam. One day, I hope to be worthy enough to call you my friend, too."

"You can call me friend," she mumbled, backtracking from her moment of confidence. "As long as you don't let Bael win."

"Wouldn't dream of it," he said without much conviction. "But right now, I need a drink. Or several. Care to join me?"

They walked in reverent silence to the basement of Kastali to a room filled with wine barrels and lined with bottles on the wall. Lotan plucked a bottle from the center of the rack and opened it with corkscrew he found nearby. Tossing the cork away, he tilted his head back and gulped down an entire glass in one breath.

"Slow down there," Cam said, pulling the bottle away from him. "Freyja said it's potent stuff."

"I need potency," he said, as a tear fell down his face. "Forgive me."

Cam gently placed the bottle on the table as he sat down on a wine barrel. He looked so forlorn and lost. She tentatively inched closer, before finally sitting down in his lap and pulling him into her arms. He embraced her, pulling her closer and pressing his wet cheek to hers. She held him, stroking his hair and wishing she had something to say to take away the pain. But words were meaningless in the face of grief. The only thing to do was to sit in it until the storm passed.

"She didn't deserve that," Lotan whispered. "She didn't deserve to be betrayed like that."

"I know," Cam said, releasing him. She wiped his cheek, and he pressed his hand against hers, closing his eyes. Her eyes filled with tears as she watched him, knowing exactly what he was going through. Remembering how she'd wanted someone to hold her like this the night she'd lost Sara.

He opened his eyes, and Cam lost herself in their sadness. Lotan kissed the inside of her palm sweetly. His lips felt like velvet against her skin, and it sent a shudder down her body. He reached behind her to pluck the bottle from the table. This time, his sip was small, and he passed the wine to her. She took a swig, and warmth spread from her stomach to her toes and fingers. She wasn't looking forward to another hangover, so she handed the bottle back to Lotan.

"I must leave in the morning," he said with a solemn look.

Cam tilted her head. "Isn't that what Bael wants you to do? Leave us? Maybe he's trying to splinter our forces."

"Bael's not nearly as smart as he thinks he is," he replied. "I'm merely a figurehead. Izel will continue to ready the troops with Mizuchi. I was already planning a return to the noxlands to find more soldiers to our cause. Now, it's a matter of finding out who betrayed us, dealing with them, and *then* finding more soldiers."

"Just don't..." Cam began softly. She shouldn't be telling the nox prince how to run his kingdom, but at the same time, he did seem kind of uninformed about the whole thing.

"Don't what?" Lotan asked.

"Don't go in guns blazing," she said, unable to help herself. "Look, as a leader, there are always going to be people who think you suck at your job. It's part of the gig. And yeah, *maybe* you've been doing yourself a disservice by wandering around the world and spying on your own people. Maybe cut down on projecting your feelings of inadequacy."

Lotan blinked at her. Insecurity screamed in her mind, but she kept talking, because once she got started, she just couldn't stop.

"You can't be a wimp, but you can't be a tyrant either. You gotta strike a balance. Go back to the noxlands, make a few heads roll—only those who were directly responsible. Tell the rest of them what's at stake. Show them you're out there fighting with them. You're gonna put your own butt on the line. That should bring the rest of them over." Then, she held her breath and waited.

His surprise turned to a sultry chuckle and he rested his free hand on her knee. "You seem well-versed in this subject. Maybe I can hire you to be my consultant."

"Yeah, I think the Division might have a problem with that,"

Cam said, glancing down at his hand. Feeling brave, she covered it with her own. Perhaps she was finally getting the upper hand with the nox. "Then again, who knows if I'm still employed there."

"They would be remiss to get rid of you, as brilliant as you are," he said, taking another sip and handing the bottle to her. "As much as I want to sit down here and get drunk with you on my lap, duty calls."

"Yeah," she said, looking up at the ceiling. "Do you think Anya's going to be okay?"

"She didn't go with Bael," he said with a shrug. "That was surprising."

"It wasn't to me," Cam said. "She's trying. But he's really fucked her up. It's going to take some time to get past that."

"Then it's a good thing she has you here to get her straight." He handed her the half-empty bottle. "Take a bottle or two for her. I'm sure she'd appreciate a friend right now."

"I will," Cam said. "But are you going to be all right?"

"In time." His eyes filled with sadness once more.

Perhaps the lilin wine was making her brave, because she leaned in to kiss him sweetly. "I'm here if you need me."

He blinked at her, the shock a welcome change from the sadness that had been hanging around his eyes. For a moment, Cam feared she might have misread the *entire* situation, until he pulled her toward him. He covered her lips with softness and passion, and she let herself swoon into him, the bottle nearly falling from her fingers. He swept his tongue against her lips, and she readily opened to him, fighting the urge take things further. But oh, how she wanted to.

"I told you," he whispered against her lips, "when I kissed you, you'd be awake for it."

Cam had nothing to say to that but idiotic stammering. So much for the upper hand.

CHAPTER TWENTY-EIGHT

The smell of broken earth, blood, and salty tears was familiar to Anya. Death had never been far from her, though it had mostly been caused by her own sword. And even when it hadn't, she still carried the blame in her heart. And now, Oce's death was on her hands. For as much as Anya had tried to keep the nox at arm's length, Freyja had been correct—there was no hiding love from Bael. Here was the proof that all her efforts had been in vain. Oce was still dead—tortured. All because Anya had decided to take a stand against Bael. Because she'd let the nox prince convince her she might have a chance. Because she'd let *Jack* fill her head with the optimistic notion that she could have a beautiful life. That she deserved to have something more than pain and misery.

But she'd learned long ago that life with Bael could never be as beautiful as she'd hoped. Good things never lasted.

After Ayumi's death, Bael had been more attentive than ever. He never mentioned the unspeakable thing he'd made her do, and she was sure to stay clear of all servants and other athtars to prevent it from occurring again. And, for a while, things calmed down.

Then came word of the nox boy.

"Are you…serious?" Bael asked his messenger, Lazlo. "That's impossible. I'm sure they found a human babe and transformed it."

"My lord," Lazlo said with a grimace. "It is…true. The birth was witnessed."

"By whom? The noxes? They are liars. Find out the truth."

Lazlo nodded and disappeared.

"What do you think of this nonsense, my lady?" Bael asked, taking her by the hand. "Demons don't have children. It's impossible."

"Of course it is," she said with a firm nod. "I'm sure it's as you said. They found a human babe."

"But…" He slid his hand up her arm. "That of course begs the question of *where* they would've found such a creature. The noxes have never used my schism, and their pack of dogs remains in their own lands. Besides that, it's been two years since the schism, and two years until the next."

"Perhaps they've kept a human as a pet," Anya said, closing her eyes when his fingertips brushed the sensitive part of her collarbone. "What does it matter?"

"What if it is as Lazlo has said," he replied, undoing the latch on her dress. She only just caught the fabric before it fell from her chest.

"Bael," she said, quickly retying her dress. "Don't focus on it. Whether they have or they haven't—it doesn't matter. You're the king of the five realms. They are mongrels in a cave. They don't hold a candle to you."

The world shifted; Anya now stood in their bedroom, Bael fiddling with her dress once more.

"Bael, what are you doing?" she asked, pushing him away gently.

"What if it's not a human babe?" he whispered against her skin. "What if they made a nox babe? What if they're more powerful than I am?"

"Bael, that's insane," she said, allowing her dress material to fall away from her body. "You are the most powerful, the most —"

His kiss came rough and unforgiving, as did his lovemaking, if Anya could even call it that. In the weeks that followed, he would take her twice, sometimes three times a day. His mania grew when Lazlo confirmed through multiple sources that the babe—Lotan—had been born a nox. Making an athtar child became Bael's compulsion, even as Anya begged him in tears to stop.

"If you can't give me a child," he snarled, yanking his pants back around his waist as she lay in trembling misery, "perhaps I'll find another athtar who will do it for me."

The door slammed behind him, and Anya let herself sob in silence. When Bael became obsessed, there was no stopping him until it ran its course. But in this case, there was nothing she could do. She was either barren or physically incapable of giving birth. Perhaps she couldn't give Bael what he wanted because she hadn't been touched by God himself.

She stumbled to the window and fell to her knees, looking toward the Nullius. And in a fit of desperation, she clasped her hands together and prayed.

"Please let me get pregnant," she whispered toward the holy place. "I can't lose him. Please, I know I'm not God-touched, but... Please..."

One week later, she felt the stirrings of something in her lower abdomen.

Bael had been ecstatic—over the moon. He'd paraded her around to every belu's house—including a rare visit to the noxes —to show her off, especially as her stomach swelled with the product of his power. Mot and Xo offered their congratulations. Xo, while little Lotan suckled at her teat, even generously offered her knowledge of childbirth and motherhood to Anya.

"She won't need it," Bael replied before Anya could. "My Lady of the Mountain needs no guidance."

That had been a falsehood, for nothing had prepared Anya for the glory and terror that came with birth and holding the tiny child in her arms. There were no doctors, no nurses, just a few kappas and elokos who'd been mothers before they'd been turned. And soon Bael banished them as well, for he didn't want them getting too close to their child.

Anya called her Asherah, a name from her childhood that she'd always liked. When she and the baby were well enough to travel, Bael carted them around for another tour of the belus, skipping the noxes entirely. Bael was a loving father, carting Asherah wherever he went with a proud smile. In the privacy of their own room, he'd become meaner toward Anya, especially as new whispers from the noxlands reached them.

Xo had created her own schism to the human world, or so it was rumored. When Lotan had been born, the force of the original's magic separating from her child had been powerful enough to break the bonds of the demonic world. And unlike Bael's, this schism remained permanently opened.

"What does it matter?" Anya said when Bael raged about it. "You create schisms every few years. They have one. It's clear you're the most powerful."

"Simple woman," Bael snarled. "If they control access to the human world, I lose power over them. But I suppose a woman who's never been God-touched wouldn't understand that. It's obvious you're a lesser creature—*you* didn't create a schism."

The baby began to cry, and Anya hurried to the crib to hush her and to hide her own tears. But even as his words cut her deeply, she found solace in her child. This tiny creature with black hair and big, round eyes, who'd squawk and burp and cry was the most wonderful thing she'd ever had. The first thing Anya could really call her own.

The years passed slowly, and the little creature turned into a young girl with curly black hair and a smile that resembled her father's. Anya loved to watch them together, especially as Bael taught her how to use a sword and defend herself. The first attempts were the clumsy efforts of a child, but it was clear to Anya that her daughter would possess the skill and grace to be a fearsome fighter.

The magic in her veins was powerful as well. Though she had nothing to compare her to except neophyte athtars, Asherah could run circles around the newer brethren Bael brought home. He would delight in having them pair off, and laugh with good-natured cheer when the pompous athtars were bested by a child.

"She is no mere babe," he'd announce proudly. "She is a princess. And she is more powerful than the nox prince."

That was a common refrain from Bael. How true it was, Anya had no idea. Mot and Xo never left the noxlands, and Anya didn't want to bring her child across the Underworld just to prove a point. But if the rumors from the servants were true, the boy was as powerful, if not more so, than his parents. Whenever Anya heard the servants discussing it, she'd make sure to quiet them—by words, or by sword, if they didn't listen. She was content to let them think she was being an unreasonable queen.

But perhaps she should've spent more time worrying about the noxes.

Bael had returned the evening before from another visit to the other belus' strongholds. He'd arrived smelling of lilin miasma and had promptly taken her to bed then fallen asleep while Anya lay awake. Something felt off to her, but she couldn't place it.

She rose from the bed and made her way to her daughter's bedroom, needing to see the child before she'd be able to sleep soundly.

The smell of blood reached Anya's nose, and her heart fell into her stomach. She couldn't reach the bedroom fast enough, even her athtar magic was too slow.

For there, in her bed of white, lay the little girl, barely half a decade old. Her eyes were open—her throat cut and crimson blood pooled around her black curls.

She screamed.

Anya opened her eyes, unable to bear the memory any longer and needing to return to the present moment. To feel the ground under her, to smell the cool air. To remind herself Asherah's death had occurred five hundred years in the past, even though her heart felt it was breaking anew.

The freshly dug grave at her feet had been blessed by her tears. Wherever Oce was now, whether with God or the Nullius or somewhere else, Anya hoped she could feel her sorrow. Prayed she might know how much Anya regretted keeping Oce at arm's length.

With one final prayer, Anya left Oce's grave and trudged

toward the castle. There wasn't another soul in the halls, but that infernal connection with the polluelo was a beacon. Did Bael feel this with her? Was their connection so powerful that he knew every whim and mood swing? Could he feel the depths of her grief, and did he care?

Anya set those questions aside for another night, or perhaps never. She pushed open the door to the bedroom she shared with her polluelo, greeting Cam with a soft nod and no eye contact.

"Hey." Cam was a mix of apprehension and sadness. "How you doing, champ?"

Anya sniffed and wiped her cheek, where a tear had escaped. "Jack used to say that, too."

"Where do you think he got it from?" Cam said. She picked up two bottles she'd set on the table and handed one to Anya. "Drink."

Anya pulled the cork and took a long swig. It was red wine, an old vintage that needed some breathing before drinking. But she didn't care about right or wrong; she just wanted to get drunk.

"Where did you get this?" she asked.

"Lotan gave it to me," Cam replied, a starstruck expression crossing her face.

"What?" Anya asked, nudging her. "Did you fuck or something?"

"*No.*" The polluelo couldn't help but smile. "But he is a good kisser."

"I could've lived another three thousand years without

knowing that," Anya said with a hearty eye roll. But it was mostly in jest. Anya might've hated the noxes and everything they were, but the prince had been an innocent bystander in all of it. He seemed genuinely smitten with Cam, and if the flutterings of lust and excitement across their bond was any indication, Cam was warming to him as well.

"I'm sorry," Cam said, playing with the bottle in her hands. "You've lost a friend, and I'm sitting here talking about kissing a guy."

"Oce would be happy to hear Lotan has met his match," Anya replied with a soft nudge. "And I wish I could call her my friend but… I never allowed it to happen. I was too scared that if I did, she'd—"

"End up like Ayumi," Cam finished for her. The girl was a good listener, Anya would give her that. And she was a good, loyal friend.

"You should fuck him until you can't see straight," Anya said, taking a sip.

"W-what?"

The shock that filtered through their connection was mixed with relief, and Anya smiled. "Somebody had better get laid in this castle before we all die or Freyja will be pissed."

Cam released a throaty laugh that was equal parts relief and surprise. "Well, I'm glad I have your blessing. And Oce's." Her smile faded. "Guess I just need Jack's now. Goddamn, why am I even talking about this when Jack's in trouble?"

"Everyone needs a release," Anya said. "And there's nothing

we can do for Jack right now."

Cam inhaled and shivered. "I thought Bael had brought Jack at first..."

"Bael won't kill him unless it's in front of us," Anya said, unable to gather any emotion. "That's not his style. He'll make a spectacle of it."

"He's depraved," Cam said. "Please tell me you're finally at the point where you want him dead?"

She dug deep for that anger—but all she felt was disgust at herself. "How can I be angry with Bael when I'm the one at fault? I knew better than to become friends with her—"

"Are you serious right now?" Cam laughed, incredulous. "*Bael* killed Oce. *Bael* is responsible for his own damned actions. Nothing you did or didn't do is ever to blame for what that man does."

"What about the thousands I did kill?" Anya said. "It was my sword that killed Ayumi. Even if Bael goaded me into it, it was my decision."

"What do you want me to say, Colibrí? Do you want me to tell you that it's all your fault, that you're garbage and should just jump off a cliff?"

Anya's eyebrows lifted in surprise. "I mean..."

"Or do you want to grow the hell up, take responsibility for your own life and the mistakes you made, and make it right?" Cam put her hands on her hips. "Physical ability aside, if you were face-to-face with Bael right now, do you have the *emotional* strength to kill him?"

"It doesn't matter. If I raise my sword, I die. It's as simple as that," Anya snapped. "That's the only reason you're here. You get Jack. I die. I thought that was pretty damned clear. I don't understand why we keep rehashing it."

"Anya—"

Anya stood and swiped the bottle out of Cam's hand. "Thanks for the booze."

She walked out the door.

CHAPTER TWENTY-NINE

Oce's death had left a dark cloud over the entire castle. Lotan left early the next morning for the noxlands, taking his most trusted lieutenants with him. Anya flat-out refused to train with Cam, disappearing into the Kastali upper levels with Freyja in tow and barely speaking when she returned to their shared room for meals and to sleep. But from the lines on the lilin's face, Cam was sure Anya wasn't faring much better against her than Lotan.

Cam spent most of her time with Mizuchi, listening to reports from the scouts and hoping to hear good news. It never was.

"Three thousand?" Mizuchi said quietly.

"Yes, Belu Kappa," the scout replied. "From our last count.

But we cannot see clearly, not without crossing the border. There may be more."

"Thank you," Mizuchi said, waving his hand and dismissing him. He sat in silence for a moment, toying with the pen and paper in front of him.

"Not good, huh?" Cam said, breaking the silence.

"It's not the best situation," Mizuchi said. "I would feel much better if Lady Anat were making more progress. But I fear she may never be ready."

Cam chewed her lip. "There's got to be something we can do. Have you heard from Lotan?"

"No, but I don't expect to. It is a tough situation, when one's spawn revolts against you," Mizuchi said. "I've been there once or twice. You usually end up killing more than you can stomach. And with Bael breathing down our necks, I'm not sure Lotan can spare many noxes."

"I hope nothing's happened to him," Cam said, "I mean, they need him alive, right?"

"In theory," Mizuchi said. "Although I have been testing some ideas around Lotan's own miraculous situation. In this new era, I can't count on Bael wanting to keep Kappanchi intact. I'd much rather make provisions for my spawn to continue without me."

Cam chewed her lip. "But Lotan—"

"Is probably fine," Mizuchi said. "If he doesn't return within the week, I'll send scouts to the noxlands. Don't worry yourself, Agent Macarro. He is a powerful demon, and the noxes that crossed him will be sorry they did so."

"I'll just worry myself about everything else, then," Cam said, looking at the map between Athtar and Liley. The mountain range spanned from the Nullius all the way to the edge of the map. There was no getting around it. "How are we going to move an army across this thing?"

"There are ways," he said simply. "But before we do that, we need a better view of where Bael is positioning his forces, and a better count." He pointed to the map. "This is where I've sent my scouts. I can't get them any closer without risking Bael taking it as an act of war."

"Do you think he was literal on that?" Cam asked.

"He always is," Mizuchi said, rubbing one of his webbed hands along his green face. "I'd hoped to send Lady Anat to the border, but I fear she may not be ready. Freyja says their training has not been progressing. In fact, she's getting worse."

"I could go," Cam said. "I'm not as strong as Anya, but I'm still an athtar."

He nodded slowly. "Perhaps. I doubt Lady Anat would allow you to travel by yourself."

"Good thing she's not allowing me to do anything," Cam said. "Tell me what you need me to do."

Mizuchi slid his finger down the map. "We need to see more of what Bael is planning, and my scouts can only see so far on the Liley side of the border. But your eyes are a bit better than ours."

"Yeah," Cam said, straightening. "Can't I just use my Sight

to do recon for you?"

"Unfortunately, no. Bael knows everything that occurs in his borders—including a magical presence. But your physical eyes are enhanced." He placed a telescope in her hand. "Take this and you should be able to see all the way to Bael's castle."

"I…guess…" Cam said. She hadn't really noticed a difference in her vision, but Mizuchi seemed convinced.

"I cannot stress enough how important it is that you do not cross the border between the lands, not even with your Athtar Sight," Mizuchi said. "Bael will not hesitate to call an immediate strike. We are not yet ready to engage."

"So…why doesn't he just come now?" Cam asked.

"Because in his heart, he doesn't want war. He wants fealty and submission," Mizuchi said. "He wants us to come to him on bended knee and beg for forgiveness."

"Would you?"

"Not now," Mizuchi said. "Because I fear he would take the apology and use it to slaughter us all. This way, at least, we'll die fighting."

Cam hastily packed a few things and grabbed her macuahuitl before descending to the docks to find herself a boat and transport to the other side. She didn't want to waste energy using magic—and she still wasn't a hundred percent on the mechanics of it without Anya's watchful eye.

"So yeah, just to the other side," Cam said to the young lilin at the docks. "Then, if you could wait for me? I don't know how long I'll be, but—"

"And where the hell do you think you're going?"

Anya stood at the base of the steps, arms crossed, swords on her back, frown on her face.

"Mizuchi asked me to do some recon at the border," Cam said. "You're busy training." *Also, you haven't spoken to me in, like, three days.*

"You aren't going by yourself."

"Well, I'm not gonna sit around and wait for Bael to strike. Mizuchi needs information, I can get it for him." Cam climbed onto the boat and sat down. "Come if you want. Or don't. Doesn't matter to me."

Anya appeared on the boat and plopped down on the front, as she had when they'd left with Lotan. Cam tried not to take offense at her attitude—she was still hurting over the loss of Oce —but it was hard when she was being difficult.

Cam struck up a conversation with the lilin, a young man named Jarrod, who was two hundred years old and came from the Austrian empire. They had a wonderful conversation about historical events, which filled the time until they reached the end of the bay and the black mountains that shot up toward the sky.

Cam tilted her head backward. How she planned to get across this monstrosity in a few hours she had no idea.

"So…uh… Did you happen to bring any climbing gear?"

Anya grunted, her cheeks redder than they had been as she set foot on the black gravel beach. "We may be able to use a spot of magic after walking for a bit. It may sound counterintuitive, but the higher we climb, the better you'll feel."

The terrain was uphill, but walkable in most spots. Anya kept a quick pace, and although Cam was sweating, she felt more invigorated than tired. The air should've been getting thinner, but to Cam, it was refreshing. Like going outside after being indoors all day. Even Anya had lost some of her scowl in favor of a more neutral expression.

So Cam tested the waters a bit.

"How are you feeling?" Cam asked. "About Oce?"

The athtar's foot slipped on a rock, but she caught herself and kept walking. "I'm all right, I suppose."

"Pissed off yet? Ready to decapitate anyone?"

Anya sighed. "I think we're close enough to use magic the rest of the way. Do you remember how?"

"Yep," Cam said, allowing her to change the subject. "Use Sight. Magic. There."

"You cannot cross into Ath-kur. Not even with your Sight. Bael will know—"

"I know, Mom, gosh," Cam said, closing her eyes. Her magic hadn't fully recovered, but it certainly felt pretty spry now. The mountains opened up around her, from the tips of the snowcapped peaks to the valleys of rivers and trees. Through the stone and the air, Cam's Sight pressed further out of Liley until that line—that very clear line between the two worlds, rose up to meet her. She made sure not to cross the line, finding a spot just at the border. The world shifted under her feet as she followed her Sight, and she opened her eyes to a brand-new world.

"Wow."

It was as Mizuchi had said: there was orange desert and black mountain sand. As far as the regular eye could see. Orange and black.

And magic. Cam could *feel* the magic emanating from every grain of sand. It penetrated her skin, zipping around her veins and giving her a level of mental clarity she hadn't had in ages. As Mizuchi had said, her physical eyes could see further, another mountain range on the other side of the world coming into focus. And a castle.

"Mount Zephon," Anya whispered.

"That's where Jack is," Cam said, her heart pounding at the thought of him being so close. Well, closer than he was before.

"We can't get him yet," Anya said. "I know it's hard. But our best chance of getting him out alive is to stick to the plan."

"Look at you, Miss Following-the-plan." Cam quirked a brow. "Feeling better so close to home? Not so eager to throw yourself on Bael's sword now?"

"I still think it would be the faster route to the same outcome," she said, leaning over the rock and pressing her hand to her forehead for shade. "But Bael might be chastened if we can defeat his army. That's what I'm pinning my hopes on."

"That was a lot of mountain," Cam said, looking behind her. "I'm worried. How are we going to bring everyone across this mountainside?"

"That's Mizuchi's worry," Anya said. "We have a job to do, remember? Help me locate this army."

Mizuchi had given Cam one of his telescopes, so she pressed the lens to her eye and scanned the horizon, focusing on the castle in the distance—as well as the gathered soldiers in tents out front.

"There," she said. "In front of the castle. Do you see it?"

"No," Anya said, pulling her hand away from her forehead. Cam handed her the telescope, and she scanned the horizon. "Shit. That's more than I thought. And just in front of the castle too."

"Do you think there are more out there?"

"Absolutely," Anya said, slowly rotating to the left. "Bael will secure his castle first, then..." She pulled the telescope away from her eye. "To the north. Look. Thousands by my count."

Cam peered through the lens, hoping Anya had been exaggerating, but she hadn't been. Although it was hard to tell specifics, the numbers sent a jolt of fear down her spine. "They're right on the border."

"Exactly," Anya said. "Waiting for us at the pass."

"Where are the athtars?" Cam asked. "I only see kappas there."

"I presume living in the castle," Anya said, taking the telescope back. "They wouldn't be amongst the rabble. They'll show up right as the battle begins."

Something odd blossomed in Cam's chest, the sensation that athtar magic was quickly approaching from somewhere far away.

"*Look out!*" Anya shoved Cam to the ground just as a sword flew by their heads.

"The old Anat would have stopped my sword," came a sultry voice from above. Cam squinted in the sunlight, making out the form of a man leaning casually against a nearby boulder.

"Lazlo," Anya snarled, rising to her feet. "What rock did you crawl out from under?"

"I could say the same of you," the man said. He was pale, with brown hair and a cocky smile that raised the hair on Cam's arms. "You're looking weak. A shadow of yourself. And you think you have any chance against our King of the Five Realms? You're deluding yourself."

"And you talk too much," Cam said, pulling her macuahuitl off her back.

"Cam, stay out of this," Anya ordered.

"Ah, Bael mentioned you'd spawned a neophyte," he said, turning his attention to Cam. "She's unimpressive."

"Fuck off," Cam said. "I'm *damned* impressive."

"Well, she certainly has the athtar pride," Lazlo said. "But it doesn't matter. You know the rules, Anat, perhaps better than anyone. There will be no thirds. Bael finds them too weak to do anything with."

"I dare you to try to hurt her," Anya said.

Lazlo moved in a blur, but Anya moved with him, stopping him with her swords. She gritted her teeth and pushed, throwing him backward. He chuckled as he took a step back.

"You aren't as dead as I thought," he said. "But I also wasn't trying very hard."

Again, they moved in blurs, so fast even Cam's athtar eyes

couldn't keep up with it. She held her macuahuitl ready, her vision dancing around as the blurs shifted from one rock to another. But they never moved onto the orange sand—when Lazlo stopped there, Anya remained on the black, her gaze fierce.

"Very impressive, very impressive. From how King Bael described you, I'd expected a washed-up ghost," the other athtar said, wiping a bit of blood from his cheek. "Still no match for me, of course. I can see you huffing and puffing. Even so close to our motherland, you're still a weakling."

Anya remained silent, but there was a light sheen of sweat on her forehead. "And you're still too impressed with yourself."

"Why don't you come and fight me here? I'm sure it pains you to be so far away from your own world," Lazlo said. "Bring your spawn with you. She should see the glory of Ath-kur before she's snuffed out."

"Cam, stay put," Anya said.

"Yeah, I got that," Cam shot back.

"Mouthy, isn't she?" Lazlo said. "If I ever took a spawn, they would bow to me. Perhaps if I bring your and your spawn's heads on a platter, Lord Bael will make an exception and let me have one."

"You'll have to kill me first," Anya said, swinging her swords.

"Oh, I don't think so," Lazlo said, his gaze turning to Cam. Her blood ran cold as his smile twisted upward. "Do you remember my special skill, Anat? In your absence, I've perfected the art. Shall I show you?"

Electric pain shot from Cam's midsection to every corner of

her body. Her insides screamed as if she were being pulled apart bit by bit, her nerve endings sizzling and popping with agony.

"*Get the fuck away from her!*"

The pain stopped, and Cam gripped the ground with weak fingers, staring at the sky. With great effort, she turned her head to the two athtars—Anya stricken, Lazlo gleeful.

"You don't like that, Anat?" Lazlo said. "You used to look the other way when I used it on the humans. Oh, how they'd scream. How they'd *beg* for death." His grin widened. "Your human begged for death. Jack is his name?"

Anya's growled. "You son of a bitch."

"He's feisty," Lazlo said with a low chuckle. "Found him trying to escape once." His smile grew cruel. "King Bael let me punish him mightily. How the man cr—"

The words had died in the athtar's throat and all movement ceased. He was frozen in time—overpowered by Anya's magic.

"It seems I'm more powerful than I gave myself credit for." Her voice was low, calm. Deadly. "Or you just pissed me off too much. Don't touch my polluelo. And don't touch my Jack."

The athtar twitched, a sign that her hold on him was weakening.

With a mighty roar, Anya sliced his head off. The energy crackled and dissipated into the air then left nothing but Anya's breathing and the painful stinging of Cam's body.

"Are you all right?" Anya said, dropping her swords and rushing over to Cam. "I'm so sorry. I couldn't stop him."

"You stopped him plenty," Cam said, allowing Anya to help

her sit up. The pain was subsiding, but slowly. "What the fuck did he do to me?"

"It's difficult to explain, but it's a way of using athtar magic for torture," Anya said. "Lazlo's specialty."

"Did that son of a bitch say he used it on Jack?" Cam asked, opening and closing her hands. They still stung like every bone was shattered, but everything seemed to be working properly.

Anya's hand twitched at her back. "It could be a lie."

"Do you want to believe that or do you actually believe that?"

"I want to," she said quietly. "I don't know how long Jack could withstand that level of torture."

"Hope he's the only asshole who can do it," Cam said, looking at the body on the ground with grim pleasure. "Otherwise, we're fucked."

"I doubt he passed on his skills to someone else," Anya said, following her gaze. "Athtars aren't the type to share."

"Well, I'll say one thing: You certainly kicked his ass."

Anya looked at the horizon, frowning. "Bael must've been on the outs with him."

"Why?"

"Because he's not here, decapitating me," Anya said, standing and helping Cam gingerly to her feet. "He would have known the moment Lazlo died and he would've been here if it wasn't what he wanted."

"Unless he's too chicken shit to face you himself," Cam said, shaking her arms to loosen the rest of the pain. Perhaps it was being so close to Ath-kur, but her body was recovering quickly. "How powerful was that athtar?"

"Fairly," Anya said, doubt creeping into her features. "Not as powerful as Bael."

"So..." Cam tilted her head. "You overpowered him. And he's more powerful than me."

"Only because..." Anya actually smiled, a self-loathing one. "Because he was hurting you. Because he hurt Jack."

"And Ekur was going to kill Jack," Cam said. "So maybe you just need to focus on killing Bael for other people? I'll dangle myself in front of him, and it'll get you all riled up."

"Cam, be serious."

"I am serious," she said. "And while I think you *should* want to take him out for *yourself,* getting angry because he's hurting other people works too. However you get there, you get there."

"Perhaps," Anya said. "Let's get back to Kastali and report what we've seen here. The good news is we only have to deal with four hundred and sixty athtars now."

"Hooray..."

CHAPTER THIRTY

It had been three sunrises and sunsets since Bael had tortured Jack with the vision of Sara's death. Or perhaps it had been ongoing. Every time Jack closed his eyes, he saw her bloody body, listened to her screams of pain. Her cries for help scratched at his mind, leaving bloody trails all the way down to his aching heart.

For weeks after Sara died, Jack had been plagued by nightmares. They became so bad that he refused to sleep, or drank so much he wouldn't remember them. Now, without whiskey as a salve, he was left with the choice of insomnia or night terrors. He had tried to stay awake to keep the visions at bay, but inevitably fell asleep after the stress and exhaustion became too much. Then, he'd awaken, his voice raw from screaming. He was sure Bael enjoyed every moment of it.

It was difficult not to succumb to despair. His options were few—any rebellion was met with swift punishment. The physical torture he could deal with. Reliving Sara's death over and over again? Even he wasn't strong enough to withstand that. Nobody would be. Submission was a tempting, but risky, option. Bael's game seemed to be predicated on breaking him; if he was broken, what fun would it be? If Jack allowed himself to believe his wife had come back from the dead, Bael might tire of him and end his misery altogether.

And as nice as that might be, Jack still had some things to do before he died.

Bael's vision had been horrific, true, but it had left a small ray of hope. When he dreamed, Jack was back in his old life. But when he opened his eyes, he came back to the present and all that he'd experienced since. It had been full of heartbreak, sure, but at the end of it, he'd found Anya. And for that, he was almost…grateful.

They'd started small in the ashes of their past loves, but it had barely taken root before Bael whisked him away. And after seeing Sara brought back to life, he'd been sure that fragile love would be stomped out for good in grief and misery. And yet, there it was. The more he thought about it, the more it grew in his heart, a reminder that although his life had disintegrated, it hadn't ended. He could be happy again.

That thought kept him fighting.

The elokos and kappas were back serving him, arriving three times a day with meals and no conversation. Perhaps Bael was giving him a breather before the next round of torture began.

As if on cue, the door opened, and Sara walked in with food and her usual sly smile. "I heard you were a bad boy, Jackie."

Seeing her now was like getting pricked with a needle after being stabbed in the heart. Bael's torture had been Jack's worst nightmare. He used to think he could never survive reliving that pain. And yet there he was. Surviving. Breathing. Allowing himself to think about Anya when Sara stood in front of him, and not feeling guilty about it.

In a way, Bael had overshot himself. He'd taken things too far, and what used to be a tortuous affair was now merely a curiosity. With a clearer head, the demon masquerading as his late wife came into focus. She was almost too thin—Sara was willowy, but she still had a strength about her thanks to kickboxing with Cam twice a week. The breasts were bigger, too, and the butt was all wrong. Her smile was off, her eyes too close together, the way she held herself was unfamiliar. He'd been so desperate to see Sara again that he'd ignored the obvious signs this woman wasn't her.

"Do you like what you see?" Sara asked, sliding her hand across her hip. "I'll take you to bed if you promise you won't try to run away again. I don't want King Bael to have to hurt you."

"No," Jack said, shaking his head. "I was just thinking that the last time I saw you, a nox was ripping your throat out."

"Jackson, that's mean," Not-Sara said with a pout.

"My wife didn't pout," Jack said, putting his hands behind his head. "She was a Macarro, and Macarros are strong-willed and get what they want through words and action. Not batting their eyelashes."

Not-Sara opened her mouth, as if she wasn't sure what to say.

"I hate to tell you that you suck at your job, but you suck at your job," Jack said. "If you're going to impersonate someone, you might as well do it right."

"If you're going to be mean, I'm leaving," she said finally, but Jack read the worry in her eyes. She would have a bad report to give to her king. Jack might've felt bad for her, except she'd agreed to this nonsense in the first place. She'd kissed him wearing his wife's face.

And yet... "You can tell Bael I'm taking the bait, if you like."

She stopped, turning to look at him. "Excuse me?"

"If it would save you a decapitation," Jack said. "I'm sure you aren't here of your own free will. Not many people are. Of course, if you are here because you want to be..." He leveled his gaze at her. "Go fuck yourself."

She took a step back, then bristled as she hurried from the room.

Jack loosened a breath as the door shut, reveling in his victory over his own grief. He could almost picture Anya's proud smile, the same one she'd worn when he'd defeated Oce. The one she'd wear when she walked in the door to come for him and found him whole.

CHAPTER THIRTY-ONE

Cam was feeling hopeful when they returned to Kastali. Anya had defeated an athtar using her magic, and perhaps they'd unlocked the secret to getting her pissed at Bael. It made sense; Anya always seemed to put others before herself. Mother Athtar seemed a little less worried than she'd been when they'd left the lilin stronghold. She even let Cam practice using athtar magic to defend herself on the boat back to Liley—although Cam was careful to let Anya win, just in case.

When the ship sailed into the bay where Kastali rose into the sky, Cam's heart skipped a beat. A thousand boats were docked around the castle.

"I hope that's Lotan," she said.

"I'm sure you do."

"I meant—"

"I know what you meant," Anya said with something of a smile. "Connection, remember?"

"Man, I'm going to be *super* happy when that goes away."

When they arrived, the castle was teeming with demons coming in and out of the boats, tripping over each other carrying tons of weapons. One passed too close to Cam and nausea washed over her.

"Watch it!" Anya barked at the eloko, who jumped at the sight of her and ran off. "You okay?"

"Yeah," Cam said, feeling better as the creatures wandered away. "What the hell happened?"

"Looks like the weapons have the talisman engraved on them," Anya said. "C'mon, let's get upstairs and out of this muck."

She did the magical honors, sliding them through rock and air to Freyja's bedchambers. The world faded into view as Lotan, Izel, Mizuchi, and Freyja stood hunched over a map in deep discussion. None of them had noticed their arrival. It was nice to be on this side of things, versus being the one surprised.

"...tomorrow, but only if they leave right now through the tunnels," Lotan said.

"Then give the order. I'd prefer to have them in place now."

"Who?" Anya said, wearing a smirk.

Both Lotan and Izel reached for their weapons. When they realized who stood before them, Izel's face melted into annoyance, but Lotan beamed, especially when his gaze landed on Cam.

"Welcome back," Mizuchi said, sounding a little winded from the scare. "I trust your mission was successful?"

"Even more than we could've anticipated," Cam said. "We encountered an athtar, and Anya kicked his ass."

"Who?" Freyja asked.

"Lazlo," Anya replied, stalking further into the room. "He gave me a little trouble, but I was able to overpower him."

"That's outstanding," Lotan said. "And what news of Bael's army?"

"It's as you suspected, Mizuchi," Anya said, leaning over the map. "There's a legion of them here, right at the border. They have the upper hand. This whole area is difficult to sneak into. They'll be able to see us coming for days."

"They haven't yet," Lotan said.

Anya removed her finger from the map. "What are you talking about?"

"I'm afraid we haven't been entirely truthful with you two," Mizuchi said, placing a chip on the table just to the north of where Anya and Cam had gone. "Izel and Tabiko have been overseeing the amassment of kappa, lilin, and nox soldiers in a pass between the mountains. We've constructed a glamour with kappa and lilin miasma to hide from Bael. There are ten thousand strong waiting on our command to move into Ath-kur."

Cam couldn't believe her ears. "So why did you send us to

spy on Bael?"

"A decoy," Mizuchi said. "With Lotan's return, we wanted to divert attention. Make Bael think we were in the beginning stages of our attack plan, versus ready to pounce."

"Do you think it worked?" Anya asked.

"We won't know until tomorrow," Lotan said. "The last soldiers I brought will be in position by daybreak."

"And how the hell are you going to do that?" Cam asked.

Freyja leaned over the map, pointing to a thin pencil line. "There's a river that flows from the bay here, all the way to this lake close to the border. It's been my secret for many centuries." Freyja smirked. "And none of my seconds have betrayed us yet."

"But time is of the essence," Lotan said. "Every day, Bael recovers more from Demon Spring. Tomorrow, we make our move."

Anya clicked her tongue, placing her hands on her hips to look at him. "You were going to go forward with this plan whether I helped or not?"

"I'll admit our chances improved dramatically when you two showed up," Lotan replied with a grim smile. "But…yes. This has always been our plan."

"It would've been suicide," she said. "It still might be."

"It's better than the alternative," Freyja said. "We have been living too long subject to his whims and tantrums. Spawn killed without a second glance. Nunzia's death was unwarranted, as was Rosemary's, and Jonathon's, and every other lilin lord he decided to slaughter." Her eyes grew white. "Thousands of their spawn reverted to human or worse. Simply because he felt the desire to show off his power."

"This war has been coming a long time," Mizuchi said with a solemn nod. "But, of course, we would prefer to have your help. Agent Macarro's talisman discovery was a welcome addition to our forces as well."

"I've spent the last few years looking for demons in the human realm sympathetic to our cause, and bringing them through our schism," Lotan said. "The latest group includes more than a few elokos from the southern United States willing to fight against Bael and their belu."

"I'm sure Parras was totally fine with that," Cam said.

"Parras is dead," Lotan replied softly. "From what I can tell, he lasted an hour after the schism was closed. Seems Bael's directives are only adhered to when the athtar is around to enforce them."

Cam shook her head. "The Division is probably having a hell of a time right now."

"I checked in on the humans as well," Lotan said with a wink. "They're still busy cleaning up after Atlanta, and paying very little mind to the intrademonic conflict. As it should be."

"Izel has nearly completed equipping our army with talismans," Mizuchi said. "Every weapon on the battlefield will have the mark inscribed on it. Bael will be expecting an army of five thousand. We will give him an army of fifteen with talisman magic."

"Plus hundreds of arrows to dull their magical abilities," Izel replied with a proud smile to Lotan.

"Sounds like we might not be so fucked after all," Cam said with a grin to Anya.

"Don't count on it," Anya said, but it was less glum than usual. "There's still Bael to contend with."

"We hope that your progress has been swift then," Lotan said cautiously.

"Not as swift as I'd like," Anya said. "But we cannot sit on this much longer. Bael will strike first if he thinks he's in danger. The only thing keeping him in Ath-kur is that he believes himself invincible. In that vein, once we attack, he will try to draw our armies into the world, believing we won't kill him as long as we all remain there."

"Why not?" Cam asked.

"Because if he's slain in Ath-kur, the armies will go down with him when the land fractures," Lotan said. "But our armies know this, and are still willing to take the chance."

Cam straightened. "Wait a minute. Are you saying that the whole 'world disintegration thing' happens *immediately*? As in... everyone who's in Ath-kur when Bael is killed will die?"

"We will do our best to minimize the casualties," Lotan said.

Cam couldn't believe what she was hearing. "How much time after the noxes were slain did you have to get out of the noxlands?"

"The fracture happened almost immediately," Anya replied quietly.

"So use your magic to get the hell out of there," Cam said.

"If I kill Bael, I, along with every athtar, will revert to human," Anya said. "And my feeling is Bael will nestle himself deep in Ath-kur to seal my fate."

"That can't be right," Cam said. "You can't all be…"

No wonder Anya had been so reticent. No wonder she'd made Cam promise to get Jack to safety. Cam was only surprised she hadn't put the pieces together sooner.

"We will do our best to retrieve you, Anat," Lotan said, although he was staring at Cam when he said it.

"Don't bother. You should ensure your armies remain close to the Liley border so they can make a hasty escape," Anya said, standing. Her face was a mask of resolute certainty as she stared at the map. "Give the signal. We're moving in at dawn."

It was as if everything in the castle went into high speed. Lotan's army rushed here and there, gathering weapons and provisions. Freyja's boats came and went from the shore, ferrying the collection of noxes, lilins, kappas, and elokos.

The presence of athtar talismans sent Cam retreating to her bedroom, watching the activity from high above. It was odd to know with certainty that war would be starting in the morning. Like the night before a big exam, only Cam and everyone she'd grown fond of might end up dead.

And even if they were successful, Anya would still die. It was grossly unfair. Despite everything, Cam had grown a little fond of the moody woman. Anya deserved the chance to be happy with Jack. She deserved to have a guy who didn't want anything from her except to love the hell out of her.

The door opened, and Anya walked in carrying a map. "I need to show you the castle."

"Castle?"

"Where to find Jack." She looked up at Cam without any emotion. "You do still want to get him back, right?"

"You're going to let me go on my own?" Cam said, although it seemed a dumb question to ask.

"I'm not letting you do anything," Anya said. "As you've said many times before. Besides that, I have other things to worry about. Namely, drawing Bael's attention so the rest of the army can get in position. He wants a show for the masses, and that's what I'll give him."

Cam's smile faded. "Are you really going to die tomorrow? Like really?"

"We could all die tomorrow, Cam."

"But I mean, even if you're successful. Especially if you're successful. You're...you're okay with dying?"

"It's a fitting end," Anya said. "Even if I kill Bael, I still killed others. Ten thousand innocent lives."

"But..." Cam frowned, but Anya squeezed her hand and smiled.

"This is what I want. And if I think for a moment that it won't be how it is, I'll lose my nerve. So let's just focus on the castle."

Anya laid out a map she'd drawn on a large piece of parchment paper. There were several circles and scratches where she'd written notes to herself and changed her mind, and three spots where "Jack?" was written.

"There's one of three places Bael would've stashed him," Anya said. "One is my old room—it's where Jack was held before. He could also choose a room on the western wing of the castle, high on the mountain. Or he could be in the bottom of the castle, if Bael's decided to let him live in squalor." She tapped the map. "I believe he's in the western side. Gut feeling."

"Listening to those now, are we?" Cam asked.

"Impending death will do that to you." Anya slid her fingers to the bottom of the map. "You won't be able to go straight into his room. The safest place to sneak into the castle using your magic is here." She pointed to a spot at the bottom of the map. "It's a wine cellar. You'll still have to go through the castle, so be careful. It's imbued with athtar magic, so if you think something looks strange, it probably is. Bael doesn't like the servants to travel too far out of their duty area, so he sets traps. Keep your hand against the stone wall to ground yourself."

"This sounds like a carnival funhouse," Cam said. "Except the clowns are athtar demons intent on killing me."

"Well, that's the good news," Anya said. "Bael will come for me. His athtars will come for the army. The castle will most likely be protected by one or two athtars, but they may rush to join the battle if they find it's not turning in their favor."

"What if they don't?" Cam said.

"You won't be that noticeable in Ath-kur," Anya said. "It will be easy for you to hide in the shadows and stay out of sight.

I'm more concerned with the others in the castle who might be guarding Jack. It's imperative that no one knows you've got Jack until you're safely back in Liley—"

"Hang on. Liley? We're going to help you guys."

"No, you're not," Anya said. "You promised me—"

"Jack won't go for that."

"Jack is human. You are an athtar neophyte. You will bring him back to Liley, then continue to the human realm. As we agreed."

Cam licked her lips, seeing right through Anya's stern look. "He'll want to see you."

"We don't always get what we want," she said, staring at the map. "Eventually, he'll understand it was in his best interest. It's important to put space between him and Bael." She closed her hand over Cam's. "Please, promise me you won't seek me out."

"I'm not going to make that promise," Cam said, wrenching her hand away. "But I'll promise you I'll guard Jack with my life. And I'll get him back to the human realm. As long as *you* promise me you'll try to meet us there. That you'll try to kill Bael and not just…die."

"Cam, that's not…" Anya sighed. "I don't want to make promises I can't keep."

"You can promise to try."

"I have been trying," Anya said. "I've been thinking a lot about our history. About the moments when I thought about leaving him for good. The times when he scared me, or when he…" She swallowed and her eyes hardened. "When he struck me in anger. But every single memory of him is surrounded by the other memories. The times when there was nothing but us and our love."

"But it was all a lie," Cam said.

"It was a good lie," Anya said. "I believed it."

"So stop believing it."

"I'm trying, Cam. I'm trying so hard. But every time I reach for that anger, all I feel is disgust at myself."

"You were abused, Anya. That shit doesn't go away in a day or a week. In your case, it may take a hundred years or more." Cam smiled. "But that doesn't mean you can't get control of your own life. You deserve to be happy."

Anya sat back and stared out the window, something uncertain in her gaze. "I could've been happy. With Jack. But I never allowed myself to be. If I'd known that the outcome would've been the same, I would've kissed him the night he saved me in Brussels."

"He saved you in Brussels?"

She nodded. "We'd been captured by an eloko lord. I'd just told him that my magic was depleted and he was furious. But he still found a way to extricate us both from the situation." Her eyes grew wet. "He could have just saved himself and let me go. He had every right to walk away. But he took my hand and promised me we'd figure out my curse together. Even though I'm sure he knew it wasn't even real. He stayed. He stayed because he cared about what happened to me. He cared about *me*." She exhaled and let a tear fall down her face before wiping it away quickly. "I don't want to die not ever knowing what it is to really be loved. Jack was right, I have…I have no idea what that feels like."

"Then don't die," Cam said. "Because I promise you, if you let him, Jack will make you forget all about Bael. Spend one week with our families and you'll have more love than you know what to do with. You think my grandmother was a lot to deal with? Just wait until you meet my mom. And oh, man, are you in for some serious fussing over when you meet Karen, Jack's mom. But first, we all have to make it back home." Her chest tightened. "For what it's worth, I do give you my seal of approval. You're allowed to date Jack."

Anya burst into laughter, something Cam had never heard from the demon. Even Cam had to admit, it sounded ridiculously normal, like something from a life long ago.

"Speaking of approvals," she said with a smile. "Lotan has requested you join him in his room for dinner. Or whatever. Be a shame not to take him up on it."

Cam's eyes bulged. "You're going to probably die in battle tomorrow and you're telling me to go get laid?" She furiously shook her head. "Nuh-uh. We're going to have a girls' night. We're going to get drunk and cry and talk about our feelings and —"

"And I need time to myself to think," Anya said. "I would regret it more if you didn't go to Lotan tonight. Don't worry." She patted her chest. "I understand all that you feel about tomorrow's events. But I also know you're holding a torch for the nox prince. Like I said, Freyja would be pissed if someone didn't get laid soon. Might as well be you and Lotan."

"Are you…" Cam swallowed. "Are you sure?"

"Go," Anya said, squeezing her hand.

CHAPTER THIRTY-TWO

The full weight of the impending battle in the morning settled on Cam as she walked away from Anya. Would that be the last time she saw her? Would Cam be successful in retrieving Jack? Would Jack even still be alive, or would Bael kill him the moment they declared war?

She was so wrapped up in her thoughts she didn't even realize she'd wandered down to Lotan's side of the castle. There was no one to tell her which door was his, but she heard voices coming out of a cracked door close to the end of the hall.

"...who gives a shit if he's encroaching? Do they not understand what we're up against right now? I can't be mediating every little spat."

"They still need an answer, Prince."

He sighed wearily, as if he thought this entire conversation was bullshit. "Cosgrove can take over the district. Dominique can take Richmond through the Virginia border." He paused. "Of course, this conversation could be moot if I die tomorrow, you realize that, right?"

"I'll pass on your direction," came the tired response.

The cracked door opened fully, and Cam froze. The nox on the other side stared at her, surprised for a moment, then looked over her shoulder.

"You have a guest, Prince."

"Oh, excellent." Lotan was seated at a large round table covered with papers. He beamed at Cam, but his cheshire cat smile was muted, tinged with worry and nerves. "Come in, Cam. I'm glad you received my message. Alain, can you tell the kitchen to send up dinner?"

Cam entered the room as the other nox left, and jumped when the door shut behind her.

"I apologize for the mess," Lotan said, running a hand through his curly locks. "And for not having dinner ready for you. Time slipped away from me. It's incredible how much monotony goes into being a nox prince." He gathered the various papers on the table. "I hadn't quite considered what would happen when I unseated Vicente, but it created a power vacuum and now his seconds are fighting amongst each other."

She chuckled. "Maybe you *should* hire me as your leadership consultant. Haven't you ever removed a lord from power before?"

"No. And that will probably be the last time I ever do it." He held up the papers. "I've spent the past three hours divvying up his properties amongst his people. I've never signed my name so many times." He deposited the papers on another table in the corner with others and turned to her with his smile fully restored. "You don't have to stay next to the wall. Unless that's where you prefer to be?"

Cam peeled herself off the wall and entered the room. "I gotta say, this is…weird to me."

"How so?" he asked, pulling a chair out for her.

"I mean tomorrow is going to be heavy," Cam said. "Anya's going to war, I'm going to get Jack. We could all be dead in twenty-four hours."

"Even more reason you and I should take tonight to have our long overdue dinner date," Lotan said, procuring a bottle of wine from a box on the other side of the room. "I know you're partial to wine, *period*, but you did enjoy that Bordeaux wine in the noxlands, right?"

"Yeah," Cam said, flushing at the thought of him remembering a throwaway comment like that. She readily took the glass from him and sipped to steady her nerves. It didn't help.

"Why do you look so nervous?" Lotan asked, taking his seat across from her. "I promise I won't eat you." He winked. "Unless you want me to."

Cam choked on her wine.

He laughed, throwing his head back. "You can relax, Cam."

"Can I? Because here we are, planning intrademonic war and you're trying to woo me with grand gestures, and sweet words, and wine, and dinner. I can do warfare or I can do romance—I can't do both."

Lotan's eyebrows lifted in surprise. Then, he leaned over the table and captured her lips in a kiss.

"Let's do romance tonight, then," he whispered.

She was too tongue-tied to respond, so with a pleased chuckle, he crossed the room once more to retrieve a garment box wrapped in brown paper, which he deposited in her lap.

"What the hell is this?" Cam said, finally finding her tongue.

"It is, as I understand it, what humans refer to as a present," he said with a devilish grin as he took his place beside her again. "I believe one is supposed to rip the paper to see the contents."

"Yes, I know," Cam said, pursing her lips at him. "But why did you get it for me?"

"Does it bother you?" he asked, toying with one of Cam's curls, sending shoots of electricity down her spine. "Why don't you open it and see what it is? Then you can decide if you're angry with me."

Cam slid her finger along the paper, carefully opening the box, then stopped. "At least give me some kind of context here. Is this a 'we're all going to die' gift? Or is it a 'maybe we'll survive'?"

He huffed and continued unwrapping the box for her. "My mother told me that a soldier should never go into battle without her armor."

Cam placed her hands on top of his. "I'm not wearing nox armor."

"Just open the damned box, Camilla."

After thumbing the flaps, she carefully peeled open the box and dug through the tissue paper until her hands hit something…familiar. Vinyl and crinkly. She lifted the object up, revealing her Division jacket.

"Your armor, my lady," Lotan said, wiping away the tear on her cheek before she even knew it was there.

"Are you serious?" she whispered, running her fingers along the material. It was her jacket, right down to the receipt for a Circle K coffee balled up in the pocket from Charleston. "I don't even remember where I left this. How did you find it? How did you *get* it here?"

"I had to pull a few strings," he said. "Sent one of my lieutenants to your grandmother's house on bended knee. Apparently she has a talisman protecting her house?"

"Yeah, she does," Cam said, another tear falling down her face. "Why'd you do this?"

"Because every lady—"

"No, Lotan," she said, clutching the jacket to her chest. "Why did you do this?"

His smirk faded, and for the first time since she'd met him, he looked uncertain of himself as he knelt in front of her. "Because despite what you might think, I'm quite taken with you, Camilla Macarro."

"You realize that if we're successful and I go back to the human realm," she said, running her finger over the patch. "I'm going to Shanghai to continue researching my talismans. Including the nox one. And if Bael dies, I'll probably turn them into standard-issue weapons for all Division agents."

"Well," he said, placing his hands on top of hers and stroking them with his thumbs, "nobody's perfect. I can only hope that you'd never use it on me."

"I'd hope you never give me a reason to," she said.

He stood and pulled her to her feet. "As long as you promise never to resort to it during our lovers' quarrels, of which I'm sure there will be many."

"Don't argue with me, and there won't be any quarrels."

"But arguing with you is half the fun," he whispered, sliding his hand along her cheek and leaning down to kiss her once more. She let him slip his tongue between her lips, sighing in happiness. She couldn't remember the last time she'd been kissed like this. When someone had put in this much effort. But this was dangerous territory—presents as thoughtful and kind as this only led to heartbreak down the road. She pushed him back.

"Lotan, I don't know if this is smart. I mean, we're like… two different species."

"You have an athtar demon implanted in here." He tapped his finger against her chest. "I've got a nox here. The rest is fairly compatible, so I assume…" He took her chin. "But if you're truly averse to this, I'll stop."

Averse? Not in the least. Cam had been thinking about

taking the nox demon from the moment she laid eyes on him. But thinking about and doing it were two different things, especially because in the thinking, Cam couldn't get hurt.

"I just really don't want to get my heart broken," she said.

"What makes you think I'd do that?"

"Because you're a nox, immortal, and the prince." Cam swallowed. "And I really like you a lot. More than I probably should."

"Mm-hm. And I've already confessed that I am very fond you, Cam. In fact, I might even be falling in love with you, if I could say that without you bolting out of the room."

She swallowed. She'd been told that someone loved her before. Usually two weeks before they headed for the exit.

He pulled her into his lap, slinging an arm low around her hips and gazing up at her with an almost longing look. "And there's a good chance Bael will kill us all, so I would hate for our last night to be us wondering whether we should or we shouldn't."

"Well, Anya told me to 'fuck him until I can't see straight,'" she said, her face growing warmer by the moment. "So how about that?"

Lotan laughed, the sound echoing in the room and filling Cam with a sense of lightness. "I have to thank Mother Athtar for her kindness. It would be a shame to disobey her, hm?"

She expected him to kiss her just then, but he didn't. For as much as he'd been insinuating, he was waiting for her to make the first move. And perhaps he was right, they could die tomorrow. Might as well have some fun before the end.

"Well, let's just get this over with," she said, pulling off her shirt and walking to his bed. She flopped onto the sheets in her bra and underwear, crawling up to the pillows and waiting.

"That has to be the first time a woman has ever said that to me." Lotan followed her to the bed, stripping down as he went. "And you've denied me the pleasure of undressing you."

"It's been a while since I've had romance, so you'll have to forgive me," Cam said, warming at his touch when he joined her on the bed. "I find it all a little ridiculous sometimes."

"I'll do my best to change your mind on the subject," he said, placing his hands on her hips. Yet even with the light touch, he hadn't. Cam supposed she would have to break the ice.

She kissed him, sliding her fingers across his cheek and tangling them in his black curls. His hair was soft and bouncy, his lips gentle against hers. There was no urgency behind it, and Cam rather liked the lazy way he moved.

"Tell me what you like," Lotan purred in her ear. "I'm very curious to see Cam with her hair down."

"It's been a while, I told you," Cam said, curling her toes as he pressed a kiss to her neck. "I might've forgotten."

"I think you know," Lotan said. "But you don't want to tell me. That's fine, I'm sure it will come out eventually. I'm a very patient man. Especially when it comes to you."

"Before we take this any further," Cam said. "Got any condoms?"

"Of course," Lotan said, rolling over onto his stomach and

digging in the bedside table drawer. Cam got a nice view of his ass, which was perfectly shaped like the rest of him.

"Take a lot of girls to your bed, then?" Cam asked, as he pulled out a long strip of them.

"Oh, no," Lotan replied coming back with one. "Freyja keeps every room stocked. She is the lust demon, you know. Safety is important."

"And how much of this," Cam said, as he placed the condom on the bed next to them, "is due to Freyja?"

"I'm sure this incessant need to be inside you is partially due to the lilin magic," Lotan said, returning to her side. "But I found you immensely attractive the moment I first laid eyes on you." He kissed the underside of her ear. "A mere human standing in a den of noxes. I thought to myself, who is this woman?"

Cam couldn't stop the grin that blossomed on her face as he trailed kisses down her neck. "You were pretty cute yourself."

"Then, when I saw you again, standing in the jungle with Anat, ordering her about," he whispered, sliding his tongue between her breasts as he trailed lines down her body. "I had to know more about you. I still want to know more about you."

"I think you know me pretty well by now," she replied, arching her back to his touch.

The kissing and stroking abruptly ceased. "I believe I've merely scratched the surface."

She tilted her head, catching his gaze. "You think so?"

He rested his chin on her stomach, and she lazily tangled a

hand in his hair. "I believe I could live another fifteen hundred years and still find more pieces of you."

"Now you're just trying to butter me up," Cam said. "And I hate to break it to you, but I'm not going to live that long, so you'd better get some Cliffs Notes or something."

He made his way back to capture her lips while slipping a finger inside her. "Less talking then, more lovemaking."

She winked at him, ready to take things a bit further. "Then lie down."

He obliged with a sly grin, and it was her turn to crawl on top of him. She wrapped her hand around his shaft, and his breath hitched with each gentle stroke. She straddled his hips, guiding him inside her slowly and breathing through the tightness until she settled against him.

"How did I know you'd end up on top?" he said, resting his hands on her hips.

"Problem?"

"I get to watch you." He smiled. "No problems at all."

She moved slowly at first, getting a rhythm down. Lotan was content to let her take control, pressing his thumbs into her hip bones as her pace quickened. She clenched around him, warmth growing from her fingers to her toes. She released a moan when he began to rub her sensitive core, just as a wave of pleasure pulsed through her. Her body shuddered, and she pressed her hands into his chest, resting for a moment.

"That was pretty good," she said with a chuckle.

"Pretty good?" Lotan asked with a frown. "Not incredible?

We will have to do better, my love." He sat up, holding onto her as they moved together. "May I take over?"

"By all means."

"No," he pulled her down to a hair's breadth from him, "may I take over?"

A chill skated down her spine, but she wasn't nervous. He had given her all the space to be nervous and cautious, and now she was ready to see what they could really do. "By all means."

He kissed her—and there was nothing sweet, gentle, or slow about it. This was passion, the way he opened her mouth against his, the way his fingers somehow reached every inch of her body. Without words, he pulled her across the bed and positioned her on her hands and knees.

"Really?" Cam said with a snort.

He answered with a deep thrust, sending a jolt all the way down to her toes. His movements came hard and quick, but Cam couldn't complain. Her knees wobbled with pleasure, so he slid a loose arm around her to hold her up—and slipped a finger through her folds. The feeling was indescribable, her head light and her body barely able to keep up as he whispered her name with every movement.

With a loud grunt that sounded more like a whine, he fell forward, surrounding her with his arms and chest. His breaths were heavy on her neck, and his sweaty stomach slid against her skin. He kissed her cheek and snaked a hand around her midsection.

"How was that?" he asked.

"Fucking awesome," she replied.

He laughed and fell to the side, taking her with him as they collapsed onto the bed together. There was a breathless, light smile on his face that took years of worry off his face. And for the first time, he wasn't the nox prince, not a powerful demon who struck fear in the hearts of humans—now, he was just Lotan, a guy she'd rather grown fond of, and one who made her feel like she was the only woman on earth.

He tilted his head toward her. There was something behind his smile, something a little terrifying. Something that told Cam if they survived all this, she was going to have a regular visitor to her house and bed. And most terrifying of all: Cam found herself excited by the prospect.

Cam needed to lighten the mood—she was getting a little too emotional. So she propped herself up on one arm and poked the nox in his sweaty chest.

"I must confess," she said, imitating his deep voice, "I take it as a point of pride that I can elicit such a face from someone so fearless."

He laughed and pulled her to him, kissing her forehead. "Make no mistake. I am woefully under-equipped to deal with you."

"I think your equipment is just fine," Cam said with a sly grin.

He kissed her roughly on the lips before leaning back into the pillows with a satisfied sigh. "You're incredible, Cam. An incredible, terrifying, amazing woman."

"Now you're just trying to get me to sleep with you again," Cam said, tracing her fingers along his chest. Tomorrow threatened to crawl into her mind, and she did her best to push it away.

"I confess, I have a burning desire to see more of you, Agent Macarro," he said, pressing his cheek to her forehead.

"I think I might like that," Cam said. She decided to ignore the questions about what might happen if she dated an immortal being when she was human, and also what might happen to her career at ICDM if they found out. Instead, she tilted her head to look at this beautiful man who seemed smitten with *just her* and let herself fall deeper into bliss. "But for now, why don't we continue this date? I think I might have remembered a few more things I like…"

CHAPTER THIRTY-THREE

Another flush of excitement and pleasure ruminated through the athtar connection and Anya rolled her eyes. How much longer Cam would continue with Lotan, she had no idea, but that certainly answered how Bael knew the intimate details about her and Jack. This connection was highly intrusive, and she wished for the millionth time she could turn it off.

The giddiness settled strangely against her present mood of morbidity, reminding her of all the things she'd missed out on in her very long life. Cam's hesitation was gone, the only thing left was the full-throated affection and acceptance of something beautiful.

Anya had been given something similarly beautiful in Jack,

and she'd spent every moment with him wondering what the consequence would be. She'd never looked at him with unfettered love, never spent a night curled in his arms without worrying what tomorrow would bring. And perhaps because she knew her fate was sealed, she found herself wondering what might have been.

She allowed herself to daydream of a utopia where she and Jack were free to live as they pleased—however far-fetched that seemed. Visions of rebuilding their lives together, of settling in a small home somewhere—eating fondue often and making love even more often.

A tear snaked down her cheek.

Jack had talked a lot about how helping her had given him something to live for. But lying in bed now, replaying memories of their brief, wonderful adventure together, Anya realized that it was *he* who'd given *her* a reason to live.

The centuries following Asherah's death had been one long, bloody nightmare. When Bael opened the schism, Anya lost her mind, killing and slaughtering as many humans as she could get her hands on. Bael reveled in her viciousness, goading and celebrating every bloody crusade. Even the athtars, who'd thought her simply Bael's whore (though not to her face), began to respect her as a warrior and a worthy companion to their king.

No matter how many humans she killed or how Bael praised her, it never filled the hole in her heart, though. She was grateful Bael had never asked her for another child, but since the noxes were dead, there was no danger of the other belus creating their own. Freyja, Mizuchi, and Biloko had spread themselves too thin across the human realm, and didn't hold a candle to Bael. The nox prince Lotan had been hidden away in the noxlands and they barely heard a peep from them in the years that followed. Not that Anya wanted to even remember they existed.

"My love, it's time for us to return to the human realm," Bael said one day, kissing her temple. "I have heard talk that the humans have been warring again. Shall we see what carnage they've wrought? See if we can make it a little worse?"

"Of course," she replied.

She'd followed their usual course of action—praising him for his show of power when he created the schism, standing beside him when he faced the humans, killing the local lilin lord who'd pissed Bael off. She added the deaths to her body count, now over ten thousand.

"I am off to speak with the humans," Bael said, adjusting his collar. "Will you be long in your destruction?"

"I always am."

It had become her escape, to leave Bael for the entirety of Demon Spring. The one time she could breathe freely and do as she pleased without him looking over her shoulder. She knew she was never truly free—not with the contingent of athtars traveling with her and reporting back to Bael. But it was something.

They sliced a bloody path through the southern United States, still rebuilding from the Civil War. Anya reveled in rubbing salt in their wounds, making her own pain less by making theirs more.

Using her magic, they arrived in New Orleans, long rumored to be a city where one could find pleasures and vices. The local demons welcomed them with open arms and Anya took to the place. She drank herself silly with the athtars, slept with the local lilins, and woke up regretting both only to do it again the next evening. Bael cared little for pure carnal relations—for that was all it was. Anya felt nothing for those she fucked or those she killed.

Until one night, she fell into bed with the wrong sort.

The man had been handsome, and said all the right words to keep Anya interested. She'd been too drunk to notice he wasn't demonic, and when he'd brought his friends, she just thought it the more the merrier.

But when she awoke the next morning, a strange necklace was around her neck.

"I wouldn't," came the voice of the man she'd shared a bed with. "If you take that off, it will cause you unimaginable pain."

"W…what the hell is it?" Anya said, sitting up. "And who the hell are you?"

"My name is Jean-Luc Broussard," he said. "And I am part of a secret society of humans who fight against demons."

"It's not so secret," Anya grunted, her head throbbing from a hangover.

"We're not with the Anti-Demon League," he said. "We believe demons should be stopped by any means possible. And you, Lady Anat, have just been stopped."

"What are you talking about?" Anya said. "What is this thing you put on me?"

"How many innocent lives have you taken, Lady? Last night you boasted ten thousand."

"Ten thousand, seven hundred, and forty-two."

"And that is the number you will have to save for that curse to be broken," he said. "Otherwise, you will die a slow and painful death."

And Anya had believed him without hesitation. Perhaps it was true was Mizuchi had said; she was always looking for an easy solution. Instead of leaving Bael on her own, she could blame the curse, and maintain deniability of her culpability.

She'd clung to this convenient excuse until she'd crossed paths with a handsome man in a coffee shop.

At the time, she'd been furious with herself for being seen by a pair of Division operatives. They'd been clumsy and that man was about ready to have his head removed, so she'd thought them innocent humans. But once ICDM caught wind she was alive, it was only a matter of time before Bael came for her.

Therefore, she couldn't understand why she kept finding excuses to meet up with the brown-eyed human with a thousand-megawatt smile. But it wasn't a happy smile—Anya saw the same sadness she carried in her heart on his face, in his eyes. Perhaps that was why she was so drawn to him, despite her smarter instincts.

And he'd been drawn to her, staying even when it was ludicrous. Even when he was a wanted fugitive. Even with the threat of Bael and death and torture, he'd stood by her side, ready to accept any punishment for the sin of loving her.

He was the exact opposite of her. Brave, loyal. He loved with every bit of his heart, even when it meant it would be shattered. He tried so hard to be the best partner, agent, son, friend he could be. And even when he fell short, he got back up and tried again.

Damn, she wished he was there to encourage her. She wished he was there so she could tell him how she really felt.

There was a very good chance that would never happen. And, maybe on some level, she was convinced Jack was too good for her. He deserved someone like his late wife, a pristine woman without any baggage. Someone who would love him with her entire heart and never look back.

But he wanted *her*.

If there was no curse, then she'd made her own decisions. Could still make her own decisions. She'd chosen to leave Bael, and she'd chosen to stay with Jack. Chosen to develop feelings for him—maybe even fall in love with him.

And now she could choose to make her wrongs right. Even if it meant she could never have the one thing she wanted.

She rose to her feet and found the weapons bag that kept appearing in her things. She hadn't taken it from the noxlands, but somehow, Lotan had returned with it in hand. Each of the weapons inside were precious now, since Oce was no longer around to make more. She was grateful Lotan or whomever had returned them to her.

The one piece Oce hadn't made was the bejeweled sword. Oce had once said she carried too much emotional baggage with it. Even now, Anya could almost see the faces of the innocents she'd killed reflected in the steel.

She fastened the sword to her hips, the weight anchoring her to her purpose. To the lives she would be repenting for. Ten thousand, seven hundred, and forty-two souls.

Numbly, she used her Sight to locate the nox Izel in the castle, then transported herself down to the docks. She appeared in the midst of a frenzy of activity, the preparations for war. It reminded Anya of Demon Springs before, when Bael would gather the demonic forces for battle.

A box of weapons passed by, and Anya swayed slightly.

"Can I help you with something, Lady Anat?" Izel said. "We're quite busy here."

"Yes," Anya said. "I'm going to the border. I'd like to scope out the area before the morning."

"The prince has given us orders to remain here," Izel responded.

Cam took that exact moment to send another glorious jolt of pleasure down Anya's spine. "Ah, I think he's a little busy right now."

Izel caught the look on her face and rolled her eyes. "About damned time. Boy has been been going on about your spawn for days now."

"I'll be sure not to tell him you called him boy," Anya said with something of a smirk.

"I call him boy to his face. I'm allowed to do that, as I let him bounce on my knee," she said. "But as for going to the camp now—"

"If I'm expected to lead an army tomorrow, I need to see what they look like," Anya said.

Izel scratched her chin and grimaced.

"I would consider it a personal favor," Anya said quietly. "As staying in this castle with my polluelo is driving me mad."

After a long pause, the nox nodded slowly. "I'll help you get past the glamour and magic. You won't be able to use your athtar magic to get inside, but you'll get close. We will walk the rest of the way."

She spoke to one of her lieutenants about the preparations, then beckoned Anya to follow her into the captain's quarters. There, laid out on the table, was a map, similar to the one in Freyja's bedchambers. The nox pointed to a spot on the map where the smallest of marks could be seen.

"There," she said. "Can you use your Sight to find it?"

Anya stared at the map, but in her mind's eye, her vision was speeding across the mountain ranges. It slowed when it neared the spot Izel pointed to, but...there was no army. Nothing but trees and rocky terrain until the border with Ath-kur, and the eloko army that lay just to the south.

"I don't see it."

"Then land somewhere nearby," Izel said. "The kappas will

have to release their glamour to let you in."

Anya nodded. "Ready?"

"Ready as I'll ever be, Lady."

With a spot in the mountain range in her Sight, Anya found a suitable location and her body slid between the air, along with the nox. The bustle of the docks echoed away, leaving nothing but a silent forest and moonlight overhead.

"That was…" The nox warrior actually looked taken aback.

"You're one of very few noxes to have experienced that," Anya said, unable to resist. "Be grateful."

"And if we're successful today, my lady, I may be the last," Izel said. "Come, we're not that far."

If Anya hadn't known there were talismans nearby, she would've missed the subtle queasiness that began as they drew further into the dark mountainside. Soon, the feeling was so strong, she was having trouble putting one foot in front of the other.

"I can see what you meant about wanting to space the talismans," Izel said, turning as Anya fell behind more. "If you wish me to carry you the rest of the way—"

"No, thank you," Anya said, straightening. She wouldn't begin her last day by being carried by a nox.

"Suit yourself," Izel said, disappearing into nothing as she passed through the glamour.

Anya inhaled a long breath and pushed herself forward, running toward the darkness. Torches flickered to life, and the sounds of warriors preparing filled her ears. She blinked, her eyes adjusting quickly to take in the view.

Thousands of demons of all shapes sat huddled in tents that stretched as far as the eye could see. They hunched over bonfires and passed bottles of alcohol amongst them. Kappas sat with lilins. Elokos and noxes. All of them, readying themselves for the battle that would occur in the morning.

Many of them would die. Most of them, probably. If not in the battle, perhaps in the aftermath—either when Bael ordered their slaughter for insurrection, or, if Anya was successful, when the world collapsed. But there they sat, ready and willing to die for a cause greater than themselves.

"Anat."

Anya turned at the sound of Tabiko's voice. The kappa wore her armor, a sword at her side, but her eyes had widened in surprise. Anya searched for words to say to her, but found nothing.

"Good luck tomorrow," the kappa said with a nod. "We will be right behind you."

Anya nodded.

"Come, lady," Izel said gently. "We should get you away from the talismans to regain your strength."

CHAPTER THIRTY-FOUR

"Prince! Prince!"

Cam jolted awake as the body under her moved. "Wha...?"

"What is it?" Lotan sat up as much as he could, keeping a warm hand pressed against Cam's back. She, slowly waking up to the realization that a nox attendant had just barged in on them naked, allowed mortification to crawl up her skin.

"The Lady Anat has disappeared! And so has Izel—no one has seen them in hours."

"Calm down, Alain. I'm sure Anat and Izel went to the front lines, although I gave her *express orders* to wait for me," Lotan said, throwing the blanket off without any care for his state of undress while leaving Cam covered.

"Jorge says he saw them talking last night," Alain said. "My prince, what if—"

"Alain, I'm fairly confident in our athtar lady," Lotan said, pulling his silk boxers back on. "I'm also fairly confident in Izel's ability to take care of herself. Are our forces in place?"

Cam, realizing she would have to dress soon, gathered the blanket around herself. As gracefully as she could, she slipped off the bed and hunted down her clothes from the night before.

"Y-yes, my prince," he said with a brief nod. "The last group left a few hours ago, and should be arriving at the battlefield by mid-morning."

"Excellent," Lotan said. He, now dressed in pants, turned around just in time to see Cam trying to put on her bra with the bedsheets still wrapped around her. Smiling, he cleared his throat. "Alain, would you be so kind as to turn around so Agent Macarro can dress?"

Cam caught an eye roll from the nox attendant but he did as he was asked. She dropped the sheet and Lotan's grin widened. Trying not to melt under his gaze, she dressed hastily, swiping her Division jacket from the chair and sliding it on. Lotan had been right; she was more confident with it on.

"Alain, you're free to look," Lotan said, walking to the wardrobe and retrieving a white shirt and a leather vest. "I had a feeling Mother Athtar would go to the battlefield early. Unfortunately, if we leave now, it will take us several hours to get to the battlefield. Unless..." He turned to Cam with a grin. "Could you do the honors for us, Cam?"

"Us?" Cam asked as the door opened. She was very grateful she'd already dressed, for Mizuchi and Freyja walked in, both looking ready for battle. The lilin belu had lost her flowing robes and fur-lined boots in favor of wearing a skin-tight leather ensemble that made her look more action star than lust demon. She carried a sword at her hips, her golden hair pulled back to reveal her pointed ears and Mizuchi wore a suit of armor that looked more fitting for feudal Japan.

"Yes, it seems Anya ignored my request to wait for us," Freyja said with a pout. Then she looked around the room, taking in disheveled sheets and a few used condom wrappers. She smiled with satisfaction. "Excellent. I hope the lovemaking was everything you wanted and more."

Cam fought a blush at the thought of everyone knowing her private business, but Lotan seemed unperturbed. "Of course it was," he said. "But to pressing matters."

"Yes, please," Cam muttered. "So you want me to take you three to the front lines? Is that advisable? I mean, if you leave Liley, Bael could...well, he could destroy all your lands."

"I'm not cowering in Liley while my spawn fight for our country," Freyja said with a fierce look.

"Nor will I," Mizuchi said.

"None of us are," Lotan said, stepping forward fully prepared for battle in leather armor. Cam had to admit—he looked sexy as hell. "Let's get going. Anat will move at dawn and it's nearly time."

The three belus surrounded Cam and she swallowed hard.

"I'm not sure...I've only ever transported Anya, and—"

"I believe in you," Lotan said with a smile reminiscent of their night together.

"Just take a deep breath. You'll be fine," Freyja said.

"Okay," Cam said. "Where am I going?"

"Search in the northern mountains. You will see a large lake in a valley. Try to aim for the shore of it, or as close as you can."

Cam closed her eyes, and her Sight did what it was supposed to do. The lake she found, but the army? "I don't see anything."

"Good," Freyja said, tightening her hold on Cam's arm. "Let's go."

The world slipped under her feet, and the warm roar of the fire in the hearth was replaced by a cold breeze that chilled Cam to the bone. She opened her eyes into a dim forest and a sky painted pink above. Still no sign of the army, though.

"Come, we're close," Freyja said, adjusting her swords at her hips and marching forward.

Cam took two steps, then felt it—the now familiar wave of talisman magic. She fell backwards, into the waiting arms of Lotan yet again. Without waiting to ask, he swept her up into his arms and carried her.

"It's easier this way," he said with a smile.

"You just want to carry me," Cam replied, her stomach roiling in misery as they crossed the thick forest.

"I look forward to carrying you many places," he said, low so only she could hear.

Cam might've found that sexy, except that her head was

threatening to split open. She also might've been hallucinating, because what had appeared to be an empty forest before was now a thriving, busy camp filled with demons. The nausea hadn't lessened at all, but the shock of what she was seeing cleared her mind a bit.

"Holy shit," she said. "You guys weren't kidding."

"My prince." Izel had appeared, wearing leather armor similar to Lotan's. "We are ready for your signal."

"Where's Anat?"

"She's been meditating at the front lines for some time," Izel said. "I apologize for—"

"It's fine," Lotan said. A demon passed by with a spear, and Cam hiccuped. "We should get Agent Macarro away from the talismans."

They marched through the camp, which stretched for longer than Cam had expected—and demons of all stripes trained with each other, shared meals, and conversed over fire pits. Many of them looked more human than demon—some could be noxes, but many of them were Lotan's acquisitions from the human world. Closer to the front lines, the soldiers stood in long lines, their weapons drawn and ready.

They'd walked for almost half an hour to get to the edge of the mountainside, where the line between Liley and Ath-kur remained clearly defined. There, Anya stood, gazing into the land she'd once called home.

"What are you all doing here?" Anya said, her gaze landing on Cam, as if she'd betrayed everyone. Lotan gingerly placed her on the ground. "You're supposed to remain in Kastali."

"And let you have all the fun? Hardly," Lotan said.

"You are putting your spawn in unimaginable danger," Anya said.

"We're doing that regardless, Anat," Freyja said. "At least this way we can give them a fighting chance."

"Very well," Anya said, looking to the belu lilin. "Just remember your only escape is into Liley."

"I do not plan to die, Anat," Mizuchi said. "Let Bael come for me, and I'll be glad to take him down along with me."

Anya turned to Ath-kur once more.

"Can you give us a moment?" Cam asked to the belus and Lotan.

They nodded and walked back toward their camp, deep in conversation. Lotan tossed one final look over his shoulder, then hurried back. He pressed his lips to Cam's in a long, soft kiss.

"For luck," he whispered, before jogging back to Freyja and Mizuchi.

"Did you have fun with your prince?" Anya asked.

"I'm sure you know the answer to that," Cam said, coming to stand beside her at the edge of the world. "Thanks for the push."

"I see he gave you his present," Anya said, glancing at her jacket. "I'm glad your grandmother willingly gave it up."

Cam chuckled. "So you had something to do with this?"

"He asked me if I thought there was something you could take with you into battle that would give you comfort," Anya said. "I know how much being an agent means to you. So I told him the last place I could recall you wearing it."

"Wow," Cam said, sliding her fingertips along the vinyl. "You really like him then?"

"I appreciate that he might not be the evil bastard I painted him to be. Especially since he's tried very hard to woo you." She smiled. "I can only assume he'll have to impress Jack. Good luck with that."

"If I like him, Jack will like him," Cam said. "Jack's never had a problem with my boyfriends."

"So why give me all that trouble about needing to get into your good graces?" Anya asked with a frown.

"Because I'm not Jack," Cam said with a laugh.

Anya didn't share her amusement, as her face had grown somber. "Can you See the elokos? Just to the south?"

Cam closed her eyes, and nodded. "They're all asleep. Does this mean we'll be able to sneak up on them?"

"If the athtars are feeling generous enough to alert them… no. They'll know the moment we set foot in their land."

"But they're athtars."

"In any other circumstance, I'd agree with you. But even Bael knows not to sacrifice too many pawns." She inhaled deeply. "The moment I step over this line, the battle will begin. The athtars will appear immediately, the elokos will be roused and arrive soon thereafter. Once the armies have met, go to the castle and get Jack. Don't take any unnecessary risks, and try to get in and out quickly."

"I could say the same for you, Colibrí." Cam turned to her.

"Just...get him home, okay?" She looked at the ground. "And tell him—"

She grabbed Anya's hand off her hilt and forced her to face her. "Listen here you little shit, I'll be *damned* if I let some colibrí-sized bitch break his heart. So you'd better come back alive or so help me God, I'll find you in the afterlife and drag you back myself, do you understand?"

Anya blinked, then pulled Cam into a hug. Cam froze, then slowly brought her arms up to return the embrace.

"It has been my great pleasure to be your friend, Cam," she whispered into Cam's ear. "I couldn't have picked a better polluelo."

"This isn't goodbye."

"If it is," Anya said, stepping back, "I don't want to leave anything unsaid." She inhaled deeply. "Tell Jack that I loved him."

Cam's eyebrows shot up. "Really?"

"Yeah..." She gazed out into the purple sky. "I still don't think I really know...what it feels like to love someone like that. But he was..." She smiled. "I really think we could have had something special."

"I look forward to you telling him yourself."

Anya smirked. "Stubborn ass. Go hide yourself."

"Right," Cam said, stepping back. "Anya... Be careful."

"I will."

Cam fell back, torn between wanting to help but knowing

she had a greater purpose. Anya wouldn't be able to do her thing unless she trusted that Cam would take care of Jack. She kept that in the forefront of her mind as she passed the throngs of waiting demons. They wore similar looks of grim resignation, and Cam had to avert her eyes to keep her stomach from flip-flopping.

"Cam, my love!" Freyja waved to her from a group of lilins. Cam jogged over to the group, slipping between two armor-clad lilins with long spears. Freyja placed a loving arm around her and held her close.

"Stay with me until the battle begins. You'll be safe here."

Cam nodded and found Anya at the edge of the land. She held both her swords, the bejeweled Sharur hanging from her hip. The wind brushed her braided hair against her face, and a ripple of apprehension swept across those nearest to her. Slowly, she raised her swords and took one step onto the orange sand.

For a breath, there was nothing. Then the chaos came.

Elokos appeared out of nowhere, carrying clubs and spears into Liley and smashing into the first army. With every breath Cam took, it seemed more arrived—and more—and more—and more. It didn't matter that they'd amassed a hundred miles to the south. The athtars were ready to airlift them in anywhere.

"Archers!" Lotan called somewhere in the distance. "Ready!"

Five hundred bowstrings went taut.

"*Fire!*"

Torrents of arrows flew overhead, landing in the center of the approaching army. Cam counted maybe twenty that hit their target, but that wasn't the point. The demons kept coming, and Cam could make out their snarling faces. This battle was really happening, and there was no stopping it now.

The first wave of noxes went barreling into the elokos, some in human form, others in their beast form. Cam didn't want to know if Lotan was among them yet—not with the way they mercilessly ripped their adversaries limb from limb.

But to Cam's eyes, the deluge of elokos had stopped—at least momentarily. "Do you think the talismans are working? I don't see the athtars bringing anyone else in."

"For now," Freyja said. "We will see how they hold when Bael makes his appearance. And the athtars can still move." She pulled her sword from her hip as the elokos pressed further into their ranks. "Now, little neophyte. Take cover. The lilin glamour will disappear and the full battle will begin."

"Are you sure you should be going in there?" Cam asked. "What about Liley?"

"I will watch her," Izel said, coming to stand next to Freyja. "You have a job to do."

Cam nodded and stepped back, hiding herself behind a nearby rock.

"Lilins," Freyja said, raising her sword. "Get ready."

The glamour faded like water down a rock, and where there had been mountains and trees were now ten thousand demons. A cry of surprise rose up from the battle—clearly, their numbers had been unexpected. Perhaps winning the day wasn't implausible.

The lilins rushed the battlefield, and it became impossible to tell which side was winning, or which side belonged to whom. Cam kept on the Liley side of the battle, Jack's knives at her hips and her macuahuitl at her back. She'd seen carnage before, but this was on a different level.

Freyja was fearsome and unrelenting. Her long sword dispatched any demon that came too close with the grace and beauty of a ballet dancer. Most of her victims were elokos—perhaps the athtars feared the belu lilin as much as their own. Izel stood next to her, fending off attacks from elokos with a sword as well as any.

Anya was still at the border, fighting whomever crossed her swords. She was grimly focused, even as blood splattered her face and arms. The arrows had done their job in keeping the athtar magic at bay, and now Anya was simply proving her superiority with a weapon. The other demons didn't stand a chance. Then again, they were all elokos, so they didn't—

Cam felt the approaching athtar before she saw her, and ducked out of the way of a sword that missed her neck by inches. She fell backward onto her hands, able to look up just as the sword came down for a second blow.

Anya's sword caught it, and with a mighty roar, she pushed the athtar back. The athtar, a black girl with long braids, swallowed then came for Anya again. She locked swords with the creature, her arms shaking with the effort. Cam pulled her macuahuitl from the ground, but Anya was quicker. The athtar's head went flying into the muck.

"Cam!" Anya cried. "*Get the hell out of here!*"
And as much as she didn't want to, Cam disappeared.

CHAPTER THIRTY-FIVE

The sounds of battle died on the wind, replaced by eerie silence. Cam's Sight had found the wine cellar and she'd landed gracefully in the center of a dark, musty room. She froze, waiting for someone—anyone—to have noticed her arrival. After a few heart-pounding moments, she relaxed and inched toward the door.

Pushing open the door, she winced as the creaking sound echoed into the empty hallway. She held her breath, listening and squinting into the darkness. But there was little activity. No servants, no bustling. Even the kitchens were deathly silent. Bael had taken his entire castle to the front lines. Or so she hoped anyway.

She crept down a long corridor lined with tapestries, keeping her fingertips to the left wall as Anya had said. Before entering a hallway, she counted the tiles to the other corner, marking them off in her mind as her toes touched down on them.

The world seemed stretched out in front of her. The tile on the floor went from a few inches to miles ahead, and the wall her fingers touched suddenly looked ten thousand feet away. If not for her touch against the wall, she would've thought her hand was reaching out into nothing.

"It's only an illusion," she whispered to herself, sliding her foot forward until she felt the grout between the tiles. That was tile number fifty-two. She dragged her fingers with her as she slid further, reaching the next tile. Fifty-three. Fifty-four. Fifty-five. There were sixty tiles on this hallway; she just needed to keep moving forward.

The wall disappeared behind her fingers, and she leaned to the left, falling face-first into an empty, dark hallway that had returned to normal-sized. Looking over her shoulder, she couldn't see evidence of the athtar magic, but she was damned sure it was there.

She jumped to her feet and re-centered herself. The hallway she'd been walking down would lead directly to the staircase, but she didn't want to chance walking back into the magic and getting lost.

"Psst!"

Cam froze. She was a sitting duck in the middle of the hallway—nowhere to hide.

"Cam! Over here!"

"Angela?"

The second to the Atlanta lord was probably the last person Cam had expected to see in Bael's castle. Her head poked out from behind a tapestry, her gaze darting this way and that as she frantically waved at Cam.

"Come on," Angela whispered. "Get out of the hallway."

"Wait a minute… are *you* Freyja's spy?"

She nodded and waved again. "Come on. We don't have much time. Bael is still in the castle."

"How do you know?" Cam asked.

"I just left him," she said, averting her gaze.

"Ew," Cam said. "I mean… Sorry. So you got the short straw, huh?"

"It was my choice," she said as they walked through the hall. "I returned with Bael during Demon Spring. He took a liking to me—especially after Anat disappeared again. I went to Belu Freyja to ask if she could give me protection, and she asked me to play along."

"What did she promise you in return?" Cam asked.

"I asked for her to protect my flock topside," Angela said. "And when this is all over, for me to be able to return to them and live in peace. They're scared, especially after what happened to Nunzia. If I can protect them in any way, I will."

"Dangerous work," Cam said. "So you've been keeping tabs on Jack?"

"As much as I can. I know where Bael's been hiding him, at

least."

"How is he?"

"He's been through a lot," Angela said. "I haven't seen him in a few weeks. The last I heard he had told the demon who'd been masquerading as his late wife that she was terrible at her job."

"That's my partner," Cam said. "How'd Bael react to that?"

"He's currently seeking her replacement," Angela said quietly. "She was a good lilin—old. Freyja was sad she'd chosen to ally herself with Bael."

A new voice echoed in the hall as an athtar appeared in front of them. "And it's sad you've chosen to betray our king."

She looked like a baby, barely eighteen with dark brown skin and black hair braided down her back. She snarled at Angela, who lifted her chin in defiance.

"Gita," the lilin said. "I thought you'd been sent to the battlefield."

"Somebody had to remain behind to make sure no one betrayed my king," she said. "I knew he was making a mistake taking you to his bed. Filthy turncoat."

"If you wish to learn how to seduce a man, I would be happy to teach you some other time," Angela replied, although her voice shook slightly. "Cam… Go."

"What?" Cam said, pulling out her macauhuitl. "No way. I'm not leaving you against this chick. You go. Join the others."

"But—"

Cam grinned at her. "I've been hankering to kick some

athtar ass recently. And I'm sure Freyja could use you on the front lines."

"There's a staircase fifty feet from here. Go three floors up, fifth door on the left," Angela said, backing up. "Good luck."

"Likewise," Cam said.

Angela's footfalls disappeared behind her, leaving Cam alone with her new target.

"She won't make it far," the athtar said. "And neither will you. Your human is as good as dead, as is everyone else on your side. Bael is unstoppable."

"Just you to protect the castle?" Cam asked. "Sure you can handle it?"

"We only need one athtar here," she said. "The vermin will take care of themselves."

"Looks like we got two athtars here," Cam said, folding her arms across her chest. Her jacket crinkled with her movements, giving her strength.

"Barely. You're a neophyte third."

"I'm also an agent with the US Division," Cam said. "And I believe you guys have some overdue punishment."

Jack's knives or her macuahuitl, there was no contest. Cam clicked the button to expose the teeth. "Let's see what a neophyte can do then, huh?"

Cam lunged first, but the pressure of time sucked the movement from her limbs. She concentrated hard—as hard as she did when she fought Anya, but she couldn't break totally free of the magic.

The athtar smiled; she hadn't gone for her weapon yet. "It is as I suspected. You aren't worth the magic in your veins. But I suppose it's to be expected, with your weak maker."

Cam found a foothold in her own magic and pushed with all her might, breaking free of the athtar's grasp. But the other woman didn't seem too concerned.

"Puh." She turned her nose up. "Pathetic. Anat's training has become lax over the years, I see."

"Oh?" Cam said. "Did she train you or something?"

"She tried," Gita replied with a shrug. "She was weak. Bael pitied her, that's why he kept her so close. She wasn't worthy to sit beside him."

"I *dare* you to say that in front of her," Cam said. "Athtars. Talk a big game, but when push comes to shove, they're a bunch of chicken shit assholes."

"And I dare you to say that to my face, you little bitch."

"I think I just did," Cam said, clicking the teeth on her weapon again. The more riled up she could get the athtar, the less focus she'd have. "And I'd say it to your little prick of a king, too. He's nothing but an insecure little asshole with a lot to prove to nobody who gives a shit. Sure the apple doesn't fall far from the tree."

That set her off. The athtar yanked her sword from the sheath and pointed it at Cam. The tip wavered as she panted in fury. "You will *not* talk about my king that way."

"Again...I just did," Cam said with a hearty chuckle. "If you'd like to stop me, I'm right here."

They lunged for each other, Cam pushing against the magic with as much of her own as she could muster. But even as her body succumbed to the magic, her club fell forward like a knife through butter, slamming into the athtar and eliciting a howl of pain and the full release of magic around Cam.

That was when Cam noticed the little symbols etched along the teeth of her weapon. All five talismans symbols had been added to the top five teeth.

"Lotan, you sneaky bastard," she muttered to herself, pulling her weapon out of her adversary as she screamed obscenities. "Or Anya. Either way. Sneaky bastards abound."

The athtar had recovered from her wound, grabbing her bleeding arm with a snarl on her face. "You little shit."

"There's more where that came from," Cam said, gripping her macauhuitl and swinging it hard. The athtar jumped out of the way, clutching her crimson arm. She fell backward, staring up at Cam with wide, fearful eyes.

Then, like the little chicken Cam knew she was, the athtar scrambled to her feet and took off running. Cam couldn't let her escape—not when she could go to Bael. Cam inhaled a breath, using her magic to place her in the athtar's path.

"Hi, precious," Cam said with a smirk as she slammed her club into the demon's chest. Then, before the demon could react, Cam pulled Jack's knives from their holster and sliced hard, severing the head. Magic fizzed out from the body, reminding Cam of a soul sliding out into the ether.

"Suck on that," Cam said. "I won third place at the US

Division Academy championships. And I would've won second place if that bitch hadn't cheated. Don't mess with me."

For good measure, she kicked the corpse.

Then, she remembered that she was in the middle of Bael's castle and had just killed an athtar directly connected to Bael.

She put her weapons back in their holders and took off running toward the staircase.

CHAPTER THIRTY-SIX

Jack's stomach rumbled, and he walked to the window, staring at the red dawn. Although he didn't have a good grasp of time, he was fairly sure he hadn't eaten since kicking Not-Sara from the room, and that had been over a day before. Perhaps Bael would let him starve to death in lieu of other punishment.

Perhaps it was just him going stir-crazy, but he was ready for more. Wanted to see Not-Sara again and prove to himself he wasn't just barely holding it together. It had been a small victory, but those had been few and far between during his captivity.

He rested his hands on the stone ledge and peering out into the darkness. The sun was rising in the distance, casting an eerie red glow across the empty desert beyond. Jack squinted, straining to see what he first thought was a trick of the light. But no—he was sure of it now. There was activity in the distance— large groups of people. Were they fighting, marching, or having a kegger?

Did this mean something was breaking?

The door handle turned behind him, but Jack didn't bother to turn around. He wouldn't dignify Not-Sara or some other servant with his attention.

"It's about time you showed up. Just put the food on the table and leave."

"Jack…"

He went stick straight. Seeing Sara had been hard enough, but Cam? Those wounds were too new. He took a deep breath, reminding himself this was Bael. It was punishment for defiance, and Jack wouldn't let the athtar win. Later, in his solitude, he would let himself feel all the pain. But now, he would remain strong.

"So what?" he said, his voice strained. "Sending Sara wasn't enough for you jackasses? Now you're torturing me with Cam?"

He finally turned to look at the creature, the sight of Cam hitting him somewhere deep in his soul.

"Jack, it's me," Not-Cam said, walking into the room. She looked about the same, with her Division jacket and hair balled behind her head. Her brown eyes were wide and pleading, filled with tears as she stumbled into the room, drinking him in.

"Goddamn, Jack. You look…" She wiped tears out of her eyes. "I'm so glad to see you."

"I'm sure you are, demon," Jack said.

"Jack, it's me," Not-Cam said. "I swear to you, it's really me."

"Well, you did a little better than with Sara," Jack said, surveying her. "At least you got the measurements a little closer. Although I don't think Cam's hips are that big."

Not-Cam stopped in the center of the room. "Ex-*cuse* me?"

"You got that look right, too," he said, crossing his feet and leaning back against the wall. "No, Cam is hopefully somewhere in Shanghai, putting together the world's best weapons program to get rid of all the demons."

"No, *Cam* decided to walk her ass down to the Underworld and rescue you, you ungrateful shithead."

"If you're *really* Cam," he said, closing his eyes. "Tell me something only she and I would know."

"We had sex in our third year."

"I told Anya that," Jack said, shaking his head. "Do better."

"You were garbage."

Jack laughed. "As if. I was great in bed."

"Not at sixteen you weren't," Not-Cam said, folding her arms across her chest. "And here's something even you don't know, dumbass. I had a massive crush on you until we slept together."

"No, Cam didn't."

"Yes, Cam did," she said, stomping her feet. "But once we slept together, I don't know. I decided you were better as a friend than a lover. Although I'm starting to doubt whether you are, since you think any demon could *ever* compare to the real thing. So wake the fuck up, because we gotta get the hell out of here."

Jack blinked once, twice, then relief welled to the surface. "C-Cam?"

"Yeah, you asshole," she said, tears spilling down her face. "Here to rescue you. *Again.* Can you just not get—"

He cut her off with a bear hug, squeezing her so tightly she complained about not being able to breathe. Oh, if this was a trick, it was a good one. But when her body trembled, and the sobbing began, he let himself believe this was reality.

"Dammit, Jack," she whispered against his shirt. "I thought I'd never see you again."

"C'mon, really?" Jack said as he held her with everything he had. "You think I'm that easy to kill?"

"I thought..." She looked up at him. "Jack, Bael was torturing you."

"He tried," Jack said with a shrug. "Turns out I'm a lot hardier than I thought. And what the *hell* are you doing here? Where's Anya? How did *you* even get here?"

"That's a long, involved story," Cam said. "One I'd be glad to tell you over sushi when we get back home. But here's the bottom line: Anya is fighting Bael, the demons are at war, and you and I have to get back to the human realm."

Jack processed what she'd said in slow motion. "Anya... One more time?"

"The demons are at war," Cam explained slowly. "They're all on the battlefield. Anya's there distracting Bael, I hope. You and I have to get back to our world before Anya kills him and this whole world implodes."

"No way," Jack said, unhooking the knives around Cam's waist and putting them around his own. They felt good. Right. "If Anya's out there fighting, I want to be out there fighting, too. I have some assholes to pay back. Namely, one dick named Lazlo—"

"We took care of him," Cam said. "We took care of everything. Anya made me promise to keep you safe, and that means we have to go."

"Cam, are you seriously telling me you're going to walk away from a fight?"

She pursed her lips. "Don't try to sway me, Grenard."

"I'm not swaying you," Jack said with a casual shrug. "I'm just saying, the Camilla Macarro I knew would never let anyone tell her she couldn't participate in a good ol' fashioned demon brawl. Maybe you aren't the real thing after all."

Her eyes narrowed, just as he'd predicted. If he'd had any doubts that this was his best friend, they were gone with that one look.

"I gave my word, Jackson."

"You can still keep me safe on the battlefield, just as you always have. Just as you always will." He gathered her hands in his. "But I need this. Please? These guys have been torturing—"

"*Gah*," Cam cried, ripping her hands away from him. "*Fine*, you son of a bitch. We will make an appearance. But if things get too rough—"

"We'll go, of course, of course." He pulled out his knives, which were covered in blood. "Um. What have you been doing with my weapons?"

"Killing bitches," Cam said, taking Jack by the arm. "They're going to get a lot messier."

Inhale. They were in the middle of the desert.

Exhale. They stood on the edge of a mountain overlooking the battle Jack had seen. The fighting was fierce, with bodies strewn across the battlefield, and yet more pouring in from the mountains above. Short eloko demons locked swords with tall lilins, fierce and terrifying. Human-looking athtars battled with froggish kappas. Black nox demons, fully transformed, barreled through the crowds, throwing demons into the air with their mouths and tails.

"Are we winning?" Jack asked.

"I have no idea," Cam said, chewing on her lip. "But the fighting has spread too far. This is as far as I can get and there's still a lot of fighting behind us."

"…Hang on a second." Jack straightened as his mind caught up with himself. He turned to Cam with wide eyes. "How the hell did we get here?"

"What?"

"Camilla Lucía Macarro, what did you do to yourself? Did you…did you…?"

"Become an athtar to save your scrawny ass? You bet I did," Cam said, pulling her macuahuitl off her back. "You can yell at me later, Jackson George. But I had to do what I had to do. I wasn't leaving your rescue up to La Colibrí."

His face softened. "Cam, were you really in love with me?"

"Oh, who knows," Cam said with a smile. "Maybe I was just nursing a teenage crush."

"And was I really garbage in bed?"

"You weren't great. It's a good thing. You make a better best friend than boyfriend."

He smiled at her. "I love you."

She smiled back, her eyes brimming with tears. "Backatcha. Let's kill some motherfucking demons."

They tapped their weapons and ran down into the fray. Despite Cam being athtar and Jack being on the receiving end of torture these past few weeks, they fell into their normal battle pattern with ease. Cam used her club to stun the demons, Jack delivered the finishing blow. They were a deadly assembly line, making progress through the throngs, even as Jack began to wonder why they were being so successful. Even during Demon Spring, their body count wasn't usually so high.

That was when he noticed the carvings inscribed on his knives.

"Cam," Jack said, nodding to the tip of his blade. "Was this you?"

"Nope," she said, pointing to the talismans on the teeth of her weapons. "I think Lotan did it."

"L-Lotan?" Jack blinked. "The nox prince?"

Just at that moment, a giant hellbeast barreled toward them, snarling and drooling with blood and spittle flying everywhere. Jack held up his knives, ready to engage, but Cam pulled him back with a rough hand on his shoulder. The beast morphed into itself, revealing a tall man with brown skin and curly black hair.

This man strode up to Cam and pulled her into a kiss worthy of the front cover of a romance novel.

"I thought you were going back to the human realm," he said, breathlessly. "Are you all right?"

"Do you really think I'd miss this party, Lotan?" she said, starry-eyed and lovestruck.

"Um." Jack cleared his throat. "You've been busy, it seems."

"You must be the famous Jack." Lotan grinned at Jack as if they were best friends. "I'm glad to see you alive and well. Cam has been very worried about you. Please take care not to die in this battle."

"What's going on?" Cam asked. "Is Bael here yet? Why is everyone all the way out here?"

"It's further than we would've liked, but we're still winning the day," he replied with a look to the battlefield. "I've counted two hundred athtars dead so far, but the eloko army is proving more difficult than we anticipated. Anat was right—Bael gave them orders to push far into the world."

"And Anya?" Cam asked.

"She's holding her own against a group of athtars. I believe she's taken down half of them herself," Lotan said with a smile. "She's quite formidable."

"I know," Jack said. "Cam, take me to her."

"No way," she and Lotan said at the same time.

"You're human," Lotan said.

"And she would absolutely murder me," Cam said. "We stay

on the edge of the fight until it's over. Then you can have your big reunion or whatever."

Lotan captured her lips once more. "I have to get back out there. Please take care of yourself. We have another date to plan."

"Be careful," Cam said, gazing into his eyes like a woman in love. Then the nox bounded away, transforming into a beast the size of a Clydesdale.

"We have a *lot* to discuss, apparently," Jack said.

"Oh, don't even go there with me," Cam said, her face turning pink. "You started it by sleeping with Colibrí."

"Anya isn't the nox prince," Jack said. "Well done, Macarro."

"Shaddup," Cam said, but Jack didn't miss the smile on her face. "We should find Mizuchi. He'll know what's going on."

"The kappa belu?" Jack said. "Since when did you hobnob with such lofty people?"

"Since we all decided to start a war," Cam said. "That sushi date is going to be a long one, I feel."

"You said it."

Cam pointed to a spot in the distance. "There. On that outcropping. Come on."

Jack followed Cam, keeping any wayward demons away from them both. It took some time to press through the crowd and avoid the dead bodies—a mix of all kinds of demons. Finally, they reached the bottom of a large hill where Mizuchi stood barking orders to the ground below. Another kappa woman was next to him, also calling orders. Jack gave Cam a boost then shimmied up behind her.

"Ah, Agent Macarro," he said with a wide smile. "I see you've found your human."

"Yeah," Cam said. "Jack, this is Mizuchi and Tabiko."

"P-pleasure," Jack said, trying not to gawk at the kappa woman in full body armor.

"Has Bael arrived yet? Where is Anya?" Cam asked.

Tabiko pointed at a spot in the distance. "Over there. She's leading the tip of the spear. The elokos and athtars have discovered our talismans and have retreated further into Ath-kur. But even without the talismans on the ground, our weapons still bear the markings, so we are at a stalemate."

"You're pretty far away from Liley, Mizuchi," Cam said, frowning. "Isn't it dangerous for you to be out here?"

"We are all in danger, but there's been no sign of Bael," Mizuchi said. "I believe he's waiting for—"

Mizuchi's eyes bulged, then his head slid off his body. A bright light blinded Jack, and he fell backward. When the spots faded, Bael stood above Mizuchi's body, his sword still raised and his eyes bright with vengeance.

"I always hated that old frog."

CHAPTER THIRTY-SEVEN

Anya moved indefatigably across the battlefield. The adrenaline and athtar magic had made her strong—stronger than she'd felt in years. She kept her purpose locked away in the middle of her chest, a reminder that if she was struck down, so many more would be in danger.

But it was hard not to think about every life she took—especially the athtar demons. She'd been there the day they'd been made—all of them. She'd never befriended any of them and spent most of her time trying to stay one step ahead, but each death was a knife in her chest.

She didn't let herself think about the others—Cam or Jack, although Freyja remained close by to cover her back. Izel, the fierce nox warrior, had been dead for some time now, struck down by an athtar when the battle had barely begun. Anya had avenged her death almost immediately then killed five more athtars for good measure.

"How many more are there?" Freyja asked, leaning on her sword. The lilin was red-faced and winded, although her magic remained powerful.

"Plenty more," Anya said, wiping the dirt and blood from her face. "Why hasn't Bael shown himself yet?"

"I don't know," Freyja said, turning in the direction of the castle. "Perhaps we'll have to attack the castle and draw him out."

Anya let that thought wash down her back. "If we press too much farther out of this area, we will lose our protection from the talismans."

Freyja nodded. "Then we should hope for a change in tide."

A nearby kappa fell to his knees then landed facedown in the mud. Then another. All across the field, kappas fell over, as if...

"No..."

She spun, scanning the mountains for Mizuchi. That was when she saw the figures standing atop the rock.

Her gaze locked with Bael's.

"Anya," Freyja said, placing a hand on her shoulder. "Steady on."

In two breaths, she and Freyja were on the outcropping. The atmosphere around them crackled with releasing electricity and magic. Anya's gaze fell from Bael to Mizuchi's body and

Tabiko's next to it, and her heart cracked in her chest.

Lingering magic oozed from the headless corpse, the head nearby still looking so painfully like the kappa Anya had known. She should never have let him or Freyja pass into Ath-kur. Another dead body, another mark to her tally. But not just his—thousands of kappas who would find themselves reverted to human, or worse, if Kappanchi disintegrated.

And yet...

Tabiko blinked and rose, her green skin and webbed feet still intact. She threw back her shoulders and glared defiantly at Bael, who frowned in confusion.

"What is this? The kappa line continues without the belu?" he said. "The frog man was more resourceful than I gave him credit for."

A sad smile grew on Anya's face. Mizuchi's experimentation had been worthwhile, it seemed. The kappas could continue without him. As much as they could without their belu.

"Tabiko," came Lotan's voice from behind Anya. He must've seen what she had and come to help. "Gather our forces and retreat. My soldiers will carry the wounded."

Tabiko nodded and slid off the outcropping. Her voice carried, calling to her kappas to retreat. Anya would give them more time, as many of them had been reverted to human.

"Yes, run away, little frogs," Bael said. "As if they'll be safe beyond the border."

"You'll have to go through Liley first," Freyja said, pulling out her sword. "And through me."

"It seems that all the lilins have betrayed me lately," Bael said, gently pushing the tip away from him. "How you poisoned Angela against me, Freyja."

"You poisoned her yourself," Freyja said with a snarl. "And you will pay for her death. As well as the death of every other demon you killed unjustly."

"The only unjust deaths today are my athtars," Bael said, turning his gaze to Anya. "Look at you. My Lady of Destruction, covered in the blood of her fellow demons. This wasn't the ending I wanted for you. You were supposed to come home to me, not engage in some useless vendetta. Now you're nothing but a bloodthirsty monster, twisted and evil. What have I ever done to you to warrant such hatred?"

Anya couldn't find her tongue, not with Mizuchi's unseeing gaze boring into her. Not in front of Bael, who was in his element. And not when she still wasn't sure she could bring herself to do what she needed to.

"Let me write you a list."

Anya's head snapped up at the sound of a voice she'd scarcely hoped to hear again. She hadn't noticed the two behind her, but now...now Jack was the most beautiful thing she'd ever seen. His pale cheeks flushed with exertion, that cocky, brash smile etched on his face. The knives Oce had given him bloody from battle. His gaze locked with hers, and his smile widened.

Relief rolled through her. Bael hadn't broken him. If anything, he looked better than he ever had. Or perhaps it was just that she'd missed him so very, very much.

"I see you found your pet," Bael said with a strained voice. "See, Anat? He's healthy. Just as I said he was."

"That's a bit of a stretch, dickhead," Jack snapped.

"Goddamn, I missed you," Cam said with a grin. "Welcome back, partner."

"I thought I told you to to take him home, Cam," Anya said, although she couldn't find the energy to be angry with her. Not when seeing Jack smiling and healthy was the most precious gift she could've ever received.

Bael snorted. "I cannot believe you've become so soft, Anat."

"Well, which is it?" Cam said, stepping forward. "Is she a bloodthirsty monster or a weak idiot? Your story keeps changing, Bael."

Bael's nostrils flared, and the smile on his face was anything but kind. "As an example of my unending grace, I'll allow you to speak to me thusly, Camilla. And I'll let you and your human return to his realm, if that's what you choose."

"Yeah, I don't believe you," Cam said. "Because literally everything that's ever come out of your mouth is a fucking lie."

Bael shrugged. "Then go. Test my grace."

"We already tested it," Jack said. "Anya told you to fuck off, and you took me instead. Pardon us if we don't believe you now."

"Her name is *Anat,* you spineless piece of pig filth," Bael growled, pulling his sword. "I should have killed you ages ago."

Bael lunged toward Jack, raising his weapon to lay a killing blow. Anya reached for her sword, but Cam was quicker, the teeth of her macauhuitl locking with Bael's. Her arms shook but she held fast, her eyes alight with fury.

"Im…possible," Bael said, his eyes wide. "You're a *third*. Barely a month old."

"And you're weak, still," Cam said. "Plus, I got these great talismans etched onto my macauhuitl. Yeah, remember that, you asshole? How afraid you were that the humans would revolt against you using those talismans?" She smirked. "Guess you were right to be scared of them." With a mighty roar, she pushed him back, his sword clattering to the rocky ground.

"This is…" Bael stepped back. Then he smiled as if the past few moments hadn't happened. "It doesn't matter. I retain my strength—"

"So soon after Demon Spring?" Freyja said, wiping blood from her cheek. "I find that hard to believe. I remember the days when you could barely get out of bed."

Bael smiled. "You've always been a liar, Freyja."

"If anyone's a liar, it's you," Lotan said. "You lied about my parents killing a little girl, just to get them out of the way."

"Mot and Xo killed Asherah," Bael said. "And even if they didn't, someone else did. I would never—"

"You killed her."

It wasn't so much a realization as an acceptance. Anya had seen the signs, heard the stories, felt the truth in the pit of her stomach. But it had been a step too far for her to accept the depths of Bael's atrocities. Mizuchi had pegged her correctly— she was a selfish coward, unwilling to face the truth because it was difficult.

She turned to Lotan, whose wide eyes reminded her of the boy she'd spared all those years ago. "I'm sorry," she said, a tear falling down her cheek. "Lotan, I'm so…so sorry."

"I can't believe you would think something so horrible of me," Bael said, pressing a hand to his chest. "Asherah was my child—"

"And I was your lady," Anya said. "And you had no problem hurting me."

His eyes widened, and he glanced at the others. "I *never* hurt you. I made you into what you are today. I gave you power and saved your life! This is how you repay me? By allying yourself with those who would take my place? How can you be so stupid as to trust the word of a nox?" He shook his head, as if the very sight of her disgusted him. "Then again, you always were a simple woman. A poor imitation of a belu."

"I may not have been God-touched," she began with more strength than she felt, "but God gave Asherah to me. I got down on my knees, and I begged Him to give me a child so you wouldn't leave. To make you happy." She closed her eyes. "This is ridiculous. I can't believe I'm having this conversation with you. She was our *child. You killed my child.*"

"I don't even know if it was my child," Bael said. "How do I know you didn't sleep with Mot? How do I know you didn't sleep with everything that moved? You were always willing to sleep with Freyja, and now this…this human man. You obviously never loved me at all."

"Bael, you were my hero, my soulmate," Anya said sadly. "All I wanted was for us to be a family—you, me, Asherah. And you were so wrapped up in your own fantasies that you couldn't see what you had. You had to destroy everything…and for what? Jealousy? Even now, all I want is for you to put down your sword and *stop* this. But you won't, will you? You'll never stop trying to hurt me for wanting nothing more than to love you."

"You don't love me," he snarled. "If you did, you never would've betrayed me like this. I never should've given you my gift. It's obvious you weren't worthy."

Once upon a time, those words might've stung. But now she saw them for what they were—the rantings of a deranged man. And just like that, the last bit of hope she'd carried that he would ever change evaporated on the wind.

"Cam," Anya said, her voice sounding hollow and resolved at once. "Do you remember what you promised me?"

"W-what?"

"Do you remember our agreement?" Anya said, not taking her eyes off Bael.

Out of the corner of her eye, Anya saw Cam nod, and blink heavily. "Good luck, Anya."

"Wait, wait—" Jack's voice died on the wind as he and Cam disappeared.

"Good luck, my lady," Lotan said, bowing low to her. Then he transformed into the hellbeast, Freyja climbing atop him. She blew Anya a kiss before they barreled into the retreating crowd.

"Is this how it ends, Anat?" Bael asked. "You kill me and you die in the rubble of Ath-kur? After all we've been through together? All the beautiful days and nights when it was just the two of us? Don't you remember how happy we were together?" He took her hands in his. "We can be that happy again."

How tempting it was. He was right—there were days when Bael was her sun and the moon, her hero. Days when he would spend hours gazing into her eyes, using every language in the world to convey the depths of his love. The beautiful music when they lay together, content to hold each other for all eternity.

But there was a shadow on every one of those memories, the knowledge that it wouldn't last. One wrong look, one question, one misstep, and the illusion came crashing down. Things were good *as long as* she kept him happy. And even then, there was no guarantee something else wouldn't set him off.

And finally—*finally*—she'd begun to understand what Cam had said. This wasn't about Asherah. Or Jack. Or Ayumi, Oce, or the litany of other deaths Anya could pin on Bael's psychotic whims. Anya needed to break the cycle for herself—to be as protective of her own heart as she was of others. To recognize that even if her life hadn't been worth much, it was still hers. And she owed it to herself to reclaim it.

She looked at the sword on her belt, the bejeweled sword Bael had given her. The symbol of her reign as the Lady of Destruction. She'd brought it, hoping it would bring her closer to the task at hand. But now, she found herself preferring the thin swords she'd been carrying for years. The ones Oce had made for her. The ones she'd been wearing when she first met Jack, and the ones she'd used to save all the humans.

Sharur fell to the ground, splatting into the mud.

"That's my lady," Bael said, sounding relieved. "I don't want to fight. I just want us to reclaim what we had."

"There's nothing to reclaim," Anya said, pulling her two swords from her back. "Our life was a lie."

"Anat—"

"I'm sorry." She looked out onto the battlefield, hoping the armies had had enough time. Hoping that Cam had already made it to Liley with Jack.

"Oh, my lady, it's all right," Bael said, taking a step toward her. "I forgive you for—"

"No," she said, readying herself for what was to come. "I'm sorry I let you hurt me. You weren't worthy."

She moved faster than she'd thought possible, praying it would happen before she'd realize what she'd done. But she experienced every second. Metal cutting flesh. The choked gurgle that would be the last sound he made. The horror and relief that crashed into her in twin waves. The sound of his body hitting the ground then the severed head. The sickness that bubbled in her stomach and the salty tears that dripped down her face.

Then it all went white.

"Stay? Or go?"

CHAPTER THIRTY-EIGHT

The world had sped up, but Cam's dark eyes remained steady. Jack realized too late what was happening.

"Cam, what the hell?" Jack said, trying to break free of her grip on his arm. "We can't leave her there!"

"We have to!" Cam barked. "Anya made me promise—"

The world stopped moving abruptly, leaving them in the center of a desert. The black mountains in the distance were closer than they had been, but at least a football field away. Between them were scores of demons fighting, unaware that Cam and Jack been dropped in the center of their battle.

Cam made a guttural sound and toppled forward, Jack catching her just in time. Her face had paled considerably, as if the very life was draining from her body.

"Cam, what's wrong? Cam!" Jack shook her, but she was unresponsive. "*Cam!*"

The earth shook under his feet, reminding him of Demon Spring all those weeks ago. Screams of terror rose from the battle, and the mass of demons began their hasty retreat.

A boom echoed across the plain, and a crack of lightning smashed into the very castle where Jack had been a prisoner. To his horror, the top spire cracked from the castle and crashed to the ground, followed by another turret. Then another.

Then the entire building collapsed on itself, disappearing into a thick cloud of dust.

"Holy shit."

Jack jumped to his feet, Cam cradled in his arms, and ran like hell. To where, he had no idea, but something told him that if he didn't get as far away from this land as possible, he was going to meet the same fate as Bael's castle.

Thundering footsteps echoed behind him as a cloud of dust kicked up in the distance. Jack glanced over his shoulder and slowed, as the belu lilin came toward them riding a massive nox.

"*Get on!*" Freyja cried.

Jack didn't need to be told twice. He handed Cam's comatose body to Freyja, then climbed on behind the lilin, holding on for dear life as the nox took off toward the barrier. To his left and right, other hellbeasts bounded as fast as their considerable legs could move them—some carrying other demons. The rest of the retreating army hoofed it on foot, dropping weapons and armor.

Behind them, the world was crumbling—into what, Jack couldn't see. He said a prayer and held on tight to Freyja and Cam, hoping the nox was faster.

With a loud howl, the beast leaped across the final crack in the ground, landing head first in the black sand of the other world. Jack, Cam, and Freyja flew into various heaps on the ground.

Gingerly, Jack sat up, rubbing the back of his head. He blinked once, twice, then shook his head. When he opened his eyes once more, he still couldn't believe what he was seeing. The orange desert was gone—completely enveloped by a white mist that ended right where the black rock began.

"It's gone," Freyja said beside him.

"G-gone?" Jack sputtered. "What do you mean *gone?*"

"Ath-kur is no more," Lotan said behind them. He was back to his human form, cradling Cam in his arms. "Bael is dead."

Jack scrambled to his feet and rushed toward the mist, but Freyja's hand on his arm stopped him short. "No," she said. "It's too dangerous for you to go in there."

"But Anya…"

"She knew what she was getting into," Freyja said, a tear sliding down her face. "She'd accepted her fate."

Jack couldn't believe that. "That's bullshit. Her fate? To just die after everything she'd been through?"

"She may not be dead," Lotan said. "But she's no longer athtar."

"How do you know?" Jack snapped, turning around. He softened when Cam's eyes fluttered then opened.

"Because Cam is human," Lotan said, smiling in relief. "Cam? Can you hear me?"

"Who are you?" she murmured. "You're very pretty."

"That happens on occasion," Lotan said, turning his head to the side as he smiled in relief. "Temporary amnesia after a demon reverts to human. I'm sure she'll remember most of her adventures as soon as the pain fades." He carefully stroked her face. "Cam? Do you remember where you are?"

She squinted at him. "Did we sleep together? And did I drink last night or something? Why do I feel like shit? And where the hell am I?" She looked at Jack. "J-Jack? What are you doing here? I thought I was going to rescue you?"

Jack walked toward her, kneeling in front of Lotan. "You did, Cam. You marched right into Bael's castle and rescued my skinny ass." He kissed her knuckles. "And I'm really glad you did."

"Here," Lotan said, gently placing Cam in Jack's arms. "Beyond this ridge, you'll find an encampment. Find a warrior named Izel—"

"Lotan," Freyja said quietly. "She didn't..."

The nox's eyes widened and he swallowed hard. "Find an empty tent, then. There should be plenty of food and water. Take as much as you and Cam need. I'll come find you after a while."

"Where are you going?" Jack asked.

He turned to the mist, straightening his back. "To look for survivors. And…others."

"Are you sure it's safe?"

"Not in the least," he said as Freyja came up beside him, ready to walk through the abyss with him. "But if there's a chance one of my noxes is alive in there, I'm going to go. Take care of Cam, will you?"

With that, he transformed back into the hellbeast and darted off into the dust with Freyja on his back.

The camp must've been a sight at one point, but now it was a ghost town. Jack could only imagine the numbers who'd had been killed on the battlefield against the athtars—and the number who'd merely been unable to get out in time. He stashed Cam in the nearest tent, staying with her until she stopped babbling and fell asleep. She'd sworn to Jack she was still in Mexico City, and that she and Anya were going to meet with the noxes. He hoped after a long nap and some food, she might remember more.

While she slept, Jack waited outside, watching the injured and healthy wander through the camp, looking for friends and loved ones. Once or twice, Jack got to witness two friends rushing toward each other, embracing with a fierce relief that spread to others around them. But those were few and far between. Most of those who called out names got no response.

And even as Jack was thankful to have Cam with him, he kept his hopes alive that Anya would emerge from the world of nothing. There'd been a handful of survivors, most of them wearing looks of wide-eyed relief that they'd reached the other side. Many of them came on the backs of noxes—there were at least ten going back and forth into the mist.

One nox came bounding toward them with three human-like creatures on his back. Jack popped upright to help them off the nox's back, noting how their heads lolled and eyes blinked vacantly in the light.

"Kappas," came Lotan's voice, tempered by the low growl of his beast. "Or former kappas. We'll get them back to the human world."

Once the humans had been offloaded and placed in tents, Lotan transformed back into the man. He looked weary and devastated, but resolved to continue the grim mission.

"What's it look like in there?" Jack asked.

"The land is broken," he said. "It's difficult to see where you're going, even as the beast. Large cracks fall into nothing. I'm afraid that has taken most of our army."

"And..." Jack swallowed. "Any sign of Anya?"

"Bael had drawn her far into the world—intentionally," Lotan said with a growl. "But if I find her, I promise I'll bring her to you. I believe, at the end, she wanted to live."

"And you're sure Bael is dead?"

He nodded. "The world disintegrating as it did—Cam reverting to human. Bael is dead. The athtars are no more." His eyes grew sad. "It was a high price for victory. Too many lives were lost."

Jack didn't disagree. "How many?"

"Of the five hundred noxes, I have counted only twenty," Lotan said with a downcast look. "The kappas may have been cut to a handful. Freyja is still counting her lilins, but I fear she has lost more than her fair share as well. Who knows what this has done to our numbers in the human world? Who knows what this will mean for us going forward?"

"Yeah, the Division's going to have a field day with all this," Jack said, then pressed his hand against his forehead. Bael was gone—things were about to change. For the better or worse, he had no idea.

"So…you aren't going to take Bael's place, right?" Jack asked. "I mean, you seem like a decent guy, but—"

"I can see why you're Cam's partner," Lotan said, squeezing Jack's shoulder. "There will be talk about how to rebuild without Bael's dictatorship. To answer your question: no, it's not my intent to assume the King of the Underworld mantle. I'd prefer to have a more symbiotic relationship with the humans."

Jack didn't miss how the nox's gaze went to the tent where Cam slept.

"But first, I have to resolve the immediate crisis." Lotan turned back to the abyss. "I'll return soon, and take you back to the human realm where you belong."

He dashed away again, disappearing into the mist. Behind Jack, the flap to the tent opened, and Cam came stumbling out.

"Did I hear Lotan?" she asked, blinking in the light.

"Got your memory back, have you?" Jack smiled and helped

her take a seat on a log in front of the campfire. "Any sordid details you want to share?"

"I'll spill as soon as you tell me what you did with Colibrí," she replied with a grin, then winced. "My head feels like it's being pried open with a jackhammer."

"But you're human again," he said. "And alive."

"Definitely human," she said, flexing her fingers. "Can't believe I was always this weak."

"Camilla Macarro, there's no one in this universe who would ever call you weak," Jack said. "Not after what you did for me." He threw an arm around her shoulder. "Thank you. For coming to get me. For…everything."

"Please. As if I'd let Colibrí get all the glory." Her breath hitched. "She hasn't…come back yet, has she?"

"No."

So there they sat, watching the steady stream of survivors come out of the mist and holding onto the same hope that Anya would be one of them. But the hours passed, and the numbers coming out of the mist dwindled. When Lotan came out of the abyss carrying only Freyja, an uncomfortable knowing settled in Jack's gut.

"Cam," Freyja said, sweeping over to them with a sad smile on her face. She took Cam's face and kissed her soundly. Before Jack could ask what that was about, the belu lilin turned to him and gave him a kiss that sent unwelcome pleasure straight down into his groin. "I'm so glad the two of you are here. It has been a horrible, horrible day. Your beautiful faces bring me peace."

"T-thank you?" Jack said.

Cam stood and pulled Freyja into a hug, and the lilin collapsed into it, taking the solace. "I'm sorry."

"The battle has been won," the lilin said, wiping tears from her eyes. "And my future spawn can live in a world without Bael's influence. But the price has been... Mizuchi. Anya. So many others..."

"Anya may not be dead," Jack said quickly. "She could still be alive."

She nodded, but couldn't speak through her tears. She excused herself, rushing away with her face in her hands.

"She'll be all right," Lotan said, although he didn't sound all right himself. "How are you feeling, Cam?"

"Much better," she said, sliding her hand through his. "Glad to see you."

He pulled her into his arms and held her tight, resting his chin on her head. For a moment, Jack watched them, before turning to the abyss beyond.

"It's time to get you two back to your realm," Lotan said, not releasing Cam.

"No," Jack said. "I want to stay until we find Anya. Either... either way."

"I promise the moment we find her, you'll be the first to know," Lotan said. "But I would feel better if you were back in the land without magic. This place is unstable. Tremors have broken into Liley. Anya made me promise I would get you two back."

"Hang on," Cam said, leaning back, "she made *me* promise that I'd rescue Jack."

"And she knew you were a damned liar," Lotan said with a not-so-innocent grin. "But if you're worried you won't see me again, I promise I'll visit you there as often as you'll have me. And then some."

Cam flushed, and Jack had to laugh. It was the first time he'd ever seen someone render his best friend speechless.

"I'll give you a few moments to say your goodbyes," Lotan said to Jack before leaving them in peace. "Don't get too close to the line."

Hand-in-hand, Jack and Cam walked to the edge of Liley. From a distance, it had seemed the mist was encroaching on the land, but at the border, it was very clearly contained. Cam released Jack's hand and poked the mist, marveling at how her finger disappeared into it.

"Careful, you'll lose a finger," Jack said. "Didn't Lotan say not to get too close?"

"Yeah," Cam said, dropping her hand. "You okay?"

He nodded and squinted at the dusty void beyond. "I don't want her to think I abandoned her."

"She'll know you didn't. Actually, I think she's probably still pissed at me for *not* getting you back to Liley like I was supposed to." Cam chuckled. "That was kind of the deal. I become athtar, I get you back to the human realm. Whoops."

He wished he could find her humor, but all he could manage was a half-smile. "Maybe I just don't want to leave her. The not knowing..."

Cam scrutinized him in that way she always did. "Are you okay?"

"Hm?"

"I mean, you seem okay, but are you okay?" She tilted her head. "After what Bael did to you?"

"Bael's torture wasn't half as effective as he thought it was," Jack said. Sara's dead face flashed before his eyes, and he shuddered. "I mean, some of it was pretty bad. But...on the other hand, it kind of helped, you know?"

"How so?"

"He made me relive...that day. The day Sara died. Multiple times."

Cam sucked in a loud breath and her upper lip curled. "That son of a bitch."

"Yeah, I know, I know," Jack said. Probably a good thing Bael was dead; Cam would've killed him otherwise. "But the oddest part was, once I'd lived through that again, I found everything else kind of paled in comparison. I'd survived. I kept living. I'd gone through hell and come back alive. And I guess... that sort of helps with everything else. I'll always miss Sara, and I'll always love her. But now I don't feel like...life's over anymore. I can move forward."

Cam's gaze turned outward, toward the nothingness. "And how are you feeling about Anya?"

"I wanted to see her happy. Truly happy. Maybe that could've been with me, or maybe it could've been with someone else. But she deserved it."

"Seeing you made her happy," Cam said. "I could tell."

"Yeah," Jack said with a sigh. He just wished they'd had more than a moment to get reacquainted. But at the end, he was happy she'd been able to finally take her life back. Even if it had ended shortly thereafter.

"I'm sorry," Cam said, pressing her cheek into his shoulder. "For what it's worth, she really did care about you."

"I know," Jack said, closing his hand over hers. "I did, too."

CHAPTER THIRTY-NINE

"I think I've changed—"

"No, you haven't," Jack replied, emotion thick in his throat. "You're going. That's final. I've already bought my ticket to visit you next month."

He and Cam stood in front of the security gate at Atlanta International Airport. Cam was teary-eyed with a bag slung from her shoulder and Jack was doing his best not to be too upset for her sake. They'd been saying their goodbyes for almost a week now, but as the date approached for her to leave, there'd been more tears on both sides.

It had been three months since Jack and Cam had appeared in Mexico City, telling tales of surviving the Underworld to everyone from their families to the full Council of Fifteen. The Council was even kind enough to drop the litany of charges against Jack, having decided he'd been punished enough. Instead, they'd allowed him to medically retire from active duty.

Cam was offered the same, but she'd taken a different route instead. Thus their presence at the international gates, and Cam's reticence.

"What if I hate it there?" she asked.

"You won't."

"What if I don't make any friends?"

"That many nerds? You'll be queen of them all."

"What if you need me?"

Jack sighed. "I thought you didn't care what happened to me anymore? Your exact words were—"

"I know, I know. But you know I say things I don't mean." She chewed her lip and adjusted the bag on her hip. "This is stupid. You're still recovering from your ordeal—"

"Camilla Macarro," Jack said, putting two hands on her shoulders. "You're looking for excuses now. There are none. Go. It's what's best for you, and you know it. Be selfish for once in your life."

Two tears slipped down her cheeks. "I'll call you every morning."

"I know you will."

"I love you, Jack."

He pulled her into a hug. "I love you, too," he said, kissing the side of her head. "I'm going to be fine. And so are you. You survived the Underworld. You can do anything."

She nodded, wiping her cheeks. "You'll let me know if...if you hear from her, right?"

Jack nodded, sadness inching up his mind. "You'll be the first to know."

As if on cue, her phone began to buzz, and for a moment, they held their breath. But the look of annoyance on her face, mixed with a bit of amusement, was telling enough.

"Your boyfriend?" Jack teased.

"I'd hardly call the nox prince my boyfriend," she said, stuffing her phone in her pocket.

Despite her half-hearted protestations, Lotan had been appearing every few weeks in Atlanta, and when he wasn't there himself, Cam would find flowers of varying species waiting at her doorstep, along with handwritten letters of affection. Jack found them a little ridiculous, but seeing Cam happy was all he really cared about.

"At least he's not trying to convince you to become a nox anymore," Jack said.

"No, now he's professing that he's making arrangements to become human, if that's even possible." She shivered. "I told him that's a level of commitment I'm not ready to make yet."

Jack just had to laugh. "Just enjoy it, Cam. You deserve to be treated like a queen."

"He says he'll come visit as soon as I'm settled," she said with a smile that said she wasn't as upset as she made out. "I'm sure that will go over well with the Weapons Institute. I'm surprised they haven't kicked me out yet."

"With all the new world order happening, they may give you an official title as nox liaison," Jack said.

"You could do great things in Charleston, you know," Cam said. "I think you should reconsider working for your grandfather."

"We'll see," he said. Frank was already knee-deep in rewriting regulations to crack down on demons and demonic transformations and had begged Jack to come join him. But Jack still didn't think ICDM HQ was for him.

"Just promise me," she took his cheeks in her hands, "Jackson, *promise me*, you won't go do that vigilante stuff anymore."

"Why not?" he asked.

"Because it's dangerous and against the law."

"So is dating the nox prince."

Cam pursed her lips, and Jack realized just how much he was going to miss her. Things had irrevocably changed between them. They would never reclaim what they'd had in D.C., but the new step was positive for both of them. Cam was going off to chart her course; Jack would stay behind and figure his own way. They would build a new relationship, too. And for once, Jack was excited to see what the future held for them both.

She wiped her face, but more tears fell. "I should go, or else I'm gonna miss my flight."

"Go." A tear fell down his cheek. "Show Shanghai who's boss."

She nodded, her face screwing up with unshed tears and marched away, her shoulders back and head held high, but Jack knew she would bawl like a baby the entire flight. As for him, it was easy to pretend he was fine when Cam stood in front of him. But without her to worry about, his eyes stung. He sniffed and stuffed his hands in his pockets, making his way to the Atlanta airport's terminal train, and out to the MARTA.

A niggling feeling of grief entered his mind as he thought about Anya, and he checked his phone out of habit and hope. Lotan had found a few survivors, none athtar.

But Jack allowed himself to hope.

He departed the MARTA at his old apartment—one he was already in the process of re-packing up. Atlanta wasn't the place for him. Neither was Charleston, or D.C. As much as it had been alternatively monotonous and terrifying, Jack missed being on the run with Anya. He was toying with the idea of sending all his belongings to a storage facility and just living out of a suitcase for a while. Amsterdam seemed like a viable option, but so did Seattle. Maybe even Richmond. But he didn't want to go just yet. Not until—

He stopped in the middle of the sidewalk.

"It...it can't be..."

The woman who stood under the awning of his apartment building was familiar, except she wasn't. The cloud of misery had dissipated, leaving a bright-eyed innocence that he'd only seen glimpses of. The bright yellow sundress was a change of pace from the black garb. Her nervous smile and fidgeting told him she'd been waiting for some time.

"Hi."

"W…where have you been?" Jack rasped. "I thought you were dead. You've been gone for weeks—"

"Yeah." She chuckled and tucked a strand of hair behind her ear as she walked up to him. "Apparently, it's a lot harder to get out of the Underworld when you're human."

His breath caught. "Human?"

She nodded. "I killed my maker, and so…" She shrugged. "Back to my original factory settings."

"You're not dead?"

"I'm not dead."

He swept her into his arms, crushing her to his body and thanking whatever God was up there that she'd come back to him—that she'd been given a second chance to find happiness.

"Jack—ow—human," she said, pushing him slightly. "More breakable than I used to be."

He released her, but only enough that her feet rested on the ground. He drank in every part of her—from her bronze skin to her green eyes, to the way her black ringlets rested against her shoulders. And her smile—still tinged with sadness, but for the first time, free of fear.

"You look like…" she began, resting her fingertips against his skin. "You look good. Recovered—"

"Enough about me," Jack said, finding his tongue again. "Where the hell have *you* been? Lotan's been looking everywhere for you—"

"And I apologized to him for making him worry," she said averting her gaze. "And I'm sorry for not telling you sooner. Freyja found me in the rubble and let me recover in her castle."

"For three months?" Jack gaped. "You could have—"

"I needed time," she said, turning her head away from him. "I just… I needed time."

He gently lifted her chin to look into her eyes again. Then he kissed her forehead. "You're here now. You're alive. That's all I care about."

"I missed you so much," she whispered, pressing her forehead into his cheek. "When it…when it happened, I remembered being given a choice to move on or come back as a human. I chose to come back." She looked up at him and smiled. "I had something to come back to."

"We do have a lot of unfinished business," he said with a grin.

"Speaking of unfinished business, where's my polluelo?" Anya asked. "I thought for sure she'd be attached to your hip after all we went through to get you back."

"Your polluelo is currently flying over the middle of the country, en route to Shanghai. Her world domination plan is back on track, it seems."

"I look forward to bowing to our new queen," Anya said with a laugh. "Especially as I hear she's got the nox prince wrapped around her finger."

"Uh, I think it's the other way around," Jack said. "Despite her better judgment."

"I did tell her to fuck him until she couldn't see straight," Anya said with a familiar smirk. "Glad she took my advice."

"How long are you staying?" he asked, hoping it would be forever.

"I don't know," she replied with a shrug. "I don't really know what I'm doing." She looked up at him through her lashes. "I think I want to figure it out with you for a while."

"That's pretty convenient," Jack said. "Because I have no idea what I'm doing either."

She grinned, and his heart skipped a beat. He'd never seen her smile that brightly before.

"We could see what Seattle looks like?" Jack offered. "Or Amsterdam?"

She laughed and slid under his arm. "How about we just not have a plan for a while and see where we end up?"

"Sounds like a plan to me."

ACKNOWLEGMENTS

Thanks to my beta readers: Emily and Chelsea. Thanks to Meli, for helping me get all my words right.

Thanks to Dani, my incredible line editor, who always takes my book from good to great.

Thanks to my typo checkers: Lisa, Vicki, Lilivette, and Mom.

Thanks to the Sushis, my street team, for being cheerleaders and all-around awesome folks. If you'd like to join the street team and make us even MORE awesome, check out www.facebook.com/groups/susherevansstreetteam/

ALSO BY S. USHER EVANS

THE MADION WAR TRILOGY

He's a prince, she's a pilot, they're at war. But when they are marooned on a deserted island hundreds of miles from either nation, they must set aside their differences and work together if they want to survive.

The Madion War Trilogy is available in eBook, paperback, and hardcover. Download the first book, The Island, for free on all eBookstores.

Empath

Lauren Dailey is in break-up hell, but if you ask her she's doing just great. She hears a mysterious voice promising an easy escape from her problems and finds herself in a brand new world where she has the power to feel what others are feeling. Just one problem—there's a dragon in the mountains that happens to eat Empaths. And it might be the source of the mysterious voice tempting her deeper into her own darkness.

Empath is a stand-alone fantasy that is available now in eBook, paperback, and hardcover.

ALSO BY S. USHER EVANS

The Razia Series

Lyssa Peate is living a double life as a planet discovering scientist and a space pirate bounty hunter. Unfortunately, neither life is going very well. She's the least wanted pirate in the universe and her brand new scientist intern is spying on her. Things get worse when her intern is mistaken for her hostage by the Universal Police.

The Razia Series is a four-book space opera series and is available now for eBook, paperback, audiobook, and hardcover. Download the first book, Double Life, for free on all eBookstores.

The Lexie Carrigan Chronicles

Lexie Carrigan thought she was weird enough until her family drops a bomb on her—she's magical. Now the girl who's never made waves is blowing up her nightstand and no one seems to want to help her. That is, until a kind gentleman shows up with all the answers. But Lexie finds out being magical is the least weird thing about her.

Spells and Sorcery is the first book in the Lexie Carrigan Chronicles, and is available now in eBook, paperback, audiobook, and hardcover.

ABOUT THE AUTHOR

S. Usher Evans was born and raised in Pensacola, Florida. After a decade of fighting bureaucratic battles as an IT consultant in Washington, DC, she suffered a massive quarter-life-crisis. She decided fighting dragons was more fun than writing policy, so she moved back to Pensacola to write books full-time. She currently resides with her husband and two dogs, Zoe and Mr. Biscuit, and frequently can be found plotting on the beach.

Find her on the internet:

www.susherevans.com

www.facebook.com/susherevans
www.twitter.com/susherevans
www.instagram.com/susherevans